THE LOST CLANS OF LYDANIA

The Lore of Lydania
Book One

By Alin Silverwood

The Lost Clans of Lydania
(The Lore of Lydania Book One)

Printed in the United States of America.

Cover Art by Howard David Johnson
Cover design by Amanda Kelsey of Razzle Dazzle Designs
Editing by Yvette Keller and Sunwalker Press
Map by Stephanie Johanesen
Formatted by PyperPress

Acknowledgments

Lots of time and encouragement passed during the writing of this book. I would especially like to thank M. Edward McNally for a heroic and helpful scrutiny, and, of course, Shéa MacLeod for editorial assists and peeling me off the ceiling on numerous occasions.

Dedication

This one is for my daughter Ali, who was told much of the early parts of the story and has had to wait far too long to be able to read it.

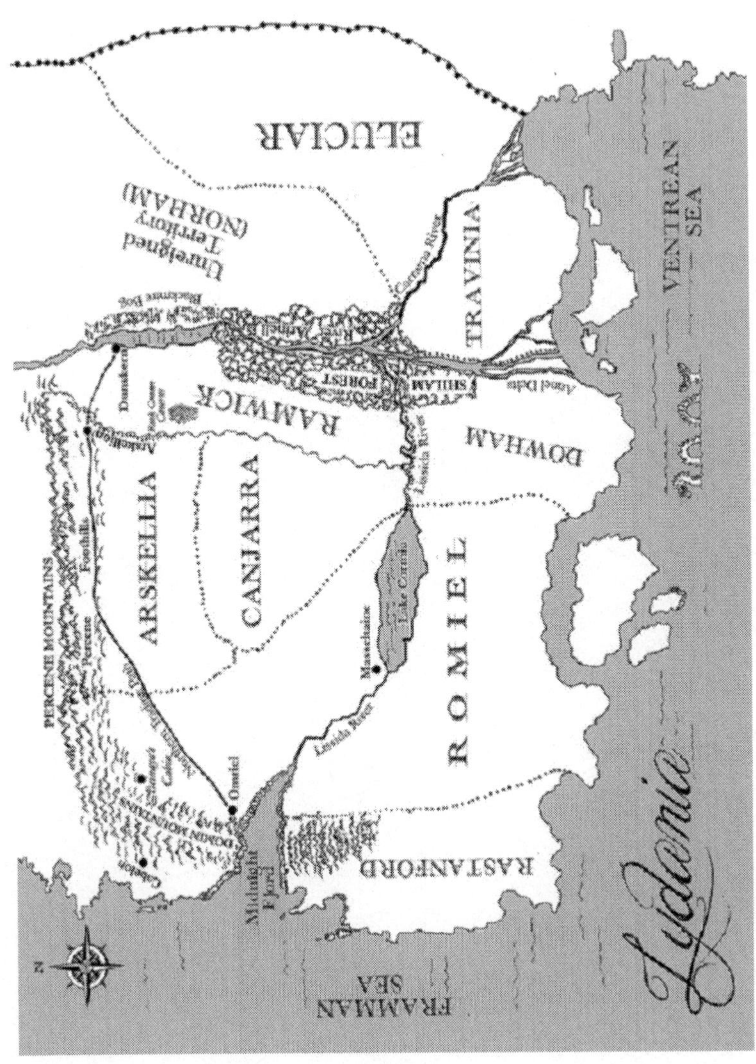
ELUCIAR
Unreigned Territory (NORHAM)
TRAVINIA
VENTREAN SEA
RAMWICK
CANJARRA
ARSKELLIA
DOWHAM
ROMIEL
RASTANFORD
FRAMMAN SEA
PERCENE MOUNTAINS
Midnight Fjord
Lydania

Notes About Pronunciation

When reading epic fantasy, I often find myself guessing at what the author meant for the pronunciation of certain names and terms. Since I find this frustrating, I offer this brief listing of names and terms with a key for their intended pronunciation. Nevertheless, feel free to refer to it or use whatever pronunciation works best for you. It's only my story, but it's *your* imagination bringing it to life.

ALTAIN CEBROS (AL-tun SĀ-brōhs)

ARINELL (AIR-in-el)

ARSKELLIA (ar-SKEL-yuh)

ARSKELLION (ar-SKEL-yun)

BRINAYA VOSS (bri-NĪ-uh VOS)

BRONDUR (BRON-dur)

BRUCCAN (BROO-kan)

CABELON (KAB-uh-lon)

CADDRYTH (KAD-rith)

CANJARRA (kan-JÄR-uh)

CARRAMA RIVER (kär-RAH-muh)

CORMIN (CORM) LYDAN (KORM-in LĪ-dun)

DALGIN (DAL-jin)

DEVRAM (DEV-rum)

DOMIN MOUNTAINS (The Domins) (DŌM-in)

DOWHAM (DOW-um)

DUNSKERN (DUNS-kurn)

ELUCIAR (i-LOO-sē-är)

ELYR (uh-LIR)

EODORR HOULT (Ā-ō-dor HULT)

ERATHO (uh-RATH-oh)

FLEK (FLEK)

FRAMMAN SEA (FRAM-un)

GAIMESH (GĀ-mish)

GETHOR DRAN (GETH-ur DRAN)

HEGANA (hā-GAH-nuh)

HERILYN ASHUIR (HAIR-i-lin A-zhur) (Last name pronounced like the color azure)

HONNARVO (hon-NÄR-voh)

INGON SUMMERHILL (ING-on)

JERRICK LYDAN (JAIR-ik LĪ-dun)

KEIRWYN DAYAS (KIR-win DĀ-os)

KILWARD (KIL-wurd)

LAKE CORMIA (KORM-ē-uh)

LISSIDA RIVER (lis-SEE-duh)

LYDANIA (lī-DĀN-yuh)

LYNARI (li-NÄR-ē)

MARAGGAN (mar-OG-un)

MARKIN ASHUIR (MAR-kin A-zhur) (Last name

pronounced like the color azure)

MASSELTAINE (MAS-ul-tān)

MERINDEL (MAIR-in-del)

MUNDON (MUN-dun)

NARKAN TANGLAS (NAR-kan TAN-glus)

NORHAM (NÔR-um)

NORRIK (NOR-rik)

ODRYN DAYAS (ŌD-rin DĀ-os)

OMRIEL (OM-rē-el)

PARAM VOSS (PAIR-um VOS)

PERCENE MOUNTAINS (The Percenes) (pur-SĒN)

PYVADIS (pi-VOD-is)

RASTANFORD (RAS-tun-furd)

RENDIFF ARSKELL (REN-dif ar-SKEL)

RHINAN ASHUIR (RĪ-nun A-zhur) (Last name pronounced like the color azure)

RIP (RIP)

ROMIEL (ROM-ē-el)

SHILAM FOREST (SHĪ-lum)

SILARRAH (sil-ÄR-uh)

SIRAS (SĪ-rus)

THURRIK (THUR-rik)

TRAVINIA (truh-VIN-yuh)

VAYLENE (VĀ-lēn)

VENELWIN (ven-EL-win)

VENTREAN SEA (VEN-trē-un)

VIMYR (VIM-eer)

WENDAM (WEN-dum)

WERALD (WAIR-uld)

YLVA (IL-vuh)

YLVAN (IL-vun)

Prologue

Echoes of laughter and gleeful screams rose above the misty hollow. The fading sun melted into the horizon, shadows stretching out and flowing over the landscape with the fluidity of blood. The heavily wooded slopes on either side of the long, narrow basin provided plenty of hiding places for the five children —and perhaps for other things.

Dashing in and out of the trees along the hollow, one boy lagged behind his four companions. Caught up in their game, he was determined to enjoy as much of it as the fading daylight would allow. Their parents would expect them home before dark. The rules about lingering too late within the woods near the small mountain town were very strict.

A flock of blackbirds suddenly took flight, startling him. The air took on an unusual chill, considering that winter had passed.

The other four were far ahead of him, vanishing in the hazy twilight. He did not want to be the last one home. His mother (or worse, his father!) would thrash him if he wandered in too late. And he was hungry.

Losing sight of the other children, he realized that he did not want to be alone in the forest, either.

The shadows deepened swiftly, and the chill intensified.

Seeing his breath in the air, the boy wished for his cloak. Was winter returning before summer made a full appearance? No, the trees were tall and thick, bursting with the fresh growth of the spring. Amid their towering presence, the boy usually felt safe and comfortable. He was a good hider and almost always the last one found when the children played his favorite game.

Unnerved, he sensed an extreme stillness in the air. It was far too hushed. The trees took on an unfamiliar appearance, dark and twisted, as they leaned menacingly over him. The light dwindled far too swiftly, and fear clenched at him. He broke into a trot, scampering up the side of the slope. The sound of his own breathing split the silent air, his heart pounding within.

Then he heard it.

Distant at first, a loud whispering crept among the trees from somewhere back along the hollow. Unlike the usual sound of the wind in the treetops, this was a random murmuring. He could not tell which direction the sounds came from; they seemed in one moment to be on one side of him, then on the other side in the next. As the sound hopped around him, beside him, before him, after him, it seemed to change. Now it reminded him of the muffled sound of the sick and dying, mumbling and moaning in their feverous delusions. The words were indistinguishable, but that there were words at all disturbed him greatly. His friends were too far ahead, and he was certain there was no one else around.

Trembling, he ran as fast as he could. Small eddies of pursuing wind whipped up, caught at him, teasing his hair and catching at his legs and arms.

He screamed.

Mist and shadow now poured out from among the trees

behind him as he ran as fast as he could. He saw faint outlines of faces watching him from the edge of his vision, transparent people it—like ghosts!—pursuing him. Their mumbling and moaning surrounded him and assaulted his senses. Drowning in panic, the boy rushed on, seeking the edge of town. He didn't know what had happened but, though it was dark now, he feared the wrath of his parents much less than the shadowy phantoms in the trees.

Just as it seemed the roiling mist and shadow would catch him, swallowing him, he saw the hazy silhouette of the abandoned blacksmith's forge at the edge of town taking shape through the trees ahead. Feeling safer at the sight of it, he chanced a look behind him. Within the mist, a throng of transparent people, or their outlines, watched him in silence. Whatever or whoever the ghosts were, they would follow him no further.

Leaving the phantom occurrence behind him within the woods, he turned toward the old forge and made his way quickly along its side. He'd been told it had once been a busy workshop, but it hadn't been used since about the time he was born. No one ever spoke of what became of the blacksmith, but no new smith appeared to breathe life into the tiny shop. The forge remained cold.

Catching his breath, he looked back one last time. To his great relief, there was no mist and no swarm of apparitions. The normal early-night sounds of the darkened wood had resumed. Had he imagined it all? He told himself it would be a long time before he went back to play in the forest. His curiosity might take him there as long as there was plenty of daylight left, but he vowed never to be the last one home again.

His friends reappeared, running toward him. Had they

seen it? He hoped they had, or they would never believe him. As they drew near, he could see that the three boys looked horrified. The face of the girl was streaked with new tears. So they *had* seen it.

"Wasn't it awful!" the boy exclaimed in nervous excitement, bravado returning now that the perceived threat had disappeared.

His exclamation seemed to puzzle his friends. They looked at each other, and then back at him. "Yes," said one of the other boys slowly and quietly, "but how could you know? You haven't been home yet."

The small boy felt his stomach drop out of him. So they *hadn't* seen the shadows. But whatever they'd seen was worse—and they associated it with his... "Home? What do you mean?"

At his question, the girl whimpered in sorrow. "It's your parents! They... they..." She sobbed too heavily to continue.

"Come on," said the older boy, putting his arm around him. "I think you should come to my house."

Confused about what may have happened, the boy allowed himself to be led by his friend. Momentarily forgetting his unnatural encounter, new fears writhing within him, he got the feeling that he would never be going home again at all.

PART ONE

Chapter One

He would later recall that the dream had been pleasant, but the details were quickly forgotten when Rhinan found himself drowning.

He awoke sputtering and gasping, still engulfed in water and soaking wet. Water splashed off him, around him, and away from him. He was only slightly relieved as he floated into consciousness to realize that he was still lying in his own straw bed in his small thatched hut at the edge of town. Shivering and rising on one elbow, he noticed with discomfort that his bedding was also thoroughly soaked. With a look out the window, latched open, Rhinan could see the hazy red glow of the impending dawn. It didn't look like rain. So where was all this water coming from? He turned over.

Standing at the foot of his bed were both Devram and Eodorr. Each one was holding an empty wooden bucket and staring cautiously at him as if ready to run. The two young men were large and powerful, but Rhinan considered them both mostly harmless. They were as opposite a pair as you could get: Devram looked like he'd just rolled out of bed himself, his straw-colored hair thrusting out in little clumps as his tall, leaner frame slouched. Eodorr, on the other hand, stood like a coiled needlebeast, his brawnier build looking for all the world as if it would spring into action at a moment's notice. He was all cord and sinew like the horses he raised, and his dark hair and close-cut beard were neatly arranged. That was Eodorr—by the regulations for the most part. He took his position far more seriously than Devram. Probably why he and Rhinan no longer got on.

Once among his closest childhood friends, the two were now the only soldiers assigned to the Constable in the little mountain village of Cabelon. Neither wore their uniform nor armor this morning. Not unusual, as being posted to a small village had its advantages, and they could afford to be casual about such formalities. They didn't even carry their weapons most of the time. Eodorr, however, at least normally wore his crisp uniform, but apparently hadn't even had time for that today. There was little trouble in Cabelon, and most of it was caused by Rhinan anyway. But this time, both had sheathed swords at their side. *So they were here officially*, Rhinan thought. And he suspected he knew why.

Initially startled at their uninvited presence, Rhinan would have been irritated with the officious duo, but for the comforting figure standing directly behind them. Constable Keirwyn Dayas wore an expression of disappointment and concern on his aging features—a dark, coppery hue—as his white facial hair appeared to droop. Seeing him, Rhinan grinned coolly. Keirwyn's presence probably meant that Rhinan was only in for another lecture of some sort, and that was never so bad. Rhinan knew just how to handle Keirwyn. The aged Constable had been like a father to him for years.

Before speaking, the Constable paused, seeming to consider something briefly. "Get up," growled Keirwyn in a harsh manner, uncharacteristic for tfhe old man.

Rhinan's grin faded, replaced by his confusion. Although he'd been out the night before, and up to no good, it was never anything serious. Why would Keirwyn be any more surprised or upset than usual?

Sitting up proved to be difficult. Rhinan now had a moment to realize that someone had inserted war drums into his skull overnight, and whoever it was now played them with full gusto. He suspected the same prankster of being responsible for the bitter whirlpool that raged in his stomach as well. He groaned. The two village guards each took one step back, apprehensive of his precarious condition. Rhinan took some satisfaction in their wariness, but it didn't alleviate his discomfort. He swung his bare feet out from under the furred, hide blanket and felt the water trickle down his shins. Had they needed to use *full* buckets to wake him?

He tried to remember the previous night. He had gotten hold of a large, old bottle of rather potent hard ale and had regrettably opened it with no one around to share it. After that, he seemed to recall a deep philosophical debate with some farm animals, but…

Oh, yes, the farm.

He had obtained the bottle of ale from one of Lord Mundon's smaller farms (Mundon was the local Baron, utterly useless for anything but ale and cheese in Rhinan's opinion), as well as another random thing or two. He had quickly hidden everything but the fine, strong ale, and he wished momentarily that he'd hidden that, as well. Ah, but what delicious ale it had been! He'd tried explaining that to the farm animals, but they'd been so sheepish and pigheaded.

Ooh, *that* hurt. He decided to leave off his sense of humor this morning.

Standing, Rhinan stretched his sturdy, broad-shouldered frame to its full six-foot height. He was lean, but by no means slight. His green eyes were bloodshot, and his rich brown hair was thick and unkempt. He hadn't shaved himself in a week, nor had he bathed. His mouth felt like he'd been chewing on dried twigs. He was certainly as nude as a farm animal. He looked at Devram and Eodorr, who seemed to find other places of interest to observe around the tiny hut. Though Rhinan had assumed a casual demeanor, hoping to diffuse Keirwyn's anger, the Constable appeared to be losing patience with the entire routine.

Rhinan reached for his gray leggings, draped over a nearby chair, and slipped them on. He then donned a green tunic that lay crumpled on the same chair and reeked of a mix of foul odors, then strapped on the leather vest over it. Sliding into his worn leather boots, Rhinan was almost ashamed to have Keirwyn see him in this condition. He would have liked to at least dip his clothing in the river first.

With a yawn, Rhinan turned to the two guards. Indicating their buckets, he said, "I don't suppose you saved any of that water for the *inside* of me?"

As the two young men looked helplessly down at the buckets, Keirwyn sighed wearily. "We can stop at the well," he snapped. "We're taking you into custody, Rhinan."

At Keirwyn's words, Eodorr stepped forward, withdrawing a short length of rope that he had tucked into his belt. Rhinan looked past him to Keirwyn, shocked and hurt.

"Ah, there's no need for that, Eodorr," Keirwyn told him. "Rhinan won't be giving us any trouble today, will you lad?"

"No, sir."

"Fine. Then come along." Keirwyn turned his back on Rhinan, and Rhinan now felt the revered Constable's disappointment like a slap in the face. And it stung. He was ashamed, a feeling not many could bring out in him.

Rhinan's nonchalance was having no effect on Keirwyn this time. As they emerged from the hut into the brisk morning air, Rhinan inhaled the rich scent of the loamy earth, the fresh trees from the surrounding forest, and the aroma of hot breakfast somewhere nearby, which did not appeal to him at the moment. As they made their way into the center of the small village, there was smoke rising from the scattered thatched cottages, no doubt in their attempts to stave off the chill of early autumn in the mountains. Though the morning was otherwise quiet, a small crowd had gathered not far away, trying to see or hear whatever was going on without looking like they were interested. The townsfolk appeared to be only half attentive to whatever business they normally had, but their individual tasks and duties conveniently took them a little closer to his dwelling this morning. He wondered just what was really going on. Could all this fuss really have anything to do with his little raid at Lord Mundon's farm last night? That greedy old codger was away on business, and wasn't expected back for a couple more days anyway. No, it couldn't be that. "Keirwyn, what—" Rhinan attempted to question.

"Hush," Keirwyn stopped him firmly. He leaned close and quickly whispered, "We can't talk here." The Constable then stepped past him without looking back. Rhinan followed, eyeing as many of the nosy townsfolk as possible and finding amusement in their inability to look away quickly enough to avoid being noticed watching him. Some of them were people he'd always ignored anyway. The town's most aggressive gossip was passing nearby, bearing a load of what appeared to be clothes for washing. She wasn't fooling anyone—everyone knew the stream passed the other side of the village, just beyond the old blacksmith's workshop.

Devram and Eodorr followed Rhinan a few paces back, allowing his aroma as much room to dissipate as possible. Despite their best efforts to keep him downwind, Rhinan dropped back to whisper a few words to Devram, eldest of the pair. "Devram, what is all this? It's not like Keirwyn to arrest me publicly. As a matter of fact, it's not like Keirwyn to arrest me at all."

Devram wrinkled his nose and made a point of exhaling. "Lord Mundon returned early. Last night, in fact, and apparently just in time to see you staggering away from the stable at one of his farms with a sack. Coincidentally, some of his best flagons of ale are now missing. Well, Mundon was annoyed enough with you *last* time when you pilfered his cheese cellar. Instead of complaining to Keirwyn this time, he's sent his steward directly to Masseltaine for an audience with the King—and he's got connections at court, Rhinan. It looks better for us if we treat this one seriously."

Apprehension spread through Rhinan, ripples on a pond.

Devram continued. "You should have left well enough alone. And you should bathe, by the way."

"I do. And frequently," Rhinan replied, offended. "Just not this week." He thought for a moment. "Is Mundon really going to miss a few flagons of ale all that much? He never has guests anyway. By the Black Halls of Norrik! No one even *likes* the old windbag."

Devram shrugged. "No one but his nephew, who happens to be the King's dog trainer. And is currently visiting him."

Rhinan smirked. "If it's that upsetting to Mundon, I can

just return it all with an apology. I was only going to tote it down to Omriel for market and sell it off to give a few coppers to Silarrah for the orphans. You'd think if Mundon had a heart, the old miser would help out anyway. All that fine ale and no one to share it with…"

"I'm afraid it's too late for that," Devram said sympathetically. "Mundon's steward left for Masseltaine at dawn. Eodorr and I saw him leaving, and we were the ones who told Keirwyn. Keirwyn was very disturbed. Believe it or not, the water was *his* idea."

Arriving at their destination moments later, Devram marched Rhinan into the small village lodge where Keirwyn kept office. Keirwyn remained outside momentarily, having a word with Eodorr, who had sneered at Rhinan as Devram guided him inside. A warm fire blazed in the hearth, and a small clay pot of porridge had grown cold left on Keirwyn's shabby, well-worn desk. The lodge was not particularly large or well lit, but there was almost a certain comfort to it. Rhinan had spent much time here since his childhood.

Alone momentarily, Devram turned to Rhinan. "Keirwyn mentioned something about how King Jerrick might take a particular interest in any… *events*"—Devram stressed the word meaningfully—"up here in Cabelon. He seemed to have you in mind when he said it. Are you in some kind of trouble, Rhinan? Besides the usual, I mean?"

Rhinan shrugged. "Not that I know of. Besides, King Jerrick can kiss my—why, welcome back, Constable." Rhinan turned a charming, boyish grin on the old man who had just entered. "So may I ask to what I owe the pleasure of your hospitality this fine morning?"

Keirwyn bristled. "Don't play games with me today, boy."

"I find it hurtful that you still refer to me as `boy'—I've

just passed my twenty-seventh summer."

"I find it hurtful that you still act like one after all I've taught you," Keirwyn snapped.

Rhinan stopped smiling. There was still something much more wrong than usual, but he just couldn't believe it was really this bad. The two looked at each other silently; he could see the pain in Keirwyn's brown eyes, around which there seemed to be more wrinkles than ever.

Keirwyn glanced to Devram. "Leave us," he muttered, his voice tired.

When Devram had gone, Rhinan began, "Look, Keirwyn, I'll make it right with Lord Mundon if it's so important to—"

"Important." Keirwyn cut him off with the statement. He exhaled through his bushy silver moustache. His straight hair was all silver, too, though Rhinan could recall when it wasn't. He suddenly felt his shame increase. He did not like to make trouble for Keirwyn, and only Keirwyn could affect him exactly this way. Like disappointing a father.

"Rhinan, you don't know," Keirwyn shook his head. "You've just kept it up until you've gone too far. I've always looked the other way for a lot of your mischief. It's been troublesome, but mostly harmless. I've managed to keep Lord Mundon very patient with your foolishness, sympathetic to your..." The Constable trailed off, but Rhinan knew. His madness. The entire village all thought him as mad as he thought himself.

"Perhaps I've been overindulgent because I think of you as the son I never had." Keirwyn sighed. "But Rhinan, I've been incautious. I'm not sure even I can get you out of this one." He looked as if he would weep. "I'm going to have to lock you up for a while. It has to look like you're being punished if we're to have any hope of getting you out of this."

"I do sincerely apologize, Keirwyn. You've never been anything but a father figure to me, and in return, I've never been anything but trouble to you." He paused, focusing his sadness elsewhere. "Or perhaps to anyone else, either."

"You don't understand, Rhinan. I've kept the King from taking any special interest in the affairs of Cabelon ever since…" Keirwyn stopped himself.

"Ever since what?" The Constable said nothing. "Ever since what, Keirwyn?"

"Since the deaths of your parents," Keirwyn stated flatly. "But now you may have drawn the King's attention."

Rhinan, puzzled, examined Keirwyn's expression, awaiting some further explanation. Keirwyn looked away. "Why would the King be so interested in *me*?" Rhinan asked. "What's the worst they'll do? I'm no more than a simple mover of excess goods, helping others who have less. I'm just a troublemaker, really. And I do make up for it with my hunting for the village. At worst, would they cart me off to the dungeons at Masseltaine? Certainly not forever."

Rhinan's concern grew. He'd been in trouble with Keirwyn before, but the Constable had never reacted like this.

Keirwyn had taken Rhinan in when he was a boy after his parents had been mysteriously murdered. Rhinan recalled being hidden for a time, for his own protection, but he didn't remember much, nor had he ever learned who killed his parents or why. All he knew was that it had happened on the same day he'd gone mad, and that had happened before he knew his parents were dead. He shuddered, stopping himself from thinking any more about *that* problem at the moment.

Despite Keirwyn's best efforts to raise him responsibly,

Rhinan had spent most of his time alone, either fooling around or worse, perfecting the art of sneaking around where he didn't belong. The few friends he'd ever had were mostly gone elsewhere now, though Devram would sometimes drink with him. Rhinan's lack of ambition or responsibility was a mystery to everyone, but Rhinan himself understood that he would never be normal—possibly even a kind of danger to those he cared about. Keirwyn had raised him with love, nevertheless, and he felt he owed his own kindheartedness to the aging Constable.

Keirwyn sat, leaning his head into one hand and rubbing his temples. He then looked up at Rhinan. "Why could you never listen to me? I've nearly *begged* you to settle down. You bring in meat, hides, furs… You're the best hunter in the area. The Lore Givers blessed you with your skills of the bow. It is partly because of those skills that this village even puts up with you. You do well enough for just yourself, but if you did a little more—and you easily could—you'd do well enough for a family. Are you not unhappy spending so much time alone on your hunts? Perhaps you might take up another trade. You've always been a sharp boy, Rhinan. Maybe it's not too late. You could still go to the Lore College in Masseltaine, become a *Sohera* of the hunting and tracking discipline…" A *Sohera* was an apprentice to becoming a Lore Trainer of the college, which Rhinan was undoubtedly qualified for if he were allowed to skip levels based on his skills.

Rhinan grinned. "You know as well as I, Keirwyn, that I've never been too adept at much of anything other than maybe avoiding people. I'm fortunate that the Lore Givers granted my skills. And a family? Me? You can't be serious."

He paused, trying (as he often had) to imagine what it would be like for anyone to be around him when his ghosts materialized, his own personal affliction. They'd first appeared, and his parents—Markin and Herilyn Lussaine—had died. Were the ghosts to blame? He'd always wondered. No one else ever saw them, but they would appear to him periodically, whispering and murmuring and hovering at the edge of his vision. He dared not mention them to anyone else, not even his closest confidants. His madness was his alone to bear. Some people endured blindness, others could not walk. But he was simply plagued by his ghosts. His only solution was to retreat in isolation as much as possible, deep in the mountain forests. If the ghosts were a danger, he was keeping others safe by his own solitude.

Then he added to Keirwyn, "But I have always dreamed of a farm for myself someday." Coaxing the land to yield up its bounties held some appeal to him as a peaceful existence. He loved the land, plants, and animals.

Keirwyn allowed himself a chuckle. "Farming is it? You've never grown so much as moss or a mushroom."

Rhinan looked offended. "I've grown… stuff. Besides, you know, I *am* good with animals. Well, sometimes."

Keirwyn smiled warmly at him. "Yes, you have a gentle spirit. Perhaps too gentle. I think that, though I've really tried to be of some comfort, you never quite got over your parents' sudden deaths." Rhinan looked down. Keirwyn did not know about the worst of it, nor did anyone else—the madness of seeing ghosts which may or may not be real and may or may not be dangerous to those he cared about. Rhinan carefully kept it strictly to himself. "Yes, too much for a young boy," Keirwyn went on. "It's been haunting you your whole life."

Rhinan looked up sharply at this. Keirwyn's face was blank. "Haunted?" Rhinan mused. "Yes, I suppose you could say that."

"Silarrah tried to be of some comfort. I'll never understand how she failed to ensnare your attentions."

A bitter pang bloomed in his chest, and Rhinan turned away. He gazed out a window from which he could see the tall trees on the mountain waving in the breeze. "You know she has my attention," Rhinan said quietly. "I just haven't done well by her, either. Couldn't."

"What *are* you waiting for?" Keirwyn suddenly demanded, standing up, pounding a fist on his desk. "Rhinan, I've seen it in her eyes. She would marry you if you would but lead a more honorable lifestyle, become responsible. Maybe just *ask* her! She's a good woman. She won't wait forever. You're both well past marrying age. Don't make the mistakes I made." He grew quiet, distant for a moment before continuing. "Don't get me wrong, Rhinan. I bless the day I took you in. I don't regret it. I just wanted better for you, and now—"

Devram burst back in at that moment, slamming the wooden door behind him. "They're coming!" he hissed.

Rhinan and Keirwyn looked at him in confusion.

"A large squadron of soldiers!" Devram exclaimed. "They're already coming. Apparently, Mundon's steward ran across them out on patrol not far from here. And Keirwyn," Devram looked seriously at the Constable. "It's the King's special force… the *Maraggan.* Gethor Dran himself."

Keirwyn paled at the name, and Rhinan felt his chest tighten in panic. Gethor Dran was well known for his reputation. Not only was he the General of the most well-trained royal unit—the *Maraggan*, and as such the chief law enforcer in Lydania—but also the King's right-hand man. Even that was less frightening than Dran's reputation: he was said to be quite unforgiving—to the point of cruelty.

Keirwyn turned quickly to Rhinan, shaking his head grimly. "I thought we'd have a few days before… This changes everything. You won't even be safe in my custody. I won't be able to keep you here." He looked lost. "Get going," he said furiously, pushing Rhinan toward the door. "Find a place out of the way and do what you do best: disappear into the woods. Hide. Just let me handle this." Rhinan began to back out, his thoughts racing.

As Rhinan left Keirwyn's lodge, Keirwyn called one last thing to him. "Whatever you do, Rhinan, *don't let them find you.* Fear for your very life."

Chapter Two

"Why is Keirwyn so sure they'll want to kill me, Devram?" Rhinan asked, scrambling around in his small hut, quickly wrapping a few provisions and shoving them into a worn satchel. "I'll be the first to admit I'm a troublemaker, maybe I'm even good for nothing. But I've never done anything so terrible as to deserve execution. I've never even met Gethor Dran or King Jerrick. Param brings stories back from his travels, but I suppose I don't really listen. Have things become so oppressed in Lydania?" Param Voss was Rhinan's best friend since childhood, an accomplished troubadour, and he would return home each winter with stories of the various regions of Lydania. Rhinan wasn't much for hearing about the unpleasant things.

"Just hurry, will you?" Devram replied in exasperation. "The only thing I can tell you is that I honestly do not know why Keirwyn is so particularly worried. Spend less time hiding away and you'd *know* how bad things are in Lydania. I'd suggest hiding now, though, given Gethor Dran's reputation. In normal times, the worst punishment you could expect for something like this would be time in the dungeons at Masseltaine, or to lose a hand perhaps."

Rhinan paused. "Oh, is that all? Well, then maybe I'll just go accept my fate."

"It's not funny, Rhinan," Devram admonished. "I've never seen Keirwyn so worried. He dotes on you, and you make light of all this."

"I am sorry, Devram," Rhinan replied, stepping toward the door. "I make light of what I don't understand." He pulled his satchel over his head, bracing it on his shoulder, then reached down beside the door and lifted his quiver of arrows over his head, bracing the strap on the opposite shoulder. Finally, he plucked a large sheath that held a hunting knife from a hook by the door and strapped it to his right thigh. Opening the door, he peered out. "I don't see any *Maraggan* yet."

"That's the idea," Devram remarked dryly. "Now let's go. Eodorr's waiting."

"Eodorr?" Rhinan was suspicious, but he grabbed his bow from where it hung on a pair of pegs above the door, quickly strung it, and he and Devram emerged from the hut. "I would expect *him* to be tempted to hand me over."

Rhinan and Eodorr had been friends in their youth, but had grown distant as they emerged into adulthood. Eodorr increasingly resented Rhinan's easy manner, and his ability to perform mischievous undertakings and wriggle his way out of any consequences for his actions. Eodorr felt as many in Cabelon did: Rhinan, though harmless, did not make a fair and consistent contribution to the community. He did, however, benefit from the community's labors, although it was through reckless means that were a regular source of irritation. Only his expert hunting skills kept Rhinan from being driven away completely. He was the finest archer in the town. Though Cabelon raised some livestock, his skills were appreciated during leaner times when he strolled into town with wild game slung over his shoulders. Though such occasions were probably too rare, he was generous with his spoils, which made people all the more inclined to look the other way when he pilfered from a garden, cellar, shed or such. Rhinan and Eodorr had often quarreled over Rhinan's behavior. He regretted that now.

Devram sighed. "He's stopped being upset about all that. Oh, he still thinks you're a worthless cur, of course. But fortunately for you, he'll do what Keirwyn asks."

The two men scrambled away from the hut, out of the village and into the mountain forest. The crunch of fallen vegetation beneath their feet was like a trumpet blast in Rhinan's ears. He placed his steps carefully, also looking for damper leaves and needles to muffle the sound of his steps, but Devram had no such stealth. Rhinan would never have called Devram simple, but he knew that Devram was unencumbered by attention to detail.

They were startled when a *linkbird* squawked, uncoiled its lengthy tail from a branch above them, and flew away with a rustling of twigs. "We'll wait at the old smithy down by the river," Devram called over his shoulder as he continued on. "Eodorr will meet us there."

Yet Rhinan barely heard his words. A familiar disturbing sound was sweeping up at him from within the forest, chilling his blood. *Oh, Divine Lore Givers, no. Not the madness… not now.*

The murmuring of a multitude of voices engulfed his senses, rising in volume that only he could hear. The voices pelted him like small wisps of wind, and dimness permeated the air like a shadow. The voices spoke only gibberish whenever they manifested, as they always had since they first came to Rhinan when he was a child.

He continued to follow Devram, but could not be sure if his friend was still speaking. Reluctantly, yet certain of what he would find, Rhinan cast a glance back over his shoulder.

And there was his entire horde of ghosts.

Flowing along behind him, like a flood among the trees, was a host of unclear, hazy forms—men, women and children, garmented only in dull, light tones of gray, tan or white, as if color did not completely exist in their realm. Their faces were either shadowed, dark blots hiding their features, or they were not completely visible. No details in their features. Rhinan was gripped by the chill of their presence, now familiar after years of such encounters, but no less horrifying.

He stopped and turned to face them. The ghosts immediately stopped as well, and their murmuring dwindled to silence as they stood before him.

But that was all they ever did. They would appear at various times, sometimes more frequently, then not at all for long periods of time. They were more likely to appear to him outside of the village, out in the woods, but had even followed him through Cabelon on a random occasion or two. He had no idea what they wanted, or if they actually existed. Only he saw them, and only he suffered them. But his own lifelong madness was always with him—even in their absence. Though he was filled with potential, he had chosen not to attend the Lore College because of this. He had not married because of this. Rhinan had chosen isolation, secretly afraid that these appearances had had something to do with the slaying of his parents, and that the ghosts' reappearances would always be a danger to others. It had not proven to be the case, but he had still never been willing to take that chance.

He wondered now if their appearance heralded some dreadful occurrence. Or was it just another trick of his imagination?

Then, for the first time in his entire life, the ghosts did something other than follow him murmuring gibberish or watch him in motionless silence.

As one, they all silently raised an arm and together they pointed in what he could only determine was eastward, which would send him the opposite direction from the smithy where they were supposed to meet Eodorr.

The sudden shock of the new gesture caused him to stumble backward. Hands grabbed him, and he turned, prepared to fight.

"This is a poor time for daydreaming, Rhinan." Devram gave him an odd look. "Are you all right? You look—"

"I'm… fine." Rhinan peeked back, and the ghosts were no longer there. He never knew if they really had been after these incidents, for they left no traces. Why had they chosen this time to appear? What were they trying to tell him? *What had caused them to take any kind of action?* "Just a bit anxious, I suppose."

"Well, hurry." Devram set a quicker pace toward the smithy, and Rhinan followed, confusion churning his thoughts. He couldn't stop wondering why the ghosts had chosen now to act, and why they were pointing the other way.

Chapter Three

Gethor Dran could not tolerate the odor of these tiny mountain villages. The smell of mud and straw assaulted his nostrils, reminding him how far from the comforts of his quarters at the palace he had come. The worst thing about damp straw, he reflected, was that it didn't burn as well as he liked it to.

The peasants of Cabelon stopped whatever meaningless task they were busy with as Dran and his men trotted their horses into the village. It pleased him to see the surprise and alarm on their dirty faces, but it would have pleased him more if he could smell their fear over their surroundings. Still, he was sure he was being shown as much respect as these worms were capable of, and he deserved it. After all, was he not the General of the *Maraggan*, the special force that acted as the very living embodiment of the King's order, justice and retribution?

Ordinarily, Dran would have had no concern for a small incident out here so far from Masseltaine. What did it matter? The local Constable could handle it or not, for all he cared. These people were of no real use to the kingdom, perhaps more of a burden than an asset. Yet the rider had come from the Baron Lord Mundon, and Dran knew the King was fond of Mundon's family. It would appear favorable for the complaint to be answered so swiftly. Not that Dran was concerned about losing Jerrick's favor, but he liked to justify his autonomy. He was free to enforce the King's laws by about any means he deemed necessary, and he wanted to keep it that way. He knew that strict enforcement was the only thing to keep the masses in line, and fear of strong penalties prevented any likelihood of open rebellion. Dran did not like to be challenged, so he made it easy on himself by treating the mere appearance of disorder as a treasonous crime.

Boredom, however, was even more of a factor in Dran's decision to ride up here to Cabelon. Their patrol of the foothills region had been dull and uneventful, and the men were itching for sport. Such lack of action always blackened his mood. Some insignificant rogue out here on the mountain frontier could be just what they needed to break up the monotony. Furthermore, these distant villages tended to be an unruly lot, and it never hurt to make a strong example when opportunity presented itself. Perhaps it just had.

Near the center of Cabelon sat a long hall of wood with a straw-thatched roof. Dran expected the Constable would be found there. There were no signs of activity as he and his *Maraggan* approached. Too quiet. *Perhaps the situation has been handled sufficiently.* Considering that brought him a touch of disappointment. If that were the case, he would have to settle for disciplining the Constable for not doing a proper job of keeping order. He checked the lash he kept tucked into his belt, and found it securely in place, as always.

Reining his horse to a halt outside the hall, he turned to

his men. The two score *Maraggan* were the sharpest soldiers to be found in the army of Lydania. He'd been allowed by the King to handpick his own regiment, the royal special force, and he'd chosen such men as could be counted on to see things his own way. The last thing Gethor Dran was willing to put up with was insubordination or even questioning of his orders. When he gave a command, nothing but immediate action with efficient results was acceptable.

"Siras, Kilward… you'll come with me," Dran ordered two of his three captains. "The rest of you mind the horses, and be alert. Anything looks like trouble, you know what to do." *Kill first, ask questions later. No point in being soft with these yokels.* "This won't take long."

He, Siras, and Kilward dismounted, their boots striking the ground with a heavy thud. *Now let's see how we can find a way to exercise our skills.*

* * * * *

Keirwyn peered out the window, his breath fogging the pane in the chill of the autumn day. He counted forty soldiers approaching on horseback with Dran, all of them in the black and gold uniforms of the King's elite force, the *Maraggan.* Dran himself wore the golden mantle, signifying his position of command. The General appeared younger than Keirwyn would have expected, given that he'd held the position for a number of years. His close-cropped hair was still dark, though by Keirwyn's reckoning, it should be revealing more gray traces of age by now than it did. He moved with authority and indifference, a cold and powerful man. He is as arrogant as ever, Keirwyn decided.

Keirwyn knew him not only by reputation, but had seen

him before. It had been long ago, and they'd never actually met. Dran had been the Captain of the Palace Guard at the time, close to the King (Jerrick had been different then, but so had many other things) but not yet a general. He doubted that Dran would know him, though. And he preferred it that way.

Keirwyn had not yet been granted the position of Constable at the time, but he was serving in the army of Lydania. He'd been decorated by the King himself, with the Lydanian army in attendance, after the sudden and drastic conclusion of the Ylvan Uprising. Jerrick had shown no mercy in an abominable act to end the Uprising and banish the Ylvan clans from the world. With the conflict ended, Keirwyn had been able to request the position of Constable in the distant, frontier town of Cabelon. It was as far from the seat of power as he could get, and a place where his obvious distaste for the King's rash choices would not betray him. And he had other reasons for heading as far from Jerrick as he could, too.

His position had enabled him to grant secret amnesty to his friend Markin Ashuir, keeping the man's family hidden and off the official records. Markin's wife Herilyn was expecting their first, and what would turn out to be their only, child. The Ashuirs were the last remaining members of the Ylvan clans, the people of the eastern-most region in Lydania: Eluciar. Rhinan was born shortly after Keirwyn took them quietly in. They assumed the name Lussaine for discretion, though no one in Cabelon would know Markin Ashuir or his connections to the King. Upon the happenstance discovery of the Ashuirs' survival and whereabouts by one of the *Maraggan* a few years later, Keirwyn had, in fact, literally taken Rhinan in like a son when his parents' murders had left the boy orphaned. The Constable had been thankful that whatever mercenary the King sent to slay them had overlooked the child. After an anxious period of time when Keirwyn successfully made every effort to keep Rhinan less visible for his protection, it appeared that the King did not know of his existence.

Filled with pity and compassion, the Constable tried to help the boy adjust, but Rhinan was filled with troubles that he refused to talk about. The time of hiding, combined with the shock of his parents' murder and whatever those unspeakable troubles were that played upon the boy's mind, left Rhinan unable to fit in with the rest of the village. As a result, he gradually came to live as something of an outcast, viewed mostly as a good-natured pest, but a pest nevertheless. Keirwyn had always believed that the boy would mature someday—as long as King Jerrick never learned of his heritage. Keirwyn had even kept the knowledge from Rhinan himself, but was certain that the King would guess should Rhinan ever be brought before him. His manner and his presence were undoubtedly Ylvan, a certain grace and affinity for communing with nature. And his resemblance to his father would not be overlooked by Jerrick. The King would see Markin in Rhinan.

And now Rhinan's only hope for survival might lay with Keirwyn's ability to play politics with a man who was known to prefer action to debate. Failing that, the Constable hoped that Devram and Eodorr could cover his escape well enough to prevent Dran's men from following too quickly. Keirwyn would have to stall the King's special force at any cost.

As he watched Dran and two of his men step down from their horses, Keirwyn silently made a request of the Lore Givers, those immortal mentors who imparted all knowledge to mortal men, to grant him the wisdom in whatever discipline he needed to diffuse this situation.

But, jaded, he had lost his faith in rationale long ago.

He removed his scabbard and sword, and hung it over the back of his chair. No point in a show of force if he could resolve this peacefully. He did, however, withdraw his polished maille shirt kept folded on a shelf in the corner. It had been polished regularly but not worn for years. He put it on, and it was a bit snug. Certainly no show of force, but a little defense could be wise.

Forcing himself to be calm, he prepared a diplomatic smile and pushed open the door, stepping out to greet the General, a man with a reputation for being one of the cruelest known. As he did so, he wondered if it was very well considered to leave his sword behind.

Chapter Four

Rhinan and Devram edged their way carefully around the outskirts of town, remaining among the trees. Down the slope sat the old smithy beside the stream that ran past it, marking what used to be the northern edge of Cabelon. The open-front stone building was crumbling; wild trees and plants twisted throughout the fragmented ruins and shaded the surrounding area. The scent of moss and fungus hung thick in the air. Behind the structure, the stream trickled weakly along in anticipation of winter, a slight mist rising from the hollow. Rhinan could recall a time when the abandoned smithy was an interesting place to explore, but for years he'd associated it with more disturbing feelings. He shuddered now as they approached the shadowy structure.

Eodorr was pacing anxiously when they arrived, now dressed in his Village Guard uniform of black and tan to look official. A bridled horse stood patiently tethered to a broken timber. "Did you stop for a picnic?" Eodorr sneered, stepping forward. Rhinan could see he had a bundle wrapped in cloth under one arm, the contents indistinguishable. "Devram, get right back to Keirwyn. He should tell Gethor

Dran that the prisoner escaped."

Devram turned to Rhinan. "Be swift, be cautious, and be smart. Maybe we'll see you again when this whole thing washes down the mountain." Eodorr snorted, but Devram turned and scampered away, disappearing among the trees.

Eodorr looked back at Rhinan, and he seemed to be considering something. "Well, I doubt you'll get far. For what it's worth, I hope they don't catch you. You're a pebble in the boot, but the *Maraggan* is real trouble."

"I'm sorry for everything, Eodorr. Seriously."

"No time for that now," Eodorr shook his head. "Here." He handed the bundle under his arm to Rhinan, who couldn't determine what all of the contents were by feel, though there seemed to be a sheathed blade among the items. "Keirwyn sent me to fetch those for you. He says they belonged to your parents, and that you should have them now. I don't know anything more about them."

Perplexed, Rhinan allowed his curiosity a moment while he dropped to one knee to open the cloth around the bundle of items. There was a sword in a scabbard, and a fist-sized wooden box with etchings on the edge of the lid that Rhinan didn't recognize. Before he could open the box, he noticed Eodorr staring at the hilt of the sword with a strange expression on his face.

"Could I…?" Eodorr asked, apparently entranced.

Rhinan nodded and handed the blade to him, still in the scabbard. Eodorr drew the blade partially out, transfixed. "I've never seen the like of it," he murmured. "With the King's decree against unauthorized weapon smithing, anyone who has this kind of skill works only for the royal army. And I don't seem to recall seeing anything this nice even among their blades." He peered at Rhinan. "What *was* your father?"

"I believe he was a Lore Trainer at one time." Rhinan was a boy when his parents were killed, and knew almost nothing of them prior to his birth. Most of what he knew he'd learned from Keirwyn. He took the weapon back from Eodorr and stood.

Both of them looked up at the long-abandoned blacksmith shop. Before his parents had died, the place had fascinated him. He'd learned later that the blacksmith made weapons, but had been taken away to work for the King before Rhinan was born. Weapon smiths had three, perhaps four, choices in Lydania: work for the King, find another discipline, or suffer imprisonment. Or worse.

"That sword didn't come from here." Eodorr then tilted his head toward the other item. "Not going to look in the box?"

"Later." Rhinan looked to the tethered horse. "For me?"

Eodorr nodded. "You'll need him. He's fleet and sure-footed. His name is Dodger." He turned and spared a long look at the horse. "Take care of him, Rhinan. You'll find a few provisions in the bags to get you away from here. After that… well, you're a fine hunter."

Rhinan acknowledged the compliment with a brief nod of gratitude.

"Now hit me," Eodorr said. "Hard."

"What?!?"

"If I'm injured, it'll look better that you escaped. It's not like there haven't been times when you wanted to anyway, right?" He grinned at Rhinan, who hesitated. "If it makes you feel any better, I hope I get the chance to return the favor someday."

Rhinan couldn't suppress a chuckle. "You know, I hope so, too," he said, moisture in his eyes. "I'd like to come home again when I can."

He noticed Eodorr was about to speak, but his swing was too quick. He caught Eodorr alongside the head with his bow, and Eodorr slumped to the ground in silence.

Rhinan looked down at the limp form. "Might as well be a convincing blow, right?"

* * * * *

The feeble Constable that strolled out to greet them was smiling. Dran thought he looked every bit the politician, and he might even look familiar. But then most of these village folk all looked the same anyway, didn't they? Except this Keirwyn was obviously Travinian by his copper-brown skin.

Once the Constable had approached, he silently dropped to one knee and bowed his head in the appropriate salute, a show of submission. "You may rise," Dran told him, already growing bored of the performance.

"General Dran," said the old man, straightening up. "We are honored by your presence. I am Keirwyn Dayas, Constable of Cabelon. I apologize for our lack of reception. We weren't expecting—"

"Never mind." Dran sighed. "We're only passing this way to look into a complaint about some persistent wretch who's been plundering the farms hereabout." He noticed the Constable pale and stiffen. "What can you tell me about him?"

"Oh… yes, of course." To Dran, it seemed that the Constable hesitated for the briefest of moments, and then he tried reasoning. "Well, it seems to have been a tricky bit of misunderstanding, really. The matter is being resolved even as we speak. Why don't we—"

"Why don't we step into your lodge?" Dran asked. "And you can provide me with a full report."

The Constable seemed to hesitate again. He then spoke quietly. "Why, yes, there is a chill to the day. Do come inside." What was his reason for such caution?

Dran and his two captains followed Constable Dayas into the lodge. It was poorly lit with an old hanging lantern—the candle burning low—and sparsely decorated with some wooden furniture that appeared as if the old man himself had hacked it out from some of the local trees with his own sword. A meager fire burned in the hearth. There was nowhere to sit, save one old chair behind a broad table being used for a desk where the Constable's sword hung uselessly. *Perhaps dulled from whittling furniture*, Dran jested to himself. He noticed no record books, and made a note to ask later about the tax keeping.

"We'll be taking your prisoner back to Masseltaine," Dran commented, circling around to sit in the chair he presumed was the seat of authority. He was growing weary of the Constable's continued silence or preoccupation, and he wanted to be done with this dreadful place as soon as possible.

There was no immediate response from the Constable, who seemed momentarily displaced. These mountain people were such simpletons, and Dran began to wonder if the Constable weren't one as well. Perhaps it was his age, though he didn't really seem much older than Dran—just perhaps not taking care of himself as well. "The prisoner," Dran repeated slowly and clearly. "You said the matter was near resolution. I assume this means you have apprehended the rascal?"

"Well, it's not that… I mean, you have to understand…

that is… well, he's dead."

"Dead?" Dran frowned.

"He was in fragile health, you see. Poor lad."

"Fine," Dran sighed. "We'll take the body, then. If you can point me to your cells, we'll retrieve it."

Now the old man looked confused. "You want the body?" he said.

He must be daft, Dran thought. Definitely too old now to be very effective. He would have to recommend the Constable be replaced.

"No disrespect, your Lordship, but surely you wouldn't want to bear such a burden. We can certainly dispose of the body. Besides, you've traveled so far. Wouldn't you prefer some of our fine provisions to carry on your trip back to Masseltaine?"

Dran felt almost as if he was being bribed. Fresh provisions were no matter. They were the *Maraggan*, and whatever supplies were available were there to suit their need. But perhaps some mountain ale and a local wench or two offered as token appreciation for services rendered might not be so bad for the men.

Then a rising commotion outside the door caught all of their attention. The door was opened, and a young man was shoved roughly inside, followed by two more of Dran's patrol. He wondered if this "poor lad" might be the "body" he was asking for. His infinite patience was dwindling. "Someone had better explain this, and make it quick," Dran snarled. "Who have we here?"

* * * * *

When he came through the door, it looked to Keirwyn as

if Devram had already been roughly handled. Keirwyn wondered if this meant Rhinan had been caught. Either way, this may or may not have been going well, but now it was likely worse.

"We saw him approaching the hall," said one of the soldiers who'd just brought Devram in. "We called for him to stop, and he turned to run."

"I was startled," Devram explained. "I actually work for the Constable. Keirwyn can tell you."

"Really?" Dran turned to Keirwyn, rubbing his chin. "He one of yours?" he asked, cocking his head toward Devram. Devram hadn't taken the time to put on his uniform. At least they hadn't caught Eodorr. They didn't mention another Village Guard, so Keirwyn hoped for the best.

Keirwyn considered carefully what response would be safest. He did not know if Rhinan was away, and he did not want to endanger Devram. He simply nodded.

"Well, then, perhaps you can tell us about your prisoner?" Dran asked, rising from the chair and circling around the table to stand over Devram.

"I have already told you—" Keirwyn began.

"Ah, ah!" Dran cut him off, turning back to him and raising a finger to his lips. "Consider this an efficiency check. I like to see if everyone has the same perspective." He returned his gaze to Devram. "Now tell me. What has become of your prisoner?"

Devram looked to Keirwyn, but Keirwyn could find no way to signal anything to him without making the situation worse. After a long silence, Devram spoke, barely audible. "He's escaped, My Lord."

At first, no one moved or made a sound, other than Dran turning to stare coldly at Keirwyn. Though relieved that this meant Rhinan had not been caught, Keirwyn feared now for more than Rhinan. If only they'd had time to prepare the same story…

At length, Dran asked Devram, "Escaped, did you say? Are you certain?"

"Yes. I believe he means to travel west over the mountains to the sea, and then south along the coast. It may not be too late to ride him down."

Under Dran's gaze, Keirwyn suddenly felt very tired. He expected Rhinan would most likely head in the opposite direction, so he assumed Devram was lying.

"That's quite an accomplishment and quite a journey," Dran mocked, "for a *dead* man." Over his shoulder, he told the two guards with Devram, "Take him outside and hold him for questioning. Have Captain Gaimesh see to it."

Even Dran's own men drew back at the thought of Gaimesh questioning a man, and that sickened Keirwyn. As Devram was lead out, Keirwyn watched in silence. He could do nothing for Devram right now, and he had now run out of ideas for delaying these men from finding Rhinan. Out of ideas save one.

"I'm out of patience," Dran warned. "I came here to take custody of a local thief. Instead, I find a Constable who seems to be protecting him or hiding him for some reason. Now I'll have an explanation and a prisoner, Constable, or I'll have to consider your loyalties suspect."

As he stood beside his table of office, Keirwyn felt himself suddenly overcome with calm and clarity. He had only one option left to help Rhinan, and he knew what he must do. Swifter than he'd moved in years, he reached for the hilt of his sword, drawing it forth from the scabbard where it hung over his chair. In one motion, he swung it around and brought it up between himself and Gethor Dran.

Fearless, silent, he stood knowing that his skills were well out of practice, and he had no chance of defeating the deadly General or his men. Yet every moment he could hold their attention, keep them distracted, was a moment for Rhinan to get further away. Keirwyn would lose this battle; of that, he had no doubt even as he drew his sword. But he was prepared to face that outcome, and he would make this battle count.

Chapter Five

Clouds nudged each other across the sky, crowding out the light of day. There was a damp chill in the air, and Rhinan knew that a mountain storm was developing. It would make his travel more difficult, but any pursuit would suffer the same inconvenience. And, he hoped, tracking him would be much harder.

The Domins, a range of short mountains in which the town of Cabelon was nestled at the far north end, ranged southward past the town of Omriel until they stopped at the Midnight Fjord which cut in from the Framman Sea. Trailing up the coast of the Framman Sea, they curled eastward at the northern end above Cabelon and folded into the larger Percene Mountain range which ran across the northern expanse of Lydania.

Fort Cabelon had been founded long ago as an outpost—far out on the frontier of the young Lydania—to watch for, warn of and delay any invading forces from the north or west. To the west of the pass of Cabelon, the Domins tumbled down to the sea, but no attacks had ever come from that route. To the north there had been scattered brigades of ice trolls in colder winters, and long ago an occasional hunting party would wander into the vicinity of Cabelon. There were few troublesome encounters, however, as the ice trolls preferred to avoid contact, rather than provoke hostility. It had been countless years since any such appearance.

Rhinan also recalled childhood stories of trees which walked and talked like men. But he'd spent so much time in the forest that he would know if that were true, and it wasn't. Which was not to say that the trees didn't move and speak in their own ways. He would hear their voices when the gentle breeze whispered among their dancing leaves, or the wild wind roared through their branches, or when their boughs would creak or their leaves would fall… or in so many other ways in which he could hear the trees speak to him that others could not.

What had actually happened was that Cabelon eventually settled into a quiet foresting community, providing lumber, hides and furs to various parts of Lydania. It was almost forgotten by the rest of the kingdom, in fact, and that seemed satisfactory to the inhabitants of the little village.

Eastward and to the south of Cabelon, in the foothills of the Domins, was the city of Omriel. Named after the brother of the first Lydan king, the city had been the seat of power in Lydania generations ago. It had once been a busy market for trading and services, though less so since the rise of Masseltaine, where King Jerrick's father had established a new palace. In its prime, Omriel was considered the jewel city in the crown of Lydania and still was to some.

Though he generally preferred to remain amid the quiet forests around Cabelon, enjoying the sunlight-dappled forest floor, moss-coated tree trunks and moss-draped branches, ferns and ivies, with upright circular root systems of toppled trees so large in diameter as to reach twice the height of a man, Rhinan traveled down the mountain fairly regularly to Omriel. He made for it now as swiftly as possible, wary of any sound or movement. He was startled a few times by small birds or animals, which darted off in one direction or another at the approach of a man on a horse.

Dodger proved to be true to his name. As the horse carried Rhinan down the mountainside, he was able to move swiftly and still avoid colliding with trees, roots, or boulders. Rhinan admired the horse, and recalled that Eodorr had raised more than a few fine beasts. Dodger was white with gray and brown patches, both swift and agile, and an agreeable creature—a fact that was most important to Rhinan, since he seldom did any riding. His trips to Omriel were normally afoot, and it would take a day, a night, and another day to reach the city. On Dodger, if he rode all day and most of the night, he might make it by morning.

After Omriel, Rhinan had no idea where to go. He had no family and had never been further from Cabelon than Omriel. It was important to him that his first stop be in that city for only one reason.

Silarrah.

After his parents' death, other children began to find him odd. He knew it was his ghosts, but he could never tell anyone. Only two of his four best friends (which had included Devram and Eodorr) stood by him during those difficult times: Param Voss, who now traveled Lydania as a troubadour, and Silarrah.

She was the one person he'd almost told about his ghosts, but she was also the one person whose friendship he couldn't afford to risk losing. She'd grown up and eventually left Cabelon to help orphaned children in Omriel, never having had any of her own. Since then, Rhinan had made frequent visits to see her and to bring gifts, and sometimes smiles, to the children in her care.

Keirwyn had been partly right—Rhinan should have married her. If only he weren't mad, he would have made the attempt to make her happy. She had not married, choosing instead to couple with her work and the children in her charge. And Rhinan could not justify inflicting his curse on her, or any children in her vicinity. So year after year, he settled for brief visits that both of them looked forward to with eager anticipation. Yet Rhinan worried that Silarrah would someday grow weary of this.

And now he would have to tell her that he was going away. He knew it would be the final spurn, the event that would at last cause her to give up on him. Unless he offered her a promise, and they came to an understanding. He had some serious thinking to do, and he would have to come to a decision. Concentrating, he hoped the Lore Givers would provide some knowledge for handling the situation.

By late afternoon, Rhinan had arrived at a site he hadn't consciously intended to reach. Two white stone arches that came together and intertwined at half a man's height. Overlooking the plains below, the monuments (placed by Keirwyn) marked the graves of his parents. He passed this way occasionally on trips to Omriel, but today seemed different. He was in a hurry, but he felt compelled to stop and pay respects.

A flash of lightning illuminated the graves as he dismounted Dodger. A moment later, a crack of thunder resounded across the darkening sky, and a light rain began to fall. The wind grew stronger, chilling him, and driving the rain into his face as he knelt beside the markers.

Unusually silent, his ghosts appeared. As Rhinan looked up, they seemed to shuffle around as if uneasy.

"What?!" He shouted at them, knowing that they never made any response. As always, they had no reaction to anything he said or did. In hopeless despair, he threw himself on the ground and wept in the rain.

Momentarily, he withdrew the box and sword that Keirwyn had sent to him with Eodorr. They came from his parents, though he had no recollection of the existence of these items. He also couldn't imagine what might be in the box, so he decided to open it there at his parents' graveside. Let the ghosts watch. Let the rain fall.

What type of wood the box was carved from was a mystery to him. He could tell it was lovely workmanship, but he didn't take the time to really admire or appreciate it. He couldn't read the markings on the box, but there were two letters on it that were clear to him: M.A. It made no sense to him, but it looked like initials, perhaps of the owner or the woodworker. It wasn't his father's initials, or it would have been M.L. He undid the catch and slid out a small drawer. There was some kind of dull gray gem in the drawer, almost the size of his palm.

Two things happened at once. The ghosts all turned in his direction, their hollow eyes immediately orienting on the gem. At almost the same instant, a searing bolt of light sizzled down from the sky, striking the gem and hurling a stunned Rhinan backwards onto the damp ground, momentarily blinded. His hands burned with pain. He sat up and noticed that his gloves were charred and smoldering, but he was otherwise unharmed.

The ghosts were now murmuring as they usually did.

"And this is why I stay away from people," he said to the ghosts. "Did you do this?" No response, which was no surprise. He shook off the impact of the lightning bolt and removed the smoldering gloves from his hands. His vision clearing, he cast a wary glance skyward and bent to retrieve the gem.

The gem itself was changed—it glowed a brilliant shade of sea blue-green. Despite the lightning strike, it was quite cool to the touch. Only now did he notice the silver chain upon which it hung. The cut of the stone was only an inch or two thick. Narrow and almost pointed at the top where the chain passed through, the gem—though crudely shaped and roughly edged—widened at the rounder base, giving it the vague shape of a flat drop of water. As Rhinan gazed into it, he had the sense that he peered into the depths of a tiny lake, extending much deeper than the stone's thickness would indicate.

Rhinan couldn't recall ever seeing either of his parents wear this about their neck. Whatever kind of family heirloom it was, he would keep it. This and the sword were the only belongings he now had from his parents. Why had Keirwyn never shared this with him before? He looked down at the wooden box, and was sorry to see that it lay charred and shattered from the lightning strike. He hung the chain around his neck, dropping the gem safely away inside his vest and tunic.

He looked down at the graves. "What did you mean for me to do? What is to become of me?"

An instant later, the ghosts moved to surround him, apparently frantic. The air rippled with their energy, swirling about him in small bursts of air he could feel, catching at him and waving his hair around! This was another new act on the part of his ghosts—

No, it wasn't. The last time they'd touched him this way had been the day his parents were killed.

"Keirwyn!" he shouted into the wind, turning to grab Dodger's reins.

The rain intensified, falling so heavily that Rhinan lost sight of the ghosts.

* * * * *

Gethor Dran stepped back when Constable Dayas brandished his sword. Both of his captains there in the Constable's office with him drew their own blades in response.

So there was to be no cooperation at all from this official. Dran sighed. He made no other move before he spoke. "Well isn't *this* an interesting turn of events? I bring my regiment up into this worthless little corner of the kingdom for a routine investigation of a local complaint, and in so doing, expose a traitor to the crown. Being a Constable, you are aware of the penalty for treason, I presume."

Dran noticed Keirwyn's quick glance at his captains. It looked as if the Constable were preparing to take all of them on at once. Neither of Dran's men advanced, but they stood ready. The Constable backed around the table, presumably in an effort to find room to maneuver for a fight. Or, Dran considered, perhaps to keep him and his men distracted and facing away from the door as long as possible. But Keirwyn did not respond to Dran's statement.

"I see," Dran continued. He drew his own blade, slowly, deliberately. "Relinquish your command, Constable. Will you lay down your sword and surrender, or must we take you by force? Resisting arrest is considered an extended act of treason. The penalty grows harsher if we have to disarm you."

Keirwyn chuckled, and Dran wondered if he might be mad. The penalty for treason was death—and it appeared the Constable was already prepared for that—but why would he resist and earn the additional penalty of torment?

The Constable finally spoke again with a sneer. "I doubt if disarming one old man will even earn you your pay, but I'll do my best to see that the King gets his money's worth."

This at last brought out Dran's wrath. He had been told that, upon his features, this was a frightening thing to behold. Keirwyn said no more, but he glared defiantly and held his position. He didn't attack, and Dran knew the man was wasting time for a reason. It was time to end this.

When Dran brought his blade to bear, the force of each of his blows striking Keirwyn's sword visibly shook throughout the Constable's elder body. Dran came on steadily, effortlessly, raining stroke after stroke with smooth motions, each clash of their blades a thunderclap.

Despite his age and obvious lack of practical exercise, Keirwyn held his own admirably well. Dran never had any doubt of the outcome, however. Entirely on the defensive, it was all the Constable could do to retain his balance. Dran drove him steadily back until he was trapped, at last pressed into the corner of the lodge. There was nowhere left for him to step, and his arm trembled with fatigue.

Then Keirwyn at last appeared to anger. Drawing a breath, the Constable returned Dran's blows, hailing one after another against the powerful General, driving him backward momentarily. Dran smiled, enjoying the sport of it. He welcomed a challenge, even a slight one. The Constable's skill was still in there, earning Dran's respect. In his youth, this

Dayas may have even bested Dran, and that impressed him.

With another surge, Dran drove the Constable back into the corner again. He then drew back and examined Keirwyn. "It's not too late to turn yourself in," he suggested. "Last chance."

Keirwyn responded with one more lunge forward, a single thrust aimed straight at Dran's heart.

Yet Dran sidestepped the thrust, bringing his own blade down on Keirwyn's sword arm, severing it cleanly at the elbow. Keirwyn cried out in agony and slumped back against the corner, clutching at the stump with his other hand.

Stepping on the severed limb, Dran reached down and pried the Constable's sword from the fingers. He examined the blade.

"Still sharp," he observed. "Not too bad." He turned back to Keirwyn, who was slumping down toward the floor, blood pooling at his feet. With a snarl, he drew the Constable's own blade back and, with a powerful thrust forward, drove it through Keirwyn's midsection, pinning him to the wall. As blood began to trickle from the Constable's mouth, Dran leaned in and patted him lightly on the cheek. "See?" he said. "*That's* how it's done."

Gethor Dran then stepped back again, regarding Keirwyn Dayas one last time. "You are hereby relieved of your position."

Chapter Six

With the rain falling heavily, Gethor Dran was most upset about one thing—there would be no way now to set the mountain village ablaze. He gazed around at the drab cottages. This dreadful place had so tried his patience that he wanted very badly to eliminate it. Perhaps, if it suited him, he might return next summer… when things were dry…

"My Lord?"

The voice of his captain interrupted his bitter musing. He hoped it would be good news. *It had better be.* "What have we learned, Siras?"

Siras pulled his cloak tighter, hesitant to respond.

Is it the weather or is it me that he's trying to avoid?

"He's not our man, My Lord."

Dran sighed. "Let me see."

Siras motioned in silence, leading Dran away from the Constable's quarters. The village seemed deserted now, as if a plague had come. The thought was almost enough to cheer Dran's spirits. Then he noticed the rest of his men huddled together against a low wooden fence, over which was draped the unmoving form of the unfortunate young man they had captured.

Dran strode past Siras and stepped close enough to examine the man. Beyond the fence lay a small patch of plants—some kind of garden—and a cottage beyond that. He thought he noticed a face peering out of a window, but then the face pulled away out of sight. He snorted with derision at such cowardice as he reached for the body. Grasping the back of the man's tunic, he gave one hard pull and the limp figure flopped back onto Dran's outstretched arm. He looked into the still face.

"This man is dead, Siras," Dran stated. "You were careless."

"I apologize, My Lord," replied the captain, sincerity in his voice. "We did not anticipate his frailty."

"Well, I suppose that's the way of it sometimes," Dran replied. He heaved the body onto the ground, and stared for a moment as blood merged into the rivulets of rain trickling along beside the body in the mud. "Aside from his frailty, what else did we learn?"

Siras cleared his throat. "It seems his name is Devram... was Devram… and he worked for the Constable. He was quite devoted to the old man, in fact. Rather concerned about his well-being. He was becoming a bit too nostalgic, so I let Captain Gaimesh work on him." He nodded toward one of the men, a dark, slender figure. Gaimesh stood silently in the rain, wearing no cloak or tunic—just a flat band of leather around each of his upper arms and around his neck. He was holding something, examining it. Dran couldn't be sure, but it looked like an eye.

"He became somewhat more conversational," Siras continued, "but not as much as we would hope for. We learned that the man we're looking for is no more than a petty thief, not to be taken seriously. Apparently, this was not the first time he'd raided Lord Mundon's larders. Oh, and he was like a *son* to the Constable."

"Ah," Dran said, folding his arms across his chest. "So *that's* it." Dran had little concern for familial bonds. He'd never known his mother, and his father had been a distant figure at the best of times, and a brute at the worst. He'd left home at a young age, joined the King's army, and never looked back. When he thought about them, which was rare, he realized he didn't know anything about his own parents—and he didn't care. "Well, did we get a name? Any hint of his whereabouts?"

"No name," Siras responded. "But in an attempt to assure us that our man is actually decent and harmless despite all his mischief, it came out that he pays visits to an orphanage in Omriel. Apparently he takes gifts to the children—and a young woman who cares for them."

Dran smiled. "Omriel. The old capitol."

"Yes, back down in the foothills."

"And did we manage to get this woman's name?"

Siras shook his head. "He was babbling by this time. Gaimesh put a bit more effort into his work, but then the man expired."

Dran nudged the body with the toe of his boot and grunted. "Well, it's a start. How many orphanages can there be in Omriel? Maybe this woman will be less frail… and more fun."

There was a twinkle in Siras' eye. "One can hope, My Lord."

"One more thing, Siras." Dran looked him in the eye to make sure he understood. "I'm going to leave a few of the men here with you. I want you to remain in the village in case the thief shows up back here. While you're here, make a thorough search of the area just in case this woman doesn't produce our man. Make sure there's no place else he may have slithered off to. I may need Gaimesh, so he'll come with my group."

Siras looked disappointed, but Dran was sure he understood.

Moments later, the men Dran had chosen to ride out with him had gathered up supplies donated generously by a few of the locals—whether the locals had wanted to or not. The rain continued steadily as they packed their horses. It was late afternoon, and Dran wanted to be on the move before dark.

A violent peal of thunder shook the earth, and the animals started. The rain was torrential, beating loudly upon all beneath its descent—man, beast, structure or ground. The men shook their heads in disbelief. They could not hear one another over the onslaught.

Dran gazed skyward. This was no ordinary storm. There was fury and anguish in it, and he knew it was more than his mind playing tricks.

They were seeking a man from this place… a man who others had died to protect. In Dran's experience, only the becharmed would be so foolish. And now a storm that would make tracking their outlaw nigh to impossible? And might this man not be angry and sorrowful? Magic. There was magic at work here, he would have gambled on it.

Given that magic was forbidden—practiced, used or performed under penalty of immediate death—Dran was touched by an emotion he rarely felt the need to consider. He was… uneasy… as something vague prickled the back of his mind, though he could not sort it out. If this man was practicing magic, where might he have acquired the skill? And if he had such skill, then he would need to be taken considerably more seriously than a common troublemaker and petty thief.

But he would need to be tracked down and stifled at all cost.

* * * * *

As the night descended, the heavy downpour and thick, murky storm clouds made the darkness complete. Shrieking wind and clattering thunder created a deafening tumult. Rhinan struggled to secure his footing on a muddy slope, tugging at Dodger's reigns, but the horse refused to continue the uphill trudge.

"You're one of Eodorr's, alright," Rhinan scolded. "You're certainly as stubborn as he is."

He hadn't made much progress back toward Cabelon. It was all uphill, and the constant rain made the going slow and treacherous. Rhinan was determined to get back and make sure that Keirwyn wasn't in any trouble because of him. The ghosts had vanished, and he feared the worst.

He wouldn't get back very quickly if he had to drag a horse up the mountain. Exasperated, he threw down the reigns and scanned the area for any kind of a knoll or cove that he could maybe coax the stubborn creature into and leave it there with some hope of safety. To the left, it was nothing but trees and rocks.

As he turned to look the other direction, a burst of lightning momentarily illuminated the sky. In that flash, Rhinan had caught a passing glimpse of a silhouetted form up the hill—a form that wasn't tree or rock, but more like beast or man.

Crouching, he ducked sideways to lean against a short tree. Positioning himself on the downhill side of it, he drew his dagger from the sheath on his right thigh and tried to peer around the tree and up the hill. He calmed himself as he had practiced so many times while hunting. He became still and silent, as if he were a branch or limb of the tree. He waited.

Only a moment passed before he heard the sound of rocks breaking loose from mud and crashing underbrush up the slope. It was followed by a muffled yelp. A small streamlet of water, mud and rock swirled past Rhinan and Dodger in the slight imprint of the trail, flowing downhill. That was followed by the mud-covered form of a man, belly-down and feet-first, clutching for a hold at the debris that was moving downhill with him.

Though unable to get a very good look, Rhinan was fairly certain this was not one of the soldiers that had come looking for him. The man and the debris came to a stop a few feet further down the slope with a thump as the man collided with a tree. He lay still for a moment, after which Rhinan could see him wriggling to get to his feet.

Once he had stood, the man turned his face skyward, allowing the rain to wash over him. The man was not wearing any uniform, only muddy garments. He put his hands to his face and wiped the mud away, then shook himself off. Rhinan had to smile. It was Eodorr, no longer in his official uniform.

Stepping away from the tree, Rhinan called down to him. "If you've come for your horse back, good luck. He won't move. I think he's stuck in the mud."

Eodorr stood still, looking up at him for a moment. Then he began to trudge toward Rhinan, who thought, *"Here's where he pays me back for that clubbing."* In truth, though they had been adversarial since childhood, Rhinan still felt bad about catching Eodorr off guard. But not too bad. It did, after all, have to be done. And Eodorr was a powerful man to tangle with.

"Forget the horse, Rhinan." Eodorr, forget a horse? That was surprising… and disturbing. "We've got to move and move fast." As Eodorr drew closer, Rhinan could see grim tidings in his expression—not to mention the lump Rhinan had left on the side of his head.

Rhinan swallowed. "Keirwyn…" he stammered.

"There's nothing you or I can do for him now." Eodorr's voice choked, solemn. "Nothing other than to get moving."

"No!" Rhinan yelled at the Constable's aide. He felt as if the mudslide had just landed on *him*. "Why did you leave him to be killed?" Rhinan shoved him.

Eodorr stepped back. "He *died* because of *you*," he snarled. "Devram, too. Lore Givers only know who all else. I'll probably be next. After what I saw them do to Devram, I fled to catch you, but they are likely not far behind."

"Devram?" Rhinan felt as if another wave of mud hit him. Keirwyn and Devram both dead… and it was his fault.

"Yes," Eodorr hissed. "And his was not an easy death. Not easy at all."

Rhinan couldn't move. He didn't even want to. His carefree world had turned upside down in one day, and now two people he cared about were dead. "Why?" he sobbed. "I can't even understand."

Eodorr shook his head. "Just move." He turned Rhinan around with a rough shove, aiming him back down the slope.

Rhinan had a sudden fearful thought and looked back up the slope. "You haven't led them—"

"In *this*?" Eodorr held out his hands for the rain.

"Besides, I'm no fool. I've learned a thing or two from you about losing pursuers. I only found you because I know exactly where you're going and how you get there."

Eodorr turned slightly and made a clicking sound, and another horse tramped carefully down the hill to meet them. Taking the reins of his own horse to lead it, he then called over his shoulder, "Come, Dodger."

With no hesitation, Rhinan's horse turned and also began to plod down the hill behind the two men.

"I would have thought you'd learned a thing or two from me about horses," Eodorr chided.

Rhinan retrieved Dodger's reins and followed, but he said nothing. He was trying to focus on all the things Keirwyn had always tried so hard to teach him. He hoped he'd learned a thing or two, or anything at all.

Chapter Seven

They were still leading the horses on foot when a powerful growl in the predawn twilight stopped them in their tracks. It came from just ahead, but neither Rhinan nor Eodorr could see what manner of beast it was.

Startled, Eodorr clambered backward. The horses were spooked as well, but Eodorr got them under control. Rhinan, however, held his ground.

"I would step back if I were you." Eodorr fumbled a torch out of his pack, getting it lit as quickly as possible, despite the potential danger behind them. Rhinan assumed Eodorr was more concerned about the danger confronting them at the moment.

The growling increased to a near roar. Whatever it was, it was big. Rhinan looked back over his shoulder. A massive beast crept forward into the dim torchlight. Covered in grayish-brown fur, it walked on all fours with massive claws. A long snout protruded from its broad head, showing enormous teeth. A short, broad tail extended from the other end of the creature. Above all, the animal was shoulder height to Rhinan on all fours. If it stood on its hind legs, it would be half again his height.

"Don't. Move." Eodorr was petrified. "It's a beardog."

The creature roared.

Rhinan turned to Eodorr, grinning.

"I'm not joking, Rhinan. He's massive."

Turning back to the animal, Rhinan reached out his hand and scratched the huge beast under the chin. "It's okay, Rip. Eodorr's a friend."

The creature sat on his rear haunches and began to pant.

"Are you *insane*?" Eodorr was incredulous. "That's a beardog, Rhinan. It will shred you with one swipe of its paw."

"Who, Rip?" Rhinan chuckled and rubbed down the chest of the beast. The beardog nuzzled his arm. "He'll do nothing of the sort. We hunt together from time to time."

Eodorr shook his head. "I should be more surprised than I am. He'll eat the horses, you damned fool." Eodorr spread his arms as if to block the beardog's access to them.

The horses, on the other hand, had calmed down once Rhinan began petting Rip. "Only if he's desperate. He doesn't actually care for horse."

Eodorr remained unmoved. "Can you send him away?"

"Why would I do that? He's very helpful when hunting. And…" Rhinan added with another grin, "he makes a great companion. Doesn't talk too much."

The beardog's appearance provided the only comfort Rhinan had had in a full day's time. Some years earlier, Rhinan had encountered the animal while hunting. Apparently, they were both stalking the same prey. When Rhinan brought down a sizeable stag, the beardog had appeared, somewhat emaciated. Enough so that Rhinan could easily see the beardog was very hungry. It had been a particularly harsh winter that year, and game was scarce. Not one to panic, Rhinan kept an eye on the beardog while carving off part of the stag. Then he took his portion and stepped aside, allowing the beardog to approach the fresh kill without a fight. At first, the beardog had crept forward slowly, eyeing Rhinan with each step. Then it reached the stag and swiftly sank its massive jaws into the warm flesh, still steaming in the crisp, cool air of the early evening. Rhinan heard the rip of flesh (and the crunch of bone), and never thought of the beardog as anything else. The next time Rhinan was out on a hunt, he awoke one morning to find the beardog sitting there watching him sleep. There was half a deer in front of the beardog, which he nudged toward Rhinan. After that, Rip would appear from time to time, and the two began to work together when hunting. Rip would never come back to Cabelon with Rhinan, always disappearing back into the forest, only to reappear again at his own choosing. It had taken some time before Rhinan could touch the creature, but when he had, the creature hadn't minded. Over the years, the beardog became what he considered a friend. And, as with everyone else, Rip made no notice whatsoever of Rhinan's ghosts when they appeared.

Eodorr was looking at Rhinan with a scowl.

"Would you like to pet him?" Rhinan stepped to the side. Rip made a groaning sound.

"No. No, I would not."

Rhinan wondered if Rip had been near Cabelon, waiting for him in the edges of the forest, and perhaps followed them all night. Aside from beardogs in general being most common in the mountains—the Domins and the western Percenes (and growing rarer even there)—Rhinan had no idea how far Rip ranged. But they were so near Omriel, it seemed unlikely that this was an area Rip would normally frequent. Rip tended to avoid clusters of people even more than Rhinan. Perhaps the beardog was more attached to him than he thought. At any rate, he welcomed the familiar animal.

Resigned to the beardog's presence, Eodorr extinguished the torches as enough light signaled morning's arrival. "Won't he make us easier to track?"

"No easier than you," Rhinan jabbed. "In fact, he's very good at leaving no trace if he doesn't want to be found. He's almost as smart as you are, too."

Eodorr's reply was shocking even to Rhinan.

* * * * *

The city of Omriel had stood for centuries, soundly nestled within a natural curve at the base of the Domin mountain range, just on the northern shore of the deep Midnight Fjord. With the rise of the Lydan kings, the highly defensible city served as the seat of power. After Corm Lydan, father of current King Jerrick, moved the seat of power to Masseltaine, Omriel remained a bustling center for trade. In fact, the Northern Trading Path itself began in Omriel and ran to the north before curving and running parallel to the great Percene Mountain range, east and west along the foothills. Often referred to as "the Sunset City," Omriel was built almost entirely from *sarett* stone, a solid reflective mineral of a light red-orange hue. Even at high noon, Omriel was tinted with the warm glow of a summer sunset. In stark and literal contrast, the dark waters of Midnight Fjord lapped a small portion of its considerable shoreline at the southern end of the city, where it ran along the base of the Domins westward to the Framman Sea.

As they descended the final slope overlooking the city

from the north, Rip wandered back into the woods. Rhinan hoped the beardog would still be around when they returned, but he never knew what was in the animal's mind. Eodorr, by contrast, seemed relieved to be rid of Rip.

Rhinan could see the rising sun reflected on the surface of Midnight Fjord far away to the south. As the dawn brought the city to life, he spared himself a moment from dwelling on Keirwyn's death, his ghosts, the new mystery of his parents' belongings and his current predicament. The morning breeze was strong and cool above the city and, though it chilled him in his damp clothing, it stirred something inside him to the surface. He always felt this way when he came to Omriel, and it wasn't because of the beauty of the city. It was Silarrah.

* * * * *

As she looked down at the city, Rhinan was careful to ensure that Silarrah was not aware he was watching her. He smelled her hair as it fluttered in the gentle breeze. She was smiling in the midday sun, but smiling was more difficult for him with the ache that grew deep inside of him.

Helping her tote her few belongings, he'd accompanied her from Cabelon to Omriel, where she'd decided to work at the orphanage. She had told him that she had no plans to return to Cabelon. One of the few people he could turn to in his usual solitary existence, her absence would add to his loneliness.

When his ghosts appeared at the same time as his parents' deaths, he feared the phantoms were somehow responsible. He kept his distance, both physically and emotionally, from everyone he could, hoping to protect them from the ghosts, his own madness, or both. For a long time after Keirwyn took him in, he would speak to no one. He would not risk their safety.

It was only Silarrah—compassionate, gentle Silarrah—that Rhinan could not bring himself to completely push away. In her persistence to reach him, it seemed that his ghosts would not harm her, yet she apparently remained completely unaware of them. She asked him questions that he wanted to answer, but she knew when to leave off those that he did not. He shared his thoughts with her and the dreams of youth, but he was always careful to keep certain secrets. He remained concerned for her safety.

Becoming closer over the years, she even joined him occasionally for some of his less reckless adventures. He still felt protective of her, honing his skills at moving silently and remaining hidden from sight. He spent countless hours practicing difficult shots with his bow. Even in his solitude, as he drew more and more into his own, silent world filled with ghosts and fears, he appointed himself her secret guardian. He knew she was aware of it—a silent protector whenever she traveled beyond the safety of the village—but she never told him so. Casually trailing her one day along the river, he spotted a needlebeast perched in a tree that Silarrah was about to pass under. Stricken with panic, he fired an arrow directly into the heart of the predator so quickly that all Silarrah heard was an unexplained splash in the river when the beast hit the water, dead. She did not look back at the sound. He always suspected this was because she did not want to spoil his illusion that she didn't know he trailed her.

Given that she was the only one he spent much time with, the villagers expected them eventually to marry. However, Rhinan spent more and more time alone in the forest and became more self-reliant. In his escalating solitude, Rhinan noticed that Silarrah increasingly took his absence as a sign of rejection. Nothing could be further from the truth, but she seemed less enthusiastic to see him on the rare occasions he appeared, and she was often too busy with other things to spend much time with him. He knew she was only hurt, but he grew bitter that his situation was pushing her away.

Still he spent even more time alone, hunting or getting into trouble, which occasionally included his friend Param Voss. Param's mother had been a friend to Rhinan's parents, and all three children had grown up together. Frustrated by Silarrah's distance, he spent more time with Param. When Param left Cabelon to apprentice with a troubadour, Rhinan turned again to Silarrah.

As time progressed, he made no move to settle down and remain by her side in the village. Silarrah grew justifiably impatient. When she announced her plan to move to Omriel and help care for children there (partly, it was assumed, because she'd given up hope of having any of her own), it came as both a blow and a relief to Rhinan. Though he would miss her painfully, he knew that she might be safer if she was further from him and his cursed ghosts.

"Are you going to miss me?" Silarrah did not turn, her gaze still fixed on the city below them.

Summoning up what he could of all the deepest feelings he would have liked to be able to convey to her, he told her what he was certain she must already know. "Your name, your whispers and your sighs are carried to my ears by every breeze." He touched her arm. "How could I not miss you?"

She turned and leaned toward him, eyes softened with emotion and filled with warmth. With a sudden surge of courage, he swept her into his arms and kissed her. He instantly regretted that he had never so much as tried to kiss her before. The warmth continued, filling him, both alleviating his sorrow and deepening it all at once.

At last she pulled back, searching his eyes. "You and I, we never belonged in Cabelon. Neither of us was like the others. I had once hoped that together, we—"

"Please don't." He stopped her. "Believe me when I tell you that I am all too aware of the hopes we share. I have always asked you to trust me, and you have, haven't you?"

She nodded.

"This is not what we wanted, but it is for the best."

She looked confused and hurt and frustrated, but she had known him long enough to know there would be no further answers. He embraced her, looking over her shoulder at the city where she would now reside. Rhinan trusted she would be safe there. Safe from him and whatever trouble was attached to him.

Fearing she was upset with him, it was some time before Rhinan began to make visits to her in Omriel. Once he did, they would spend time talking, and he would help out or play with the children in her care. He even brought gifts from his hunting prizes—one of the few memories he had of his father was being taught to carve fancy objects from wood or bone. Sometimes, when he could afford it, he even brought items from Cabelon merchants. But he and Silarrah had remained close—though no more than special friends—as the years passed.

* * * * *

"It's been a long, cold night." Eodorr interrupted Rhinan's reflections. "I'm tired, I'm wet, and I'm hungry. So are the horses. If Dran's men didn't get here ahead of us, they're surely not far behind. If you're going to see her, get on with it. Make it quick and be discreet—for her sake, if not for your own."

Rhinan scowled at Eodorr, but said nothing. He was right, and Rhinan considered his options. He could stop in Omriel for provisions without seeing Silarrah, or he could pass the city by altogether. He decided that he needed to say something to her. He owed her that much. He owed her *at least* that much.

The morning sky was blue, speckled with scattered, puffy clouds. The wild storm of the night before had moved on, and a strong wind had taken its place. Afraid that he would never be able to return, Rhinan inhaled. The fresh scents of the earth and trees of the mountains he had been raised in lifted his spirits. He followed Eodorr down into the city. There was no time to lose.

Unstopped by the city guards as they blended in with the early morning merchants, they slipped into Omriel uneventfully. They led the horses past merchants setting up tables, stands, and blankets from which to peddle their wares. The morning sun reflected off the buildings, casting a rosy pallor into the streets. The sweet and savory aromas of hot breakfasts teased the two travelers, and Rhinan felt his stomach begging for acknowledgment. Twice Eodorr slapped his hand away harshly as he made sly attempts to pilfer pastries from the shelf of a flour-dusted baker.

"You'll certainly leave an impression if you get caught stealing here," Eodorr warned. "Let's just get where we're going, and I'll take care of our provisions while you take care of whatever it is you need to with Silarrah."

The city was waking up, and more people dotted the streets as they wound further into the city. The morning was chill, so they didn't look out of place trotting along with cloaks and caps obscuring their faces. Rhinan worried that Eodorr would panic when a pair of city guards strolled past and took a particular interest in their horses and their muddy appearance. He launched into an artificial coughing spasm, and the two guards hurried away, apparently eager to avoid whatever plague this traveler may be carrying.

"Very subtle," Eodorr commented.

Rhinan ignored the sarcastic remark.

Chapter Eight

With an eye toward eluding any pursuers from the streets, Rhinan surveyed the orphanage in Omriel. He could see two or three women tending to children of various ages, serving breakfast and welcoming the day with comforting conversation. The children smiled or nodded as they received their portions. Nothing seemed amiss, so he began to approach the door.

"That's far enough, you."

Her voice startled him, but he smiled as he turned. Silarrah stood holding a bucket of water by the handle with both hands, flashing an admonishing smile as a lock of her chestnut brown hair tumbled down over her right eye. She wore a plain, pale brown dress with a scarlet apron which, Rhinan noticed, nearly matched the rich hue of her full lips. "Silarrah." He spoke her name but, seeing her again, was otherwise immobilized with enchantment.

Silarrah exhaled a puff of her breath, aiming it at the lock of hair over her eye, but the lock merely lifted and then fell back where it had been. A familiar gesture of hers, it always charmed Rhinan to behold.

She nodded down at the bucket in her arms. "A little help here?" she said, and Rhinan was stirred to motion, aware suddenly that the bucket was heavy for her to carry. He took it from her, and easily carried it with one arm. "You look awful, Rhinan. But it still warms my heart to see you here this morning. It's been too long."

She hugged him, and he saw that the sparkle in her deep brown eyes was still there. Keirwyn had always said that it was only there when she looked at Rhinan, but he was certain that was not true. For a moment, he felt as if the troubles of the last couple of days were no longer a concern. The moment passed, and he recalled the potential danger of being sighted. Glancing around quickly, he said, "Let's get inside."

"Oh, Rhinan," she whispered, a tone of worry emerging in her voice as her brows creased. "What have you done this time?"

* * * * *

The children were mostly sons and daughters of tradesmen or merchants, orphaned due to misfortune, or abandoned due to necessity. Despite their unfortunate circumstances, the women at the orphanage managed to keep the children's spirits lifted as much as could be expected.

Rhinan quickly helped Silarrah make sure that they were all taken care of. Despite the few moments it took, he was still concerned that he was spending far too much time in one place.

He realized that Silarrah noticed his edginess, as she finally beckoned him to follow her into a storage room of unused furnishings where they could speak in private.

"Since you seem like you're about to leap out of your

own skin, maybe you should tell me what's going on." She pointed to a short stool for Rhinan to sit, and curled herself up into a well-worn wide chair, leaning to one side with her legs drawn up. She looked him over as he sat. "You're a mess."

"Sil… I don't know how to say this gently. Keirwyn is dead."

She sat up straight, her mouth hung open in shock. "What do you mean? What's happened?"

"It's my fault. He was protecting me. Devram, too. It was Gethor Dran."

"Devram, too?" It seemed too much for her. The composure of a few moments ago had already faded, and a teardrop fell from her eye, running down her fair countenance.

Rhinan nodded, looked down in shame.

Silarrah sniffed, reached out her hand and gently lifted his face with a finger. "Why would the King's *Maraggan* be looking for you, Rhinan? You mustn't draw that kind of attention to yourself. *What did you do*?" She asked the last question slowly and clearly, as if commanding a child to tell the truth.

As quickly as he could, Rhinan told her of pillaging Lord Mundon's farm, his arrest, and of Dran's appearance. He shared what he'd learned from Eodorr about Devram's murder and the beloved Constable's death. He told her of his parents' items, brought to him by Eodorr at Keirwyn's direction. "And Eodorr is with me now. He's looking after the horses."

She dropped her head into her hands, sobbing for a moment. Then she looked up at him, saying angrily, "You *know* Mundon has royal connections. What were you thinking?"

"I… I guess I wasn't."

"You were drunk." It was a statement. Rhinan only nodded in confirmation.

Sighing, Silarrah rose to her feet, showing concern. "You need to go, Rhinan. Now. You won't be safe here, and what will I say if they question me?"

"I know. I have to go away for a long time. Maybe forever. But I had to say goodbye first. I had to see you, to talk to you."

She stared into his eyes for a long time, and he could see the pain he felt was also in her eyes. "You've always had the biggest heart, Rhinan. But you seldom use your head. You've been a child all your life. It's as if you refused to grow up after—" She stopped suddenly. He knew she meant to refer to when his parents were killed, but no one ever spoke to him of that. Not ever.

Apparently changing her approach to the lecture she was giving him, she said, "Slipping away to the woods for hunting is all well and good. But you can't hide out there forever. It's no way to take care of yourself, and it's no way to take care of a family. Haven't you ever wanted a family? Why must you choose to be so alone and so reckless?"

He still couldn't tell her about the ghosts. Not even her. "I *want* to be different than I am, Sil." His strong feelings toward her surged, and he continued. "I'm going to be gone, and I don't know for how long. But I *want* to come back, and I *want* to be the kind of man you can respect." He also wanted to say more, but he stopped himself. Did he deserve her love? Could she love him, knowing that his foolishness had cost the lives of people close to them?

She studied him for a moment of contemplation. "Do you know what I always liked best about you? You always treated me differently than the other boys. As we grew, you viewed me differently than did other men. While they considered me a thing to possess, you acted like I was someone to be respected. And more importantly, you didn't just look at me. You *heard* me. I was more than one thing to you. To you, I had substance and depth."

"Why should it be any other way? You were always more complex—" He watched her raise an eyebrow and purse her lips, a sure sign he was entering sensitive territory. Correcting himself, he continued, "—less simple, rather, than any of them." This seemed to be the correct course, as it brought a grin from her. "You always had more to say than anyone else." The expression of doubt and frustration returned to Silarrah's face, and Rhinan reached quickly for words to clarify his meaning. "For me, you had more *interesting* things to say."

She gave him a self-satisfied look that was playfully smug. "Well, *I* always thought so as well." Now it was Rhinan's turn to squint at her. She flushed red and made her own revised statement. "I meant *you.* I felt more interest in what you had to say than what other boys or men said. It was always... disappointing... that it seemed you chose to say so little."

Rhinan felt an ache at the thought of disappointing her in any way, but he knew it couldn't be helped. It was for her own good. He could see the moisture well up in her eyes, the pain in her expression, as she realized her words had hurt him. She gently placed the palm of her hand on his cheek. "I was always thankful for the words you chose to share with me. I still am." She smiled tearfully. "I'll happily take what I can get."

Pure sorrow overcame her expression. "But I prefer

better news than this." She looked down for a moment, clasping her hands together and bringing them to her lips, seriously considering the heartbreaking news about Keirwyn and Devram. When she looked up again, the intensity in her eyes was fierce. "Just be careful. Stop looking for trouble, and start accepting friendship and companionship. It's no good you being so alone so much. I've always felt that…" She paused and closed her eyes for a moment. "I hope I can be here for you when you come back. But Rhinan, you *have* to *change*. For your *own* good."

She was weeping openly now, and he didn't know what else to say. Finally, he said, "I just don't know where to go."

Standing, they remained silent for a moment, Silarrah dabbing at her eyes with her apron. "Maybe that's something I can help you with," she said finally.

"Disguise me as an orphan?" Rhinan suggested.

Silarrah squinted at him, pursing her lips. "You *are* an orphan." She then grew contemplative. "But that's what I want to speak of. It's about your parents, and maybe about what they gave Keirwyn to keep for you."

"Do you know something about it? Tell me."

"Not so much *know* as *wonder*," she mused. "It's something I overheard, or thought I heard, but I wasn't meant to. It was a long, long time ago when… well, when we were children. Right after…"

"When my parents were slain," he finished for her. "It's alright to mention. It was long ago." His curiosity was raging. What could she have overheard at the time when the ghosts began to visit him? Could she know something that would help him to finally be rid of them? "What did you hear, Silarrah? I need to know."

"When did you last see Param?"

"Quite some time. I haven't seen him since I last saw you." Param always came to see Rhinan and have drinks when he was home for the winters. Where Rhinan was quiet and solitary, Param was loud and boisterous, living for as much attention as he could get. He was slightly older than Rhinan, one of Rhinan's strongest role models. Param lived a carefree life, traveling where he wished, performing in taverns, inns and palaces. "Why? What's it got to do with Param?"

"Not Param. His mother. Brinaya." Silarrah turned away, peering out a window, her arms folded. "Keirwyn was speaking to her about you, about what to do with you, being that your parents were gone." Her voice broke and her tears returned now as she mentioned the man who became Rhinan's surrogate parent.

"Yes, that makes sense." Rhinan thought back to that terribly difficult and frightening time. "I stayed with Param and his mother for quite some time. Their cottage was remote, and I think everyone assumed it was best for me to be away from people for a while. I think they were right, too. Look how I endanger the people I'm around—"

"That's the thing, Rhinan. They made it sound as if *you* were the one in danger. They wanted to *hide* you."

"Well, I can see that. Someone killed my parents. Better to be cautious—"

"No!" She looked straight at him, shaking her head. "This was more than that. There was something about your parents and something about the King. I don't remember much about it, because I didn't understand it then any more than I do now. I'd forgotten all about it until you just mentioned those things that belonged to your parents. But I think you should go see Brinaya Voss. You should show her and ask her about your parents."

Rhinan was stunned by all that Silarrah had told him. He had only childhood memories of his parents, but knew nothing about where they had come from, what they had done before they had him, or… or anything. In all the years since their deaths, neither Keirwyn nor Brinaya Voss nor anyone else had said a word to him about them. Even when he asked, he was told very little other than that they had loved him. Now, it seemed, there was something to know. It might even be something that could help him.

He looked long at Silarrah. She was standing in front of the window, watching him, and the morning sunlight streamed in, forming a glow around her. As enchanted by her as he ever was, he stepped forward. "That's where I'll start, then. Thank you, Sil." He brushed the lock of her hair back from her eye with a delicate motion, and kissed her—something he'd only done once before, years ago. "I promise you that I will change, and that I will see you again if possible."

More concern flickered on her face, and then was replaced with a serious gaze. "Change for the better, Rhinan. Or else I'm not sure I *should* see you again."

It was like a slap, but he felt that he deserved it.

"I work with orphans because I knew one once. He became withdrawn and solitary and unhappy, and I couldn't help him. Maybe I can help some of them, Rhinan. But you? You aren't happy. Something is missing in you. I don't want them to know how that feels."

There was a quick, urgent knock on the door. Silarrah crossed and opened it cautiously.

"Hi, Sil." Eodorr flashed a quick, sad smile at her, and they embraced. He then looked past her to Rhinan. "Time to go if you still want to have your head when you do. The city patrol is drawing near. And you don't want to lead them here."

Rhinan turned to Silarrah, his heart breaking. "I'm sorry… I'm so sorry. As my father used to say, the Lore Givers will always bring you what you need to know." And then he forced himself to move, pushing past Eodorr and out the door.

As they left the orphanage, Eodorr asked, "How did it go?"

Without looking at him, Rhinan replied, "No better than I had any right to expect."

* * * * *

Staring out the window, Silarrah watched the two men mount and ride their horses away. She had no idea what Rhinan's fate would be, but she did hope he would keep his promise to change. She just didn't know if he could.

"They're leaving now," she said over her shoulder.

A cloaked and hooded figure emerged from behind a stack of crates and supplies. "You handled this very well, Silarrah. You've done the right thing. That little bit of information… that was interesting. I wonder, however, if you were holding anything back about what you remember."

Silarrah turned to face the figure. "If I *did* remember anything else, I'm not sure I would tell *you*."

There was a slight chuckle. "No matter. I'll find out soon enough. Brinaya Voss, was it?" Silarrah made no reply. "You've done what's best for *everyone*, Silarrah. Just remember that."

The figure then slipped out the door, leaving Silarrah alone with her doubts and regrets.

Chapter Nine

"Bring me the Captain of the city guard," Dran growled. "Now."

He considered Omriel to be a run-down place filled with undesirables, but Dran knew that Hodrak—the Captain stationed here—was a competent soldier. Hodrak could help him find the orphanage he was looking for, and might even have information regarding any recent visitors to the place. He did not yet know the name of the thief he sought, but he was sure someone at this orphanage would be accommodating on that issue. Perhaps one of the children... children were so... pliable. Easy to work with.

Dran waited on his horse while one of his men went to retrieve Hodrak. He longed for the comforts of his quarters in the capital city of Masseltaine, and perhaps two or three of the castle maids. Dilapidated though it seemed to him, he felt that at least Omriel was closer to civilization. He had no use for those little mountain communities, and hoped that nothing he uncovered would send him back that way anytime soon.

It had been a wretched night, traveling in that atrocious

storm. He had no doubt that it was unnatural, and made a mental note to question some of those educators at the Lore College who might be aware of any unauthorized use of magic. Such a visit would serve another purpose as well. He would make it a menacing reminder that King Jerrick had banned the use of magic, and the penalty for breaking that law was nothing less than death.

"My Lord." Hodrak approached. His black Lydanian military uniform was impeccable. This was a man who took his position seriously. At his side was one of Hodrak's own aides and the *Maraggan* Dran had sent to retrieve Hodrak. All three stood gazing up at Dran, attentive and ready for orders. Just the way Dran liked it. He momentarily considered promoting Hodrak to a better location, but quickly dismissed the idea. For one thing, who else would so efficiently oversee such a dilapidated city as Omriel? And for another, if his recollection was correct, Dran seemed to remember that Hodrak was happy in Omriel. There was no accounting for taste. But if the man was satisfied and doing a sufficient job against such odds…

"Captain Hodrak," Dran nodded to the man. "We've just come down from the mountain villages, and we require information and provisions. We are pursuing a dangerous criminal, and we have reason to believe he may have slithered down into this city."

Hodrak raised his eyebrows. "I will have the watchmen report at once, My Lord. If one of your men will see our clerk, he will ensure that all the provisions you require are supplied." The city Captain swept an arm toward the building he'd emerged from and bowed to Dran.

"Good," Dran replied, dismounting his horse. He handed the reins to Hodrak's aide, motioned for his own man to follow, and went inside with Hodrak. There was one more city guard stationed inside, seated over a steaming beverage. He glanced up with a casual air as Dran entered, then he looked up again, his recognition of Dran now apparent. He jumped up quickly and stood at crisp attention.

"Bring in the watchmen," Hodrak commanded as he walked by. "We need a full report… *immediately*." The man turned and left without hesitation, apparently relieved to escape Dran's presence. Dran grinned at the efficiency. These men knew their place, despite the shabby condition of the city in which they dwelled.

Hodrak turned to Dran. "I apologize, My Lord, for not being better prepared for your visit. Please excuse me for a moment while I have a fulfilling meal prepared for you and your men. And if you wish to bathe…"

"Thank you, Captain." Dran removed his gloves and sank into a cushioned chair. "We won't have time for any luxuries, but a quick meal would be most welcome."

Hodrak bowed again, left the room for a moment, and returned soon carrying a tray of steaming mugs. Dran took one, and looked to his own soldier, indicating with a wave that he should take the rest outside to the others. The *Maraggan* took the tray from Hodrak and exited.

"So… this criminal…" Hodrak prompted.

"It seemed at first like a petty thief," Dran explained. "King Jerrick buys dogs from a cousin of one of the mountain village Lords, Baron Mundon. Mundon was robbed. The King felt it necessary for me personally to lead the *Maraggan* up there and apprehend the rogue. Yet, when we got to the village—Cabelon—the local Constable was more concerned with protecting the villain than he was with preserving his own life."

Hodrak looked shocked. "Keirwyn? He's dead?"

Dran peered at Hodrak over his mug. "You knew him?"

Hodrak squirmed, but he answered promptly. "Served under him for a time, long ago. He was a good man." When Dran's eyebrow arched, Hodrak corrected himself. "Er, *seemed* to be, that is. How is it that a royal Constable comes to protect a thief?"

"Exactly what we're hoping to find out here. I have my suspicions, though. We rode through an unnatural storm last night, which would indicate that someone is using magic to help this thief—perhaps the thief himself."

Hodrak looked shocked at this. "*Magic*? I had thought it eradicated. Especially since it's outlawed under a strict mandate by King Jerrick himself!"

"Now you see why this man is so dangerous and why we must find him at once."

At that moment, Hodrak's guard returned with two more members of the city guard. "South watch and west watch, reporting, sir," he announced, and the two men stepped forward. "North and east will be here momentarily."

"Thank you, Forin," Hodrak said. "That will be all." Dismissed, the guard went back outside.

"This is Gethor Dran, General of the King's special force, the *Maraggan*," Hodrak told the two watchmen. "He's trailing a criminal and believes the man may have slipped into Omriel during that horrible storm last night or early this morning."

"We had a merchant party up from Masseltaine at the south gate just this morning, sir," said the south watchman. "Do you think he would have slipped in with them?"

"Doubtful," Dran said with a shake of his head. "We've followed him down from the Domins, so it's more likely he's come in from the west or the north."

"There's been no activity on the west side, sir," reported the west watchman.

After looking to Dran for confirmation, Hodrak dismissed the two.

Dran thought a moment, and then addressed Hodrak. "Somewhere in town there's an orphanage. We have information that this man is friendly with one of the maidens there."

Hodrak hesitated. "Uh, yes. Yes, there is an orphanage—"

"Not far from my watch," said a man who had just limped in the door. "North watch reporting, My Lords."

Hodrak eyed the watchman coolly, and Dran noticed it but chose to ignore it. It would not be uncommon for the Captain assigned to a town to become sympathetic to the locals. As long as the Captain didn't try to interfere with the investigation. Dran had already had enough of that with this chase. He turned to the limping watchman. "Did anyone come into the city from the north last night? Or this morning perhaps? He would have been making for that orphanage."

The watchman looked back and forth between Dran and Hodrak for a moment, but Dran gave him a severe look, which seemed to convince him to continue. "Why, yes, My Lord. There was two men spotted at daybreak. I think they was believed to be beggars. From the worn and dirty look of them, they'd probably slept out in that uncommon weather last night."

"*Two* men?" Dran became urgent. "Did they make for the orphanage?"

"Might have done," the watchman considered. "Come to think of it, they was supposed to have had horses. Not as likely to be beggars if they have their own horses. Be they horse thieves, My Lord?"

"Lead me to that orphanage at once," Dran said through clenched teeth. "If they've been there, I'll know about it, or those children will be twice orphaned. One of those maidens knows this man."

Hodrak swallowed, and Dran kept an expectant eye on him. Hodrak led the limping north watchman out the door as Dran followed.

* * * * *

When she heard the urgent knock at the door, Silarrah hung her head. She'd already had two visitors this morning and—given the nature of her visitors—a third would very likely be of the most unwelcome sort. She reminded herself that the children's safety was the most important thing. Fortunately, they were out playing games in the back area. She rose and moved toward the door.

Opening the door, she saw Captain Hodrak of the city watch. With him was one of his city watchmen, plus a third man whom she instantly recognized, though she'd never had any occasion to speak with him. She considered herself fortunate in that regard.

Fortunate, until now. The man was Gethor Dran. And she already knew he was looking for Rhinan.

He stood tall, his dark curly hair flecked with the slightest bits of gray. He gazed at her with piercing blue-gray eyes, and she wanted to turn away. He was dressed in black, with the golden mantle worn by the General of the King's special force. She knew she was in trouble—trouble she could not avoid.

Before she could speak, Hodrak addressed her. "Silarrah,

this is Gethor Dran, General of the King's *Maraggan.* He's looking for a man who may have come here this morning, a man from Cabelon who knows one of the maidens working here. Did you happen to have a visitor or two today?"

Silarrah almost laughed at the question. Would have laughed if the situation were not so dire. Hodrak knew that Rhinan occasionally visited her from Cabelon, but she didn't think he knew Rhinan by name. She wondered what Dran would do to get information from her. She was shaking when she answered and knew that her lie would not fool Dran. "Only a delivery," she said, staring directly into Hodrak's eyes, hoping that she might not give anything else away to Dran. "One of our benefactors dropped off some clothing for the children."

Hodrak stared back at her without responding, and she could see the worry in his eyes. The silence seemed to wear on until Dran nudged Hodrak aside. "I see your concern for children and maidens has softened your attention to your duties, Captain. I find that very disappointing." Hodrak stepped back, allowing Dran to face Silarrah directly. She refused to flinch, although inside she wanted to run, hide, get away from this menacing figure. He seemed the type to harm her to get to Rhinan if it came to that.

"Silarrah, was it?" Dran continued. He smiled, and Silarrah felt a shiver run up her spine. There was no warmth in the smile. She felt as if he was about to bite her like a vicious dog. "Step outside so we can speak." His tone was rude. He drew aside, giving her room to pass through the doorway.

She wanted to say something, but could not find a voice. Her legs were so weak, she wasn't sure she could step forward without collapsing. Grasping the doorway, she pushed herself outside.

Beyond the three men, Silarrah could now see several more of the *Maraggan* on horseback, all watching her. There would be no running from this. She knew she was doomed. As doomed as Keirwyn and Devram.

And then she hardened. She thought of her friends, killed by this cruel and bloodthirsty fool of an oppressive king, and a surge of defiance rose within her. She looked up at Dran, and she could tell he saw the change in her demeanor. She knew it was probably foolish for her own sake, but she didn't care anymore. She carefully restrained the pain and fury she felt and spoke.

"I certainly hope, My Lord, that whatever you're looking for warrants your lack of manners."

Silarrah heard Hodrak's intake of breath at her words. She saw Dran tense up, couldn't be sure, but thought she might have seen him draw back to strike her. She was dizzy with the tension of the situation.

"Do not attempt to school me as if I were one of your orphans," Dran told her, his words measured carefully and firm. She felt her brief surge of courage eroding, and then she drew Keirwyn back into her thoughts. Was this how Dran had treated the dear Constable before killing him? She fumed, but she said nothing.

Dran put his hands on his hips, stepped away, and then turned back to her. "I am here on King's business. The man we seek is a threat to the King's laws, and it would be entirely foolhardy to protect him or assist him." Dran stepped forward, looming over her. "We are prepared to take whatever measures are necessary to find the man." He made sure that Silarrah noticed him place his hand on the pommel of his sword, but she tried to pretend not to notice the gesture.

Hodrak spoke up. "Silarrah, it is my job to keep peace in this city. Let me urge you to offer us any knowledge you have for the sake of that peace." His eyes were pleading. Silarrah knew Hodrak to be a good man, but she didn't want him to protect her. There was no reason for him to be put in the middle of this.

"We can always question the children." Dran said it quietly, casually, appearing unconcerned. It was clear to Silarrah that it didn't matter to him who he tortured to get what he wanted. She hadn't expected him to consider anything so abysmal, and it took her by surprise. This caused her to respond too quickly, without thinking.

"The children didn't see anyone!"

Dran's gaze met her eyes, a cold grin on his lips. "So we're getting somewhere now. Good. It will be much easier this way. If the children didn't see anyone, someone else must have. Please, continue."

"I…" Silarrah was thinking as fast as she could. Now all she could do was provide delay, stall, and give Rhinan more time to get further away from this monster. As Keirwyn had, she thought. She knew how that had ended, and expected no less for herself.

Then a desperate thought occurred to her, a way she might create delay and yet spare herself. She could throw herself on the King's mercy, though from what she had heard and seen, he had no more mercy than Dran himself. "I will speak only to the King," she said flatly. "You may take me to him."

As she stood defiant once more, Dran chuckled, but she heard no pleasure in it. "You wish to barter with information while I am conducting an investigation?" He stepped closer to her and, so fast she didn't see the move, he grabbed a handful of her long hair and roughly tugged her head back, exposing her neck. She could not help the wince that escaped her lips at the pain. "Listen carefully to me, woman," he snarled. "I have no time for games, and I am in no mood for them." A dagger appeared in his other hand, and she felt the cold point touch her throat. "I will have what you know here and now, or I will leave your flesh here to rot and continue to question every woman and child remaining in this orphanage!"

His voice rose to a shout by the time he finished speaking, and Silarrah could see a crowd had gathered. She feared the children would come out soon, and she didn't want them to see this, let alone be a part of it. She gulped and spoke.

"No one else in that orphanage can provide you with any information about the man you seek. If you kill me, your King will be very disappointed when he hears that I offered to give him the information directly and you chose to throw it away instead." She flicked her eyes toward Hodrak, intending Dran to see it and consider that there were witnesses to what she had just said—witnesses he could not so easily make a case for eliminating.

A moment passed, and she watched the shimmer of fire in Dran's eyes. She was almost certain that all she'd done was anger him further, ensuring that he would kill her now. Then she saw him glance at Hodrak, and the cruel grin on his lips faded. He shoved her to the ground and stomped away with a growl. She saw him look up at the orphanage, and then he turned back to her.

"So be it," he said. Then, to one of his men, "Bind her. And Lore Givers help you if she slips out of her bonds."

Silarrah's hands were jerked behind her, and she realized

she was bleeding. Dran's dagger must have cut her arm when he shoved her. She felt weak again, yet she struggled with the soldier rather than surrender to the binding. She knew it was a futile gesture, and it only resulted in a knock on her head from the pommel of the soldier's own dagger.

As she felt herself losing consciousness, she heard one last heartbreaking command from Dran to his men. "And burn this orphanage to the ground. Nothing must be left of any place that harbors traitors."

Chapter Ten

"I certainly hope you haven't put her in any danger, Rhinan," Eodorr commented as they rode away from Omriel. "So far, you've managed to get a lot of people who care about you killed."

Rhinan opened his mouth to snap at Eodorr, but he didn't have the heart. In truth, he'd been wondering the same thing. People *were* dying to protect him, and he didn't even know why. They'd been careful, hoping not to add Silarrah to that list. But Silarrah was a resourceful girl and had always been good at getting herself out of trouble. Though Rhinan was sure she could handle herself if trouble came along, he couldn't stop himself from worrying.

The visit to Silarrah turned out to be vital to Rhinan. More than just clearing the air and informing her that he needed to go away for a while, she'd given him a clue to whatever made him more interesting to the King than a common thief. If the conversation she'd overheard so many years ago held any answers, he would have to go find out from Brinaya herself. And warn her as well. The hunt for him seemed so intense that his best friend's mother could even be in danger if anyone connected him to her.

As if his solitary existence hadn't been miserable enough—protecting others from any potential harm by the ghosts that first appeared when his own parents had been slain—now Rhinan had to be concerned with more tangible threats to anyone he cared about. What if his very existence was the problem, a problem that couldn't be solved? He had spent his life trying to keep others safe from him, and now he'd failed. He didn't know if he could deal with it, and maybe Eodorr was right. And, although he and Eodorr hadn't been close since they were children, perhaps Eodorr…

"You're right, Eodorr," Rhinan said with a sigh. "I don't know what's going on here and, until I do, no friend of mine is safe. It might be better if you went home—"

"Are you serious?" Eodorr glared at him. "I am not with you because I am your friend. Our childhood friendship ended when your parents died. I don't know why, but it was your choice, and I've never understood. And I am not with you out of sympathy, though many extend that to you because of what happened to your parents. I felt sorry for you, and I still do at times. And I am with you despite my position as an authority of the King. I'm inclined to think you may deserve whatever you'd get if you were delivered to him. I'm also with you despite the fact that I hold you responsible for Keirwyn and Devram. Don't misunderstand why I'm with you, because I am only with you for one reason. I am with you because I made a promise to Keirwyn, and I keep my promises. And he meant very much to me."

Eodorr's voice broke a little, but he continued. "He saw something in you that I never could. Keirwyn wanted you safe, and I remain in his service until we ensure that. I will see it done or die trying, if only for Keirwyn's sake and for that reason only. Whatever happens now, unless I help you through it, then those people who happen to mean something to me have suffered and sacrificed in vain. I'd be letting them all down if I didn't see this through, wherever it leads us. Besides, I'm sure I've no safe place at this point either. No, Rhinan… you're as stuck with me as I am with you."

Rhinan hid his reaction, stifling a smile. This was a tongue-lashing worthy of Keirwyn himself. Whatever disagreements they had had, Eodorr Hoult was loyal once he'd attached himself to you. He'd been this way with Keirwyn and had clearly learned much from the Constable. He'd always seemed so simple and uncomplicated to Rhinan. But now, Rhinan saw an analytic side to his critic which he had previously overlooked, and it pleased him. Perhaps Keirwyn had been right all these years to put his faith in Eodorr.

Rhinan could easily admit that Eodorr may be an asset as a travel companion. Besides his skill with a sword, Eodorr was, and had always been, an excellent horseman. He had been breaking and riding horses even before Rhinan's parents had been killed. Most of the horses in their village had been raised by Eodorr by the time he was an adult. With him along, Rhinan knew that the horses would be kept healthy and in line. Something Rhinan had little experience with.

"Thank you, Eodorr. If not for your concern about *my* safety, at least for your service to those who I care about and who care about me."

Eodorr grunted an acknowledgement, ignoring Rhinan's sarcasm, but said no more.

They rode without speaking, heading northward along the foothills of the Domin Mountains. Brinaya's cabin was about a day's ride northeast of Cabelon, near where the

Domins met the Percenes. It was almost the same distance north from Omriel. They would have to keep moving, a very dangerous prospect, as Eodorr said that Dran's men would undoubtedly be patrolling up and down the foothills east of Cabelon, but agreed that Brinaya sounded like their best bet. Rhinan decided to worry about that when the time came.

With Eodorr in the lead, his horse following placidly, Rhinan had a moment to regard the gem that hung around his neck. After the lightning strike, it had retained its luminescence, the light within flowing around in waves as if it were liquid. He again marveled at the apparent depth that extended beyond the stone's actual size. As he stared at it, focusing, Rhinan thought he could faintly hear the haunting murmurs of his horde of ghosts as he concentrated on the gem alone. No, he was almost sure of it.

"Do you hear that, Eodorr?"

Eodorr reined in his horse and listened. "No, but I trust your skills in the wild. If you hear something, we'd best find a hiding place or prepare to make a stand."

Listening carefully, Rhinan gazed around at the steep, grassy hills strewn with large, jutting boulders. So much of his life, spent alone in the wilds, had honed his senses and his skills to a sharp degree. If something were out of place, he would know. Nothing struck him as such, so he could only deduce that he was the only one hearing the sound. And it was coming from the gem.

"No, I guess I'm just a bit on edge now," he told Eodorr, drawing his horse away from grazing in the grass and nudging him forward. "We should keep going."

Experimenting with the gem, Rhinan could still hear the faint murmuring if he concentrated on it. When he stopped focusing on the stone, the sound faded. The haunting sound gave him chills, just as his ghosts did when they appeared. He felt like he had more control over the gem's sounds, with an ability to make them go away. He'd tried to ignore the ghostly appearances for years, and he wished that had been as effective, making them fade as well. But alas, they had as of yet to cease their visitations.

He couldn't help wondering where this odd stone came from and where his parents had gotten it. He'd never seen its like. And either it had shielded him when he was struck by lightning, or it had—all on its own—called the lightning to itself. If it were the latter, it was a frightening thought. For one thing, he didn't want a stone around with that kind of power when he didn't understand it or know how to control it. Far too dangerous. But he was especially concerned that it was magic. Magic was expressly forbidden by King Jerrick under penalty of death. Rhinan was in enough trouble already without adding any further charges to his name. He reflected that he still wasn't even aware of what all the charges were.

He considered tossing the gem behind a boulder or under a tree. But he didn't want to part with what was one of the only heirlooms he had from his parents. Until Keirwyn had sent these to him via Eodorr, he had no legacy of any kind. It was like his parents had hoped he would forget them when they died. And who was M.A.?

The stone also seemed connected with his ghosts. What if it was the key to finally dispelling them, ridding himself of whatever threat they posed? He decided he would keep the gem unless it became real trouble, but he took it off and placed in his pack. At least he'd think less about it if he weren't wearing it.

The blade was another mystery. Rhinan was far better with a bow and arrows than he was with a sword, but

Keirwyn had taught him swordplay. He wasn't nearly as proficient as, say, Eodorr… but he could defend himself capably with a blade if the need should arise. And with a blade like that, perhaps even better than capably.

Droplets of water pelted him, rousing him from his thoughts. The sky had grown dark, and more rain was falling. This was good on one hand, as it would make the efforts of their trackers difficult. On the other hand, it would slow their own progress as well. Somewhere behind the clouds, the sun was directly overhead.

There was a gurgling noise from Eodorr' stomach. Rhinan chuckled.

"I could eat, too," he said.

"About time," Eodorr replied. "We haven't eaten since I caught up to you last night."

They led the horses in amongst a grouping of large boulders reclining against the hillside, where they could lean in tight enough to gain some shelter from the drizzle.

However, an odd little bird stood before them, blocking their way in to the small boulder-encircled spot. The small bird was narrow and ovular shaped, muddled red, as of sunset, with black stripes under its wings. It stood facing them down rather than taking flight at the sight of them. Eodorr appeared amused at the bird's stubborn refusal to give way, but Rhinan issued him a warning through pursed lips. "Keep your mouth closed and stand still."

"Why?" Eodorr snorted, taking a step toward the creature. "What do the two of us have to fear from such a little bird, odd one that he is? Fly away, small—" With the speed of a lightning bolt, the bird shot swiftly and directly into Eodorr's mouth, toppling him backward with the impact and the surprise.

Rhinan was upon him in an instant, as Eodorr grasped at his throat, his eyes wide. He was choking. Rhinan drew his dagger. Eodorr's eyes widened further as he squirmed away. "Don't move!" Rhinan commanded.

The bird had puffed up in Eodorr's mouth, preventing him from closing it. The creature pushed outward with strong, sinewy wings and burrowed further, obstructing his ability to breathe. Quickly, Rhinan jammed his dagger under the bird's tail, twisting and carefully spearing upward toward the roof of Eodorr's mouth. The bird struggled, and Eodorr writhed.

"Hold still!" Rhinan reached deep into his companion's mouth with two fingers, wrapped them around the skewered bird, and pulled it out. Eodorr shuddered with a spasm, then rolled over and vomited. Rhinan wiped the bird off of his dagger onto the ground, stomping on it for good measure.

When he was able to speak, Eodorr sat up and rasped, "Wen's tongue! What was that cursed thing?" He continued to cough and spit.

"It's a Mouth Breeder," Rhinan explained casually. "They burrow into your windpipe and suffocate you, then lay their eggs in there until they hatch. They peck away at your dead flesh for meat during that time, and then the fledglings in turn feed upon what's left of you when they hatch. If you've ever come across the remains of one of their victims, it is not a pretty sight, I assure you. Nasty little creatures. Also, fortunately, very rare. I've only ever seen one or two."

Eodorr cringed, disgust on his face. "Why in all of creation would such a thing exist?"

"I could ask the same question about certain people I've known." Rhinan laughed and, after a moment, Eodorr joined him.

"In any event," Eodorr continued, standing and brushing himself off, "I prefer my birds plucked and roasted."

"As do I." Rhinan nodded in agreement.

After a bit more coughing and spitting, Eodorr assumed a more serious tone. "I'm grateful."

Rhinan grunted and nodded in response.

"I suppose this means you expect me to keep my mouth shut if you tell me to from now on." Eodorr was half grinning.

"That would be wise."

"How can I be a wise man and yet such a fool at same time?" Eodorr lamented. "If I'd thought to grab some of my own money, I could have purchased more supplies in Omriel." As it was, they had only the horse saddles, tackle and packs. The packs held their cloaks, a bit of dried food for travel, and leather pouches for water. Rhinan had his parents' belongings in his, while Eodorr had stuffed his own sword into his. It wouldn't do to be seen with the blade strapped on out of uniform.

"Wisdom is a divine gift of the Lore Givers, and knowledge is taught by the Lore Masters and Lore Trainers they have imparted it to in this world," Rhinan said. "Knowledge can be learned, but you can't teach wisdom. I think my father always said that."

While Eodorr worked out whether he'd been insulted and exactly how, they crouched beside the rocks in cold, wet silence, and they withdrew dried meat from their packs. As they settled down to eat, a large, familiar form wandered into their tiny encampment. Rip made a noise and dropped a hunk of meat at their feet. Eodorr grimaced at the sight of it or perhaps at the wet beardog's odor. Rhinan was happy to see the creature despite the assault on his nostrils, and he felt it would be rude to turn away the offering.

"You're not seriously going to eat that, are you?"

Rhinan looked sidewise at Eodorr, and tore off a chunk of the raw flesh, popping it into his mouth. "Don't insult our donor." He handed the meat to Eodorr who accepted it with a look of horror. Rip nudged him with his great snout. Seeing no choice, Eodorr tore a small bit off for himself and put it in his mouth. It was gamey and unidentifiable, and at the very least it could have used some roasting.

"Very good, Rip," he lied to the beardog. "Thank you." He handed the meat back to Rhinan. "I suppose it's my day to have awful things in my mouth."

When the wind shifted direction, they found they had lost any shelter from the rain. Bracing themselves against the worsening weather, the two men and the beardog were soon on their way again.

Chapter Eleven

The rain continued all day as they rode toward Brinaya's place. The light dimmed early in the dreadful weather and the air grew thick with a chilly mist. Rhinan hoped they could make it before they wound up having to find a place to camp that would provide some shelter from both the elements and their pursuers.

Eodorr sneezed. Rhinan was used to being out in any type of weather, but Eodorr should be in his cottage, with a nice fire roaring and something hot in the cauldron. The need to reach Brinaya now seemed more urgent, or Rhinan worried about keeping Eodorr healthy.

"I know what you're thinking," Eodorr grumbled without looking at Rhinan. "But we can't stop. We have to keep moving, no matter what. The weather may be awful, but we can't assume Dran won't be making good time. With this fog, we might not even see them until they are upon us."

Rhinan opened his mouth to object, but Eodorr cut him off. "And I'll be fine. You needn't worry about me."

"Rip will warn us if anyone is near."

"He's a mighty beardog, I get it. But the three of us

would still be hopelessly outnumbered."

Rhinan said no more, but spurred Dodger on to pick up their pace. If they could cover more ground, at least there was some chance of reaching Brinaya's cabin before Eodorr collapsed.

"You know, Rhinan, you need to take this situation seriously. I know it's not your usual way, but this is far beyond anything you've had to deal with before. I don't know what this is all about, but it's clearly more than stealing a few bottles of Lord Mundon's best brew. Is there something you can tell me to help me understand why Keirwyn would have to *die* protecting you? What else have you done that would make them kill him? I've known you since we were children, but I can't think of anything you've ever done that should cause all this."

"I've been wondering the same thing myself. I know *you* think I lie every time I open my mouth, and I don't, but the absolute truth is that I don't know. There aren't many things about me that you don't know and, other than Keirwyn and Silarrah, I don't think anyone else knows more than you. There's nothing I can think of that would make the King's *Maraggan* so anxious to track me down. If it were just the thievery, I'd expect to be too much trouble for them to dedicate this much effort. Whatever it is, there must be some mistake."

Or, he thought, *something more than I know myself.* A sense of dread crept up inside of him at that thought. How could he get away with something if he didn't even know what it was? Was it possible that he was condemned for something he could never change, perhaps nothing aside from pure happenstance? Something to do with his father? Just how doomed was he? He'd avoided his village his whole life to keep others safe from his ghosts, but how far would he have to go to reach safety himself now, and how hard would Dran continue his pursuit to catch him?

He glanced over at Eodorr again and saw him nodding off on his horse. The solid man was exhausted, and this flight was taking a toll on him in many ways. Rhinan wondered if it might not be better to ride hard and leave Eodorr behind. But the truth was, he needed him. He'd spent life as a loner and a rogue with a mysterious horde of ghosts for companions, but now? Though he'd begrudgingly accepted his companion at first, Rhinan had begun to appreciate him for his usefulness if nothing else.

Besides, what Eodorr had said earlier was true. He had risked his life for Rhinan and he, too, saw Keirwyn as a fatherly figure. Perhaps their separate relationships with the Constable made them brothers of a sort. Eodorr deserved more than to be abandoned to whatever the elements might do to him.

As the darkness settled in over them, the fog condensed. Rhinan could no longer see more than a few feet ahead and had lost track of Rip, too. Even relying on the beardog, the hiss of steady drizzle drowned out their chance of hearing sounds of a search party. The foothills lay to their left, and the plains to their right. Their only hope was to climb further up into the foothills for cover. But the way would be slick with mud, and fraught with peril. It would only slow them down.

"Eodorr?" Rhinan nudged him. "We've got to get out of this weather. No one can follow us in this, and we'll have to stop completely if either of us falls too ill to continue."

Eodorr didn't look up, but nodded. His acceptance signaled that he was feeling worse than he wanted Rhinan to know. He needed food, warmth, and sleep soon.

"Stop where you are!" The gruff voice came from ahead of them, rather than behind. Eodorr's head snapped up, surprisingly alert so swiftly, and Rhinan's hand went to the bow strapped across his back.

"Don't do that," said the voice. "Dismount."

Rhinan dropped his hand to his side, and peered ahead into the foggy mist. He could make out the form of a man on a horse, an arrow nocked in a bow and aimed right at him. Two other men sat on their horses behind the man, swords drawn. They were not Dran's men, although if they were coming down from Cabelon, the *Maraggan* could have turned up in front of them.

"We're not looking for trouble here," Rhinan said. "But we need to keep moving."

"If you're not looking for trouble, then dismount," the man repeated. "We won't keep you long."

Something in the man's voice seemed familiar to Rhinan now. Eodorr slung a leg over and dropped to the ground, keeping hold of his reins. Reluctantly, Rhinan followed suit. "I hope not," Rhinan replied. "I would be very upset if your delay causes us any trouble."

The men chuckled. "We're all the trouble you need be concerned with at the moment, lad," said the man with the bow. "But we'll lighten your load so you can travel faster. Your horses you can keep."

Highway robbers. Rhinan cast a sidelong glance at Eodorr, who made a slight move toward the pommel of his blade.

"Ah, ah, ah," said the man. "Hands up, or I loose this arrow."

Suddenly Rhinan recognized the voice. "Jaskar Heeth?"

The man aimed the bow directly at Rhinan. "Who's that?"

"It's Rhinan Lussaine."

Jaskar Heeth had a nasty reputation as a foothills bandit, but Rhinan had had dealings with him and his band in the past. They had turned out to be too rough, untrustworthy and ruthless for Rhinan to remain associated with. When they'd first met, Heeth had been amused by Rhinan and impressed with his archery skills, so he'd taught Rhinan a few thieving tricks. In return, Rhinan had used those skills to acquire a few items that Heeth had desired in payment. When Rhinan had refused to join Heeth's band, Heeth had been displeased, but he had never tried to kill Rhinan. He hoped that wouldn't change now.

"Rhinan? Well, well! The rain has washed the weasels down the mountain. Who's your friend?" Heeth did not lower the bow, but pointed it at Eodorr.

"One of Constable Keirwyn's aides. He's not worth the trouble." Rhinan gambled that the news of Keirwyn's death had not yet reached this far down the mountain yet, and he knew that Heeth avoided incurring the Constable's direct wrath. He kept his band in the foothills, preferring not to cross into Keirwyn's territory and therefore never had to face the tough law keeper. This was an area one might expect to encounter Heeth, but any encounter with him hadn't occurred to Rhinan with everything else on his mind. He felt as if the whole of the land was just upon his heels.

"Is that right?" Heeth paused. "You still owe me, Rhinan."

"I paid you and then some!" Rhinan snapped. "Please, Heeth. This is not the time."

"Oh? In a spot of trouble, are we? Well, Rhinan, I'm not

going to kill you on account of our past. And as a courtesy to Constable Keirwyn, I'm not going to take any of your friend's belongings. But *you*, Rhinan… You'll give me the contents of your pack, and we'll call it even."

"Heeth… I can't do that. All I have with me are a couple of sentimental keepsakes left to me by my parents, and I've only just recently been given them myself. You remember about my parents, don't you?"

"Then you won't miss them much, will you?" Heeth snarled. "Or do we need to convince you?"

"They're worthless to anyone but me, Heeth," Rhinan pleaded. "Only to me."

"I'll decide that," Heeth said. "Your pack. Now."

Eodorr kept his eyes on the thieves. Rhinan reached for his pack, his mind racing for a way to escape the band. He could see no way out at the moment, so handed the pack to Heeth. As the big thief dismounted and stepped forward, Rhinan could smell him despite the rain. He wore scruffy furs and had a scraggly gray beard. *Fallen on hard times.* His gnarled hands reached out and snatched the pack.

Rhinan's ghosts began to moan and mumble. They were loud… so loud Rhinan could barely hear what Heeth said next.

"So what have we here?" Heeth reached into the pack, withdrawing the large gemstone. It glowed in his hands, and his eyes widened. "Nothing of value, eh? What's this, then? I ought to carve you up right now!"

The air in front of Rhinan was abruptly shredded by light and sound as a bolt of lightning blasted down from the sky, striking Heeth. The blinding flash knocked Rhinan off his feet. The horses of the other two thieves whinnied and reared, anxiously stepping backward, uncontrollable.

There was a tremendous roar, and Rip leapt out of the foggy darkness, taking one of the men off his horse. The man screamed, there was a terrible ripping sound that Rhinan recognized well, and then the man fell silent.

As the other thief turned his horse to flee, Eodorr—moving like a bolt of lightning himself—drew his sword and struck the thief from his horse with a deadly thrust to his side.

In the tumult, Rhinan saw Heeth on the ground smoldering, the glowing stone still clutched in his hand. Rhinan crawled to him, pried the gem loose, and returned it to his pack.

"I won't ask you how you know Jaskar Heeth." Eodorr coughed as he wiped his blade and slipped it back into his scabbard. "But what in all worldly Lore was *that*?" He gestured toward Rhinan's pack.

"That…" Rhinan began. "I don't know. I just don't."

Rhinan climbed back on his horse, his hands shaking, the ghosts gone once again. His desire to know about the stone was much stronger than Eodorr's could possibly be. The stone had interacted with the storm twice now, calling lightning from the sky. Why didn't it kill him as it had Jaskar Heeth? Was it possible that it still would kill him at some point? Perhaps he should reconsider ridding himself of it.

"We're going to have to get some answers if I'm going to help you," Eodorr said, mounting his own horse. "I just don't know where we're going to get them if Brinaya doesn't have any."

Rhinan had no reply. He hoped Brinaya would know something, but his fear of finding out was almost enough to hold him back. Almost.

* * * * *

The girl was sobbing quietly as Captain Siras called her to him. He paused, watching her momentarily. Women made him uncomfortable when they cried. Why did they cry so much? He reached for her dress, tugging her forward to land in his lap. "Here, now," he said. The girl looked up, tears glistening on her cheeks. "Drink this." He forced her to take the last long swallow of ale from the mug in his hand. At least she'd provide some entertainment for him while he waited in this filthy nest—was it called Cabelon?—for further orders from Dran.

As ordered, he'd sent his men out in small groups to scout the area, but they had found nothing so far. This rebel was likely well on his way to the Unreigned Territories by now. It was a waste of his skills to be left sitting here with nothing but the daughters of farmers and herders to amuse himself. Meanwhile Captains Kilward and Gaimesh, that idiot, had gone on with Dran. At least the ale wasn't too bad. "Fetch me another ale, girl," he snapped. As she quickly stepped away, the sound of hoof beats outside the little cottage caught his attention. The afternoon patrol reporting in. "Make it two."

Heavy mist hung in the early evening air as he stepped out into the small village. The scout was just dismounting his horse. His boots sank in the mud as he trudged breathlessly toward Siras with a sweat darkened mount. He'd ridden hard.

"News, sir," the scout reported. Siras waited as the man caught his breath. "We discovered the bodies of three men, slain in some sort of confrontation. Robbers of the lower hill country, most likely. But one of them was burned badly."

Siras stiffened. "You searched them, of course?"

The scout nodded. "We found nothing on them, but there were signs of horses leading away from the site, moving northward."

"How far from here?"

"Just down to the foothills."

Siras himself was supposed to wait in Cabelon in case the thief returned, only sending some of the men out on searches. His instincts were proven right with this discovery. All he had to do now was ride down and capture the thief, and he'd be rewarded when he delivered him up to Dran, finally proving himself to the intimidating General. "Tell the men we all ride immediately," Siras commanded. "We're going to catch this rat yet."

The scout climbed back onto his horse and turned toward the center of the village, drawing a horn from his belt and blowing three blasts.

Siras turned back to the cottage, where his own horse was tethered. As he mounted, the girl emerged carrying two mugs of ale, her head hung low. Siras snorted at her and rode away. *Now there would have been action of another kind.*

* * * * *

The cloaked and hooded figure watched as the King's *Maraggan* streamed out of Cabelon. The information obtained from Silarrah hadn't been very specific, perhaps by Silarrah's intention. But this was certainly the proper path to follow to find Rhinan. From the pace of the special forces, it would likely be soon. The only remaining question was what to do when that happened. *Possibilities.* The figure followed, careful to remain far enough back to escape notice by the soldiers.

Chapter Twelve

It was quite late at night when they reached the cabin of Brinaya Voss. It sat in a small dell upon a foothill to the east of Cabelon, well secluded from those traveling south to Omriel, and far enough north of Omriel to avoid the foot traffic heading east and west on the Northern Trading Path that led up from Omriel, then curved eastward all the way to Dunskern on the great Arinell River. Param's unconventional mother had always been something of a recluse herself.

But to Rhinan's eyes, it was home. More home than anything else since that heart-wrenching day when his parents were killed.

He'd trekked down the mountains many times in his youth to spend warm summer evenings listening to Param play and sing, and to drink Brinaya's rich brews. He often delivered the meat for their suppers, having hunted within the woods on the way down. Brinaya would prepare it perfectly, and accompany it with the fresh vegetables she grew alongside her cabin. Recalling the sweet and savory meals he'd been served there, his mouth began to water. He could almost smell grilled meat in the air. He suddenly felt shame, realizing he hadn't taken the time to bring down a beast for this unexpected visit. But then, he'd been a little busy. Knowing Brinaya, he was sure she'd understand the situation. Just as Keirwyn had been almost like a father to him, Brinaya had been the next best thing to his own mother. Yet he'd seen her so seldom since Param went travelling. He felt a pang of guilt, realizing just how neglectful he had been of those about whom he cared the most.

Despite the miserable weather and the lateness of the hour, Rhinan could still make out the old place. The trees around Brinaya's cabin—some of them with fruits she'd grown herself—looked less trimmed than he remembered, not as well attended to. She'd removed herself all this way out from the village because she preferred privacy (something they had in common), but he wondered if, given what her age must be, she'd perhaps grown too frail to properly care for the place. With Param gone for so long, and so often, the old woman almost certainly had no help with it. Rhinan cursed his selfish negligence.

Eodorr looked sideways at him. "What is it?"

"Been a while since I checked in on her," Rhinan said. "I just hope she's well."

They rode up the slope to the cabin, which seemed much too quiet. He could not recall a visit where Brinaya wasn't busy with something as he approached, and busy with many things during his stay, and yet still busy with other things as he departed. Smoke trailed skyward in the night from the chimney, obscuring the stars where it drifted. Rhinan smiled, taking it as a good sign.

Before Rhinan could stop him, Eodorr had dismounted, tying his horse to a post in the yard, and strode toward the cabin door. With his hand raised to knock, the door was pulled open from within in a swift motion and a crossbow aimed straight into his face. "State your purpose," said the old woman. The stunned look on Eodorr's face made Rhinan laugh as he dismounted.

"I'm funny, am I?" Brinaya continued. "Will you laugh as hard with a hole in you?"

"Not quite the hospitality of Brinaya Voss that I recall," Rhinan said, still grinning. "I've always been filled here, rather than emptied from a bloody hole."

The old woman squinted at him. Her once plump and rosy cheeks had faded and sagged, and there were far more wrinkles around her eyes and mouth than he remembered. Her stringy hair was completely white now, and her hands shook a bit with the weight of the crossbow. A pipe hung from her lips, tiny wisps of smoke curling away past eyes that still twinkled with mischief, just as they always had. She wore an apron, dirtier than he ever remembered her allowing it to get.

"Rhinan, is that you, you little scoundrel?" She tipped her head and winked, a grin of her own starting to appear.

"Yes, ma'am," he replied, reverence in his voice. "Sorry to surprise you this way."

She grunted, but kept the crossbow aimed at Eodorr. "Sorry? If you're going to be sorry for anything, be sorry for how long it's been since you *last* surprised me."

"I do apologize." Rhinan shrugged.

Eodorr cleared his throat.

"Brinaya," Rhinan continued, "You remember Eodorr Hoult, don't you?"

Brinaya eyed Eodorr up and down. "The horse master? You look a fine man now." She lowered the crossbow at last, reaching out to squeeze his muscular arm. "Very imposing."

"Thank you, ma'am," Eodorr said with a bow of his

head, obviously relieved that the weapon was no longer aimed at him.

"Well, if the two of you are here to rob me, I suppose you'll want some supper first." She chuckled, and stood back, motioning them inside. "It's late. You look tired, damp and hungry."

Before they could enter the cabin, Rip sauntered up behind them, prepared to follow. Brinaya squeaked and raised the crossbow once more. Rip sat down and uttered a whine of protest.

"It's okay, Brinaya. He's with us."

"You still hunting around with that dusty old thing? You realize that's a beardog, don't you? It can kill a man with a swipe of one great paw or a crunch of those mighty jaws and large teeth." The old woman shook her head. "You had so few friends, I suppose I shouldn't wonder." She lowered the crossbow. "But he's not coming in here."

Rhinan nodded. "Rip… hunt."

The beardog stood, turned, and slowly walked off into the forest, glancing back one last time as if to see if Rhinan had changed his mind.

As he stepped into the cabin, aromas carried Rhinan backward in his memory to kinder times. Brinaya had aged, but her cabin was frozen in time. The fire in the hearth, something in the cauldron—a savory stew, maybe—and the worn wood of the floor and furniture were all exactly as they had been when Rhinan would accompany Param here in their youth. There was the dark stone hearth, carved by Param's father who had died beneath a felled tree one terrible winter shortly after Param was born. There was the worn table and chairs, and Brinaya's knitting laid across the padded sitting chair in the corner, the green cloth faded nearly colorless. An undusted shelf in the corner displayed old trinkets of Brinaya's and a few treasured books.

When he wasn't with Keirwyn, Rhinan had practically lived here after his parents had been killed. It had been Brinaya that taught him some of the Lore of Leatherworking, such as how to beat and stitch hides for boots and clothes and such. There was a tanner in Cabelon, so Rhinan would sell meat at the market and hides to the tanner. He could have made a good trade of it, but he was unreliable, hunting more when it met his own needs and avoiding contact with the village unless absolutely necessary. Or when he was pilfering from the wealthy, such as Baron Mundon. But she'd helped him become capable of caring for himself in some of the ways that Keirwyn couldn't.

She'd also been the one to teach him to read on stormy days when inside was better than out. He was quick to learn, she had told him, and she always threatened to send him away to the Lore College at Masseltaine one day. When the time finally came, Param went there to delve into the music he loved so well, but Rhinan had his ghosts to deal with and was sure they would follow him if he went. So he had withdrawn to the woods and solitude.

"It's good to see you boys," Brinaya said, moving the cauldron back over the fire. She opened it, reaching in with a long wooden spoon to stir the contents, and the herby aroma that permeated the cabin set Rhinan's mouth to watering. He heard Eodorr's stomach gurgle in agreement. The old woman turned and eyed them. "Or is it good? Something's amiss, unless I'm growing daft in my ancient years."

"There's terrible news," Rhinan said. "And it's my fault."

Brinaya snorted, left the cauldron to bubble, and pulled a chair over and sat down. "Well, you better sit down and tell me. I'm not getting any younger."

Rhinan and Eodorr took turns telling her about the events that had led them here. The arrival of Gethor Dran, the death of Keirwyn, the delivery of items from Rhinan's parents, and the apparent magical properties of the gemstone (which Eodorr could confirm after the event with Heeth), how they thought that they had lost Dran's men after they'd visited Silarrah, but Rhinan knew he could not return to Cabelon. He didn't know where to go. Cabelon had been his only home.

Brinaya listened carefully to all they had to tell her. Now she peered at Rhinan. "Now that isn't quite true, is it? You spent a lot of time right here before you outgrew your wits." She shook her head. "Poor dear Keirwyn. I tried to tell that old fool this day would come. He was all heart and no head. In his way, I suppose, he was trying to protect you."

Rhinan sat forward, yearning for answers the old woman may have if Silarrah's suspicions bore out. "Protect me? From what?" He thought a moment, then added, "Why would King Jerrick be so particularly interested in *me*?"

Brinaya spooned a thick soup of vegetables and legumes into a trio of bowls, handing one to each of them before bringing the third to the table for herself. She retrieved a loaf of bread from a cupboard beside the table, uncovered a dish of creamy butter, then sat down. "Tuck in," she told them. "Then get some rest. You can dry off and we'll talk in the morning."

Eodorr did not hesitate in his condition, but Rhinan still wanted an answer. But he knew it was no use rushing Brinaya, so he, too ate his fill and—feeling safe if only for the night—he and Eodorr slept for a while warm and dry.

*   *   *   *   *

They were all awake in the dark predawn hours, and Rhinan was relieved to see that Eodorr seemed himself again. One night of Brinaya's hospitality would do that for you.

Still waking up, the questions that burned in Rhinan's mind immediately returned. Unless Silarrah had misunderstood, Brinaya, like Keirwyn, knew something about him that he had never known himself. It would seem to be the case from her comments of the previous night. What would Keirwyn and Brinaya have discussed about him in the past, and why those two? Just because they were close to him? And just exactly what "day had come" was she referring to?

Serving them a hot breakfast of grains and smoked meats, Brinaya looked him in the face. He knew she could tell he wouldn't be satisfied until he got his answers. She sighed. "You may have been born in Cabelon, boy, but it's not where you come from, not your true home" she said. Was it a riddle? "Your parents came here to hide following the Ylvan Uprising."

He was shocked to hear that his parents had been in hiding. Why?

"Remember what you know about the Uprising," Brinaya continued, looking out her window, perhaps seeing the past. With an ominous tone to her voice, "After that time, many, many things were changed."

Eating the nourishing breakfast she'd prepared, Rhinan considered what he'd heard of the legendary Ylvan Uprising. It had happened just before the time of his birth. The Ylvan Clans, from the region of Eluciar at the eastern end of Lydania, were led by the powerful sorcerer Narkan Tanglas.

Behind Tanglas, they had risen up against the King of Lydania, presumably because Tanglas was seeking power beyond his station. Many believed that most of the Ylvans only participated because they had been ensorcelled in some way. They were previously known primarily as a peaceful clan. Throughout Lydania, their relationship with the natural world and their fine artisan crafts and workmanship defined them.

As the conflict wore on, King Jerrick Lydan, much younger at the time, lost his queen and son to an assassination which the Ylvan sorcerer was believed to have been behind. No assassin was ever apprehended, so it was accepted that Tanglas somehow committed the murders himself. However, grief stricken and mad with rage, Jerrick had resorted to drastic measures by retaliating in an extreme act—he mysteriously vanquished the entirety of the Ylvan Clans from existence. All of them. And the region of Eluciar was made barren, unfit for habitation. It ended the Uprising.

No Ylvans had been seen since that day. None existed. Following the Uprising, Jerrick had banned the discipline of magic from the Lore College, and the practice of Magic Lore anywhere in Lydania was punishable by death. In further extreme, Jerrick had banned the crafting or smithing of weaponry not used expressly for survival. Bows for hunting or farming tools were approved, but possession of any existing swords and the like was strictly outlawed unless permitted directly by the royal house. The fallout from the Ylvan Uprising had made Lydania what it was today—a repressive kingdom ruled by a paranoid regent with a corrupt court.

Besides his own madness—the ghosts he frequently imagined—Rhinan wondered if this repressive society was part of the reason he spent so much time alone. Especially considering his penchant for mischief. Perhaps knowing and encountering less of it had been his way of avoiding finding himself in just the kind of trouble he now found himself in. He knew the King's laws, but he had never owned more than a bow, had never fought or killed, and certainly had never tried to learn any magic. Now, however, he found himself carrying both a sword and a gemstone that had what resembled magical properties. Yet he had gotten the impression from some of Keirwyn's final words that he probably had as much to fear from the King *before* he had those items as he *knew* he did now with them in his possession. But why? And he still wanted to know what this had to do with his parents.

He realized Brinaya was watching him. "It's no coincidence you grew up in Cabelon, a small village so far from the King's palace," she continued. "And you do resemble your father. Markin Ashuir would have been identified by those close to the King, you see."

"I'm afraid I don't," Rhinan said. "Who is Markin Ashuir? My father was Markin Lussaine."

Brinaya snorted. "You don't even know who you are, boy. Your parents took the name of Lussaine when they came to Cabelon."

Further confused, Rhinan asked, "Was my father a rebel? Did he side with the Ylvans during the Uprising?"

Brinaya chuckled without humor. "There's the irony, lad. Few are those who know this, but your father was *faithful* to the King."

He couldn't identify why, but he was uncomfortable with the direction this conversation was taking. "Why would it be ironic if my father were faithful to the King?"

Brinaya looked over to Eodorr, who was as bewildered as Rhinan. It seemed she was deciding whether or not he could be trusted. Apparently concluding that he could, she leaned forward, speaking in a hushed tone.

"Because your parents *were* the only Ylvans who were loyal to the King, but that loyalty was repaid by the King having them assassinated later when you were a boy."

Unable to speak, his mouth hanging open, Rhinan tried to process everything Brinaya was telling him.

"Yes, Rhinan Ashuir. This makes you the very last survivor of the Ylvan Clans."

Chapter Thirteen

Silarrah smelled wet horse and damp earth. The ground was above and the sky below. Her face was sore, and she was certain her head would burst open. She couldn't feel her hands at all. Had they been severed? She twisted and felt the sharp pain in the area that might be her wrists. Bound tight, but still there.

"Stop squirming, or I'll give you another lump on the head."

She looked sideways and could see one of Dran's men walking beside her, leering down at her. She was slung over a horse, and the saddle was digging into her stomach. Her mouth was dry and she felt dizzy. She was slipping, and she expected to meet the ground face-first—and hard—and perhaps be trampled by the horse. The soldier reached up, grabbed her by the buttocks, and hoisted her back to center. She glared at him, and he grinned at her.

Initially, they'd dragged her along on her feet, hauling her by the ropes binding her hands. She understood that Dran was making a point. As she stumbled, fell, was dragged, her clothes—and the flesh beneath—were tattered and shredded, and she had become too weak to stay on her feet. Since that slowed their progress too much, Dran had ordered her slung over one of the pack horses and tied there. She'd been unconscious off and on with no idea how long they'd been traveling at this point.

Twisting her head slightly, she could see the brute—Captain Gaimesh, she thought they'd called him—not far away. He stared at her with the cold, blank eyes of a reptile. She shuddered. She knew it would be the end if they turned him loose on her. The only thing keeping her alive now was whatever she knew about Rhinan, and she didn't even know if what she knew about him would satisfy them. It didn't matter. Whatever they wanted from her, whether they got it or not, she would be killed when they were through. She hoped that would be all they would do with her; living in their captivity would be worse than death.

"Halt!"

The command sounded like it came directly from Dran. Everything stopped, and the jolt caused the saddle horn to dig into her ribs so harshly she thought she would pass out again. A moment later, she heard steps approaching.

"Bring her down." Dran's voice again. Hands grasped her, ungently, and she was hauled backward off the horse and set on her feet. The hands released her, and her legs collapsed, sending up a cloud of road dust as she hit the ground. When it cleared, she looked up, and Dran was sneering down at her. He turned to the guard who had been keeping her on the horse. "Give her water," he ordered. "And wash her down a bit."

The guard shoved a leather container in her mouth, and she drank thirstily. He pulled it away before she was through, and she lunged forward, but he shoved her back. "Keep still," he growled.

She was shocked when a sudden torrent of cold water hit her from the right. Shrugging off as much of the water as she could, her muscles and her head cried out in pain. She turned to see a soldier holding an empty bucket. He examined her as if to determine what sort of creature she was. She was drenched and immediately felt a chill. She began to shiver.

"That's enough." Dran turned and walked away.

The two guards stood over her, watching her carefully as if she might try to escape. She couldn't even stand, let alone run.

The sun was setting. They were not in the foothills of the Domins; the horizon had flattened. She noticed scattered trees off to the side of the road and assumed they must be nearing Masseltaine, though she didn't see any other travelers on the dusty road in either direction.

She could hear the other soldiers stomping around, setting up camp. The activity was behind her, but after a time she smelled the fire and cooking food. She was ravenous; they hadn't fed her at all on the journey. She wondered again how long they'd traveled. Probably all of the one day. She didn't think Masseltaine was further than a couple of days from Omriel, more easterly but a bit to the south as well.

A plate of roasted meat strips, grilled roots and a hunk of crusty bread was placed on her lap. One of the *Maraggan* untied her hands and she reached for the plate, but she dropped it on the ground. Her hands were too numb to grasp it. The soldier scowled at her, his patience tested. He picked up the food, put it back on the plate and put the plate back in her lap. She rubbed her hands until she could feel them. Once she got past the prickling discomfort as feeling returned, she brushed the dirty food off and shoved it into her mouth in rapid handfuls. When she began to choke, the man gave her some more water.

When she finished, the plate was taken away. A few moments later, Dran approached.

"Well, are you enjoying your journey?" He wore a smug grin. "It won't get better. Are you sure you still want to go all the way to Masseltaine? You could tell me what I want right now and find your own way home. It might be easier on you." He eyed her up and down. "You look terrible. I don't think traveling agrees with you."

Silarrah glared at him but did not respond. It might be torture, but she wouldn't help this demon if she could avoid it.

"Your choice." He shrugged casually. Then, to the men, "Bind her, watch her. It will be cold tonight." He looked hard at them. "See that no one tries to keep her warm." Then he walked away.

Chapter Fourteen

“So my real name is Rhinan Ashuir? And I’m supposedly an Ylvan?” Rhinan wished he didn't believe Brinaya, but as soon as she said it, he felt the truth of it. His parents were Ylvan. It explained everything. If King Jerrick had a particular interest in him, he must suspect that Rhinan was Ylvan. That was a death sentence, so it explained his parents' murders. The thought suddenly occurred to him that the King himself must have been responsible for their deaths. Fury ignited within him. He had never known so much fury as sorrow.

Brinaya watched him carefully. "Yes, you begin to understand. What no one knows is how you and your parents survived the spell that ended the Ylvan Clans. Show me this gemstone you spoke of."

Hesitant, Rhinan reached for his pack and withdrew the gem. It had proven dangerous for others to touch, so he would not let her hold it. It had brought lightning down from the sky twice; maybe it would be something he could eventually use to avenge his parents. Tucked into his pack, it had not caused any more trouble or pain. The hum emitting from it was muffled enough for him to ignore, and no one else was aware of it as far as he could determine. And if it could provide him no other use, it might prove to be highly valuable. If so, what help might he be able to provide to Silarrah's orphans?

As Rhinan held it out, Brinaya leaned closer, squinting. She herself was careful not to touch it, but regarded it carefully. "I haven't seen one of those in a long time," she finally said, a curious expression on her face. "You see the depth within? It's a *Pyvadis.* It is a gem imbued with magic, and if the King's men catch you with it, it will mean your death.

"But," she continued, "as it was held for you in secret by your parents, it must have significance. You need to learn what that is. It is part of your heritage, and I for one have no idea where you might turn to learn much more of that. I can only tell you what everyone knows, what you yourself undoubtedly know of the Ylvan Clans and the Uprising."

"I would say bury it and run as far and as fast away from it as you can," Eodorr quipped. "Though since you can't go home—and neither can I, now, I might add—we may as well try to find some explanation for it."

"There is no 'we,' Eodorr," Rhinan replied. "You've done more than enough, endangered yourself, and no one is safe with me. I would ask dear Brinaya here to allow you to stay on, maybe help with chores for a while." He felt so cozy in her old cabin he wished he could stay there himself.

"No." Eodorr was adamant. "You meant something to Keirwyn and, to honor him, I will see you safely to whatever destination you decide upon, as I said. If that requires answers first, then that's what we look for."

"But you should be safe here. I think in time you could return to Cabelon. It's me they'll be hunting."

"By now, I'm a wanted man, too. No, Rhinan, I believe we are sharing a path for the foreseeable future. You may be good in the woods alone, but you need someone with a better head for people. You won't make it far without me."

Rhinan considered the truth in what Eodorr was saying. Eodorr was certainly more diplomatic than Rhinan, who had spent much of his life avoiding the company of others, albeit for their own protection. He was, after all, mad. Either that or his ghosts were real and may present a danger. He shuddered, recalling his first encounter with them. Were they some evil thing unleashed by the King to harass Ylvans?

Brinaya chimed in. "He's right, Rhinan. You would do well to abandon your solitary ways and accept whatever help you can get now. This is bigger than anything in your experience. You'll have to discover much, and that means contact with people. Not your strongest skill, and you know I don't tell you this to be hurtful. You and my son Param have been friends for many years, but how many do you count among your true friends? Silarrah? And Keirwyn is gone know, may the Lore Givers share knowledge with him in peace."

Rhinan stood and paced Brinaya's tiny cabin. Having always endured solitude, he was uncomfortable with the idea of having too much of the company of others. And there was the ever-present possibility that being in Rhinan's presence was a danger, now more than ever. But Eodorr, though never a friend, had not proven to be an enemy. He could easily have turned Rhinan in and been done with it. Eodorr was devoted to Keirwyn, and he knew Keirwyn loved Rhinan like a son. This likely made Eodorr a solid ally. And Rhinan's own love for Keirwyn, he realized, obligated him to Eodorr as well. It was settled.

"But where do we go, Brinaya?" he asked her, anguish

overtaking him. "I can think of no place where such answers may lie and no one alive who could possibly hold any relevant truths about me." He needed to journey to some place safe, but he knew that would never be without more information.

"Oh, can't you?" Brinaya prodded. "I can think of nothing further, but the Lore Masters at the College would almost certainly have some answers, if only to point you to other people and places where such answers may lie."

"I can’t go there, Brinaya. The Lore College is in Masseltaine, as is the King. I would surely be caught and executed were I to venture anywhere near there."

"So we must find a way to bring the Lore College to you, then," Brinaya said simply.

Rhinan and Eodorr both laughed without humor. "That will take some doing."

As he tucked the *Pyvadis* back into his pack, Rhinan's ghosts appeared to him, murmuring, filling the cabin, drifting through the walls.

And then there was a firm knock at the cabin door.

* * * * *

After riding and searching most of the night by torchlight, they spotted the little cabin in the predawn darkness. Captain Siras immediately dispatched the young scout Flek to inform Dran that they had found the thief. He then motioned for his men to surround the cabin without coming too close. It looked old and simple, but the smoke rising from the chimney and dim light shining from within meant it was certainly inhabited.

Once the men had spread out, Siras looked carefully for any signs of other travelers in the area. He was thorough in his appraisal of the situation, but the two horses tethered out front made it obvious. He listened for movement within the cabin, considering what and who may be inside besides their thief. As Dran's most trusted squad leader, Siras felt the pressure to impress the General. For his own good, if for no other reason. Dran was not one to suffer incompetence and inefficiency, and Siras had not risen to his level at Dran's side without considerable skills. But this would be a routine arrest, and Siras would look good having accomplished it.

Prepared at last to approach the cabin, he motioned one of his men forward. The man drew his blade and stepped lightly up to the cabin's door. He knocked, and then stepped back. "Open up, in the name of the King."

* * * * *

They jumped to their feet at the *Maraggan's* proclamation. Rhinan reached for his bow and Eodorr drew his sword. Ghosts were everywhere, but as usual only Rhinan could see them. They were unnerving and frightening to a certain degree, even after all these years. He had learned to concentrate and tune them out as much as possible, but their appearance never failed to startle him at first, and often distract. It had never been as successful as it had been with the gem—*Pyvadis.*

"Be still," Brinaya said calmly. She motioned them into another room, her bed chamber. "Just wait there silently. You'll know if I need you."

They did as she said, but Rhinan nocked an arrow and stood ready just out of sight. Eodorr stood behind him, still gripping his sword. They both had a view of what came next.

Brinaya stooped a bit and shambled to the door, feigning

more frailty than was true of her. She opened it just as the soldier raised his free hand to knock again. She looked down at his sword and cried, "What is this? Disturbing an old woman's breakfast in such a manner! I see by your finery that you are with the King's special force. Do they not teach manners to the *Maraggan* anymore?"

The soldier was taken aback for a moment at being admonished by the old woman. Brinaya was playing her role well, but then Rhinan saw her cast a quick glance over her shoulder. The *Maraggan* looked beyond her into the cabin. His eye caught sight of her table… where clearly sat the evidence that she was not alone. Three serving places at the table, and the *Maraggan* gave the old woman a knowing look. She wasn't fooling him; he already knew she had guests.

Seeing only the one soldier, Brinaya acted much more quickly than Rhinan would have expected her age to allow. She reached into her apron pocket. In a singular motion, she withdrew her hand and flicked a cloud of powder into the *Maraggan*'s face. When it came in contact with him, the powder ignited in a flash. Thrown backward, the soldier dropped his sword and clutched at his eyes.

Rhinan and Eodorr rushed forward to finish the soldier. Before they could reach him, they heard the cry of "Magic!" from outside. There were more soldiers… but how many? Was Dran out there?

The first arrow came through the open door, catching Brinaya just under her breastbone, and to the left. She fell backward into Rhinan and Eodorr. They pulled her away from the open door, out of the line of fire, and Eodorr kicked it shut.

Rhinan held Brinaya, and she looked into his eyes. She tried to speak, but there was no sound. She grabbed his hand

and squeezed, smiling. Before he could respond, she went limp in his arms. A gasp escaped his lips as a spear of pure anguish pierced his heart. How could this have happened? What had he done? Would it ever stop? Catching his breath, he laid her gently on the floor.

There was a commotion outside as more *Maraggan* closed in on the cabin. Rhinan picked his bow up, snarling as he nocked an arrow and drew back on the string. Eodorr stood ready with his sword. The two men cast a grim expression at each another and nodded.

"Step outside!" they heard one of the soldiers call. "No more magic, or we'll burn you in there where you stand."

Squatting and peeking out a window, Rhinan saw lit torches.

"I could take a few with arrows, but you may never get close enough to any of them to use that sword." In pain from the loss of Brinaya, he pleaded with Eodorr. "If you surrender, they may spare you."

Before Eodorr could protest, they heard a familiar roar followed by a soldier's gurgled cry. "Rip!" Rhinan feared the beardog would be killed out there.

Another soldier cried out, but it came from the opposite side of the cabin. Rhinan knew Rip could move swiftly, but that was a leap even for the beardog.

Peeking out again, Rhinan could only see the light of torches moving erratically. There had to be some confusion among the *Maraggan*. Had the beardog created panic, causing them to mistake each other for enemies in the dark and turn on one another?

On his side of the cabin, Rhinan counted four torches. He saw an opportunity; the torches made the shots easy. He took down all four within seconds, knowing despite the darkness that he had hit his marks when the torches fell to the ground, sparking fire in the brush and grass where they landed.

There were more cries from soldiers, coming from various directions. One soldier came rushing in, shoving the front door open in panic, and impaled himself on Eodorr's sword without much effort from Eodorr. Eodorr shoved him backward, withdrawing his blade, leaving the dead soldier lying over the threshold, his body half in and half out of the cabin.

There was a *thunk* as something hit the side of the cabin. Then another and another. Rhinan smelled smoke. The cabin had been set ablaze. Now the matter was more urgent—dashing out would mean being cut down by *Maraggan's* arrows, but staying within meant death by fire as the back of the cabin was swiftly engulfed in flame.

There were two more cries from soldiers outside, one from each side of the cabin. His heart racing, Rhinan could no longer wait. Grabbing his pack, he motioned to Eodorr to follow. Crouching low, he stepped over the body in the threshold, out into the night. With any luck, the smoke would provide enough cover to give them the chance to fight before they were shot and killed by arrows.

But no arrows were fired at them. No *Maraggan* appeared. What had happened?

* * * * *

When the soldier at the door was flung backward with a flash of some kind of magic light, Siras had been angry. Burn his men, would you? He would burn the cabin to the ground. He called out a final warning to the occupants, and then commanded his men to light torches.

As they did so, he heard a noise that sounded like a wild animal from the other side of the cabin, followed by the scream of one of his men. They had definitely come upon something serious.

Then the two men on his right and his left went down as arrows were fired from inside the cabin. He saw one of his men charge into the front of the cabin, as some of his men at the rear fired flaming arrows into the little structure.

He began to circle around toward the front of the cabin, then stopped when he heard the men at the back of the cabin cry out. He looked back but, in the predawn darkness, it was impossible to see what had happened. More arrows? Magic?

He turned to move forward again, but a cloaked figure blocked him. Two daggers plunged into either side of his neck as the figure leapt over him, flipping as it did so. The figure was unbelievably swift. As Siras hit the ground, the figure landed on its feet like some kind of wildcat, stood over him, and drew back its hood. The last thing Captain Siras knew was surprise.

* * * * *

Upon a quick inspection around the cabin, there had to be a dozen dead *Maraggan* scattered about. Even with Rip approaching him, Rhinan could not surmise what had happened without closer examination. The cabin was burning, the deceased Brinaya inside. He and Eodorr could only watch in sadness. *Another person I love dead because of me*, Rhinan thought. *I am poison.*

The ghosts were gone now. Rhinan collapsed in front of the blazing cabin, overtaken by grief and sorrow. Rip sat beside him, nuzzling his hair. Eodorr placed a hand on his shoulder as he wept.

Rhinan choked on smoke and tears. It was still not over. This would continue until he was far away or dead himself. But there was so much he needed to know. He felt as if he'd never known anything, his life a lie. All this magic… He'd never known Brinaya to practice it, but that was clearly some magic stunt she'd pulled on that soldier. Had she always used magic? Would Param know?

There was a slight sound behind them, and both men turned swiftly, weapons ready. Rip, however, seemed unconcerned.

Before them stood a dark-cloaked figure, clearly intending to get their attention, but making no attempt to threaten. Before Rhinan could speak, the figure shrugged back the hood of the cloak.

By the light of the burning cabin, Rhinan saw a lithe young woman with dark hair. She held a pair of daggers at her side, both dripping blood. Strapped at an angle across her back was a quarterstaff, the top end sharpened and also dripping blood. Here, apparently, was another ally in the battle they'd just won.

"Rhinan Ashuir?" she asked. "I am Lynari, a *Hegana* of the Lore College. I've been sent to assist you."

Speechless, Rhinan could only recall some of Brinaya's final words to him. "*So we must find a way to bring the Lore College to you, then.*"

And… here she was?

Chapter Fifteen

When she was presented to the King, the strangest thoughts ran through Silarrah's mind.

King Jerrick wore a deep burgundy robe of silk, trimmed in gold and silver and black. A golden tunic, black satin breeches and shiny silver slippers completed his outfit. Upon his head of gray-dusted hair rested a circular crown of gold and black velvet, the top of which was mounted with a golden carving of the royal emblem—the great fanged wildcat known as a *mogas*. A mighty sword was sheathed at his side, the jeweled pommel glittering in the light which streamed into the throne room from arched windows set very high. The ceiling was so far up that she imagined you would have to be a bird to reach those windows. On a raised dais, he sat on a polished throne carved of gold-marbled stone so black that it did not reveal its curves. Colorful cushions lay on the seat, and great tapestries adorned the walls to either side of the throne, extending nearly up to the base of the high windows.

She had never met a king. She hadn't been allowed the opportunity to clean up after the journey to Masseltaine. She was rushed right to this throne room, still wearing the same dress as when she was abducted, though it was now dirty and frayed. No one had done anything to prepare her in any way before thrusting her into the King's presence.

What struck her as funny was that he would probably have her killed. He would sentence her to be executed in some horrible way, and here she was worrying about her appearance. Still disoriented, dazed and exhausted from the journey, she didn't even realize it when a slight chuckle escaped her lips.

King Jerrick leaned forward on his throne, his elbow on his knee, one side of his mouth curling into what she might have otherwise mistaken for a grin. "Well, it's a relief to discover that I amuse you." The almost-grin disappeared, replaced with a blank look. He leaned back, folding his hands together.

Silarrah had just enough time to realize what she had done, and to think that this wasn't going well, before Dran—standing at her side—poked her in the ribs with his elbow. Her knees nearly buckled at the jab, but she recovered and held her head up high. *Curse them both*, she thought. *I'm not in* their *presence… they're in* mine.

Jerrick gave Dran an admonishing look, to which Dran raised his hands in apology. Silarrah could detect no animosity on either's part, however. Just a speechless communication between two people who were used to each other's ways and apparently had no issue working with it.

"So we know our guest can laugh. Let's see if she can speak." The King fixed her with his gaze. "I am told your name is Silarrah. You work with children in Omriel." He paused, waiting for her to reply.

In her condition, it took her a moment to realize these

were questions and not statements. "Y-yes... Yes... Your Highness?" Her voice did not come easily; her throat hurt from dryness and she wished she could have some water. She hoped she'd used the proper term of reference, or she may be losing her head even sooner than expected.

The King's gaze was no easy thing to endure. It was a hard gaze, and it made her feel violated. She hoped Rhinan was far, far away from this man. *Oh, please*, she thought. *Please let him be beyond the reach of these beasts.* But that had been her plan. By refusing to speak to anyone but the King, she'd hoped she'd bought Rhinan that time. She would pay with her life, but it was all she could do for him now.

The King winced and looked at Dran. "Have you brought me a simpleton, Gethor? Is this our best lead for finding that... *wizard?*" The last word was forced out in disgust.

"I assure you, my liege, she is no simpleton. Wiley enough to play at being one, perhaps." Dran gave her a cold look that chilled her to her bones. Then he turned and called to one of his men who stood assembled behind them. "Fetch water." One of the soldiers immediately disappeared to obey the order.

Wizard?!? Silarrah thought. *They think Rhinan is a wizard? That can't be. There are no more wizards. Not since before I was born. They must be looking for someone else! Maybe this was all a huge mistake. Wait a minute. Did he just call me a simpleton—?*

The almost-grin reappeared on the King's face. "Smart enough to know when she's been insulted, at least."

Silarrah tried to tell herself to control her expressions. Weak as she was, it was hard to control anything. She could barely stand.

The soldier reappeared with a carved wooden bowl of

water and handed it to Dran. Silarrah found herself marveling at the bowl's beauty as Dran handed it to her. "Drink," he commanded.

She drank it down thirstily, no attempt to maintain any decorum. She even spilled a little on herself, but she didn't care. She was parched. It wasn't enough, but it helped.

And yet it didn't. The water had the effect of making her a bit sharper, and so she was suddenly more aware of the grave peril she was in. She'd found a way to keep herself separated from the moment until now. It had given her more control, but now fear gripped her, growing stronger as it crept through her every sense.

Her head spun. She threw up. She saw the floor coming toward her face, and thought the tiles were lovely. Everything was lovely here. And then it hurt.

* * * * *

She was seated in an ornate wooden chair. *Still lovely*, she thought. She looked up, and she was still before the King. Only moments could have passed.

King Jerrick sighed. "Silarrah, let's begin again. Can you do that?" He cocked his head and, for a moment, seemed paternal.

She wondered if she should stand in his presence. Just the thought of trying made her head start to spin again, and she abandoned the idea. If they wanted to speak to her, they would now have to do it while she sat. How much worse could it be? They could only behead her once. Or hang her. And then she began to imagine all the terrible things they could do to her. The fear returned, clenching the breath out of her.

She nodded. She would need to find her voice again, but it would take a moment.

"Good," said the King, who looked anything but convinced. "It was you who requested an audience with me. Do not forget that."

"We need you to answer some questions," he continued. "A man who is very, very dangerous… We have reason to believe he visited you in Omriel, that you know him. We need you to tell us everything about him. Hold nothing back, and tell no lies. Fail me in any of these things, and you will know the King's justice. No need to fear if you simply obey your King."

Rhinan? Dangerous? Only if he were hunting you. Or if you were in love—but no, she couldn't see that. She nodded. Maybe she had a chance to convince them and survive this ordeal.

"I think you are looking for the wrong man," she managed to say at last. "You are looking for a dangerous wizard? I was not aware that any had survived. The man who visited me the day your soldiers"—she shot a disgusted look at Dran—"took me from my home? I have known him since childhood and he may be… unusual, but he is certainly not dangerous. And he can't be a wizard, because there are no more. I've never seen him practice any Magic Lore. Whoever you are looking for, it must be someone else."

King Jerrick waited to see if she would go on. She could think of nothing else to say. Nothing else she knew would be of any help to them or to Rhinan. That was the end of it all in her mind.

She was wrong.

"So this man…" The King stood, crossed his arms behind his back, and began to pace back and forth in front of his throne. "You have known him since childhood. You grew up in Cabelon, is that right?"

"Yes." She had been born there and lived there until first her mother and then later her father had died. With no marriage proposals (people had always assumed she and Rhinan would marry, given their propensity for spending time together), she had moved to Omriel to work with children. It looked as if she'd have none of her own.

"And… did you know *his* parents?" He stopped pacing and turned on her suddenly. He lowered his head and stared intently at her.

Rhinan's parents? Well, of course. Until…

"Yes," she answered. "When we were children."

"*Only* when you were children? Why do you say that?" The King's voice rose, and he spoke faster.

Silarrah thought perhaps she had made a mistake, but she couldn't see how. She had to answer. "Because they… died… when we were very young."

King Jerrick and Dran exchanged a look she did not understand. Was it fear? In these two men? The King drew closer to her. "They *both* died? Do you recall *how* they died?"

Silarrah could not see how this was important. She did not wish to recall such unpleasantness. She would never forget that day. That day had been the day that changed Rhinan. He had been a ray of sunshine… a fun boy, warm and jovial and a leader of their childhood group of friends. After that, he'd become withdrawn, less social, and quite solitary. That had remained true for the rest of his life, even now. But a thing like that… how could it not change a person at any age?

"They were killed," she whispered. "Someone tried to rob them in their home. We had been out playing, and when we came back, the Constable..." She could not go on. She remembered how Keirwyn had tried to intercept them, but they saw... She quaked at the memory. Param had taken Rhinan to his home to wait for Keirwyn. When the Constable came for him, the entire village had watched as poor Rhinan was led quietly to a place where he would be given the worst news of his life.

Again, a look passed between the King and Dran. This time, she knew they suspected something, as if they were resigned to some horribly unpleasant truth. "So he was not home when this attack took place." The King was somewhere far away in his mind, staring into nothingness.

Silarrah was sure that whatever she had unwittingly revealed had made things worse for Rhinan. Possibly much worse. She hoped there were no more questions. But she would be disappointed. The agony continued when the King spoke again.

"Was anything left after the robbery? Did anything pass to him from his parents?"

She could think of nothing specific. There were household items, but he'd never taken any of them. Not even their cottage. He'd never gone back into it as far as she knew. "Nothing that I know of. He never even went back for anything left behind by whoever killed his parents."

King Jerrick seemed satisfied at this answer, perhaps even relieved?

"How did he act after losing his parents? Did you ever see him do anything unexpected? Unusual? Strange?"

Strange? Everything about Rhinan had been strange since that day. What was the King looking for? She went for straight honesty.

"I think he was always a bit unusual after that. He was

orphaned. He was lonely. How could he be otherwise? But I wouldn't say it was anything unexpected after such a tragedy. He didn't mix well with people after that. He kept to himself. But he was never unkind, and often helped out the rest of the villagers in difficult times. He is a good hunter—"

"Is he good at anything else?" The King seemed particularly intrigued.

She wouldn't want to say he was good at anything else that might create problems for him, but she couldn't honestly say she knew of anything in particular besides his bowmanship. It was unparalleled. But everything that had to do with hunting—tracking, forestry… he knew a lot about the wilds and the animals. But that all came under "hunting" in her mind, and she had already said he was a good hunter, so she just said, "Nothing I can think of."

The King frowned.

"Do you recall their names? His parents?"

Silarrah did. She didn't see how it could matter. "Markin and Herilyn Lussaine."

The King howled in fury. "The Ashuirs!"

"He's an Ylvan!" Dran was even shocked.

Now Silarrah was even more confused. Ylvans were even more gone than those who used the Lore of Magic. They were wiped out at the end of the Ylvan Uprising. Everyone knew that. There was no way Rhinan was Ylvan. She was careful not to laugh. This King was mad, and so was Dran. This whole thing was madness. Magic? Ylvans?

"Siblings?" The King sounded very worn at this point.

"He was their only child," Silarrah replied honestly, as quick as she could, while the King seemed less angry.

"We need to find him. Do you know where he might be going?"

She paused a moment too long before she lied. "I don't."

Glaring at her, the King reached down and grabbed her by both arms, hauling her to her feet. His grip was strong, his expression angry. "I ordered you not to lie to me," he snarled, his face close to hers. Too close. She felt the heat of his breath. She thought this was the moment… this was when he would kill her.

"I don't know," she said firmly, telling herself that she couldn't be sure where Rhinan was now, or where he was going. "He is probably going as far away from here as he can. Why wouldn't he run? Your men have scared him. He's done nothing!"

The King's grip relaxed, and he pushed her gently back into the chair, perhaps satisfied. He rubbed his head above his eyes and stepped back. "Maybe. Maybe not."

Having spoken little during the interrogation, Dran finally asked her a question. "What is *his* name?"

Silarrah froze. They didn't *know*? She couldn't tell them. Could she lie? Would they know if she did?

She felt her hair seized from behind, and her head was snapped backward. She was looking up at Dran's face, his expression cool, emotionless. His other hand appeared, a dagger pointed at her throat.

"You've told us less than you know, and the King's orders were to tell us everything. You know his name. You will tell us now who this man is. We can find this answer from others back in Cabelon. If we have to go back there, we may have to kill them all one by one, but we *will* have his name. If you tell us now, you may save many lives—starting with your own."

She struggled to turn her gaze toward the King, who stood watching Dran's display with an expression that appeared to be a mixture of tired and sad. And perhaps… more fear?... in his eyes.

Silarrah could read people. She had always had a gift for it, even as a young girl. There was something in the King's expression that told her he was genuinely worried, concerned, afraid of something. Once again, she started to believe this had to be some big mistake. There had to be someone else they wanted, not Rhinan. If there were some way for them to speak with him, for him to remain safe as they did so, she was sure this could be cleared up. There was certainly nothing to fear from Rhinan. Maybe if they knew his name, they would know he was not the man they were seeking. He could not be.

With that thought, she relented under the terrifying threat. She looked Dran in the eyes. "His name is Rhinan."

There was a satisfied expression on Dran's face. He released her hair and stepped backward, the dagger still pointed at her.

The King spat out the name. "Rhinan Ashuir!"

“No!” she cried. “Rhinan Lussaine! You have the wrong man!”

The King hung his head, and Dran gave her a hard look, shaking his head. She didn't know what it meant, but she felt in her heart that she had somehow doomed Rhinan. Nothing else she could say would help him now, she was sure. She hoped her own death would be swift and painless. They'd said they wouldn't kill her if she obeyed, and she had. Sort of. But she doubted them. Dran did not seem an honorable man, and the King was… detached, distant. She felt that what happened to her did not matter to him in any way. No, they would kill her now, and hunt Rhinan all the more, and she had no idea why. Unless he *was* the man they were looking for? Could it all be true? Stunned at the possibility, she began to weep.

It occurred to her, however, that she had won a victory. She had managed to get herself taken to the King, stood before King Jerrick himself, all as a delaying tactic to give Rhinan the chance to get far away and be safe. She loved Rhinan, Ylvan or not, and she had willingly sacrificed herself for a man that was badly damaged and could not be what she wanted him, needed him, to be. Whatever she'd given them in information, she'd taken away in time.

She alone had defeated both a general and a king and all their men.

"Lock her in the dungeon," the King said, sitting back on his throne, his eyes wild. He slumped backward. "But in the upper cells." He looked hard at Dran. "No one is to harm her, or they will know my wrath. We must investigate and verify what she has told us. Determine if she has obeyed her King. If she has lied, she will meet with justice. If she has been truthful, she will remain here as our guest until this Rhinan—Ylvan offspring of Markin and Herilyn Ashuir—is found. She may still prove to be of further use."

The King sat on his throne, staring into the distance, still wild eyed. Dran nodded, and grabbed her by an arm, lifting her back out of the chair. One of Dran's men took her other arm, and she was dragged out of the King's presence.

Chapter Sixteen

Dran re-entered the throne room. Without looking up, King Jerrick moaned. "So your far-fetched suspicions of magic were accurate. I tested her. I even accused her of knowing a living Ylvan, and she had no idea. You could see her surprise. But Markin and Herilyn left a child?"

Dran hesitated. The King's melancholy was legendary, and unpredictable. Even Dran did not want to be on Jerrick's bad side. "So it would appear, Your Highness. Perhaps hidden with magic."

The King sat up and snarled. "There *is* no more magic! I saw to that years ago. Its very existence is far too dangerous. The Ashuirs' deaths were supposed to be the end of it."

"Yet it appears that an Ylvan lives, Your Highness." Dran pronounced the conclusion gingerly.

"As long as he does, it means the possibility of another Ylvan sorcerer yet exists in my kingdom." King Jerrick stood. "I will not have it, Gethor. The practice of magic once nearly destroyed us all. It must be extinguished as would a candle before a peaceful night's slumber."

Dran nodded in agreement. "It cannot be trusted. No one can be trusted with it. And no one with a potential skill for it, or a bloodline of such potential skill, must be spared."

The King turned away. Dran knew he was lost in his complicated thoughts. "But tell me, Gethor. How is this even possible? We eliminated the Ashuirs almost 20 years ago. We understood that was the end of it. There were none left. No Ylvan Clan members."

"That is perhaps easier to explain, Your Highness." Dran chose his next words carefully. The King saw conspiracies everywhere, often where there were none. He would make improbable and unlikely leaps in logic, and one never wanted to be on the receiving end of any such theory. "Someone either failed or lied to us, and then others lied, and we were deceived. The surviving Ashuir had to have been kept hidden these many years."

The King faced him, that wild look in his eyes. "Who, Gethor? Who lied? How many in this conspiracy?" His anger rose. He was working himself up. "I want them all lined up in front of me. I will show them that they obey the King's laws for a reason, and that actions to the contrary are treason and will be met with the fiercest response!"

Dran stepped back from the King's tirade. He knew how to handle him, but it was always a delicate matter.

"The Constable of Cabelon would be your first traitor," Dran said firmly. "He defended the man when questioned, and it is clear to me now that he knew who Ashuir was."

"And who is this Constable? Where is he now?"

"It was Keirwyn Dayas."

"Dayas…" The King grew distant. Dran waited as the King thought about it. "You mean Keirwyn? The hero of Ramwick?"

"The same." Dran feigned disappointment and sadness, though he didn't care about Keirwyn's illustrious history.

"The Ashuirs must have fled to Cabelon about the same time as he was assigned as its Constable. He and Markin had been friendly, if you recall."

The King shook his head. "Those days are… evasive to my recollections."

"Well, some years after you assigned Keirwyn to Cabelon, you heard that Markin Ashuir was somehow alive, despite your elimination of the Ylvan clans. You dispatched a man to find the Ashuirs…" Dran watched the King searching his own mind for the memories.

"Of course," the King said, eyes narrowed. "It was Cabelon. The couple was in Cabelon. That is when the Ashuirs were assassinated, and the last threat of magic finally ended. We confirmed their deaths."

"What we hadn't known at the time, but we can now surmise, is that the Ashuirs were expecting a child when the rest of the Ylvans were extinguished. By the time they were discovered in Cabelon, the child had been born. But since we did not know about the child until now, we only *assumed* the Ashuirs, and the threat, had been ended."

"So you're saying it's not a conspiracy?" King Jerrick seemed confused.

"Oh, no," Dran shook his head. "Others must have known of the child and kept it from you."

"Besides Keirwyn?"

Dran nodded.

"Why did you not bring Keirwyn to me?" The King peered sharply at Dran.

"He… did not survive the encounter, regrettably, Your Highness." Dran laid his hand on the hilt of the sword buckled at his side. "He will not be deceiving you—or anyone—again."

"Regrettable. But necessary, I suppose." The King paused, returning to his thoughts as he sat back down on his throne. "And who else? You think this Silarrah knew? She seemed quite surprised."

Dran shook his head. "No, Your Highness. There is no reason to think she knew of his Ylvan origins." He was usually suspicious of anyone, but he did not think this woman had any idea. He actually felt she was just a stupid cow with some feeble emotional attachment to the missing Ylvan. "However, I left Captain Siras with some of the *Maraggan* to follow up in the area around Cabelon. Having grown up there, Ashuir may have close acquaintances to turn to. We questioned one of the Constable's aides, but we got very little from him before we were through. There was also another soldier assigned to the Constable, but we've not seen him. If there are others helping Ashuir or hiding him, we will find them. There can't be many."

King Jerrick sighed. "Gethor, I know you've just returned to Masseltaine, but I must ask you to handle this matter yourself." He stood, approached Dran. "You were there in the Uprising. You recall the disastrous consequences of magic. Particularly of Ylvans using magic. It nearly destroyed the kingdom. It was used somehow to get to my wife… my son…" The King's voice cracked as he turned away.

Dran remembered well. After the death of Jerrick's father, King Corm Lydan, Jerrick himself was seeking ancient Lore—lost magic—with the help of Markin Ashuir. The Ylvan sorcerer Narkan Tanglas believed them to be in possession of it, and sought it for himself. Tanglas ensorcelled an army of his own people to rise against the young Jerrick Lydan. As part of his attempts to weaken the

King, the power-hungry Tanglas had used magic to get himself or an unknown assassin close enough to the King to slay his wife and son. The King's own secret magic council had been able to save Jerrick from the attempt that would have taken his life as well, but it was too late for his family. He'd been devastated by the loss and—horrified at its darker potential—never trusted anyone with the use of magic again.

"Find this Ylvan. Track him down. Bring him to me alive if at all possible. We *need* to know that he is the last of his kind. But find out, either way. I must entrust you with this, Gethor. You are the only one I can trust."

Dran had spent years cultivating that trust. With a man as badly damaged as King Jerrick, it hadn't been easy. It had taken hard work and hard approaches with many, some of whom might have deserved less cruel force than Dran had employed. Not that the use of force was of any consequence to Dran anyway; it was effective, after all. But he'd also needed to demonstrate to the King that he would suffer no insubordination of the King's orders, no matter how slight. Silarrah was a good example. After that unnatural storm in Cabelon, he'd begun to suspect magic, despite the improbability. Once they'd begun to suspect the man might be Ylvan, Dran still never suspected that Silarrah knew anything about it, but the use of force had elicited the answers from her that they required to confirm it. Dran had purpose. Above all, one thing was certain in Dran's mind: as mad as he was, the King was right about magic. It was dangerous, and must never be allowed to flourish again.

"And Dran?"

"Yes, Your Highness?"

"Whatever else, this man *must not* be allowed to reach Eluciar at any cost. Is that clear?"

Dran stood straight in salute. "I will ride back north at once, Your Highness. Wherever this Ylvan has fled, we will track him down and bring him to you." He bowed and left.

He thought again about the King's madness. Though Jerrick's fears were not unfounded, they were pathetic. The King was aging, He was not well, and he had no heirs. No royal blood of any Lydanian clan held a higher claim to the throne than Dran himself. Jerrick was the last of the Lydans. When the time came, other clans may step forth and vie for the crown, but Dran had as strong a claim as any. And much better means to defend it. It was a waiting game.

While he waited, it would be a worthwhile use of his time to hunt this Ylvan down. Ashuir could provide a complication he did not need. It would be good sport. And he would succeed. He never failed when it came to a manhunt.

Chapter Seventeen

The dungeon smelled of many things—straw, stone, rust, urine—but most of all, death. It was cold and dark. A slight rectangular opening allowed a sliver of sunlight to illuminate a loaf-sized space on the floor of her cell. Silarrah felt grateful she'd been placed in the "upper" dungeons. She could imagine the lower dungeons had no such slender ray of hope.

After the guards left her, she'd paced the cell, determining it was just wide enough and long enough for her to lie down flat if she chose to. There was some foul-smelling straw on the floor and that was it. Nothing else to sit or lie down on. She'd kicked the straw around, fully expecting rats or insects to skitter out, but nothing had moved into the ray of light. She couldn't be sure about anything beyond that, but she had the feeling that she was alone in the cell. She'd grown weak and vomited in a corner from the odor, and then she sat on the straw in the stream of light, her head on her knees. She may have passed out for a time in that position but wasn't sure.

She turned to other thoughts to keep her mind busy. How far had Rhinan gotten? It occurred to her that she may never know if he got away or not. She wished they'd had more time to talk in Omriel.

She wondered if the mysterious cloaked figure had reached him, been able to help him. When the figure turned up at the orphanage, Silarrah had been surprised it was a woman. But she was like no woman Silarrah had ever met. She was more like a small, swift warrior than any lady of the town. She was still unsure if telling the woman what she had would help Rhinan, but it certainly seemed the best option. Above all, Silarrah was pleased that she'd managed to keep the appearance of this woman to herself when questioned by the King. The only way she'd managed to keep it a secret was because the King hadn't asked any direct questions that would lead to her having to give up that information. And the woman had sworn her to secrecy in a way that made it seem as if Rhinan's life gravely depended upon it.

Silarrah could only hope for the best possible outcomes. She allowed herself to imagine that Rhinan had escaped the remainder of Dran's special force. That the cloaked woman had found Rhinan and helped him either escape the *Maraggan* or clear himself of the outrageous charges aimed at him. Ylvan? Silarrah knew that no Ylvan Clan members had survived the Uprising. To her, King Jerrick had seemed… mad, perhaps? She worried that it might not make a difference how wrong he was about Rhinan. If the King *were* mad and decided Rhinan was a threat, it was possible nothing could save him if he was captured.

And then there was her own predicament. She wondered what had happened to the orphans. She had heard Dran order his men to burn the orphanage down. Would the other women and the children be safe in Omriel? But here she was in a cell in the King's dungeons in Masseltaine. She could do nothing now but wait. If they found Rhinan, would they kill her, too? Would they kill her if they didn't? Would she spend the rest of her life in this cell?

She tried standing and found that she could. She turned and tried to see out of the rectangular sliver of an opening, only then noticing that there were thick iron bars at regular intervals along the width, which was probably about two feet. It was only inches high. The bars seemed superfluous. No one would be squeezing out through that, bars or no. Whatever lay beyond it, she could not completely tell. It looked like more stone paving, and then eventually perhaps a stone wall.

The dungeons were deathly silent. There would have to be prisoners in other cells, but perhaps she was the only prisoner in the upper dungeons. The silence would be the thing, she thought. The thing that would drive her mad.

But then she heard something.

The outer door to the upper dungeons creaked. Footsteps came toward her cell, and a lighted torch gradually approached, illuminating a man who carried a bowl in his other hand. He stopped in front of her cell, the torchlight shining in through the bars. She squinted against the light and did not approach the bars.

The man looked back over his shoulder. He was clearly not a guard, as he was dressed in a simple tunic and breeches. He turned back to her, trying to get a good look at her in the torchlight. She still felt ragged and filthy, wishing she could bathe. *Oh*, she thought, *not bathing? That might be worse than the silence.*

"You must be hungry," said the man quietly. "Eat this. It isn't much, but it will nourish you." He leaned down and slid the bowl through a small opening at the base of the bars.

Silarrah was, in fact, ravenous. She looked down at the bowl. There was a chunk of what appeared to be bread floating in it. She stepped forward, picked up the bowl and grabbed the bread, shoving it into her mouth. It was partially soggy, but tasted good enough. Eying the man, she quickly withdrew from the bars, out of his reach.

He chuckled softly. "It's all right. You're safe enough from me."

She waited to see if he would leave, but he stood watching her. She finally tipped the bowl, pouring herself a mouthful of the broth. It had bits—of what she didn't know—but she still found it edible. She crouched back in her spot where the light came in, watching the man with the torch as he watched her eat.

He glanced behind himself one more time. "You are the girl from Omriel, correct?" His voice was hushed.

Silarrah wondered whether or not to answer the man. He probably knew anyway, and he seemed harmless enough, so it probably didn't make any difference. "Mm-hmm," she acknowledged with her mouth full of another bite of the bread.

"My name is Werald," he told her, leaning closer. "I'm a *Sohera* of the Lore College, in the Lore of Cuisine."

So not only was he a cook, but he was studying to become a Lore Trainer of cooking? She wondered if he'd prepared what she was eating. Considering it was dungeon food, it was pretty good.

"I'm to thank you for helping Lynari," he nearly whispered. She wasn't sure she'd understood the last word.

"Who?" she asked.

"She visited you in Omriel."

The cloaked woman. Did this man have any news of

her? Of Rhinan? Silarrah stood and moved closer to the bars, but not too close. She looked the man over more carefully now. He was smiling at her, and he had a kind face. This was definitely not one of her guards.

"What did you say her name was?" She kept her voice just above a whisper, following the man's example.

"Lynari. But that's not important. She moves quickly and will probably reach your friend in time to be of use to him, thanks to you."

Silarrah felt as if her heart had not been beating, but now it began to beat again. This man brought her more than nourishment for her body—he brought her hope.

"Finish your dinner," the man said, indicating the bowl in her hands. "I'll need to take that back with me. I can't stay long, but you'll see me again."

She hastened to do as she was told. Werald then removed a flagon hanging at his side on a belt, and gave her a long draught of water. Then he took the flagon back from her.

Werald took another furtive look behind him before turning to Silarrah one more time. He closed his eyes, held out his hand, palm down, and the cell became warmer. Beneath her feet, the straw softened. It was all surprisingly comfortable.

"Sleep well," he said softly. "See you tomorrow." And then he turned, and the torchlight disappeared down the hall, back toward the main door to the dungeons.

Silarrah watched until the light completely faded. She was astonished and had no idea what to make of the man. But she had hope! Not only hope for Rhinan, but for herself. She couldn't escape the feeling that she was well-fed and comfortable. Her foul little cell was now almost cozy somehow, and her exhaustion began to overtake her. She curled up in her spot of light, which had almost entirely faded now. It must be night.

She yawned and thought of the cloaked woman's name. *Lynari.* She'd forgotten if the woman had even told her in the tumult of the moment back in Omriel. She had no idea what Lynari could do for Rhinan, but if Werald could make her cell cozy, who knew what Lynari was capable of? The last thing she remembered before falling asleep was thinking again that perhaps there was some hope after all.

Chapter Eighteen

"Explain again how you found us, exactly?" Eodorr stood over the cloaked woman, rubbing his chin. "You were sent to Silarrah, and she *told* you of Brinaya?"

Rhinan was standing a bit away from them, staring at the remains of Brinaya's cabin. The acrid scent of smoke was still rising from the embers which glowed in the darkness of night, casting a faint glow on the three survivors of the small battle. He had led those men here, and now his friend's mother was dead. Another dead for his sake.

He brooded, still trying to understand that Brinaya had obviously used magic in the attack. He had never suspected Brinaya of anything of the sort. He wondered if Param knew about his mother's abilities.

The thought of his friend made Rhinan's blood run cold. Param was out there somewhere traveling, and Rhinan was trying to find him to ask for his help. But now he would also have to be the one to tell him that his mother was dead. Things were getting worse and worse. It was a painful dilemma. Everyone who helped him wound up dead, so he should stay away from Param. Yet it was his duty, and his alone, to let his friend know what had happened here. And he needed Param's help if he was to escape the *Maraggan.* But how could he keep his friend safe?

He had discovered one thing in the battle. He could kill with deadly accuracy and efficiency. He'd never taken any life but game before; now he'd killed men. And not just any men. *Maraggan*, the King's most elite troops. Rhinan was a dead man… but he'd learned he could be deadly, too. He didn't like the feeling, and he liked feeling that it was necessary even less. It angered him that he'd had to kill those men. But he knew, now, that he would do it again if it came to it.

He turned back to Eodorr and the cloaked woman. Lynari, she'd said was her name. She stood looking up defiantly at Eodorr, he a foot taller than she.

"Silarrah expected Rhinan to seek Param's help, and this was where she thought he would go."

Had Silarrah told anyone else? Rhinan feared for her safety. If Silarrah had been taken, and had been… forced… to speak… That would be the only way. Now he was afraid his dearest friend… no, more than friend… could be gone like Keirwyn, Devram and now Brinaya.

"You!" he snapped, abruptly lunging toward Lynari with such intensity that she stepped back, drawing her quarterstaff and holding it in front of her in a defensive position.

"I did not come to fight you," Lynari said. "I need you to understand. I'm here to help you."

Rhinan looked into her eyes and relaxed. There was no doubt she had helped them. She had eliminated many of the soldiers that had surrounded them in Brinaya's cottage. She just hadn't gotten there soon enough to save Brinaya, but that wasn't her fault. And Rip was standing near her, panting contentedly. No sense of concern from the big beardog.

"Tell me about Silarrah. Is she safe?"

"She was when I left her," Lynari said. "But I can't say if that is still the case. It's possible that you were seen leaving. Some of the *Maraggan* were there in Omriel. They were looking for you, so—I won't lie to you—she may have been in some danger."

Rhinan stalked back and forth. He looked at Eodorr. "We have to go back," he said, panic in his voice. "And we have to find Param. How can we do both?"

Eodorr shook his head sadly. "We can't go back, Rhinan. It's too late. If anything has happened to Silarrah, it was to protect you. If you go back, you'd be throwing away her sacrifice, just as you would be throwing away Keirwyn's and Devram's. It's not an option."

Lynari spoke up. "He's right, Rhinan. You won't be safe traveling south. And I can't allow it."

"You can't *allow* it?" Rhinan snapped at her. "Who are you to tell me where I can and cannot go?"

"I told you. I am a *Hegana* from the Lore College at Masseltaine." She withdrew a pouch from somewhere within her cloak and began to rifle through it. She looked hard at Eodorr for a moment then shrugged. Handing a small bundle to Rhinan, she continued. "The *Hegana* are a secret group of warrior students who defend the College. We are dedicated to preserving all Lore, even the outlawed practice of magic. Those in charge of the secret Lore-sharing of Magic have divined that you in some way are a key to that preservation, possibly its restoration, to practical use. Therefore, I was sent to find you and protect you. I put my own life in your hands even telling you this."

Rhinan opened the small bundle, which was wrapped in cloth. It was bread and dried meat. He sniffed it but did not eat. Lynari rolled her eyes at him and tore off a piece of each, popping it into her mouth to indicate it was safe.

Rhinan snorted, turning away. He handed the bundle to Eodorr who quickly began to tear off pieces and eat them. "As it turns out, I can protect myself just fine. It's just people who 'put their own life in my hands' that tend to wind up dead. And I have nothing whatsoever to do with magic. I can't even imagine myself practicing it if that's what you've got in mind."

"She *was* helpful with the *Maraggan*," Eodorr pointed out sheepishly, his mouth full. "And Rip likes her." The beardog had curled up beside the newcomer, Lynari scratching him behind one enormous ear.

"And now we are both in worse trouble than before." Rhinan gestured toward where a couple of the dead soldiers lay. They had searched them, but found no sign of Gethor Dran among the dead. According to Eodorr, there were far fewer here than he'd seen back in Cabelon. There was possibly a larger force of these soldiers almost upon them, for all they knew. "This is the King's special force, Eodorr. The King wanted me before. Now they will want us to answer for this as well, let there be no doubt. Dran and more of these *Maraggan* will be upon us, and I can only shoot so many. I am doomed. And so are you."

"Then we will see to it that you do not fall into the hands of the King," Lynari said. "Or any of his *Maraggan* or other soldiers. We must hide you until we can determine what role you are destined to play in the preservation of magic."

"Do not speak to me anymore of magic!" Rhinan snapped, turning back to her. Grabbing up his pack, he reached within it and withdrew the droplet-shaped *Pyvadis*. He threw it at her feet. "If I've any magic, it's *that* thing," he told her. "It belonged to my parents. Do you have any idea what it is?"

As she bent to pick it up, Eodorr rushed forward to block her. Rip sat up—as tall as Lynari from that position—sniffing to see if it was food. "Careful!" Eodorr warned.

The *Hegana* scrutinized the stone for a moment. Then she simply picked it up.

There was no lightning strike as there had been with Jaskar Heeth. However, all at once, the ghosts emerged from the darkness of the trees around the remains of the burnt cottage. The murmuring was loud. Rhinan winced and shook his head. He felt them closing in on him, and there was a pressure, an imposing he rarely felt. Wide-eyed, he crouched and turned round and round, unsure what to do.

"Rhinan!" Eodorr called to him. "What is it? Are you well? Injured?"

Eodorr's voice brought Rhinan's attention back to his companions, but the ghosts persisted, their murmuring a distraction. Only he knew they were there—if in fact they really were—but he did not know if these beings would harm his companions. He looked at the gemstone in Lynari's hands and snatched it back. Almost instantly, the ghost-like beings began to quiet and fade. Well, he thought, the stone had produced yet another new revelation about his madness. His delusions were now apparently tied to this stone, and he must not allow it to fall into other hands. He did not yet know what connections there were, but it would have something to do with his parents, his heritage, and… yes, most likely magic.

Both Eodorr and Lynari were staring at him as if he'd just lost his mind. He had, but long ago. "I'm sorry," he apologized to Lynari as he hung the *Pyvadis* back around his neck now. "I have so little left to remember my parents by."

He feigned sentiment, but he did not feel it at that moment.

Lynari gave him a brief, curious look. "I can't say exactly what it is, but there's something… There is no question that it has been ensorcelled. You must protect it. I am sure it is of powerful importance."

Eodorr shook his head and wandered over to the cabin. Without turning back to them, he spoke. "We should give her a proper burial."

* * * * *

When they had finished, Rhinan remained solemn. Eodorr asked, "Where do you think Param would be now?"

Rhinan thought for a moment. "Somewhere along the Northern Trading Path, stopping in towns and villages. He would most likely be well on his way back here for the winter by this time."

"That's good," Lynari said. "We can't travel south, but we can travel eastward along the northern villages. We'll be moving away from the King. Perhaps we can find your friend."

"I still don't see where you get the idea you'll be coming with us," Rhinan said, his voice tired.

Eodorr cleared his throat. "As I said, Rhinan, she was helpful to us. We can probably use the extra hands if we encounter more trouble. And she seems to have your best interests in mind. If she meant us any harm, she's had plenty of opportunity."

"I assure you," Lynari said. "I mean you no harm. And I can be *very* useful."

"Do you know the Northern Trading Path?" Rhinan asked. "Because, beyond here, I do not. That would be helpful, if only to avoid being on it."

Lynari shook her head. "No, Rhinan. I am afraid that is not a way in which I can be useful. But I won't mislead you; I won't pretend to know something which I don't."

"Sounds fair to me," Eodorr said. Rhinan glowered at him.

"We should move soon." Lynari stood. "If these men found this place, others will as well."

For the first time, Rhinan studied Lynari with an open mind. She was neither small nor large for a woman, but she did appear solid. She wore a black cloak, breeches and boots. Her hood thrown back, he could see she had short, dark hair and light eyes. Were they blue? She was hearty, but attractive. He knew she could fight, could probably hunt as well if she'd come this far alone. There was clearly more to her than one would expect. And she represented secret magic users from the Lore College at Masseltaine? This was all more than he had imagined happening in the kingdom while he spent all his time hunting and lurking in the quiet, quaint region near Cabelon. But… did she know any magic? "I know that magic is forbidden in Lydania by King Jerrick," he addressed her, "but I am an outlaw now—*we* are outlaws now—so as long as you're here—"

Lynari smiled. "Yes, I have had some secret magic training. I have a few spells that may help us."

Rhinan looked to Eodorr. Eodorr merely smiled and shrugged. Rhinan grinned. It was clear that Eodorr was charmed by this strange woman. Was that some of her magic or just Eodorr? Rhinan couldn't recall Eodorr ever having a girlfriend, though many of the available women in Cabelon had certainly been interested. Rhinan may not have paid much attention to Eodorr over the years, but he knew that much.

"We can travel… but *off* the path," he told them at last. "Above it, in the foothills of the Percene Mountains. Put some distance between us and this place, and then rest for a bit. We continue eastward, find a town, and ask directions. Maybe someone will have heard of Param's whereabouts. If we can find him, he is well-traveled beyond this part of Lydania. He will know what to do."

Eodorr spoke up. "Though he will not be glad to hear the news we bear."

Rhinan was not eager to dwell any further on delivering that news. Fortunately, Lynari changed the subject.

"It sounds like a wise course." She slung her quarterstaff across her back.

Rhinan snorted. Mocking Eodorr's statement of the day before, he said, "How can I be wise and yet such a fool at the same time?"

"Wisdom is a divine gift, Rhinan," Eodorr reminded him in retort. "Of course, you'd know that if the Lore Givers had blessed you with any." He winked at Rhinan.

Rhinan squinted back at him. "I've never been a big believer in wisdoms. I prefer to rely on common sense."

"Oh?" Eodorr mocked. "I hadn't noticed you to be a sharp student of either one."

In response to Eodorr's badgering, Rhinan spoke to their new companion. "Tell me something, Lynari. I can move silently, cover our tracks so well that we cannot be followed, find hunting trails and trading paths in the darkness, and look for signs of towns in the vicinity. Eodorr can do none of these things, but I assume you can?"

She nodded.

"So… can any of your magic make Eodorr move more quietly? He could not sneak up on a deaf and blind old man."

Eodorr was not amused. He walked away.

"We'll need supplies, as well," Rhinan continued, looking back at the smoldering ruins of the cabin. "There is nothing to be salvaged here."

Lynari began to speak, but Eodorr returned with the two horses. "We're not out of supplies just yet," Eodorr said, patting the pack on his horse. He looked at Lynari and cocked an eyebrow. "Can you ride?"

Lynari looked up at the horses. "You wish to move silently and cover our tracks… riding horses?"

"She's right," Rhinan said. "We'll move quicker on foot among the tree line from here, and we'll remain less visible. This was not all of the *Maraggan*, and we have no idea where the rest of them may be."

"You mean to leave two perfectly good horses just standing here?" Eodorr was aghast.

"I may be able to… suggest… that they return to the last place they felt safe," Lynari offered.

"We'll carry our own packs," Rhinan said. "No one who finds them, if anyone does, will do them any harm. They will just be two lost horses."

Eodorr shook his head. "You're right, of course. But I don't have to like it."

Once the two horses were stripped of their harnesses and saddles, Lynari stood before them and gently whispered something to them. They hesitated for a moment, and then they turned and plodded back westward.

Rip watched them go, making a brief whimpering sound.

Eodorr looked at the beardog, his own eyes filled with concern. "I agree."

Rhinan had altered the packs to make them easier for him and Eodorr to carry over their shoulders. He knew better than to try to put anything on Rip, and Lynari already had a pouch of her own slung around her waist. There was only a bit of bread and dried meat left in his pack, a leather bag for water, and some animal fat he'd saved to condition his bowstring. Eodorr had food and a water bag in his pack, plus a small coil of rope.

The sword that had belonged to Rhinan's father had a belt and scabbard. Weapons not used expressly for hunting were forbidden by the King; they could only be carried by someone in a position of authority. Eodorr had been a Vice-Constable and so had his own sword, but was surely no longer authorized to carry it. He did so anyway. But now Rhinan strapped the belt around his own waist, carrying his father's sword in an act of pure defiance. *If I am truly an outlaw now*, he thought, *then let me be a complete outlaw. Magic, fighting weapons… and stealing a bottle of ale at the first opportunity.*

Rhinan watched Eodorr playing with Rip as the sun rose higher into the sky. The morning had passed as they debated and performed all of the preparation tasks required and, though they were weary, they knew they must leave at once. They would travel up in the foothills, concealed by the tree line as much as possible, by night or by day. But for now, they would have to just get moving.

The foothills of the Percene Mountains, the large northern range, wasn't far north for them from where they were. They could turn eastward once they got there, but there were several reasons why that would not be convenient. The weather was turning colder, the terrain would be rougher and rocky, and the northern mountain range was wild, unsettled, and filled with many dangers.

He gazed southward as they set out, realizing that his concern for Silarrah was nothing he could assuage. He had no assurance of her safety or knowledge of her survival. He wanted to go back, but he could only hope.

As if sensing his thoughts, Lynari touched his arm. She seemed far away somehow, her mind in another place in some way. "Your feet are now set upon a path which you must follow," she told him. "This will be a most difficult path, and the possibility exists that you may not reach its end. But you *must* go forward; you cannot go back. That path is closed to you now and represents nothing but an end of *all* your paths."

He looked at her, puzzled.

"It is how we found you," Lynari explained. "We see the possibilities of various paths... but only so far. Especially if a possibility leads to the end of a path."

He found no comfort in her words, but he did find himself trusting the strange woman.

Eodorr and Rip drew up next to Rhinan and Lynari as the four of them aimed northward, the huge beardog prancing slightly ahead of them. Rhinan wondered when the independent creature would wander off again, but he wished he could share the beardog's carefree optimism as he once had.

Chapter Nineteen

Dran considered himself a patient man, though he knew that others did not. Being patient meant he had to humor the peculiarities of his men on occasion, the most skilled and loyal of the Lydanian army.

Before they could set off in pursuit of Rhinan Ashuir, the inquisitor Gaimesh felt it necessary to complete whatever strange ritual of study he practiced for his obscure Lore Giver. Captain Gaimesh had specialized in the Lore of Combat, just as all soldiers. Yet there was a minor Lore Giver (Dran could not even recall the Lore Giver's name) who'd delivered the particular knowledge of "information extraction" to the world. There were so many minor Lore Givers that Dran could not keep track of them all. But if it made Gaimesh better at his job, then Dran was all for it. As long as it was quick. Fortunately, it was. Gaimesh joined them looking as if he'd practiced some of his own work on himself. He showed up with new scars all the time. Dran never asked about the practice, but he thought over time Gaimesh began to look like cracked, dried mud.

Despite the delay leaving Masseltaine, the *Maraggan* made

good time. They rode directly northward aiming for the Northern Trading Path to avoid wasting time heading back eastward to Omriel or further. The western plains of the Romiel region of Lydania allowed for a swift ride. A concession to the two brothers who founded the kingdom, the region of Romiel was named after the first Lydan king. The city of Omriel was named after his twin brother. The Romiel region of Lydania stretched east from Omriel, covering a large portion of the territory to the north of Masseltaine. It was primarily grassy plains, farms, and scattered forests.

Dran had hoped to have some news from Captain Siras by that point. He would have been perfectly satisfied to meet Siras heading south with the scoundrel bound and slung over a packhorse. He'd told Siras that it was important to take the man alive, and he hoped that this was one of those times when Siras would be too afraid not to take him literally. It seemed more important now than ever that this Ashuir be captured alive. They would need to confirm that he was, in fact, an Ylvan (and son of Markin), and that Silarrah had not lied about there being any further offspring. And if there were, they would need to be found and eliminated once and for all.

Astounding though it was, Dran did not find it impossible to accept that an Ylvan remained alive in Lydania after so many years. After the wizard Markin Ashuir fashioned the spell that vanquished Narkan Tanglas, the King had other wizards alter the spell to eliminate the Ylvan Clans altogether. He knew Ashuir would never go along with it, because, though allied with the King, he was an Ylvan himself. However, it ended the Ylvan Uprising, and Markin and his wife Herilyn vanished when had the other Ylvans. At first believed destroyed with the rest of the Ylvan Clans, the couple had been discovered almost ten years later hiding in the small village of Cabelon, once an outpost at the northwest corner of Lydania. A trusted ally to Jerrick, Markin had called his loyalties into question by disappearing with no explanation. Being the last of the Ylvans, Markin and Herilyn represented a vague threat of Ylvan revival that King Jerrick could ill afford… especially with Markin's considerable magical skills. Both Dran and Jerrick had assumed the matter finally concluded when an agent had been dispatched, and their deaths had been confirmed. They had apparently been wrong.

Working as it did, Dran's suspicious mind could easily draw the obvious conclusions that led to the current situation. Had Herilyn borne a child at any point after they disappeared, but before they were slain, the child could have remained hidden. He did not know the age of this Rhinan, but Constable Keirwyn's defense of him—to his very own death—signified a strong bond that would likely have come from a lifetime. Had Keirwyn, himself childless, raised an Ylvan orphan, the child of the Ashuirs? This now seemed likely to Dran.

If Siras was doing his job effectively (and he'd better be), Dran would see this issue soon resolved. Yet no messenger had arrived from the group Dran had left with Siras, and this concerned Dran. With magic being used by a man who was possibly the son of one of the greatest wizards of the last generation of Ylvans, there was much to be concerned about.

They stopped in a town near the border of the region of Canjarra, just a bit south of the Northern Trading Path, for an evening meal. The town reflected the intricate Canjarran architecture that predated the kingdom of Lydania, having been conquered as part of the formation of the kingdom. The Canjarrans, in fact, were darker in flesh than most Lydanians. It was a much older place filled with a much older people and culture. But the exotic and flavorful cuisine? Dran loved it.

When the rider reached them, he leapt from his horse and rushed to Dran. He was road weary and had obviously traveled swiftly. It was one of the men Dran had left with Siras. Young Flek, one of their best scouts. His horse was worn completely out.

"My Lord," Flek gasped. Dran held out a chalice and the pitcher of water that sat before him. Seated outdoors in a shady courtyard in front of a large tavern, Dran's men surrounded a long, oak table topped with platters of stewed meats, seasoned vegetables, breads and fruits. Flek gratefully took the chalice, filled it, drained it, and handed the pitcher back to Dran. "I'm sorry. I rode first to Omriel and then I just missed you in Masseltaine. But we've found him!"

Dran jumped to his feet. "Tell me, boy!"

"There's a cabin, due north from here in the foothills where the Domins and the Percenes meet. The man has a companion, and they went inside. They appeared to be putting up there, but no way to tell for how long. Captain Siras sent me to inform you at once."

Dran ordered his men. "We ride now!" Turning back to Flek, he said, "Can you still ride?"

"Never doubt it, My Lord."

"Good. Get a fresh horse and lead the way."

Without hesitation, each of them scrambled to follow Dran to their horses. In moments, the *Maraggan* was galloping north, following Flek.

Flek had ridden all night and a full day. If the Ylvan had stayed at the cabin overnight and left the following morning, it would put him within striking distance. Dran tasted blood, and drove his men hard. Even at that, he knew they would not reach the cabin until the next morning. Flek hadn't known if Siras would try to take the prisoner or follow him. Dran hoped Siras wouldn't do anything foolish. Ideally, the scenario Dran imagined earlier would come to pass, and they'd meet Siras coming down out of the foothills with the live prisoner. If all went well. And Dran had to admit that it did not always all go well, even for him. It was rare for him to worry, but he noticed the annoying feeling. He did not like it.

Chapter Twenty

The dungeon was cold in the morning, and it stank again. Whatever strange yet comforting thing Werald had done the night before had apparently worn off.

But it was the screams that had woken her.

Silarrah sat up on the pile of straw and scooted back against the wall, away from the bars. The screams were coming from some distance, despite the loudness of them. She imagined the lower dungeons. She was again grateful, at the very least, that she hadn't been placed down there. She covered her ears and tucked her head against her knees, sobbing.

The screams stopped suddenly. She felt sick, and she had to relieve herself. There was no bucket in the cell. No privacy either, yet it was dark and there was no one at the bars. She settled for squatting in the corner where she'd vomited the night before, hoping she could avoid her own filth as long as she had to.

Time passed, and she watched the patch of light on the floor as it grew and became brighter. There was nothing else to do. She tried to occupy her mind with the hope Werald had delivered the night before, but she began to doubt that it had even happened. Thinking upon it, it made no sense. She'd obviously had a moment of madness, hallucinating some comfort in this awful place to put herself to sleep. Waking had only restored the terror of her true situation. She tried to remember what she could of the odd man, hoping that she could focus and make that illusion happen again. If she could pretend she was comfortable, spend more time in sleep, then perhaps she could survive this horrendous ordeal.

If the King decided not to kill her.

She had no idea if he would kill her or not. She did not doubt that, if he wanted to, he would do it without a second thought. She was an insect to him, to be crushed or swatted. If he could see no further use for her, was there any chance he'd release her? Would he even bother to—mercifully—put her to death? Or would this dark, terrifying existence be hers for a long time to come?

She had thought the silence was bad, but the screaming was worse. And worst of all: she did not know if this would ever end, how it would end, or if it would change.

"I'm sorry I'm late, my dear." It was Werald's voice at her cell. He sounded sad.

She looked up, not believing. Wouldn't she have heard him coming? Yet he was there, with a torch and a bowl, just as he had been the night before.

"Were you able to sleep? I'm sure this morning was of no comfort to you."

As she leaned toward the bars, he slipped the bowl under them where she could reach it. There was no bread, so she dipped a couple of fingers into it, trying not to think of what horrid things her fingers may have touched in the tiny cell. It was some kind of cold porridge, but again it was palatable.

"Werald."

"It's me, yes."

"Are you real, or am I imagining you?"

There was a cackle, and the slight torchlight seemed to waver about momentarily. "If I were your imagination, would I tell you otherwise? No, I'm afraid I'm real. I hope your imagination would do better."

She wanted to laugh, but found that her throat was sore and dry. Probably hearing her struggle, he passed her the flagon of water.

"Thank you."

"You're welcome."

"May I ask you something?"

"Well, you just did, so it would seem so."

"Did you make my cell more comfortable last night? Or did I imagine that?"

"Hush, child." His voice was almost silent but severe, and his presence as still as the grave. "Don't get old Werald into trouble, hmm? Can we agree to that?"

He was practicing magic. Right here in the dungeons. Practically under the King's own nose. Silarrah was stunned. "But how—yes. Yes, I agree."

She finished the porridge and handed the bowl back to the old man. "Would you happen to know how long I am to be kept here?"

"That is the question, isn't it?" The old man paused, and she felt his eyes upon her more than she could actually see them in the faint torchlight. "You've asked one question, but it is the answer to another that you seek."

She considered this. "Yes, I suppose it is."

"Your situation may soon change. That is all I can tell you."

She wasn't sure what that meant. But she felt certain he

would say no more. He'd sounded very definite about that. The man was a puzzle, and she could not solve it in the dark in her condition. She realized it was still very cold.

As if sensing her discomfort, Werald once again reached out his hand, palm down, and her cell became warmer and softer once again.

"Thank you... for bringing me food and water." She was careful not to allude to anything else out loud, but she knew he'd understand.

"Of course." As if there was nothing he would be doing otherwise. "Rest if you can, now. Sleep, perhaps." And he was gone.

And she did.

* * * * *

Silarrah felt someone watching her.

She was facing away from the bars of her cell, but positioned as far into the cell as she could be so as to avoid any possibility of being reached through them. She opened her eyes, but there was no dim, flickering light of a torch upon the wall as there had been when Werald appeared. All was dark.

But she was not alone.

Fighting the urge to panic, she tried not to breathe loudly, but to listen. There was only silence.

Something skittered across her foot. Probably a rat. She swallowed a scream in a feat of the utmost effort. Whatever was behind her must not know that she was awake, for it hadn't disturbed her sleep. Maybe it would go away.

Moments passed, and she calmed herself. No longer startled, she began to feel that there was no ill intention on the part of who or whatever was there. Could it be Werald? He seemed kind enough, perhaps decent enough, to allow her to continue to sleep.

But hadn't Werald put her to sleep? What did he want of her?

No. It wasn't Werald. The realization came to her, but she did not know from where.

"Interesting." The voice was at her cell, but it was not Werald's voice. It was just above a whisper, but it had a presence, an air of authority.

It wasn't that awful Dran. And it wasn't the King, either.

At last, curiosity compelled her to stretch her limbs. She shook her leg to make sure whatever had crawled across her foot was gone. She swung her legs around in a sudden motion to face whoever was watching her in the darkness.

There was the patch of light on the floor, dimming in what she guessed must be late afternoon. The glow emanated outward, partially illuminating a robed and hooded figure standing just outside the bars. She could make out no further details.

"Dran has left the city, and the King will… forget… that you are here. Others, however, will not. You must come quickly." A man's voice.

The narrow door to her cell swung open with a smooth, even motion, completely silent. Once open, it came to a stop without a sound.

Silarrah blinked. She looked at the robed man again, but he had not moved. This must be a dream.

"Stand, girl," the man hissed at her. "We must make haste."

Deciding to see where this dream would lead, she rose to her feet. She was surprised to find that she had regained some of her strength while trapped in the tiny cell. *Thank you,*

Werald, for the sustenance.

A gloved hand reached out to her, beckoning. The robed man stepped back. Silarrah moved forward, but the step resulted in dizziness. She was still not fully recovered from her ordeal, if recovery were even possible in a cold, filthy dungeon. She reached out and caught herself on his arm.

"Careful now." The voice was gentler this time, but the arm was sturdy. "This way." The man gripped her by the arm and drew her completely out of the cell. There was an instant of hesitation, and then they were walking swiftly, silently, along the stone flooring, past other cells, too fast for her to see if they were occupied or not. There were turns, and then there were stairs. Downward. Horrible smells. Silarrah could see nothing, relying entirely on the mysterious stranger to prevent her from stumbling or bumping into things. More turns, more stairs. Downward again. She did not want to go downward, further into the depths of the dungeon, but there was no option. She was not in that cell anymore, and she did not want to be in another. She could only follow and hope that this was a journey out of the darkness. She would have to trust this robed man.

A door of bars opened, and she feared the worst. A deeper cell in the bowels of the dungeons. Was this the man's plan? Had this been ordered by Dran or the King? She made to resist, but he pulled her through the door, her shoulder scraping the doorway. She was propelled in front of him as he closed the door silently behind them. Then the journey continued for a long walk that seemed endless. Their path straightened now, and she could tell that the ground was sloping upward. And it was unpaved dirt. No more hard stone.

The trek continued with a few more curves, but it also angled upward. When at last it leveled off, they stopped. The man opened another door, but this one was not made of bars. It was thick, solid wood. And when it opened, there was light beyond.

They emerged into a small cavern. Lit sconces lined the walls on either side, and Silarrah's eyes took a few moments to adjust to what light there was. The room had been partially carved out of the rock by hand. There were barrels stacked on the floor, a few crates beyond. There was a musty, damp smell to the chamber, but nothing unpleasant, certainly nothing like the dungeons, which she was clearly no longer in. It was still quite cool, and she shivered in the dampness.

"Oh, I'm sorry." The mysterious man turned to her, removed his outer robe and draped it around her shoulders. She sank into the warmth, realizing at last with certainty that this man was her rescuer and not something worse. She looked up to see who had guided her out of darkness, her salvation his intent. But why save *her*?

The man was as old as Keirwyn, with short white hair of small, tight curls, though bald on top. He had a kind smile, and the dark brown skin of either the older clans around Canjarra or from some of the distant lands beyond Lydania. He did not return her gaze.

Then she noticed the scar that ran across from the side of his left eye, across the bridge of his nose, and finished beyond his right eye. His colorless eyes.

The old man who had led her out of the darkness was blind.

Chapter Twenty-One

As they continued eastward through the misty foothills of the Percenes, daylight dissolved into the shadows of early evening. A dense fog grew around them, and Rhinan felt a sharp chill in the air. He drew his cloak tighter and watched wisps of his breath trail away from him. Then he heard Rip growling a significant warning. Something or someone was near.

* * * * *

They had travelled all day, picking their way along the rocky foothills of the great northern mountain range, moving among the scattered needle-bearing trees. The gentle upward slope remained on their left, and beyond that they could make out high, sharp peaks already covered in early snows. On their right, stretching away to the south was grassy terrain dotted with copses of trees over smaller, edged hills that jutted up and down. Shallow ravines and crevices between the jagged land masses offered plenty of cover and potential opportunity to hide should the need arise.

Their plan was to follow the Percene foothills eastward,

and Lynari knew of a northern town along the base of the mountains that would almost certainly be a stop for any troubadour coming westward. Though she had not been there, she was certain they could find it if they kept to this course above the Northern Trading Path.

Rhinan found himself impressed with the young woman, trusting her. He watched her pull small plant stems from her pouch, twist them up, speak an incantation, and drop them on the ground behind them. Some magic to confuse pursuers, he presumed. But that would be helpful.

She was probably only a summer or two younger than he, closer to Eodorr's age, but she had accumulated so much knowledge. They discovered this because she was all too happy to share it for long periods of time as they hiked, even when Rhinan might have preferred some quiet time with his own thoughts. Eodorr encouraged her, asking all sorts of questions about her time at the Lore College in Masseltaine.

"How did you come to study… what is it you study besides magic?" Eodorr had started the conversation.

She snorted. "My father sent me there to learn weaving. He didn't like that I was more interested in old tales of the Lore Givers, the early wars over man's right to lore, and our ancestors. I would tell these stories to my younger brothers, and he would scoff. I would make up tales, and he would admonish. He hoped I would learn something 'useful' by attending the College, pushing me toward a discipline I showed no affinity or affection toward.

"But the Lore Masters at the College quickly recognized I was not skilled in the lore for which I had enrolled. Then one of them noticed me acting out the story of Wendam, the first Lore Keeper—who taught language so that all could share lore—for some of the students. I enacted the battle between Norrik and Ylva, and he liked the way I moved. I was invited to study what weapon play is allowed." She wiggled her quarterstaff at Eodorr. "My agility, coupled with unusual strength for my size, caught the attention of the Lore Master in charge of the secret study of sacred magic. That and my love for that particular lore of Lydania drew me further in."

Lynari explained how the Lore of Magic was the source for all other lores. Magic enhanced and perfected all lores when applied properly to their study and use. Unlike the wild magic of old, the magic practiced in hiding by these Lore Masters was subtle, mostly by necessity. Magic use, just as the use of weapons by anyone not in the King's employ, was against the King's decree and punishable by death.

"I see you carry a sword and seem familiar with its use." Lynari tilted her head and looked sidelong at Eodorr, turning the tables on him. This amused Rhinan as he watched Eodorr, who had always taken his law-keeping duties so seriously, engaged with the woman who openly proclaimed to break the most severe law in the land: using magic.

"Well, uh, yes..." he stammered. Then he drew himself up straight. "I was trained by our Constable as one of the village guards, so I'm an official."

Rhinan chuckled at this puffed up pronouncement.

Eodorr scowled at him. "Some of us made ourselves useful in Cabelon."

"Oh, that's unfair." Rhinan placed his hand over his chest, feigning a wound. "Many's the time the town would have been much hungrier if not for my hunting skills."

"Yours and the beardog who adopted you."

Rip woofed quietly at Eodorr's mention of him.

Eodorr grinned and continued to mock. "And don't

forget your thieving skills."

"*Tsk.*" Rhinan wrinkled his nose at Eodorr. "Well, you can't say I didn't contribute to the village."

Eodorr sighed in defeat. "No, I don't suppose that was fair. I apologize, but your methods were more mischievous than they ought to have been." Eodorr then went on to extoll the prowess of Rhinan's archery to Lynari, astonishing Rhinan. "Rhinan was once challenged to bring down a linkbird expressly by hitting its eye. He brought down the linkbird, but not through the eye. But then another linkbird passed overhead, and Rhinan pierced it *directly* through the eye." Eodorr looked thoughtfully at Rhinan. "I was always impressed with your bow skills, but I never told you so."

Lynari tried to hide a grin. She seemed to truly enjoy their barbs. Rhinan couldn't be sure, but he suspected she was enjoying Eodorr's company almost as much as he was hers. Perhaps she was admiring the honesty of Eodorr, telling such a wild story when he was clearly not the type to embellish stories, thereby giving it credence. It made Rhinan glad he'd relented and acquiesced to her joining them. Eodorr was, after all, kind-hearted and a loyal soul. He'd served Keirwyn well and had now thrown that loyalty begrudgingly to Rhinan at great risk to himself. It was well to see him pleased.

When it came time for a midday repast, he discovered that Lynari's tracking skills nearly matched his own as they tracked and felled a wild boar in a grassy ravine. Even Rip was willing to work with her. Unusual for the beardog, who was wary of any hunters besides Rhinan.

The afternoon trek passed with fewer questions, allowing Rhinan time to ponder more of what Brinaya had said. He found it hard to accept that he was the lone surviving member of the Ylvan Clans. All of them wiped out by some magic, and yet his father and mother had survived? But how? He had no reason to doubt Brinaya, but it was a lot to consider. His solitary life had never seemed as lonely as it did now. Was he truly the last of his people?

A thought occurred to him. Might the ghosts that haunted him since the death of his parents be the dead Ylvan Clans? As the last surviving Ylvan, was this a curse which only he could bear? It made sense, but it brought him no comfort.

And now he found himself on a path eastward, seeking safe haven where the King could not find him. Some distant and unfamiliar region of Lydania, or the world beyond, even more unknown. Far enough from the King to… do what? Live out his days in more solitude, haunted by the dead of the Ylvan Clans? He knew that Eluciar, the abandoned Ylvan region, was far to the east. His feet were now pointed that direction. Could it be that he would be safe there and perhaps find answers? Was that his destination *and* his destiny?

He didn't want to continue. He wanted to turn back to Cabelon. Go home and find Keirwyn alive and well. Spend more time with Silarrah.

He did not want to be an Ylvan. He constantly found himself in the uncomfortable, and dangerous, position of having to rely on others. And yet, to his surprise, he realized that he no longer wished to be as alone as he always had been.

* * * * *

Rhinan knew what it meant when Rip made that growling sound. It meant there was something or someone nearby that the beardog did not like. It also meant that something was about to experience the jaws which had led Rhinan to give the beardog that name.

Holding a hand up to stop Eodorr and Lynari, Rhinan drew an arrow and crept forward to where the beardog stood bristling. In the shadows and heavy mist of the early evening, wind whipping his cloak into his face, Rhinan couldn't tell which direction Rip was snarling toward. His vision was obscured.

To make matters worse, the ghosts began to stir, ever a distraction, and he needed a moment to try his best to ignore them. It wasn't much help to guess if they were there as a warning of some kind or if they were the cause of some impending doom. It had never been clear to him, and it increased his resentment of the phantoms.

The Needlebeast heaved itself upon Rhinan from a tree.

His bow knocked to the side by the weight of the Needlebeast upon impact, Rhinan was crushed backward to the ground. As it was useless at that point, he let go of the bow and pushed forward with both hands. That was the mistake you did not want to make with a needlebeast, and he knew it. Yet there was no other immediate option to prevent the creature from sinking its teeth and claws into him. He had no time to go for the large hunting knife strapped to his right leg, or to draw the sword he now carried. He screamed as his hands were punctured by the quills, and claws ripped into his sides.

Half the size of Rip, a full-grown needlebeast such as this one was still larger than a man. Covered in mottled green spiny quills that blended in with the trees, needlebeasts were particularly hard to spot at this time of day. With the claws and teeth of a wildcat in addition to their quills, they were aggressive, ferocious and deadly. Once one of these rare creatures was upon you, Rhinan knew it was unusual to survive the attack.

There was a mighty roar and the needlebeast was off of him. He saw Rip had sunk his own teeth into the creature's backside, receiving a face full of quills in the process. The beardog was able to hang on long enough to tear the creature away from Rhinan, but the needlebeast turned on the beardog. The battle then became a flurry of claws and teeth and snarling, kicking up a flurry of damp turf so it was impossible for Rhinan to see what was happening.

Eodorr leapt past him on one side, his sword drawn, as Lynari dashed past on the other side swinging her quarterstaff. The needlebeast was outnumbered, and it resorted to its final attack, rolling itself backward onto Rip and leaping away into the trees before Eodorr and Lynari could reach it and finish it. Rhinan heard Rip yelp in pain at the needlebeast's last maneuver.

Rhinan tried to sit up. Blood flowed down his arms from deep punctures in both hands, and his ribs hurt where the needlebeast had clawed him. Everywhere, the pain burned. He looked down to see that his vest and tunic were soaked in his own blood. He stopped trying to struggle up as Eodorr and Lynari reached his side, urging him not to move.

It had all happened so fast, and Rhinan cursed himself for falling prey to the savage animal. And Rip…

"Rip?" he asked with a weak voice, looking up to Eodorr and Lynari. The two looked away for the beardog, then to one another, and back down at him. Before they could speak, the world went black.

Chapter Twenty-Two

The old blind man said nothing more to Silarrah. He turned and seized a staff that was leaning against the wall and rapped upon a door on the far side of the cellar in a certain rhythm.

The door opened inward to reveal a staircase leading up. A bearded man of about Rhinan's age was standing there, wearing a gray robe like the white one now draped around her. Seeing them, the man nodded in apparent relief, and led them up the stairs.

They emerged in a small courtyard surrounded by large stone buildings. There were a few plants, a bench, a couple of barrels like the ones down in the cellar, but nothing more. It was a chilly evening, just at twilight, but despite the cold Silarrah felt invigorated. She inhaled the fresh air. Her light-headedness still clung to her and caused her to wobble. The bearded man caught her arm and turned to the old blind man. "I'll take her to Caddryth." It was almost a question, and the old blind man nodded. "This way," the bearded man said to her, not releasing her arm. He looked up and around at the surrounding buildings. Candlelight flickered in a few windows. "Quickly."

As she was led through a door into one of the buildings, she looked back to see the old blind man. He did not follow. He appeared lost in thought. Perhaps tired.

The bearded man closed the door behind them. They were in a long hallway, lit sconces on the walls and closed doors down either side.

"Where is Caddryth?" Silarrah asked him. "I've never heard of it."

The man smiled. "Right this way."

They walked to the far end of the hall. Silarrah noticed each door they passed was wood marked with a different symbol. She recognized them as the various disciplines of lore. There was Planting – symbolized by a cornucopia of fruits and vegetables, Cooking – symbolized by a cauldron, Weaving – symbolized by a loom. There were several more, but they passed by too fast for her to identify each one. Though she had never been in this place, she assumed this must be one of the hallways in the Lore College.

They came to the end of the hall, and the man opened a door with a symbol she recognized as representing Lore itself. Knowledge. It was symbolized by a book.

Within was a modest-sized chamber, again lit by sconces on the wall. In the center of the chamber was a broad table, beside which sat a pair of wooden stools. Stretched out upon the table were numerous books and parchments. Shelves against each of the walls were filled with books. One side of the chamber had a small window, and Silarrah could see that the last of the daylight had now faded. Back to darkness. She shuddered, despite the light in the room.

There was no one in the chamber. Walking past her, the man came to a smaller shelf on the back wall of the chamber. He looked back at her and grinned, placing his finger to his lips in the motion indicating quiet or a secret… or both. Then he turned and reached behind the shelf. That section of the wall, along with the shelf, pivoted to reveal a dimly lit passage beyond.

He beckoned to her, and she walked toward him. The passage was another set of stairs leading downward, though the walls resembled those of the hallway outside of this chamber rather than the roughhewn walls of the previous chamber. He took her again by the arm, and they descended the long staircase. There were sconces on the walls, but no doors. It was a long staircase down. This concerned Silarrah, but she was better off so far than she had been earlier this day, so she followed the man without resistance.

When they reached the bottom of the staircase, she noticed the air didn't smell musty as it had in the cellar. Quite the opposite. There was a fragrant, herbal perfumed aroma in the air. They turned a corner, and she found herself facing a large, round chamber with a high, arched ceiling. Four closed doors were at equal intervals around the circular wall of the chamber. There were long, cushioned benches to the right and left side and a massive desk in the center of the room. Upon the desk a candle burned and next to that a smoldering stick that was the source of the fragrance. A large book lay open on the desk, and seated on the far side of the desk, reading the book, was a woman, dark-haired with streaks of silver. She, too, wore a robe of gray.

The woman looked up as they entered the chamber. She was a stunning beauty, several summers older than Silarrah. Her dark eyes glittered in the candlelight as she smiled. "At last." She stood up and came around the desk. She was almost a head taller than Silarrah, unusual for a woman of Lydania. She looked Silarrah up and down with concern.

"Silarrah, correct?"

Silarrah could not find her voice, so she merely nodded.

"I am Caddryth. Welcome to the Lore College of Lydania." Caddryth turned to the bearded man. "Will you send Thissul down for us, Habb?"

Habb nodded. "Of course. Right away." He tipped his head to Silarrah and departed back up the long staircase.

Caddryth took Silarrah's hands and led her to one of the cushioned benches, urging her to sit before taking a seat next to her. The look of concern was still on her face.

"I won't pretend to know what you've been through." Caddryth looked her facial features over, presumably for injuries. "But you are safe here for now. If or when he decides he wants anything further from you, the King will not look for you here."

A small measure of relief passed through Silarrah, and she took a deep breath, finally able to relax just a bit for the first time since before Dran had shown up at the orphanage in Omriel. But she was still very confused. "Why am I here? I don't understand how you know who I am, or why you would take such risks to free a prisoner from the dungeons. I don't wish to sound ungrateful. Please don't think that. But there must be something you expect of me to go to such great efforts."

"Very direct." Caddryth nodded. "I appreciate your candor. I cannot, however, answer all of your questions. I'm telling you that I *cannot*—not that I *will* not. Because I do not know all of the answers. Maybe you can help us with those."

"You want to know why I'm here?" Silarrah asked. "I mean, in Masseltaine?"

"We know that much. The King questioned you about Rhinan." Caddryth was poised, confident. She exuded an air of authority that made Silarrah flinch.

They knew about Rhinan. Did they know that the King thought he was an Ylvan?

"Rhinan may be a surviving child of the Ylvan Clans." It was as if Caddryth could read her thoughts. Could she?

"No, no," Silarrah shook her head vehemently. "We grew up together in Cabelon. *After* the Ylvans were destroyed by King Jerrick in the Ylvan Uprising. It cannot be."

"I see." Caddryth looked at her with pity. "Do you remember when Rhinan was born?"

"Well, no. Of course not. He was born before I was."

"Then how do you *know*?"

"He was born in Cabelon," Silarrah stated with certainty. "Everyone knows that."

Caddryth lifted an eyebrow. "And his parents?"

Silarrah hesitated. She had known they weren't from Cabelon. But now that Caddryth asked, Silarrah realized that no one ever said where they came to Cabelon from. But it didn't matter. "There were no Ylvans left after the Uprising. They were wiped out to a man."

Now Caddryth smiled sadly at her again. At that moment, a girl much younger than Silarrah appeared at the bottom of the steps. She wore simple clothing rather than gray robes. She carried a basket of fabrics under one arm, and another basket with bread and food in her other hand.

"You should rest," Caddryth said, standing. "We can speak at length later. Thissul has brought something for you to eat, and she will help you get cleaned up and show you where you'll be staying." Caddryth returned to the desk, where she resumed her interest in the large book.

At the sight of the food, Silarrah lost interest in the conversation for the time being, but she definitely looked forward to resuming it.

After Silarrah stuffed herself with bread, cold meats and an assortment of vegetables and fruit, Thissul led her to one of the doors off of the central chamber. Beyond it was a small chamber with a hearth, where a large kettle was suspended over a small fire. Off to the side was a barrel that had been cut in half lengthwise, mounted open-side-up on a crosspiece at either end, and coated inside with a ceramic application to create a bathing tub. Silarrah could scarcely contain her enthusiasm. She removed the white robe and hung it on a rack beside the tub. Then, finally able to shed her tattered and filthy clothing, she sank into the warm water that Thissul had poured from the kettle into the bath. Vigorous scrubbing ensued, and then a long soak until Silarrah was drowsy.

Once she had dried off, Thissul attended her without a word, helping her into a simple gown. They left the bathing chamber and crossed to a door that Caddryth indicated with a wave of her hand without looking up from the book. Within was what Silarrah recognized as a simple down-filled bed. She exhaled with pleasure at the sight of it. Once she was comfortably settled into the bed for the night, Thissul silently bade her good evening and left, closing the door behind her.

Silarrah wondered if she was still a prisoner, although of a different kind. But the hospitality was certainly much improved. She fell asleep still curious about what they wanted with her—especially since they already seemed to know more about Rhinan than she could tell them. But she did feel safe.

Though something left her feeling certain that she would not be allowed to leave. Not at this time, and perhaps not for a long time.

Chapter Twenty-Three

Dran cursed in a way that made his men cower.

Damn Siras and his ambition. Whatever had happened here, it was a foolish waste of resources.

Looking around at the *Maraggan* bodies, Dran was more than furious. It was clear that Siras had attempted to apprehend the Ylvan, and had not measured up to the task. But what had the Captain encountered? The remains of the cabin were still smoldering, robbing Dran not only of clues, but also of the pleasure of burning it down himself.

He stalked the premises and found Siras. Or rather, what was left of him. "Damn fool!" He kicked the body and spat.

Whirling on the young Flek, Dran could tell that the fury on his countenance must be a terrible thing to behold. This was good. Fearing his wrath might discourage poor decisions like this by any of the rest of the guard.

"Did Captain Siras not comprehend that he should wait here until you brought me back? What made him so reckless?"

Flek backed up, flinching, and said nothing.

"That was not rhetorical, boy!" Dran barked. "Why

would Siras have thought it safe to approach an enclosed building with little to no cover? And no reconnaissance as to what may lie within the enclosure? He knew better. What did you see?"

Left with no choice but to respond, Flek spoke. "Two men went in, My Lord. And there was only one old woman inside."

"Do you mean to tell me that two men and one old woman defeated a dozen well-trained *Maraggan*? There was *nothing* else here to indicate any more danger than that? Think!"

Flek shook his head. "Not when I was dispatched to report to you, sir. It was too dark to identify the men, but Captain Siras was certain one of them was our man. There'd been an incident with them down the mountain with what seemed to be magic."

Looking around again, Dran ran a hand through his hair. Wide-eyed with anger, he scanned the ground for any other signs of an ambush or traps. Magic. Were there others helping this Ylvan? Clearly he had at least one companion. Probably the Constable's other aide, whom he'd never gotten a look at. Had others come to their rescue?

He did not find any indication of more men, but he did note the tracks of two horses leading back to the west. This seemed odd to him. Would the fool actually try to return to the little mountain village? No, he would not be that stupid. This was a diversion. Dran concluded that they must have turned their horses loose and were traveling on foot. That might be good or bad, depending on the terrain they followed.

Magic. Flek had said Siras had an indication of its usage. *Almost certainly more magic. Two men and an old woman didn't defeat a dozen Maraggan on their own, and there were no tracks here save animals, wild or domestic. Nothing else to indicate they'd received any help.*

"General!"

Dran turned.

"You may want to see this."

Stepping over to a spot behind the cabin, underneath a tree, Dran saw what the soldier was pointing out. A fresh grave.

Crossing his arms and standing back, Dran studied it for a moment. So Siras had scored one of the enemy's number.

“Captain Kilward,” he called, waving the man over. "Have a couple of your squad dig this up."

“Right away, sir.”

It took longer than Dran wanted to spend. The Ylvan was on the move. If they could determine which direction to follow, they could close in on him, assuming they could move soon. Eventually, his men withdrew the charred remains of a body from the grave.

"It's a woman," said one of the men.

Dran was relieved that it wasn’t the Ylvan. He needed him alive. Needed questions answered.

"Very well." He was exhausted from watching his men work. His patience was thin. "Leave it. Let the scavengers feast on her. She harbored a fugitive from the King. She is not entitled to a proper burial."

The men looked at him, as if they had something to say but were afraid to say it. He got that a lot, but he took it as an indication of his efficiency as a general. He looked around, and realized what they wanted. "And bury *our* men. But be quick about it."

As the men dug graves, he paced the area again. There

were the corpses of all of the horses of Siras and his men. They'd apparently been set upon by a wild animal or animals and had not survived the encounter.

There were the tracks of two horses heading west, but he'd ruled out that the fugitives would head west. The great northern mountain range of the Percenes rose sharply to the north. That would be a hard path. South would bring them closer to the King. That also seemed unlikely.

To the east, if you traveled far enough on the Northern Trading Path, lay the Unreigned Territory. And beyond that, Eluciar—that deadened realm of Lydania which the Ylvan Clans had once called home. Yes, that was the only path left to Rhinan Ashuir. Gazing eastward, Dran could see where two men on foot might travel just off the path, within the tree line, and hope to make good time while still remaining well hidden. That is what *he* would do. Still, it was rough along the northern foothills and worse if you ventured too high up into the mountains. But the terrain to the south was cut with sharp, grassy ravines and low jagged hills. Plenty of shelter there.

When the men finished burying their dead, Dran was exasperated. Most likely wild animals would simply rip the dead from their resting places as soon as they left. But the men needed this, and he could be patient with their needs. He found it strategic when he later needed them to respond to him with loyalty.

"We head east!" His shout gathered the men, impelled them onto their horses. Dran climbed onto his steed. Seated, he turned to Flek. The young scout looked as if he'd done something wrong. "Flek."

Flek looked up, fear in his eyes.

"You take point. Guide us among these foothills, hmm?

They won't be on the Northern Trading Path, but likely alongside of it. There's a good lad."

Dran reined his horse to the side and let Flek pass by. Flek nodded solemnly and rode forward, scanning the ground and flora for signs of their prey.

Doing his best to renew his confidence in his men after the mistakes of Siras, Dran felt optimistic. They were on horseback, pursuing two men on foot. They could normally catch the outlaws within a day. He looked at the terrain ahead, and his optimism waned. Catch them, possibly, or ride right by them. Besides the many opportunities for hiding, if the two men were using magic to mask their trail, what should be a simple pursuit and capture became far more complicated. The two men would know there would be pursuit, and from which direction it was likely to come. Yet, if they used efficient spells, Dran would not know if the two men turned, stopped, or continued onward. How much magic might these men have at their disposal? How powerful? Dran would have to use every bit of his instincts to avoid being misled, tricked, or lost. The inconvenience and the doubt…

As they rode on until nightfall, his fury burned hotter with every league of progress they made. When the King was through with the Ylvan, Dran would see this thief skinned alive.

Chapter Twenty-Four

When he awoke, Rhinan found himself in a sturdy shelter made of branches, logs, vines and earth. Enough light seeped in to tell him it was day. He was covered with blankets, and his clothing was folded on the ground next to him. The tears and bloodstains on them brought the dreadful needlebeast attack back to his mind.

He sat up too fast, and his ribs burned in agony. He winced, and pulled the blankets down to look. As he did so, he was relieved to note the *Pyvadis* still hung around his neck.

Both sides of his torso were covered with large poultices of herbs, held in place by a pair of thin straps that went all the way around him. His hands suffered from the burning sensation, as well. They had both been punctured through by needlebeast spines, yet now only bore the scars. He flexed them, and was relieved that he could move them normally. Needlebeast spines were coated with a poison that caused sleep and, over time, decay of the flesh. If it were not removed or treated fairly soon after an attack, the results could not be reversed.

How long had he been out? Someone had saved him, yet he was alone in this shelter. He'd been hidden in it, probably for his own protection. Had he attempted to stand, he would have had to remain on his knees to avoid hitting his head against the top of the shelter. With Dran's men still out there, likely pursuing him, it would be best to remain quiet for the moment. Whoever had placed him here would return or, if not, he would emerge carefully when he felt better.

It had to be Lynari. She claimed to have some magic, and this healing of his hands was certainly magic. He hadn't gotten the impression her knowledge of Magic Lore was that broad from her discussions with Eodorr. But this shelter? That could be her handiwork.

The needlebeast had gotten the best of him in the misty evening. He was alive now, and it seemed Lynari must have survived the attack as well. And he was pretty sure he'd seen the needlebeast creep away without any confrontation with Eodorr. Thank the Lore Givers.

But what about Rip? Rip had saved his life but taken the worst of the needlebeast's attack. The needlebeast was almost half the beardog's size, but those needles did severe damage.

Rhinan speculated that, after healing and hiding him, it was possible that Lynari and Eodorr had foolishly tried to draw the *Maraggan* in another direction. They would be sacrificing themselves, possibly even as he lay healing.

He could not bear it. Too many people had been murdered for him. Good people. Good people were dying at the hands of bad people who served the authority of the King. Something new inside of Rhinan began to stir. Was it rage? Something more?

He flinched as the front of the shelter swung open.

He reached for his bow, found it just next to his clothes, but had no time to nock an arrow. And the shelter was too low to draw a bow.

"I see you are awake." In the shelter's entrance crouched a woman clad in a gray robe with the gray tunic and leggings of the Lore College underneath it. She had golden hair and brown eyes. There was a leather pouch in her hand. He thought she could be an acquaintance of Lynari. Had she come all the way from Masseltaine? He wondered again how long he'd been out?

"Eodorr… Lynari… Rip…" He spurted names, feeling as if the effort were too much for him to breathe. He tried to rise.

"Don't do that." She reached out her hand and eased him firmly, yet gently, back down. She was very strong. He was too weak to fight her. She brought the pouch to his lips, and he drank. He had not realized how thirsty he was. He drained it and immediately felt better. "Yes, you'll need plenty of water as you recover."

"Thank you. My friends…"

"…are fine. I am Vaylene. We were travelling west along the foothills when we encountered you, or you might be dead now."

"'We'?"

"I and my *Sohera.* We are healers." *Sohera* were apprentices to the Lore Masters, studying beyond the normal levels, hoping to become Lore Trainers or even a Lore Master themselves someday. Vaylene must be the Lore Master of healing. There could be only one Lore Master of any discipline, but they could take on several *Sohera.* Rhinan looked down at his hands again and did not doubt her claim.

"Where are my friends?"

She reached out and placed a hand on his chest, closing her eyes. He felt warmth spread through his body, the effect of which was like waking up. Rhinan marveled at her skills.

She was more than a healer; she was a magic-wielding healer. He felt stronger but she advised, "Don't try to rise just yet. I'll send them in to you."

She frowned at the exposed *Pyvadis*, then noticed him seeing her looking at it. Without a word, she exited into the daylight.

Rhinan recalled what Lynari had said about other disciplines, all other lores, being enhanced by magic. If this were true, this woman was a criminal for her magic use, even though it served a helpful purpose.

Interrupting his thoughts, Eodorr knelt in the opening, creeping forward to sit at Rhinan's feet with a grin. "It's good to see you. You look well. You were turning green when Vaylene showed up. I thought you were sure to die."

"It's good to see you, too. What about Rip?"

Eodorr's smile faded. "He was bad, Rhinan. Vaylene wasn't sure what to do for him. He wasn't very cooperative. It took several of us to calm and hold him while she did what she could—"

"Several?"

"Vaylene travels with a number of *Sohera*. You'd think she was a Lore Giver. They are quite devoted."

"But Rip?"

"He wandered off. We haven't been able to find him. I'm sorry, Rhinan. I've tried. All day."

"All day? How long have I been out?"

"All night and most of the day."

Rhinan exhaled and leaned back, exasperated. "What about Dran? The *Maraggan* cannot be far behind us!"

"They are not far. But Lynari warded the camp to keep it hidden. And Vaylene's people are not without impressive skills of their own."

Rhinan almost laughed to hear these words coming from Eodorr's mouth. Speaking of magic as if it were a common thing, not unlawful at all. It still amused him. Eodorr who, only a couple of days ago, had been a Vice-Constable, sworn to uphold the King's laws. *We're all changing, I suppose.*

"You won't find him unless he wants you to."

"Who?" Eodorr seemed puzzled.

"Rip. Even I can't track him. But if you haven't found him, that's encouraging. He's able to hide. If he weren't, you'd have found him. So it might be a good sign."

"Oh." Eodorr thought for a moment. "Well, I'm glad I haven't found him then."

Rhinan smiled. *Changing indeed.* "Thank you for looking."

* * * * *

Vaylene allowed Rhinan to dress and emerge from the shelter to stretch his legs as the camp prepared supper. Outside he found about twenty brown-robed young men and women all busy with various tasks: preparing food, stoking a central multi-purpose fire for cooking and heat, reviewing their equipment for upkeep, repairing if necessary or practicing if possible (he saw some archery practice in progress, in fact), and rubbing down horses. This was quite the company Vaylene had at her disposal.

Lynari was meditating, presumably restoring the energies she'd used in the magics employed on their journey. When she opened her eyes and saw him, she approached him with a broad smile. "You look well."

"I feel better than I would expect."

"You were treated by Vaylene the Healer." Lynari said it with a tone of reverence. "She was once the Lore Master of the healing discipline at Masseltaine. Rare and honored are those directly administered by her unparalleled skills. It is said that Death himself cannot defeat her in direct battle for the life of those she would save."

"'Was?'" From Rhinan's experience, this was a woman who should still be the Lore Master, sharing her knowledge and training those who came to the Lore College to learn that skill.

"You cannot remain in Masseltaine and rise above a certain level within your discipline," explained Vaylene, who had walked up behind them as they spoke. "If you wish to enhance your discipline with magic, you must defy the King's edicts. After reaching the mundane peak of my discipline, I chose to leave and continue to learn, rather than to stay in Masseltaine and share only limited knowledge."

"But magic is explored in Masseltaine," Lynari quietly reminded her, referring to the secret *Hegana.*

"I practice it openly." Vaylene was proud, defiant. "I can neither condone nor condemn what others do, but it was not my way to defy the King privately. I continue to study how magic may help the Lore of Healing, and I teach this to my *Sohera.*" She gestured at those around them. "I am an outlaw for so doing, but I would be a traitor to the Lore Givers if I did not pursue my discipline to its fullest potential."

Lynari looked ashamed hearing Vaylene's words. Rhinan wanted to console her, tell her that it was acceptable to practice in secrecy if one must. Would the Lore Givers benefit from students who lost their heads? Who would spread the knowledge then? Yet he respected Vaylene's position as well. This was a woman who did not fear the King. She was willing to risk her freedom and her life in her devotion to the mastery of lore. Rhinan supposed there was no more noble cause.

A beautiful young woman with darkly-tanned skin—almost the color of a dim sunset—approached them. She had straight, black hair and brown eyes. Perhaps a native of the region of Travinia? It was supposed to be the region south of Eluciar, wherever that all was. Rhinan recalled that Keirwyn himself had come from there. "All who are hungry are welcome to eat now."

"This is Merindel," Vaylene introduced her. "She is one of our most skilled *Sohera.*"

Merindel bowed, and Rhinan noticed the muscle tone in her arms. She was an archer, like himself. He wondered how her skills would measure up, and if he would have the opportunity to find out. She indicated where everyone was gathering around the fire with baskets of bread, fruit, platters of roasted meat, and fire-baked sweets.

The aromas made Rhinan's mouth water. He hadn't eaten for a full day, and his stomach now reminded him loudly of that fact. Eodorr, Lynari and Vaylene laughed.

"Yes, and Rhinan needs nourishment." The Healer led them to the circle around the fire where everyone sat on grassy earth, rocks, or fallen trees. The camp was situated in a wooded draw of the foothills, a sharp cut into the slopes that provided some natural cover. Rhinan assumed Lynari and Vaylene had used enough magic to keep Dran's forces away.

As they sat somewhat apart from her *Sohera*, Vaylene leaned in to speak confidentially with Rhinan and his companions. "I must tell you that it gives my heart such a gift to learn that an Ylvan survives. Your people were done a great injustice, Rhinan."

It was hard for him to think of the Ylvan Clans as "his people." He had always felt he had no people at all. Keirwyn and Silarrah and, if Rip counted as people, then the beardog. But that was it.

"The Ylvan Clans had a gift. They were called Rain-callers or Leaf-bringers. And those that chose to practice magic? It was wonderful, natural magic. The purest form. I use some of their magic myself."

"How?" Rhinan did not see how Ylvan magic could be used by anyone but an Ylvan.

"Oh, it's Ylvan lore, but they spread knowledge. Shared what they learned. You must understand that Loregiving is the very first of the Primary Lores—the ability to effectively impart knowledge to others is how we begin the process that allows us to survive and thrive. Loregiving is a lore of its own. But of course it was the first Lore Giver, Wendam, that gave us the tool to share Lore. You recall the story of Wen?"

Rhinan did not. He knew "Wen's tongue!" as an exclamation, but he didn't know the story.

Vaylene rose and stoked the central fire. "When the Lore Givers were given the lives of men and beasts to tend, they did not know what to do with them. Men and beasts could not speak, and they were not to be taught this divine knowledge. But Wendam saw the potential of some of the beings, including man." She turned to the gathered *Sohera*, spreading her arms in front of the fire as she related their history. They listened to a tale they'd obviously heard, but Rhinan found it interesting that they were still so engrossed. "Without approval, Wendam taught speech to man and a few other beings. But Wen soon found while men were quick to learn, they were slow to understand. This would be his undoing."

Vaylene paused, staring into the night as if she recalled the incident herself. "But Wen pressed the other Lore Givers to allow him to teach hunting and farming and fishing and building. They acquiesced and allowed Wen his experiment with one condition: Delena, the Lore Giver of Justice, would observe and determine if the experiment was going well."

She took on a mystical quality, backlit by the fire at twilight as she was. "However, Norrik, the Dark Lore Giver of Sorcery, was jealous of Wen's success. He searched until he found the original pupil of Wendam, and made sure Delena discovered that Wen had begun to teach their divine knowledge without consent. She told the other Lore Givers. The Lore Givers would forgive Wendam, but Norrik saw an opportunity. He found a man and taught him a little bit of his own Dark Magic Lore, and he convinced the man to share that lore and to use it. Man and other beings now fought, seeking to use the Lore of Battle."

Norrik then pointed this out to the Lore Givers, claiming that Wen's experiment was dangerous and out of control. He tried to convince the Lore Givers to destroy all beings which had learned speech, but Delena would not allow it. However, in order to prevent Wendam from teaching speech to any other creatures, she removed his tongue. And she decreed that every Lore Giver would choose a discipline and see to it that man would learn it properly so he would not fight. They would appoint Lore Masters among men to share lore."

Now Vaylene looked directly at Rhinan. "It was Ylva, Lore Giver of Natural Magic, who discovered Norrik's misdeeds and turned him over to Delena. Her punishment was to seal Norrik into a black hall with no windows for all eternity. The only Dark Lore known to man would be what Norrik had already taught. Unfortunately, it was still too much. Men still sought it for power, and so men still fight."

She finished and returned to Rhinan, Lynari and Eodorr. The *Sohera* began their after-dinner chores and respectfully left their Lore Master with her guests.

"Narkan Tanglas was an exception, Rhinan. The Ylvans were good students of the Lore Givers. Why, your father—"

"You knew my father?"

"Markin Ashuir. No, not personally. But he was the Lore Master of the discipline of Magic at the college. As a young *Genesa*, I once overheard a conversation that led me to believe Markin served the King, in fact."

Rhinan frowned. "My father *served* the King?" He did not know how to reconcile this. Brinaya had said his parents were *loyal* to the King, but this was another level. He remembered his father as a kind man, but he had come to think of most of the King's servants as anything *but* kind. And he remembered no demonstration of magic from his childhood.

"Obviously, there was a time when magic was not outlawed by Jerrick. There were rumors of a secret council of wizards, and that Markin may have been one of Jerrick's top advisors before the Ylvan Uprising. After the Ylvans were destroyed by the King, Markin vanished. Everyone assumed he was eliminated with the rest of them. But here you sit, delightful proof that he eluded that horrible fate. At least for some time."

"They were… friends?" Rhinan could not imagine it.

"Possibly." Vaylene shrugged. "I suppose one never knows. King Jerrick felt betrayed by the Ylvans when Tanglas led the Uprising. Your father probably felt betrayed by the King's unbelievable response. Those were difficult times. As I said, I was just a girl starting at the Lore College at the time—a *Genesa*—so I remember very little." She did not much look it, but Rhinan estimated by this that she must be about ten or fifteen years his senior. "Now the King is a man who lets his fears control him. Because he is the King, he controls us, and we pay the price for his fears. We *are* his fears. He sees enemies everywhere.

"At any rate," the Healer continued, "your magic could be quite strong if you chose to pursue that discipline. Lynari, wouldn't you agree?"

The *Hegana* had remained silent, introspective since their conversation before the meal. "One cannot say with any certainty unless he studied the lore."

“I am not interested.” Rhinan was emphatic.

Vaylene looked at Rhinan with a mischievous smile. "Well, that's for you to decide. You would have much to learn, but would most likely progress and, in time, have much to teach. This is why you must continue your journey and reach your destination in safety. You may be the key to a resurgence of magic, to overturning King Jerrick’s ban on its study and usage. You see yourself its benefits." She indicated his hands.

Lynari nodded in agreement. "That is but one possibility of many."

With a quick glance at his hands, Rhinan chose to change the subject. "Speaking of the journey, we should be moving. Vaylene, I cannot pay you for your services or thank you enough for what you have done for me here. For us." He stood.

"I do not do what I do for payment. Healing others is its own reward. Together, we are better when we are at our strongest. It is the same with Lore Sharing. That is why I continue to teach all of my disciplines."

"How many disciplines do you have?" Eodorr now stood with Rhinan. It was still amusing to Rhinan that Eodorr had so much interest in this. It had to be Lynari's influence.

"Magic opens doors." Vaylene stood. "But it also creates danger. If you're going to practice it for any discipline, you must also practice some defensive discipline. Lynari is a combat expert of one sort. I am a warrior." She reached under her robe, drawing a sword from a sheath. Rhinan understood now the great strength she had used to push him back down inside the shelter earlier.

The Healer placed her free hand on Rhinan's chest again, and he felt the warmth as he had earlier. She looked down at his chest, obviously considering the *Pyvadis* she'd seen hanging there earlier. "You can travel, but you will be slowed. Do your best. The King's *Maraggan* is near, but we will delay them."

"No!" Rhinan held his hands out in a warning. "I don't want you to fight them. If Dran is with them now—"

"Hush, Ylvan. What we do, we do for a higher purpose. But I agree with Lynari's assessment, and that of the Lore Masters. You must continue safely. We are your best option to leave this place without being seized. If we can delay them without a fight, we will. If we cannot, then we are well trained for it."

The evening was soaked in shadows. Night was approaching. Rhinan had rested most of the day, and Vaylene's care had strengthened him.

"We can travel by night, remember?" Lynari had her own weapons drawn, her gaze fixed back toward the west. "My spell work is fading. It's time for us to move." Eodorr nodded, his hand on the pommel of his own sword.

Rhinan looked to Vaylene, a former Lore Master of the Lore College, turned outlaw and practicing magic at large. He had so many questions. What could she know of this *Pyvadis*?

"Lore Givers keep you safe," she said, then turned and rallied her *Sohera.* They all mounted horses, each drawing their own weapons, and followed her out of the gorge and westward.

As Rhinan and his two companions started eastward at a brisk pace, his ghosts stirred. Ignoring them, he looked back over his shoulder. He was inspired by Vaylene, but not in the way he thought she had meant to inspire him.

Chapter Twenty-Five

When the woman and her followers rode out of the gorge, Dran recognized her at once. The King had charged him with hunting Vaylene the Healer, former Lore Master, some years back. The King had received word that she traveled with followers, practicing magic healing arts in defiance of his edicts. Dran had never been able to find her. She used magic to hide, and common folk were overly charmed by her, giving her aid and safe passage as she wandered Lydania.

The Ylvan was his priority, but Vaylene stood in his way. So be it. He would satisfy two pursuits on this journey. He wanted Ashuir alive, but there was no such restriction on the capture of Vaylene.

He counted at least a dozen in her company, all mounted and armed. They projected strength and skill. His men outnumbered them by more than twice, but the outlaws showed no sign of fear. He would exploit their foolish confidence.

Though they had ridden and searched most of the day, Dran had allowed a brief rest stop in the night. The men were tired, but they were not too exhausted for a battle.

They had come across the site of a scuffle earlier in the day and searched the area thoroughly. There were needlebeast quills and blood, so someone had been injured, but neither man nor beast had left their opponent's remains. There were tracks to follow for a time, and then those, too, disappeared. Dran knew this was the result of magic, and he concluded that Rhinan and his companions must be hiding nearby, perhaps resting and recovering from the encounter. He'd fanned his men out and kept the area under watch as the day wore on.

As evening approached, his patience was rewarded. Vaylene had long been an irritating and elusive problem for Dran, and here she was. Probably in league now with the Ylvan.

He scanned the followers behind her, wondering if any of them could in fact be the Ylvan. They had no real description of him, other than what had originally been reported by Baron Mundon's steward, but it did not appear that Ashuir was among her company. This was a diversion, then… a delaying tactic. He cursed, knowing that even with a victory, he was in a losing position as the Ylvan was almost certainly on the move.

"Gethor Dran…" Vaylene called out to him, holding her small force back. They seemed prepared to fight, but she wished to speak? There was little to say.

"Surrender, Vaylene. You are accused of the unauthorized practice of magic in disobedience of King Jerrick's edicts. You are also bearing weapons that are restricted to the King's army. You will be taken prisoner if you surrender. If you do not, you will face a more immediate penalty." As if to illustrate his point, Dran drew his sword.

When he did, all of his men did likewise as one fighting unit. This always made a formidable impression, and Dran grinned to see that some among Vaylene's company appeared less confident in the face of that gesture.

"My terms are this: I will surrender myself once my *Sohera* have been allowed safe passage away. They are not responsible for my actions, and are only here under my encouragement. They are innocents."

Dran laughed. "They are not innocents. They are willfully consorting with a wanted outlaw. You are in no position to demand terms."

"General!" Dran jerked around at the shout from one of his men.

There was a twang of bowstrings, the hiss of arrows, and a half dozen of his men tumbled from their horses, slain. Dran could not spot the archers among the trees. They dared to attack the *Maraggan*? He could scarcely believe it.

"That was a warning, General. If you turn back, your men will be allowed to leave safely."

The brash woman would die at his own hands.

"Gaimesh, to the left! Target those archers!" Dran shouted orders, and led several men to the right, scanning for archers on that side.

Another twang of bowstrings, and an arrow whistled past his head. Under this second onslaught, some of their horses fell. Even if the healer did not intend to kill them, she could certainly leave them on foot.

"Flek, ride!"

From the right, away behind Vaylene and her mounted followers, Dran's young scout burst forth with a half dozen men. Dran had held them in reserve. They crashed into the rear-most of the healer's *Sohera*, attacking from the rear and quickly dispatching several of them.

Vaylene charged forward, riding directly at Dran. He sneered and brought his sword up, prepared to meet her.

Having veered to the right to find archers, Dran had ridden downhill. As he charged toward Vaylene, he was moving up slope as she rode down at him, her face a determined mask of concentration. She had the high ground, and he was at a disadvantage.

As they neared impact, Dran dropped from his horse to the opposite side of Vaylene's passing. Her sword swipe missed him. Before he could roll to his feet, she had passed, and his opportunity to strike was lost. His horse screeched and tumbled forward on the slope. She had downed his horse. He yelled in rage.

"Kill them all, but Vaylene is mine!"

He turned, seeing Vaylene swing her horse around to come back at him. However, one of her followers was closer and almost upon him. Dran brought his sword up as the young man's own blade hammered down at him. The blow was not strong enough to unbalance Dran, who turned and swung his own blade again. It caught the young man's horse on the rear quarters, nearly severing a hind leg. The horse went down and the young man tumbled between Vaylene and Dran, causing her to swerve to avoid trampling him with her own horse.

Glancing beyond, Dran could see Flek's squad engaged with half of the healer's mounted followers. The rest of her mounted *Sohera* had pursued Gaimesh and those with him. There had been another volley of arrows, but Gaimesh and his squad had leapt from their horses for cover. The result was that their horses took the arrows, leaving the men on foot and in danger of being ridden down by the few *Sohera* pursuing them.

Dran plunged his sword deep into the young man he'd unhorsed. He hauled the young man upward, still pierced on his blade, and crouched behind him as Vaylene turned for another pass.

Dran heard human screams, but could not determine if they were his men or the healer's *Sohera.* Meeting her gaze, Dran held Vaylene's focus as she came back to finish him. Flek's squad seemed to have dispatched their immediate foes and drawn bows. Dran sensed triumph over the healer's forces was within his grasp.

Vaylene charged him again in what had to be a desperate maneuver, but Dran used the dead *Sohera* on his sword as a shield. As she passed, she swung to the side, hanging low in her saddle, and Dran felt her blade slice his right hip. The pain was agonizing, and he went down with a grunt. The wound was not too deep. Had it been, she might have severed his right leg.

He staggered to his feet to assess the battle, leaning on his sword to stand.

Flek and his squad loosed arrows, taking the remainder of the mounted *Sohera* from their horses before they could reach Gaimesh. Led by a dark-haired woman, the handful of concealed *Sohera* archers broke from the trees and seized the horses of their fallen companions. They fired at Flek's squad, turning them back to seek cover. The archers then rode away swiftly, escaping Dran's men altogether.

Dran turned to find Vaylene surrounded by Gaimesh and his squad. She wielded her sword about her with great skill, but she could not escape. She was disarmed and pulled from her horse.

Grasping the cut in his hip, Dran limped forward. Several men held the struggling healer.

He'd lost Siras and his squad. He was injured and

another half dozen men were dead. The *Maraggan* was reduced by half its number, and most of those remaining no longer had mounts. His fury rose, but he fought it. He would need to be calm here in front of his men to maintain morale.

Still leaning on his sword, he glowered down at the woman he'd been tasked with capturing. She'd been elusive, and she was no coward. If there was one thing he couldn't stand, it was a coward. No, the bold healer was a worthy adversary. He did not want to give her to Gaimesh, but he needed answers.

"Tell me where Ashuir is going."

Vaylene stopped struggling. "I can tell you nothing you do not already know."

Dran realized she was partly right. The Ylvan would try to find his way to the Unreigned Territory, possibly the dead lands of Eluciar beyond that, where the Ylvan Clans hailed from. He had hoped to extract Ashuir's chosen route from her, but that was unlikely. She would not break.

"How many companions are with him now? How far ahead of us are they?"

"These are things I cannot answer with certainty. Nor would I if I could. You cannot gain anything from questioning me."

Dran felt his rage rise again, transforming his expression. He struggled to remain patient. He tried one more question. "How powerful is he?"

Vaylene laughed. "You fear him."

"I am wary of magic. Have you forgotten how the Ylvan sorcerer led his clans in the Uprising? The death he caused? It is unpredictable. It cannot be trusted."

"Not if you make an enemy of it." The healer was still challenging him.

Knowing that he would get nothing further from the healer, and that any further repartee only made him appear weaker before his men, he calmly brought his sword back over his left shoulder and swung down at her with one powerful backhanded stroke. As her head rolled to the ground, his men stepped away from her twitching body.

"*I* am the enemy you do not want to make."

He limped away, planning how he would pursue the Ylvan with more men than horses. The Ylvan had to be remaining within the tree line as he moved east, while Dran kept his men on horseback below the tree line to move quicker. Without that advantage, Dran might well be eluded by the Ylvan.

The pain in his hip was finally taking its toll. He cursed his age for making him the slightest bit slower, despite intensive daily training, or he would have avoided Vaylene's blow. Night was upon them now as well. Before he collapsed, he informed the men that they would have to make camp. But he set a sharp-eyed watch against those few *Sohera* who had escaped in case they returned.

He looked over at the healer's head on the ground, its lifeless eyes gazing up at the stars. "Put that in a sack. We'll take it to King Jerrick. It will please him to know she is no longer at large."

Chapter Twenty-Six

A fire crackled in the hearth as Silarrah emerged from a deep sleep, fully refreshed. A hot bath, a good meal, a soft bed and a warm room had left her feeling human for the first time since Dran arrested her.

There was a gentle knock at the chamber door. Still wary, she had no idea what to expect next. She sat up, wearing only the sleeping gown Thissul had brought her. Her tattered clothes were not in the tiny room. Besides the bed and the hearth, there was only a small desk and chair on the far side of the chamber. Very plain.

She yawned. "I'm awake."

The door opened, and the silent Thissul entered. Yet again, the girl was laden with two baskets—one held food and the other fabric. She smiled at Silarrah and sat the basket of food on the small desk, then turned to stoke the fire in the hearth. Silarrah must have slept through at least one visit; she could not recall a fire being lit the night before.

Ravenous, Silarrah sat at the desk and began to eat the fruits and breads in the basket. "Thank you," she mumbled to Thissul with her mouth full. *Spend a night in a dungeon and lose all your manners, Silarrah.* Thissul only smiled.

Lifting the other basket, Thissul sat it on the bed. She withdrew the fabric and showed it to Silarrah. It was a brown robe. Thissul laid it on the bed, curtsied, and left the room, closing the door behind her.

Silarrah finished eating and slipped into the brown robe. There was another knock, and she wondered who it might be. Beyond the door was the round chamber with Caddryth's desk, so she had an idea. She pulled the door open.

Caddryth stood there appraising her for a moment. "The brown robes of the *Sohera* suit you. How is it that you never came to us before?"

"I had meant to, once." Bittersweet memories washed through Silarrah's mind. "I was preparing to come when my mother died. I stayed home to look after my father. He was devastated by her loss. When he died some time later, I felt the opportunity had passed. I was used to caring for others, so I began to work at an orphanage in Omriel."

"Always caring for others." Caddryth placed a sympathetic hand on her shoulder. "But you know, a year doesn't end after one season. There is yet time."

Silarrah considered this. She had no place else to go. Probably couldn't safely go anywhere after all this trouble with Rhinan and the King. She started at the thought. "Am I safe here? Should I be leaving? When they discover I've escaped the dungeons…"

"The King will likely forget you for some time. The guards ignored you. Only Werald would notice your absence, and he's sworn to protect you, just as I am. It is a risk for him not to report you gone, but he will be long gone before you are missed."

"Protect *me*?" Silarrah was surprised. "I suppose I've angered the King, and I'm grateful to you for having me rescued. But I cannot ask any of you to take risks on my behalf. It is Rhinan who needs your help."

Caddryth smiled and shrugged. "My dear, you are safer here than you would be one step outside of the College. Until we hear from Lynari that Rhinan is safe, you must remain hidden for his sake. After that, you may still need to remain hidden for yours."

It was as Silarrah had feared. She was in a better dungeon, but it was still a dungeon. Caddryth was right. It would be risky for her to go anywhere or be seen by anyone. She couldn't risk being noticed by someone who might remind the unstable King that she existed.

"So what am I to do? I must make myself useful if you are to shelter me."

"Are you ready to begin your education? It would please the Lore Givers to have you study with us as long as you are here. Perhaps help share what you learn with others."

It was a generous offer. What lore would she study? She had long ago given up on any hope of a Lore College sojourn, but now it seemed inevitable. And she couldn't even decide what lore would be right for her! She was filled with an anxious excitement at the opportunity to choose.

In her situation, Silarrah could not turn it down, and she didn't want to. Any discipline at all would be a heart-lifting thrill now that she was here. "It would be a privilege to learn one of the lores. And to share that knowledge would be an honor."

Caddryth brightened. "See? I knew that *Sohera* robe was right for you. Follow me."

Silarrah followed Caddryth out of the little bed chamber. So she would begin as a *Sohera*? From what Silarrah knew, that was unusual. New students at the Lore College began as *Genesa*, choosing a lore to learn and studying in silence until they mastered it. Thissul was obviously a *Genesa*; *Genesa* did not speak unless they had a question pertaining directly to the lore they studied, and then they were only permitted to ask their Lore Trainer or possibly the Lore Master. Once they mastered a lore, they were free to go practice it in the world. However, if they wanted to remain at the College and share their knowledge of the lore, they could apply to become *Sohera*. *Sohera* learned to share knowledge and become Lore Trainers. Recommended by a specific Lore Trainer and approved by the Lore Trainer of Lore Sharing, few were accepted as *Sohera*. It was the first step to becoming a Lore Master one day and, if the Lore Trainer did not see you as a potential replacement for them, you were rejected. But of course, most Lore Masters had more than one *Sohera* studying under their Lore Trainers. It encouraged competition and provided options.

The Lore Master was the singular figurehead of a specific lore. Once the Lore Master of a discipline could no longer maintain that position for whatever reason, the Lore Keeper would choose a Lore Trainer who had risen to the top of their discipline to become the new Lore Master.

Silarrah had studied no lore, had not put in her time as *Genesa*. She did not qualify as *Sohera*, yet it seemed Caddryth, a Lore Master, had already ascertained her worthy of the apprentice Lore Trainer position. But for what lore?

They were now in the central chamber where Silarrah had first seen Caddryth at the large desk the previous night. Caddryth sat at the desk and scrutinized Silarrah. "You don't feel like a worthy *Sohera*?"

"Pardon, but no. I have mastered no lore." As with the King, Caddryth's gaze penetrated Silarrah in a way that made her feel uncomfortable.

"You're going to have to get over that." Silarrah wasn't sure if Caddryth meant her feeling of worth or her discomfort under the gaze of these powerful people. Neither would be easy. "Besides," Caddryth continued, "I'll put in a word for you with the Lore Keeper. In all of his knowledge and wisdom, he trusts my judgment, so I will expect nothing less of you."

Silarrah could not argue with her.

"I trust your judgment, Caddryth, when it does not conflict directly with my own."

Caddryth stood in silent response, her gaze focused behind Silarrah. Turning around, Silarrah found the blind old man in the white robes standing behind her. He'd descended the stairs into the chamber with such stealth that she hadn't heard him until he spoke.

Caddryth giggled. Silarrah found that an odd way for a woman of Caddryth's age to show respect to someone of the old man's stature, but everything here was odd. "Though you've met, I don't believe the two of you have been properly introduced. Silarrah, this is Altain Cebros, Lore Keeper of the Lore College."

More stature than Silarrah had figured. The headmaster himself had been the one to deliver her from the King's dungeons. Silarrah nearly staggered with the implications of the importance they placed on Rhinan, her, their relationship, or all three.

"Pleased to officially make your acquaintance, young lady." The blind headmaster extended a hand. Silarrah took it and squeezed.

"Thank you, Lore Keeper. Thank you." A tear dropped from her eye, landing on the headmaster's hand.

"Here, now." Altain cooed at her gently. "Tears hold magic. Don't waste them on nothing."

"I would like to ask your permission for something,

Keeper." Caddryth stepped forward, and Silarrah was grateful for the distraction.

"You want to keep the stray we've taken in." The Lore Keeper grinned, winking in Silarrah's direction.

"She's been caring for orphans. I would like to start her as a *Sohera*."

The Lore Keeper's eyebrows rose. "Are you quite sure? She will have much to learn."

"We have nothing but time."

Silarrah watched their debate, excitement mingling with fear. She did not want to disappoint either of them. And she also feared the King. She did not know if she would ever feel safe again after her ordeal with Dran, the King, and the dungeons.

"Silarrah," the headmaster of the Lore College addressed her directly. "I think you are a very smart young lady. Capable. You must realize by now that you're safest remaining here for the foreseeable future. I wouldn't want you to feel obligated or pressured, but does this offer appeal to you?"

"Very much, Keeper Cebros."

"Will you swear to the Lore Giver's oath? The First Lore is the earnest and competent sharing of lore itself. Knowledge is sacred, and sharing it is our sacred duty. That is the path of the *Sohera*… to be entrusted one day as a Lore Trainer."

"I so swear." Silarrah discovered herself swelling with pride that she had never felt before, did not realize she possessed.

"And you will honor *all* lore, and protect the practice of each distinct discipline with full discretion."

"I will."

"Then as Lore Keeper of the Lore College,

representative of the Lore Givers and the knowledge they imparted to the world, I grant you permission to study Lore Sharing. I also want you to find another lore to specialize in. You may not have completed a cycle as a *Genesa*, but choosing a specialty is a foundation of lore study."

Caddryth spoke up. "I have a recommendation."

Silarrah was curious. "Thank you, Caddryth. What lore do you recommend?"

"Rather than a Lore Trainer, you'd be studying at my side. Studying directly under a *Lore Master* won't be easy."

"I understand." So Caddryth wasn't a Lore Trainer, but a Lore Master! Silarrah had suspected as much. But of what discipline?

"Then it's 'Lore Master Caddryth' from now on, or just 'Master'."

"Yes, Lore Master Caddryth." Silarrah hoped it would be a lore she could excel at. "What lore will be my specialty?"

A sparkle in her eye, Caddryth's smile twisted to the side. "The Lore of Magic."

PART TWO

Chapter Twenty-Seven

By morning, the town of Arskellion was visible on a flat plain to the south of Rhinan, Eodorr and Lynari. Weary from the night's hard march and suffering from wounds not completely healed, Rhinan could not have been more relieved. They had to have been in the region of Arskellia for some time, and its capitol city was Arskellion. Rhinan recalled Param telling him of performing there often, painting a picture of it as a rough place where miners and foresters came down out of the mountains to squander their pay on drinking and gaming. It was at least worth the risk to search there, for this might be a good chance to find his friend. But they would have to be cautious.

The peaks of the Percenes began to curve away to the north here, and they were already covered in snow at the end of autumn. The rising sun tinted them the orange of flame, but brought no heat. It had been a cold night, but at least there had been no rain. Surely with the onset of winter, Param would be here sooner rather than later. Optimistically, he could be down there right now, Rhinan thought. Probably sleeping off the previous night's revelry.

"Well, I can't speak for you two, but I could use

breakfast." Eodorr stood next to him, tendrils of breath curling away in the chill air.

Rhinan leaned on him. "Eodorr, sometimes I like the way you think."

Aroused from her morning meditation, Lynari gave them a reminder. "We have no idea if Vaylene and her *Sohera* were able to delay Dran, or even better, turn him back." She began to pick around the flora for useful plants and herbs she would pick and save in her pouch, especially important now with winter settling in. She seemed satisfied with her findings. "If the *Maraggan* are still on our heels, they will certainly stop here for supplies and replenishment." The Northern Trading Path passed right through the town.

"You've been into my thoughts, *Hegana*," Rhinan teased her. "While this will be a good place to wait for Param heading westward, we're going to have to remain as inconspicuous as possible. Blend in. And I can't be sure how soon he may come through here, but he almost certainly will." The thing of it was, this was almost as far as any of them could get without Param. They could follow the Northern Trading Path into the region of Ramwick and the city of Dunskern on the River Arinell, but with Dran behind them, their chances of being caught on the Path was increased.

A trail extended down from the mountains into the town. Before they headed down, Rhinan took a moment to walk back deeper into the forest looking for Rip. The beardog had not appeared during the night, and Rhinan was concerned about his hunting companion. Rip had saved his life. He hoped the big animal was well. He could find no trace of him, though. All he could do was hope that maybe Rip had wandered back westward or perhaps was just keeping to the deeper forest while healing from his own wounds.

The damages in his wake were mounting: Keirwyn, Devram, Brinaya, possibly Silarrah and Vaylene, and poor Rip. All for what? Because he was an Ylvan? If the King didn't go to such lengths to hurt an Ylvan, he may not have so many reasons to fear one. But, Rhinan thought bitterly, perhaps now there would come a day when the King's fear of him would be justified. His anger rose, and he imagined striking back at this man, King though he may be. But he would have to face Dran and the *Maraggan*, plus there was the entire Lydanian army, and the palace at Masseltaine was surely heavily defended. There was no way for him to reach the King without an army of his own, even if he weren't still suffering from the needlebeast attack. Hungry and still in pain, he focused on moving forward.

"All right, let's go." The sorrow in his voice could not be disguised. Eodorr gave him a pitying look, and Lynari took him by the arm. Rhinan did not want to lean on the *Hegana*; she was strong, but exhaustion was showing in her features.

"Are you alright?" he asked her, careful not to put any of his own weight on her.

"Just tired. I may have overextended myself a little." She smiled, brushing his concern aside. "Using magic involves a great deal of concentration, and my magic ability is limited. But I used it to help keep us hidden and to make us harder to track. I was moved by Vaylene's boldness to practice magic openly, despite the potential consequences." She appeared to Rhinan as though more time had passed since they'd slept or eaten than actually had. At least there was a possibility of some rest while in Arskellion.

Once both Rhinan and Eodorr tucked and secured their swords under their cloaks, slipping into Arskellion was easy enough. They followed the trail down into the town, uneventfully passing through the busy city gates without being challenged by any of the city guard. The trail became the main thoroughfare amidst the larger buildings. The denizens were moving up and down the thoroughfare, busy with their daily routines and making preparations for winter. No one paid them much attention.

As they descended the slope, they noticed that some of these buildings were partially cut into the sides of low, rocky hills. This made them appear as if they were growing out of the slopes like giant mushrooms. Seeing it for the first time, Rhinan found it was as large as he would have expected from Param's descriptions, but still not as large as Omriel. But there were plenty of people, and he hoped that would help make them less noticeable. They looked exactly like what they were: ragged travelers. It was likely this town saw its share of those.

Rhinan stiffened when he spotted a half dozen soldiers of the Lydanian army on the thoroughfare. They wore maille with the black and crimson uniforms of the standard army, rather than the flashy black and gold of the *Maraggan.* He relaxed when the soldiers ducked into one of the taverns. Still, he did not want to be noticed by anyone who would likely be consulted by Dran's men should the King's special force reach Arskellion. Spotting a small inn to their right, he tugged Lynari and Eodorr into it.

As they entered the inn, they were greeted by the aroma of hot food and warmth emanating from the huge blazing hearth on the opposite side of the room. The back end of the room and the hearth were carved into the white rock of the hillside. Across the room directly to the left was a counter. A doorway in the wall at the far end behind the counter led to what Rhinan assumed would be the kitchen. To the right, a staircase led upward, presumably to rooms. There were several tables and chairs on the floor, hewn roughly from logs obviously brought down from the mountains. There were a few patrons at some of the tables. They looked like foresters for the most part, but there were a couple of families—probably local residents—as well.

A short, burly man emerged from the kitchen doorway, passing the counter on his right as he carried platters of steaming food to one of the tables.

"That's for me," Eodorr joked, drawing up a seat at the nearest empty table. Lynari collapsed into the seat next to him, and Rhinan waved to catch the burly man's attention before taking a seat for himself.

After delivering the food to its rightful recipients, the burly man came over to them. He was bald and had rough, red scarring which appeared to be from a burn on the left side of his face. "Breakfast?" His tone was surly and he said nothing more.

"That will be fine," Rhinan acknowledged. "And rooms, if you have any."

The man's eyebrows raised. "Only one."

Rhinan looked to Eodorr and Lynari. They both shrugged.

"We'll take it." They would have to work out sleeping arrangements later.

The man headed to the kitchen doorway, called out something to someone that they couldn't make out—like codes—and then stepped behind the counter. He reached under it and lifted out a tiny wooden chest, plunking it down on the counter top. Flipping open the lid, he withdrew a large key. He closed the lid on the chest and replaced it under the counter, then he brought the key over to Rhinan.

"Pay first." He quoted them the price, which seemed fair, and the act reminded Rhinan that he had no coin on him whatsoever. He looked questioningly at Eodorr who, in return, dropped his shoulders and smirked.

There was a jingling and the thump of coins hitting the table. Lynari took the key from the burly man, who simply shook his head and walked away.

"Think nothing of it." She smiled at them. "It's not like you planned to be making this trip. On the other hand, I prepared for it."

When they finished their meal, they hurried upstairs to their room. It was no more than a cloth-covered straw bed and a chamber pot in the corner. "Fine lodgings indeed," Rhinan set his pack on the floor in a corner, stripped off his quiver, and leaned the sword and his bow next to it. He then lay down on the bed and stretched out. Eodorr shot him a look of contempt, but Rhinan's only response was to rub himself down both sides, indicating where the needlebeast had scratched him up. In truth, he did still ache, despite the application of Vaylene's considerable healing skills. In fact, Rhinan realized it was probably safe to drop the *Pyvadis* into his pouch, so he removed it from around his neck and placed it there. It would be a relief to give himself a break from trying to avoid the faint hum which persisted from it to him alone.

Lynari, following healing instructions Vaylene had given her, examined Rhinan's hands and reapplied herbal poultices. She then touched Eodorr on the arm. "He should rest. Besides, I don't think either of you should be outside the inn more than necessary. I will go out and ask around, see if there's any entertainment later this afternoon. If your friend is in town, someone will know."

Once she'd gone, Eodorr snapped at Rhinan. "The proper thing to do would be to give the bed to Lynari."

"Oh? Not to the man recovering from being nearly shredded to death by a needlebeast?" Rhinan needled Eodorr, fighting to restrain a grin.

"You're hopeless." With that, Eodorr laid his pack and weapons next to Rhinan's. "I suppose I can curl up on the floor." He sat in the opposite corner, in the spot where the door would strike him if opened all the way.

Rhinan muttered something about Eodorr's hopeless infatuation with the *Hegana* as he closed his eyes.

* * * * *

He opened them what seemed like moments later. Eodorr had fallen asleep, tipped over, and now lay on the floor. Rhinan couldn't tell if he'd been out for long; there was no window in the room. Lynari had not returned yet, but he knew she would if she'd discovered anything.

He could hear the tavern downstairs, and it sounded quite lively. Drawn to the idea of a pint of ale and perhaps a bit of gaming, he stood up and found that he felt much better. He silently thanked Vaylene. Then he nudged Eodorr with his boot.

"Fancy an ale?"

Eodorr stirred and grumbled, but he did not move.

"Well, as long as you're pleased."

Scampering down the stairs, Rhinan found the tavern bustling with foresters, miners and other men. But no soldiers. The fire still roared in the hearth, and the inn smelled of sweat and ale. Outside, it was late afternoon. He'd slept most of the day. This would be the time troubadours would begin their performances, so he expected Lynari back soon with a report. While waiting for her, Rhinan ordered ale. The taciturn inn keeper was now assisted by two maidens as well. There was a dice game in progress back in the alcove under the stairs, and Rhinan thought he could get in on that and earn a few coins.

After flagging down the inn keeper for his ale, Rhinan shouldered his way into the group playing the dice game. He watched to see if it was a game he was familiar with, but it wasn't. A few moments of observation, and it was easy enough for him to learn. The men were all drinking heavily. In fact, a "penalty" of the game seemed to be taking an unusually deep swig of ale. Rhinan liked his odds. He'd always been very lucky at dice games. He eyed the coins on the table. He hadn't felt right letting Lynari pay for their room and breakfast. Perhaps he could pay her back. When the dice were passed to him, he prepared to roll them.

"Wait a minute." One of the men slurred at him. "Where's your money?"

Rhinan laughed and clapped him on the back. "How about if I put up a round of ale for each of you if I lose?"

Nobody objected to that. In fact, it made them all the happier to give him the opportunity to roll the dice.

A few rounds later, and the other men were drunker and poorer. None of them had even noticed a few coins "slip off the table." Rhinan felt he was doing well when he felt the tap on his shoulder.

"That might be enough for one day." Eodorr glared at him.

"You may be right." Rhinan felt the effects of the ale he'd consumed; he'd lost track of how many. As they tried to step away from the table, one of the men pulled Eodorr into the mix and put a mug of ale into his hands.

"C'mon, now. Your friend has been winning. Maybe we can recoup our losses against you." The men all laughed at Eodorr's bewildered expression, but Rhinan stepped forward.

"It's been a pleasure drinking with you gentlemen, but my friend is right. Thank you for the game." He tipped the coins on the table he'd won "legitimately" into a small pouch tied to his belt.

The men all shrugged and turned back to the dice.

"Has Lynari not returned?" Eodorr sounded worried.

"I'm sure she'll be along soon." Rhinan tried to reassure him. "If she's checking taverns for Param, it could take a while. But this is the time he'd be performing."

"Why don't we wait upstairs?" Eodorr grabbed him by the arm and pulled him in that direction. Then he stopped suddenly. "I don't like the look of that." He pointed to four soldiers that had just entered the inn. They were speaking to the inn keeper.

"Travelers, are we?"

Rhinan and Eodorr turned. Two soldiers stood behind them, waiting for an answer. Rhinan resisted the urge to throw fists at them and run. He tried deceit instead. "We're foresters."

"Are you?" One of the soldiers asked. "We haven't seen you here before."

"We're new." The soldiers exchanged dubious looks. This answer hadn't satisfied them, so Rhinan continued. "We're looking for work, actually, but we're foresters by trade."

They didn't seem to be specifically looking for Rhinan, so word must not have reached Arskellion about the renegade Ylvan. This meant that Vaylene had successfully delayed Dran. Rhinan was feeling good about his chances of talking his way out of this, but then it might be the ale. Eodorr was no help, remaining silent throughout the discourse.

"Ever done any mining?" asked the first soldier.

"Well, no." Rhinan laughed. "As foresters, we wouldn't be any good at that."

"Better hope you're wrong about that." It came from behind them. The other four soldiers had approached. Rhinan and Eodorr were now surrounded. "We're going to need you to come with us. Royal decree. Travelers are subject to conscription for work in the King's mines."

Suddenly feeling very sober, Rhinan realized if these men took them now, they would certainly discover sooner or later that he was wanted by the King. His heart raced as he looked for an exit route, considering their options for a fight and escape.

"Don't even think about it." One of the soldiers pointed a long dagger into his ribs. Eodorr was facing the point of a dagger from another soldier. There was no opportunity to fight them off in the crowded room.

Rhinan's hands were grabbed and roughly bound behind him. Eodorr struggled to move away from the dagger, but he was outnumbered, overwhelmed, and bound the same as Rhinan.

There was a tug at Rhinan's side. It was the man he'd first spoken to at the dice game. He'd just used a dagger to cut the small pouch loose from Rhinan's belt. The man grinned. "Doesn't look like you'll be needing this." Then the man's expression turned serious. "You may be good at it, but we've had enough experience around here with thieves to recognize one, even drunk."

Hoping to apologize for his error in judgment, Rhinan tried to catch Eodorr's eye, but Eodorr just looked away in disappointment. With firm grips, the soldiers hauled them out of the inn, nearly dragging them off of their feet. They were caught.

Chapter Twenty-Eight

Dran was even more furious when dawn came. Gaimesh had attended to his wound, but he could not ride for a few days. And between the foolhardy Siras and the rebellious Vaylene, the *Maraggan* had been cut in half. How was he going to continue the pursuit of Ashuir?

First, he dispatched a scout to Masseltaine with a report and to secure reinforcements, leaving him with twenty men and a dozen horses. He wasn't at all confident that reinforcements would catch up to him in time to be of use, but he could spare one man and one horse to find out.

They needed more horses, and they couldn't wait for the reinforcements from Masseltaine. There were farms to the south, so that at least could be resolved. He wasn't sure how far to the nearest farms, or if the nearest ones had horses, but there would definitely be horses to be had. He called Captain Kilward and one of his men over.

"My Lord?" He could tell they wanted to help, but none of them had any training in healing. Ironic that he'd killed probably the best healer in the area.

"Ride south. Find farms with horses. Commandeer ten

good riding steeds. Bring them back here and be quick about it."

The two men affirmed the orders, mounted and rode southward in search of farms. Dran was now down to ten horses and eighteen men. With the possibility that Vaylene's archers were still out there in the forest, and that the Ylvan was drawing further away, he had to make some difficult choices.

Gaimesh approached. "Sir, we've found their camp. There's not much there of use, but there is a shelter we could put you in to keep you warm and hasten your recovery."

Cursing, Dran allowed the big man to help him to his feet. With the assistance of another man, they carried him. Dran called to have his pack brought to him from his own dead horse.

They made their way into the gorge from which the healer and her renegades had emerged. The remains of a fire still smoldered. Magic had been employed to hide them in this place, Dran had no doubt.

Pulling back a tangle of leaved branches, Gaimesh exposed a small shelter. Dran eased into it, realizing that it was possible the Ylvan himself had been in here just hours earlier. They had, after all, found signs earlier of a struggle, and someone had been injured. If it were Ashuir or any of his companions, that someone may have been healed in this very shelter by Vaylene. Ashuir was on his way, but Dran would be stuck here for a few days. He seethed.

"Flek!"

Sitting half out of the shelter, Dran watched as most of the men huddled around the remains of the fire, stoking it back to life and keeping warm. The young scout Flek, however, had been seeing to the horses that remained. Upon being called, he brushed himself off and came over to Dran. "My Lord?"

Dran was impressed with the scout's performance—his long ride to catch up to Dran, and even a small detail such as seeing to the horses. With Captain Siras gone, he needed another squad leader besides Gaimesh and Kilward. "I'm promoting you to Captain."

The young man's eyes widened in surprise and excitement. It had clearly been unexpected. "Thank you, My Lord. What are my orders?" Dran was pleased with the appropriate responses.

"Take five men with you on horses and continue the pursuit."

A look of concern crossed Flek's face.

"I know," Dran grumbled in his weakened condition. "I hate to split us up, but it can't be helped," he confided in his newest Captain. "We'll still have four horses here until more arrive, and a dozen good men. The six of you *must* catch up to that thief. *Do not engage him.* Send a man back to report. Don't let the thief out of your sight. We'll follow and meet you as soon as we can."

"I understand, My Lord. We'll leave at once."

"Beware of magic, Flek. And ride hard. I'm counting on you."

The new Captain spoke to five of his comrades, and they mounted horses, heading east in pursuit of Ashuir. It pleased Dran to see that Flek had chosen good men for a nimble search party. As they rode out, Dran was confident that the Ylvan couldn't have gained much distance on them.

Dran addressed the rest of the men. "Our numbers may be temporarily depleted, but I've sent a rider to Masseltaine for reinforcements. We hold this position until they arrive.

The pursuit cannot be delayed, so I have dispatched Captain Flek to continue tracking the criminal. He will report back, and we will rejoin the pursuit as soon as we are able with all due speed."

He pulled Gaimesh aside. "I'll need you here to see to my injury. You are the only one of us with any skill at preserving the wounded." Dran did not add that this skill was normally used by Gaimesh to keep a suspect alive for further questioning.

"Of course, My Lord."

"Set a watch. I don't want to be surprised by any more of Vaylene's people. We can easily defend this gorge, but we risk being cornered if numbers are not in our favor."

"Wise, My Lord. I will see to it."

"If any of them dare show their faces, we take no prisoners. It is time to put an end to this."

As he listened to Gaimesh organize the men into shifts, Dran withdrew a map from his pack. He counted towns along the northern road. When he could ride again, he would turn every one of them inside out if need be, unless Flek turned up the fleeing Ylvan.

His biggest concern was the Ylvan's use of magic. It was interfering with what should be an easy capture. Dran began to wonder if having magic in the King's employ might not be useful. He decided that it might be, but he knew Jerrick would have none of it.

He leaned back into the shelter with a sigh. Next to him, one of the men had placed the sack that contained the healer's head. His triumph at her death was overshadowed by his fury. "Not so defiant now, are you, witch?" Nothing was more frustrating to him than being inactive at a time like this. But all he could do was gloat over a vanquished enemy.

* * * * *

Vaylene's *Sohera* kept a safe distance from Dran's camp, but they had watched it all night. Some of them wanted to attack, but the camp was well-guarded, and they were outnumbered. Five against twenty-two were poor odds. Paralyzed by disbelief that their Lore Master had fallen, the *Sohera* were trained to heal themselves of any wounds received in battle, and that included emotional scars.

All they knew was that the special enforcers of Jerrick's mad oppression were hunting for the Ylvan. As practitioners of magic, Vaylene's healers were just as much targets. Dran was a ruthless adversary. Until now, the *Sohera* had avoided capture by roaming Lydania as far as possible from Masseltaine. They would do as much good as they could, lending as much aide to their countrymen as their abilities allowed, and as often as possible.

With Vaylene fallen, they had a choice to make. Avenge her if they could, or continue to study the combined Lores of Healing and Magic, and share that with new devotees. There was some argument over this, but Merindel stood up and settled it.

She knew what Vaylene would want. "Avenging her will not bring Vaylene back." The other four *Sohera* gave her their attention when she spoke. "We cannot attack the *Maraggan*. She would want us to survive, move on, and continue her work. We must find others to join us." She paused for effect. "Then we can see about vengeance."

Everyone agreed. They also decided that Merindel was the best choice to lead them now that they had lost their Lore Master, despite the fact that Merindel was not a Lore Master herself. Merindel was probably qualified to be a Lore Master, or at least certainly a Lore Trainer, but since Vaylene had no longer been affiliated with the Lore College in any official way, none of them had assumed the gray robes.

Merindel felt thrust into the position, but she was determined to make Vaylene and the Lore Givers proud. "We will become stronger than before," she told the others. "There are older lores that we must find if we can."

The older lores she referred to were magic, and Merindel had heard they included extremely powerful spells for combat. After all, were she and her fellow *Sohera* not also warriors? Magic could heal, but it could also be used for defense. The Lore of Magic was considered wizardry and a natural lore. The *lost* Lores of Magic, however, were deemed sorcery and *supernatural*. She had always heard they were to be feared, and that even the Lore Givers supposedly regretted sharing that knowledge with the world. But Merindel could now see that, against oppressors like this King and his men, stronger measures would be required.

"Look!" One of the other four pointed as a rider headed west in the morning light. It was almost certainly Dran sending for reinforcements.

Merindel grabbed her bow and leapt onto her horse. Behind her, the others scrambled to catch up to her as she rode down the scout.

The *Maraggan* scout looked back and saw her. He sped up. Merindel kept pace, waving her companions to speed up as well. If she could get them on his left, he might be steered up into the rougher terrain there and slowed.

The *Maraggan* turned back again, saw the *Sohera* riding him down from the left, but he kept on a straight course. He either didn't see the maneuver or he thought he could outride them. It didn't matter to Merindel; they were gaining on him.

One of the *Sohera* fired an arrow, but it missed the man, landing in the horse's haunches instead. Horse and rider went down in a rolling tumble of man, animal and terrain. The chase ended in a heap with the horse lying on top of the scout, pinning him down.

Merindel rode closer and found the horse was still alive, struggling to get to its feet. It had broken at least two legs. She could not bear the animal's torture, and fired an arrow into its heart.

Beneath the dead horse, the man was broken as well. Blood trickled from a corner of his mouth. "Please," he gasped.

Merindel drew another arrow. She fired it into his eye, and he was still.

She turned to the others. "We may not be able to attack Gethor Dran, but he will not be receiving any reinforcements from the King."

Chapter Twenty-Nine

When Param Voss was introduced to the audience, Lynari had to admit, the man was quite becoming. His lush, golden hair glinted in the light of the lanterns hung about the tavern, his carefully cut tunic the color of wheat and adorned with fine brocade work. His voice was sweet, with a slight touch of something primal. As he sang the tragic saga of Elyr, the Lore Giver of Music who was swallowed by the sea while his wife, the Lore Giver of Dance, waited for him at home, Param strummed his mandolute with great skill. The patrons were transfixed, moved by the tale and the troubadour's delivery.

His fine features intensely conveyed the emotional impact of the song. Moved herself, Lynari would not interrupt Rhinan's friend while he performed. With Rhinan and Eodorr safe in their room at the inn, Lynari allowed herself the brief moment of pleasure.

Her journey had been difficult. As a *Hegana*, it was imperative to avoid the Lydanian army or the *Maraggan*. She belonged to a secret society of the Lore College, and any encounter which resulted in her being questioned would create problems to put it mildly. Besides—and partly due to—their use of magic, a large part of the training of a *Hegana* was stealth. She had avoided soldiers while leaving Masseltaine, traveling alone and through lesser trails to reach Omriel.

The clandestine Lore Masters who supported the use of magic had been explicit: Follow the path of possibilities. By their divination, they discovered that the strongest possibilities for a renewal of magic in Lydania rested with Rhinan Ashuir. They believed he was the son of Markin Ashuir, the former Lore Master of magic and a counselor to the King prior to and during the Ylvan Uprising. As Markin himself was Ylvan, this meant Rhinan was the last of his race. The Ylvan Clans had vanished at the end of the Uprising, and their disappearance was a mystery that had never been fully resolved. Lynari herself had originally doubted Rhinan could truly be Ylvan.

But an ally of this secret cadre of Lore Masters had gotten word to them to find a specific woman in the orphanage at Omriel, and the man they sought would be delivered to them for their protection. The tip had come from the Constable in the village where Rhinan grew up, a man who believed, as did these Lore Masters, that the King was oppressive and that only magic might bring about a change for Lydania. She was sad to learn from Rhinan that this man, Keirwyn Dayas, was now dead at the hands of Gethor Dran.

Silarrah had presented a problem. The woman was stubborn, and it took all of Lynari's cunning to convince her that it was Rhinan's best hope for survival to trust Lynari. She'd had precious little time to achieve that. Her intention was not to interact with the man, but to follow him and watch over him. She was cautioned by the Lore Masters that the man himself was not aware of his Ylvan background, and it might be safer to keep it that way.

It wasn't until the *Maraggan* attacked the cabin of Brinaya Voss that Lynari had been forced to change her plan. Rhinan and his friend were outnumbered. Her considerable combat skills were required to prevent a disastrous outcome. She had succeeded in protecting Rhinan, but it had left her with no choice but to approach him and reveal what little she could. There were always things she could not tell him, but most of those had been working themselves out. This was a sure sign she was on the right path.

The next step on that path finished his performance, and the crowd roared with delight. They wanted more, but Param bowed gracefully and retrieved his azure cap now filled with coin. He tipped the contents into a pouch at his side and strode right up to Lynari.

He was tall, slender, broad-shouldered. He smiled at her, his white teeth glimmering. *Was that a dimple in his chin?* "I hope you enjoyed the performance." His blue eyes were full of mirth. *Yes, he was very charming.* Lynari made up her mind not to be taken in.

"It was lovely." She did not want to gush, so she said little. Instead, she felt her own cheeks betray her with a flush.

"As are you, *Hegana*." Param leaned in close, and he said it so quietly that she almost didn't hear him above the din of the rowdy patrons. She was shocked that he used the term, since it was not generally known, a secret to all but a select few. But then, a well-traveled troubadour might not only have heard it, but if he were astute, might even identify one. Lynari considered feigning ignorance, or denying any such affiliation, or some combination thereof. Then she recalled that the passage of time was critical and took the direct approach.

"Perhaps we might speak in private?"

"I thought you'd never ask." The troubadour grinned at her in a way that made her uncomfortable and excited all at the same time. Ignoring the feelings, she squinted at him.

"Follow me, troubadour." She led him out of the tavern, Param following without hesitation. It occurred to her that she might have the upper hand on the wandering performer. She never thought of herself as charming, and she often overlooked it when others reacted to her in this way, but this was one of those moments when she felt confident about her effect on the man. It pleased her, though she had no intention of using this allure for any recreational purpose.

Once outside, she led him toward the inn. Though the dark of night had woven itself among the buildings of the town, wound around the flickering lights cast out through windows and dimly lit lanterns hanging on posts, Lynari was able to spot a handful of the *Maraggan* entering the inn. Dran's men!

She tugged Param around a corner and into an alleyway, blocking the view of the inn. As she pulled him in, they came face-to-face in very close quarters.

"Well, this is sudden, but very nice." He proceeded to slip his arms about her waist.

"What—?!? No!" She grabbed his arm, heaved him to her side, turned him, and brought him to his knees. She held his hand behind his back, his arm twisted to prevent him from rising.

"So you're going to rob me?" Param sounded more confused than concerned.

"Hush." She chanced a glance back out of the alleyway toward the tavern and saw the *Maraggan* had entered. She hoped Rhinan and Eodorr had remained hidden in the room.

Distracted as she was, she loosened her grip on the troubadour. He twisted, rolled to his back, and brought her down to the ground with him. There was a clatter as his mandolute hit the cobblestones, but it wasn't loud enough to draw attention. They grappled for a moment, but Lynari was able to get an elbow into Param's chin. He released her and sat up, rubbing it.

"Look, I don't know what you want from me, but you won't find it easy to obtain. I haven't known the *Hegana* of the Lore College to be such low characters."

"And how many *Hegana* have you known, exactly?" She drew her quarterstaff and held it ready to strike if the need should arise. It didn't. Param remained seated in the face of her tactical fighting skills. "And how did you know I was one?"

"Well, to answer your first question." He eyed her quarterstaff. "I could see the markings on your staff, slung over your back as it was. With your dark robes and those symbols, you could have been *Hegana*, so I took the chance and used the term. You've now confirmed my suspicion."

It would not be obvious to anyone who hadn't been informed of the *Hegana's* existence, but Param said he had known one. She wondered if it was anyone she knew and what might lead a *Hegana* to reveal signs of the order to a wandering performer.

"Are you going to tell me what you want with me? And why you're so concerned with whatever's going on down at that inn?"

"Your friend, Rhinan. I am traveling in his company to keep him safe."

Param glared at her suspiciously. "How fortunate for him, but I've never heard of this man."

"Listen to me, Param Voss son of Brinaya, we do not have time to establish trust between us. I need you to hear me. Your friend is being hunted by the King's elite force, and they have just entered the inn where we have a room. If they search it, he will be taken and likely put to death. We need your help, and we need it immediately."

Hesitating but a moment, Param rose to his feet. "Tell me your name."

"I am called Lynari."

Param peered around the corner. "Rhinan is here? Why?"

"We haven't time for the whole story. We're trying to make our way east, but we need a guide. We are here looking for you."

"I know all the towns and villages from here to the Unreigned Territory, but you could find that by following the Northern Trading Path. But tell me he's not going there. It lies across the River Arinell. If you mean to keep him safe, that's no place to do it. Most do not cross the River into the Unreigned Territory unless they wish to cause death, or to meet it."

"We have no choice. Rhinan can tell you the rest. But we must get them out of that inn first."

"I will always help Rhinan in any way I can, of course," the troubadour told her. "I have since we were children." He looked at her with concern. "Are the *Maraggan* looking for you as well?"

"I don't think they've seen me." *None that yet live*, Lynari added to herself.

"Good. Come on then." Param picked up his mandolute and strode out into the open toward the inn as if he had no care in the world.

Lynari followed as they walked into the inn. There were revelers enjoying meat and drink, some gaming, but no music. Param looked around, and approached the inn keeper. Lynari slipped upstairs to check the room.

She opened the door, but Rhinan and Eodorr were gone. Their packs were still in the room, Rhinan's bow leaning against the wall, so they couldn't be far. Perhaps they'd seen the *Maraggan* enter the inn and were hiding somewhere downstairs or possibly even slipped out a back exit. She closed the door and made her way back down to the common room.

At the base of the stairs, she turned and surveyed the patrons. There were six members of the King's special force seated at one of the tables being served by the only two maids in the house. The inn keeper was nervously fussing over them, no doubt hoping to ensure that his humble inn was well-represented to those in high authority.

Param approached her. "All right, I believe you now. But he's not here," he whispered.

"If they saw the *Maraggan*, they would have slipped out." Lynari craned her neck to see beyond the moving patrons in the crowded inn, but the only exit from this room was the doorway she'd seen before which presumably led into the kitchen.

"No." Param shook his head grimly. "He and a friend were taken by soldiers. Conscripted. Off to the mines up in the Percenes."

Lynari's heart sank. If they were already prisoners… "Do the *Maraggan* know?"

"The innkeeper didn't say, but it's possible. They've asked for rooms for a few days."

Lynari couldn't decide if this was a gift or a complication.

On the one hand, it could mean that there was no more urgency to the pursuit of Rhinan and Eodorr if the *Maraggan* had found out that Rhinan and Eodorr had been conscripted. The special force may feel the outlaws were secured, and they had the luxury of waiting here in Arskellion. Dran was not among them, so there may be a few days to plan a rescue.

On the other hand, if the *Maraggan* didn't already know about the conscriptions and just planned to wait for Dran, but then found out from the local soldiers, they could dash right off up the mountains to retrieve them. Rhinan and Eodorr would have no chance to escape.

Lynari decided that, either way, they couldn't take the chance of having these *Maraggan* here.

"What friend is with him?" Param asked.

"Eodorr."

"Wen's tongue!" Param hissed, then lowered his voice. "How ever did poor Eodorr get mixed up in this?"

"He came with Rhinan when Rhinan fled Cabelon."

Param appeared to consider this. "Well, I suppose that's Eodorr for you."

Lynari shot him a stern look. "He is a staunch and loyal companion."

Param held up his hands. "I'm not saying otherwise."

Watching the *Maraggan* enjoying themselves, Lynari said, "If they do not already know, we cannot allow them to find out that Rhinan and Eodorr have been taken prisoner."

"And if they already have? It's possible they have learned of it and now are in no hurry to leave the comfort of the inn for the night. There is no urgency if Rhinan and Eodorr have already been captured."

Param had clearly arrived at the same conclusions as Lynari. But again, if this were the case, it could provide them an opportunity to plan a rescue. But the *Maraggan* would have to be dealt with. There were too many of them as it was, and this was a chance to reduce their numbers. "Good. Let them eat and drink their fill. We will see that they never follow Rhinan beyond this inn under any circumstances."

Param jerked back in astonishment. "Are you suggesting we murder a half dozen of the King's special force?"

She placed her hands on her hips. "Are you going to help me save your friend Rhinan or not? It's dangerous, yes. But if you're not going to help us, then I will have to look for someone who will."

"I've only just met you. And while I can't say I haven't foreseen a day like this would come where he's in more trouble than usual, I need confirmation before I turn myself into an outlaw. Well, a murderous outlaw, anyway. I would do it if he needs me, but how do I know you're telling me everything?"

Before she could think about it, Lynari blurted it out. "They killed your mother, Param. I'm sorry, but Brinaya is dead."

Param stiffened and his eyes lost focus. She watched as he struggled with this news. He staggered back a step. "The *Maraggan*?"

"Yes." She didn't feel it would be helpful to tell him right now that it wasn't these men, or that the ones responsible had already been paid back for the deed. "They were after Rhinan. They will stop at nothing."

Param stared at the *Maraggan*, muttering under his breath some harsh language not usually uttered by men in her presence. "So, *Hegana*, what's your plan?"

* * * * *

Param played late into the night, the other patrons of the inn having either left or retired to rooms upstairs. But he did as Lynari asked and kept the *Maraggan* engrossed, with a little help from her use of a minor enchantment. He almost didn't need it, but she could not take the chance.

However, at one point after their meal, the captain of the squad dispatched one of their number, who left the inn and rode away on horseback. Drained as she was from using her enchantments on them, she barely had enough energy to emit a curse that would cause the rider's horse to become lame. They would still have to deal with him, but she hoped it would delay him enough for them to have that opportunity.

As the remaining *Maraggan*, all very young men, became increasingly influenced by drink, Param approached her. "Are you doing what I think you're doing? Because I am good, but even I'm not *that* good. You take great risks if anyone discovers you're using magic."

"I've already taken far worse risks, and I will take more before this night is through. Besides, it's working, isn't it?" She was beginning to have doubts about this troubadour. A friend of Rhinan's he may be, but she thought he displayed a measure of cowardice. Could he be counted on?

"I suppose it is. Their attention has remained focused on me, and they've had a good amount of ale. I've even gotten a few answers out of them. Apparently, their General—Gethor Dran himself—was injured and is having to make camp about a day's ride west of here."

Lynari had to restrain a cheer of exultation. This was great news. Vaylene must have injured Dran! She hoped Vaylene had fared well in whatever confrontation that led to Dran's injury. But this was the scenario she had hoped for, and it did indeed buy them some valuable time.

The *Maraggan* had risen from the table near the hearth, staggering their direction.

"Well, looks like their night is finished." Param turned to greet them.

The squad captain, who they learned was named Flek, approached. He dropped a few coins into Param's hand. "Thank you." The drunken young soldier slurred as he spoke. "Your songs and tales have reminded me of my home. It was enshoyable." The other four followed him up the stairs to their rooms.

Lynari removed an herb from a pouch at her waist and whispered an incantation of rest as the elite soldiers passed her. The five would be sleeping soundly in no time. She led Param up the stairs behind them.

At the top of the stairs, the hallway led off to the left. They watched as Flek went into one room, and the other four split into pairs and went into two other rooms. Lynari silently cursed the inn keeper who'd told them he only had one room for them. They'd been travelling and appeared rough, so he assumed they were vagabonds. He probably wanted them out of his inn as soon as possible. Well, he was going to get his wish.

The first door on the right was their own room, now devoid of Rhinan and Eodorr. She led Param inside. His eyes went immediately to Rhinan's bow where it leaned against the wall, and he picked it up, studying it.

"I'm with you, *Hegana*. But even though they've killed my mother"—his voice choked referring to her—"they're just lads. Is there no other way?"

Lynari felt guilty having told Param about his mother's death. It was not her place. She knew Rhinan would prefer to be the one to tell his friend about what had happened. Weary from the energy required for her limited use of magic, she had no more time to spend convincing the troubadour to help her. When she spoke, she was harsher than she wanted to be.

"They would not hesitate to kill Rhinan or Eodorr or you or me, either. At the moment, they may appear to be simple young soldiers who've had too much to drink, but if they leave this inn tomorrow, it means the end of Rhinan and Eodorr. My assignment is to ensure your friend's safety no matter what it costs me. I take no pleasure in some aspects of this assignment, but I am committed to the cause I serve. I swore an oath. And I knew when I did that there would be difficult circumstances. These will not be the first young *Maraggan* I have dealt with." She reflected on the slaughter at Param's mother's cabin, and wished to explain no further. To spare his feelings if for no other reason.

As a *Hegana*, there was no telling what act your duty might call on you to perform. If you were given a task, your commitment to it would need to be absolute. In the end, your sacred responsibility was to the Lore College and the Lore Givers. Anything that endangered the Lore of Lydania was subject to whatever means necessary. Since it had been determined that Rhinan was valuable to the preservation—and restoration—of that lore, Lynari would have to protect him from these men. She knew the King was mad and yet these men served him. Therefore, their fates were sealed. This was an opportunity, one of the possibilities that lay before her. As she had told Param, she would take no pleasure in this act. An assassin now? She would carry out the executions, but wrestling with her conscience would have to wait for another time.

After a moment in which Param did not respond, she

continued. "We will have to leave this town immediately. In the morning, the *Maraggan* will be found and we cannot be here." She picked up Rhinan's and Eodorr's packs. She handed Eodorr's to Param, recalling what lay in Rhinan's pack. She would not chance it in Param's hands. "When we've finished, we'll come back here, get these, and be on our way."

"It's a shame." Param examined Eodorr's pack. "I always did well in Arskellion. But now I think I will have to bypass it for a while." She heard the sorrow and the distance in his voice, but she had no comfort to give him.

After a few moments, they slipped back out into the hall. All was silent. A couple of sconces burned low on each side of the hall, about halfway to the other end. Lynari stepped to the door of one of the pairs of elite soldiers in complete silence, Param right behind her. She positioned herself in front of the door and removed one of her daggers from its sheath. Looking over her shoulder, she saw Param doing the same thing at the door across the hallway where the other pair had entered. He looked back at her with a grim nod.

Without a sound, Lynari pried open the door in front of her. The room was very dark, but she could feel that it was larger than the one she and Rhinan and Eodorr had been given. She allowed her eyes to adjust, using a soft incantation willing them to see more in the darkness than would normally be possible. There were two beds, one *Maraggan* sleeping solidly on each.

Stepping between the beds, she lifted the first soldier's head by his long hair, drawing her dagger across his throat as he lay face down. There was no sound. He did not wake and never would.

She turned to the other soldier to find him sitting up.

Their gazes met, and the young soldier's eyes flew open wide. As he opened his mouth to release a call, Lynari moved with the speed and stealth of a wild animal. As she leapt upon him, her dagger went right into the man's mouth and down his throat. With a thrust and a twist, she prevented any cry from escaping his lips. He died in complete silence, his eyes still fixed on her.

As she slipped back out in the hall, she found Param emerging from the other room, wiping his dagger on a cloth. They locked glances, and then faced the final room: that of the squad captain, Flek.

Param positioned himself next to the door, waiting for her to open it. As she produced her dagger, her hands shook. Param reached down and put his own hands gently upon hers. He faced her with a look indicating sympathy. She felt no better about the killings, but she did feel better about counting on him to be of aid. With a deep breath, she slid her dagger in the door jam and quietly opened it.

The young squad captain lay sleeping peacefully. Lynari wondered what he might be doing under another king, in other circumstances. The silly grin he'd flashed Param in gratitude for his performance was still on the man's face.

The grin never faded when she cut his throat.

Back in her room, Lynari lifted Rhinan's pack and bow and quiver in a rush. She could hear Param behind her, grabbing Eodorr's pack and his own mandolute. She avoided facing him as tears dripped down her cheeks. This hadn't been the battle at the cabin, where several men outnumbered two men and one old woman. This had been murder, and she did not like it.

Then she felt Param's arms around her, and she began to sob quietly. He held her tight for a brief few moments, neither of them saying a word. She might have enjoyed it at another time, but now it was just something she needed. She was grateful.

At last, she regained her composure. "Let's go."

In the middle of the night, they slipped out of the inn and out of Arskellion, leaving five brave young men of the King's *Maraggan* dead in their beds. Five less on their trail, or five less to face later. Either way, Lynari had made the difficult choice of a *Hegana.* But she knew what had to be done, and she'd risen to the task regardless of the conflicted feelings it left her with.

Chapter Thirty

With the town of Arskellion behind them, the question of which direction to take arose immediately. There was enough moonlight to travel, but the cold of winter was setting in. Fortunately, Lynari had begun her journey prepared for this: She knew a spell of warmth. Param, on the other hand, had likely been expecting to be home or almost there by now, lying beside a blazing hearth enjoying his mother's cooking.

Lynari was still troubled by the extreme actions they had taken in Arskellion, and also troubled by them, Param now seemed lost in his own grief after having learned of his mother's death. Neither of them were in the best place to take charge and make a decision, but Lynari had one advantage that Param did not.

"We must travel west as quickly as we can," she urged.

Param gazed sidelong at her. "You told me your priority was to rescue Rhinan and Eodorr, and yet you want to travel west? Back the way you came? Perhaps you don't realize that they were conscripted into a mining camp that lies northward up in the mountains. I've been there. I know the way." He pointed up the slope for emphasis. "I tell you this only because it is apparently less obvious than I would have expected."

Exhausted, exasperated, and distressed, Lynari snapped at him. "And how many soldiers are in this camp? Do we have a good plan for setting Rhinan and Eodorr free, or do we just expect to walk in and politely ask the soldiers to let them go?"

Param glared at her, but said nothing.

"If we're going to rescue them, we need to make sure that Dran never finds out they're being held there. Because if he does, they're his."

"But we just saw to that, did we not?" Quietly he said this, knowing the murders were still painful to her.

"Besides the possibility of witnesses in Arskellion, perhaps you've forgotten the rider dispatched by the *Maraggan* Captain?"

"Of course I haven't! All the more reason for us to hurry up to the camp and find some way of sneaking them out of there."

"Param, if we travel west as quickly as we can, we will come to a lame horse. He will either be accompanied by one lone *Maraggan*, or he will be left standing beside the path. Or, and I hope not, he will have been put down."

A glint of understanding flashed in Param's eyes. "Now I see. You've done something to prevent the rider from reaching Dran. I keep underestimating you, and I apologize. I have a hard time trusting women who are always right."

Lynari shot him a violent look and snorted. "We should hurry. The night is half over and there's no telling how fast that scout can travel, even on foot. But the first thing we can do to help Rhinan and Eodorr at this moment is ensure that he does not reach Dran."

Param's teeth chattered in the cold. Lynari withdrew a pair of dried *jugem* berries from her pouch, spoke a couple of incantations over them, and handed one to Param. "Eat this." She ate the other one, and within moments felt the warmth of a summer day upon her body. Param paused, shrugged, and did as he was told. Lynari watched as a smile spread across his face a moment later.

"You're certainly full of surprises." He winked at her.

"Not really," she said. "I only know a lot of basic magic. You're woefully inadequate." They had stopped to argue, but now they resumed walking, westward along the path she'd taken to come into Arskellion. She heard Param's light steps behind her and grinned to herself.

They scrambled onward in the cold night, enough moonlight allowing them to step safely along the sloped pathway. For caution's sake, they remained silent. Lynari could not imagine how Param was feeling as he dealt silently with his loss. A tinge of guilt struck her as she thought about how long it had been since she'd been to see her own mother. Not since she became a *Hegana.*

She herself was finding the strength within to realize she had been left with no choice but to kill young men in their sleep. They served an oppressive tyrant, and she was sworn to many things for which this King would kill her. She, as all *Hegana*, was an outlaw. The secret association had not come to the notice of the King, or they would surely be hunted to the last member and executed for their support of magic to begin with. Whatever Rhinan had to do with all of this (beyond what she knew so far), there was even more in it for her in saving him—it was personal. For her to continue learning and training in ways she wanted to improve, she knew that somehow Rhinan would have to survive. He would have to reach safety. If he did not, there was far more at stake than just one mischievous archer from an obscure little village in the far corner of Lydania. There were many lives, and much knowledge, and much of importance to the people of Lydania that would suffer or fail without his continued existence. She was not given details about why that was, and it was a good bet that those who sent her to him knew no more about it themselves. They just knew that he represented more than great importance; he was perhaps a last hope.

When she heard a noise ahead, she reached a hand back to stop Param. He'd already stilled, which she took as an indication that he, too, had heard it. It was the sound of a horse coughing. This pleased her. Obviously, the *Maraggan* had not seen fit to put the animal down. The slight injury she'd inflicted would easily be healed, so she knew the horse had a good chance of survival.

The problem, of course, was the *Maraggan*. Was he with the horse? What level of alert was he on? If he were sleeping, this would be easy. If he were awake, it would be complicated. Worst of all, if he'd left the horse and continued onward, could they catch him before he reached Dran?

Lynari turned to Param, withdrawing Rhinan's sheathed sword from his pack and handing it to the troubadour. She then waved a hand to indicate that he should move off the path. She wanted him less visible as he waited for her to survey the situation. He gave her an angry look and shook his head in protest. In response, she cocked her head and dropped her shoulders, returning the frown. Param briefly covered his face with his hands, then looked into her eyes with intention. He drew the blade slowly, quietly, indicating that he would be waiting with it ready to fight should the need arise. She nodded in understanding and waved him to the side of the path again.

Creeping forward, Lynari realized that dawn was

approaching, and the light of day was just beginning to spread the slightest glow across the sky. This was not in her favor. Furthermore, not just lack of sleep and walking all night, but exhaustion from the energy spent on her little spells was catching up with her. She was not at her best. This was one soldier. If it came to it, she counted on holding him off until Param could reach her and assist in dispatching him. If not, this would be the end of her journey.

She drew a deep breath, withdrew her quarterstaff from its sling across her back, and crept up into the tree line, moving westward in order to come down toward the path where the horse sounds were coming from.

When she caught sight of the horse, he was tethered to a tree. No soldier lay nearby in makeshift bedding for sleep. None stood guard. This was the worst case scenario. He'd continued onward, and she had no way of gauging how far he might be ahead of them. She slipped down to the horse, which remained calm as she soothed him and uttered an incantation that removed the pain she'd put in his leg. She asked his forgiveness. The horse seemed to enjoy her stroking, so she took that as being forgiven.

"He doesn't look lame to me."

She turned on Param. He stood with Rhinan's sword in hand, surveying the woods on either side of the path.

"You were supposed to wait."

"I don't always do what I'm supposed to do."

Without a comment, Lynari leapt onto the horse.

Param sighed. "I'm going to guess you plan to continue westward, riding down this *Maraggan* in the hope of reaching him before he gets to Dran."

"Well, it seems you're capable of learning," she teased. Lynari grinned and held out a hand. "This fellow will support us both." She patted the horse. "One soldier on foot should be easier to catch on horseback, even with two riders." She eyed him up and down. "I'm pretty light, and you're slender. I think we'll make good time."

Param grinned, leaping onto the horse behind Lynari. "It will be full daylight any minute. You do realize the risk we face if he does, in fact, reach Dran before we reach him?"

"You gamble in your travels, do you not?"

"Oh, extensively."

"Well, I don't." She spurred the horse forward. "I'm hoping you can think of an alternative for us should that be the case."

She heard another sigh from Param, this one heavier and deeper than the last.

Chapter Thirty-One

"We'll get out of this, Eodorr. Eodorr…" It was no use. Rhinan's friend would not look at him or speak to him.

Bound and marched for several hours up deep into the mountains by a dozen or more Lydanian soldiers, they were deposited into a large encampment of other prisoners conscripted for mining by the army. There were at least a dozen more soldiers guarding the workers already at the camp. It was late and cold and dark, but Rhinan counted about as many workers as there were soldiers. The soldiers, however, were heavily armed and the miners looked weary and hopeless. Their eyes were unfocused, their backs hunched and their bones protruding. All of them were shackled at the wrists by chains . Though apparently allowed to rest for the night, these poor men were being worked to death. More of King Jerrick's idea of "justice."

The campsite itself was set on a flat expanse, dotted by a few trees not yet cut down for use in the mine. There were plenty of trees surrounding the area, so lumber was plentiful. Directly into the side of the mountain was an opening no taller than Rhinan. It was pitch black inside. To the right of the mine entrance and down the slope was a heap of rock and dirt that had been carried out of the mine and discarded.

One of the soldiers from the camp approached them when they arrived. He tossed each of them a bundle of furs. "It's cold at night. I suggest you wrap up and stay close to one of the fires. Get as much rest as you can. At sunrise, you go in. Have either of you been in a mine before?"

Both Rhinan and Eodorr shook their heads.

"You'll be fine. It's not hard to shovel, swing a pick or a hammer, or haul out piles of ore. The other men will see to it that you keep pace." He snickered and walked away. Rhinan had the feeling he was being put on, and it was obvious Eodorr felt the same when he rolled his eyes.

Several of the guards paced the camp throughout the night, taking shifts keeping an eye on the sleeping prisoners. Rhinan didn't think any of these prisoners had any fight in them and probably could not get far on the run. Unable to sleep, he tried to speak to Eodorr again. Not only did Eodorr continue to ignore him, but he got the boot of a guard in his sore ribs and was told to shut up. Resolved to wait for morning, he wracked his brain for ideas of escape. Probably some of these men had tried when they first arrived, so he would question them if he got the chance. If he found out what didn't work, it might help him come up with something that would. He also tried to wriggle loose from his binding, but to no avail.

* * * * *

Another soldier's boot found his ribs in the morning. Rhinan was surprised that he had drifted off to sleep given the discomfort of his situation. The sun was up, and the miners were already devouring whatever slop the soldiers were serving them for breakfast. It smelled terrible, but Rhinan was sure that eating would be better than not.

He looked for Eodorr, but his companion was sitting among the miners, tipping a bowl of the slop into his mouth. His hands were now shackled in front of him just as the rest of the miners.

"Are we a princess?" The soldier who had kicked him awake unbound his hands from behind him, brought them around front, and clamped them into the chained shackles. There was just enough play in the chain to allow Rhinan to move his hands around, presumably for mine work, but for little else. "You might want to get over there and eat. You're going to need your strength if you're going to last." The soldier handed him a wooden bowl.

Rhinan rose and stalked over to the cauldron that was planted on the central fire in the campsite. One of the miners, a very large fellow who looked less starved than the others, scooped his bowl deep into the cauldron, withdrawing the last of the gruel that it contained. He'd obviously had at least a portion before that. He noticed Rhinan glowering at him and chuckled, shaking his head as he walked away. He sat among a group of miners, and they began to speak and laugh, casting glances at Rhinan.

"Here." Eodorr held out a chunk of crusty bread to him. "There wasn't much, and it was gone before the gruel was ready, but I saved you a bit."

His mouth hanging open, Rhinan took the bread from Eodorr. "Thank you." As Eodorr walked away, Rhinan brushed dirty bits and bugs off and out of the bread and ate what he could of it.

"Fall in!" One of soldiers shouted, and the miners stood

and lined up at the mine entrance. A handful of soldiers unlocked and opened a large, wooden chest. As each miner approached, he was handed a tool from the chest: picks, hammers, shovels, and buckets. "Dig deep," the soldier warned. "Your King needs silver."

Near the end of the line, Rhinan was handed a shovel. Behind him, he saw Eodorr and another miner each receive a bucket and a torch, which meant they would be making hard trips out of the mine carrying heavy loads. There were no good jobs, but Rhinan did not envy Eodorr.

The first two miners into the hole were handed lit torches, and spares for later were handed to the men behind them. As Rhinan entered the darkness, he could make out the two flames ahead. All of the miners followed closely, unwilling to lose sight of the scarce bit of illumination they would be provided. The last two men, of which Eodorr was one, carried torches which would presumably be lit only when ascending out of the mine with full buckets.

As they descended, the shaft sloped downward and into the mountain. At the entrance, Rhinan could stand up straight but, gradually, he was hunching over to avoid hitting his head on the top of the tunnel. Periodically, they passed thick support beams cut from the wood of the surrounding trees. At other times, they passed additional shafts leading off to either side.

Rhinan had found and explored caves not far from Cabelon upon occasion. He never enjoyed it. He couldn't shake the uneasy feeling that he got from being underground. The dead were underground, and he imagined that he felt the stillness of death when deep in such places.

At last the sound of thumps ahead indicated that the miners had reached the point of the mine they were working.

At that point, the tunnel opened out into a wide circle. Picks and hammers swung with what force the weakened men could muster, shovels bit into earth, and little crumbles of rock and dirt slid to the floor of the tunnel. Eodorr and the other man with a bucket began to scoop up the debris and, once their buckets were full, the other man lit the two spare torches and led Eodorr back out of the mine. Two lit torches and the spares remained with the diggers.

"You ever use one of those?" It was the big man who'd finished the gruel. He leaned on a pick in the shadowy tunnel, eyeing Rhinan and the shovel in his hands. Stooped though he was, the man was clearly a head and shoulders taller than Rhinan.

"I can't say that I have." Rhinan wasn't sure if these rough men, though weakened, might attack him. He tried to step back from the man, but met with the side of the tunnel.

The man chuckled again. "I'm Brondur of Dowham." He held out a huge hand which Rhinan reluctantly shook. The grip was strong enough to crush his own hand had Brondur wanted to.

"Rhinan." He didn't feel the need to point out he was from Cabelon or use his last name. He could ill afford any chance the soldiers might learn who he was. If they knew the King was looking for him, he was finished. And whether or not any of the miners could be trusted remained to be seen.

Though his long, straight hair was pure white, the big man looked perhaps only ten years older than Rhinan, still young. His face was all sharp angles, but he was not an ugly brute. There was kindness in his eyes. "Come on," the big man said. "Let's get you started."

He led Rhinan past the other miners as they worked the sides of the open space. "I'm a forester by trade," Brondur explained. "Or I was, until the Lydanian army found me drunk in Arskellion and conscripted me though I had done nothing wrong. I've been a miner for about a year now. Haven't seen my family since. They probably think me dead by now."

"You have a family? And yet they imprison you here and force you to mine, though you broke no laws?" Rhinan could not believe this was happening in Lydania. Param would bring home tales of King Jerrick's oppression, but he'd never mentioned anything like this. Or, perhaps, Rhinan had avoided listening.

"And they took my axe."

The mention of Brondur's axe called to Rhinan's mind his own sword and the *Pyvadis*, left in his pack in his room at the inn. Would Lynari retrieve it, or would that foul innkeeper take it? The thought would gnaw at him now.

A small miner, no taller than Rhinan's midriff, was swinging a hammer into a large boulder in the wall at the furthest end of the tunnel. His powerful blows shattered bits of rock away as the other miners kept their distance.

"Come meet Wogen." Brondur led Rhinan to the diminutive worker. "Wogen! Take a break."

Wogen turned around, the big hammer resting on his shoulder. His bearded face was crowned with a bald head. A round nose and pointed ears told Rhinan this was no ordinary little man. And even in the dim torchlight, the stone-gray pallor of his skin was visible. "New grinder, huh?" His voice rumbled like a rockslide.

"Rhinan, meet Wogen the rock gnome." Brondur waved a big hand at Wogen.

"You're a Rock Walker!" Rhinan had heard of them, but he had never believed they existed. And here he was, being introduced to one.

The gnome smiled bitterly. "I was." He held out his shackled hands, but the cuffs and chain looked very different from what everyone else was wearing. Only slightly thicker, but of a lighter-colored metal and etched with symbols. "If it weren't for this blasted piece of magical claptrap, I'd rock walk right out of here."

Rhinan observed the manacles carefully. "Why not use that hammer or a pick and smash them off?"

"Oh, of course we've tried." Brondur wagged his own pick. "Nothing short of magic will shatter them. If we could do that, Wogen would lead us all out of here."

"And I would, too." The gnome scoffed. "The King's mines be damned."

"Magic is outlawed by the King, but his soldiers imprison you with it?" Rhinan was incredulous. His ire at King Jerrick reached a new depth, the hypocrisy lending itself to his further disrespect of royal authority.

"We doubt the King even knows." Brondur stepped back, allowing Wogen to continue his work. "Even without being able to use his ability to rock walk, Wogen is a powerful miner. They would hate to lose his labor, so they likely don't tell the King they've used some magical artifact to imprison a rock gnome."

Brondur showed Rhinan a vein of silver in the side of the tunnel where they'd been extracting a good amount of ore. "It's mostly played out," the big man explained. "Wogen is delving further in hopes of finding more. The soldiers are kinder when we have something to show for a day's work down here."

Rhinan recalled the side tunnels he'd seen as they came down. "Is that what those other passage ways are? Veins you followed until they played out?"

"Mostly." Brondur lowered his voice. "Some of them we sealed to prevent the Eyeless Ones from taking us." His words quavered and he swallowed, casting a glance back up the tunnel.

"Eyeless Ones?" This was something Rhinan had never heard of. Whatever they were, it made Rhinan uncomfortable to see that the big man was concerned about them.

"If you are fortunate, you will never see one. The demons dwell within the mountain. They do not suffer our intrusions peacefully."

Rhinan spent his day digging around the vein of ore and shoveling the discarded material into the buckets. Eodorr and the other man made several trips to the surface to empty the buckets, then eventually switched off with other miners. The only upside of being a bucketman is that you spent some time topside, examining and sorting the rocks you brought out for silver. Everyone continued work until at last a pair of miners returned with the buckets and told them the day was over. They all returned to the surface to find that night had fallen.

Another meal waited for them in the cauldron. It was terrible, lumpy stew, but Rhinan was too hungry to care. He'd been of little use in the mine, though his wounds from the needlebeast attack were almost fully healed thanks to Vaylene. The scars on his hands from the needlebeast's quills were vanishing, but he'd developed blisters in their place. The other men were patient with him as a new addition to the crew, but Rhinan suspected that wouldn't last long. They would probably turn on him if he did not perform his fair share of the workload. Maybe they would feed him to the Eyeless Ones, whatever they were.

Under the watchful soldiers, the men sat around eating and saying little. He sat beside Eodorr, hoping to repair the friendship they'd lost in their youth but rekindled on this journey. As he sat, he noticed that Brondur and Wogen seemed to stick together, the largest and the smallest of all the men there.

"It's all right, Rhinan." Eodorr stared into one of the camp fires. "You didn't ask for any of this. I blamed you when they took us, but I was wrong."

"I was foolish to leave the room at the inn." Rhinan felt he needed Eodorr's forgiveness.

"Well, yes," Eodorr agreed. "But then, it's more than that, isn't it? This is terrible. You, hunted merely for your bloodline. These men, imprisoned for no other reason than the King's greed. Don't you see? I was part of this. I served Keirwyn in an official capacity. We *served* the King. This is what our service was in support of." He seemed as lost as Rhinan felt.

"No, Eodorr. Keirwyn had a good heart. You have a good heart… a little naïve, perhaps, but neither of you knew—"

"We *should* have!" Eodorr snapped, and a couple of the soldiers took notice. He kept silent until they looked away. "It was easy in Cabelon. *You* were our worst problem. Had we ventured out, seen how bad Lydania has become under Jerrick's rule…"

"It would have done no good. And dwelling on it does no good at this moment. Right now, we have to get out of here. Dran won't be far unless Vaylene defeated him, and neither of us thinks that's true, do we?"

Eodorr shook his head.

"So let's work on a plan." Rhinan pointed his chin at Brondur and Wogen. "I think we're going to need those two to help us."

Soldiers called out from beyond the firelight. There was a familiar roar, a scream, and all of the soldiers drew in closer to the fires, their eyes searching the dark forest. All of the shackled miners were alarmed, and one of them called out "What is it?"

"Wild beardog, I think," one of the soldiers answered. "Though odd to be this far east. Nothing to worry over. He won't come too close to our fires. If he does, we'll skin him." Several of the soldiers had bows drawn, prepared to fire at anything that crept into the light.

Rhinan made to stand up, but Eodorr restrained him with a hand on his arm. "If it's Rip, he's smart enough not to wander into the firelight."

This was true. Rhinan couldn't help hoping that it was, in fact, Rip out there. What the soldier had said was true: beardogs were increasingly rare, especially this far east. The beardog could have followed their trail to Arskellion, even picked it up and followed them here.

And the big beast would be another useful ally when they made their escape.

Chapter Thirty-Two

The light of dawn had not yet broken when, as Dran had dispatched south to farmlands to look for mounts, Captain Kilward and his aide returned with ten fine horses. The rest of the men were already up making preparations for the day, so Dran heard their cheers before he emerged from the little shelter to see what the fuss was about.

When he saw the new horses, Dran felt for the first time in days like things were beginning to go his way again. It had been a rough journey up from Masseltaine, and he'd lost good men. He had hope for reinforcements from Jerrick, having dispatched a scout, and he also expected word from Flek early this morning, whom he'd sent to scout Arskellion for the Ylvan.

Gaimesh had seen to his injured leg and, though wobbly, Dran could limp about with the help of a sturdy staff one of the men had carved for him. He might even be able to ride within a day.

It was a cold morning, but a warm fire roared in the center of the camp and food was being prepared. The sun would be up soon and the men could spend this day repairing and improving their weapons, armor, and tack damaged in the battle with Vaylene.

Dran had a good feeling, and the men were all in good spirits. A hot breakfast of meats, bread, and fruit energized them, and soon everyone was hard at work. At the urging of Gaimesh, Dran returned to the little shelter to rest his injured leg.

By this time, the sun was up, but it did not bring much warmth this late in the year. In fact, dark clouds gathered and it was the only thing that could lower Dran's spirits. More rain meant more mud, and more mud meant slower travel. He sat in the entranceway of the little covered safe spot and looked out at his men.

Taking quick stock of the camp, Dran's party now consisted of fourteen men, now with a complement of sixteen horses. Plus six more men and horses in Arskellion. If these clouds didn't unleash too much rain, they would leave as soon as he was able and make up a lot of time. Unless, of course, there was more magic in this storm, as he suspected of the storm they'd experienced outside Cabelon. He was still concerned about facing magic at the hands of the Ylvan outlaw, but even that could not bring his spirits low this morning. It would take something highly unexpected and unpleasant to change Dran's mood this day. He determined this would not happen. He would simply not allow it.

As the men completed their breakfasts and began their daily training, preparing to work on their equipment after the standard regimen, Dran was impressed with their vigor and enthusiasm. These men were the best of the best, hand-picked by him from the Lydanian army. Few men had the honor of saying they served in the *Maraggan.* These men took pride in their positions. Dran worked them hard, but he treated them fairly. Not every soldier in the army deserved that. In fact, in Dran's opinion, very few did.

It was shortly after sunrise when the first unexpected thing of the day occurred. Venelwin, one of the men who'd accompanied Flek to Arskellion, staggered into camp. He was exhausted, on foot, and obviously hadn't slept. Venelwin reported that his horse had become lame, and—being one of the swiftest of the *Maraggan*—he was able to continue at a rapid pace on foot to deliver Flek's report.

What Flek had learned was just the thing to make Dran's day even better. Two strange men had been picked up by the local soldiers and conscripted into working the King's mines up in the mountains north of town. There had been no reports of their escape, so it was assumed the two men remained in captivity. One of the men even matched what description they had gotten from Baron Mundon's steward. It had to be the Ylvan and his companion!

Dran was so delighted by the news that he urged Venelwin to take first choice of the new horses. Honored, Venelwin examined the horses and made a choice, then asked if there was perhaps something he could eat, for he was famished. Then, if possible, he hoped there was a stream nearby where he could bathe and refresh himself after his long night. Dran was happy to oblige, and even sent him to get some sleep rather than assign him any duties for the day. After all, the man had traveled all night. He would need his strength.

The next unexpected thing happened shortly thereafter. As Venelwin finished his meal, an odd young woman and a troubadour walked into camp leading Venelwin's lame horse. Except the horse wasn't lame at all.

This was when Dran's outlook for the day changed from

good to questionable. Aside from an innocent and honest mistake, which Dran did not at all expect was the case, several possibilities occurred to him, and he knew he would have to find an answer for each one in order to be satisfied. But his suspicions were aroused, and that was never a good thing. Dran didn't trust much, but he trusted his suspicions.

The first thing that seemed possible was that this pair weren't just wandering performers, but that they were also thieves. Perhaps they even used their performing talents to distract unwitting audiences while they robbed them. Dran had heard of such things, and it wasn't uncommon. That also meant that they may have had something to do with Venelwin's horse becoming lame so they could steal it, and possibly rob him. They may have even smelled the opportunity for more loot and followed him here, not realizing they were walking into a dozen men of the King's special force, the most highly trained men in Lydania.

Another possibility was that they were allies of Vaylene, here to seek vengeance and assassinate Dran himself. The young woman did not appear to be one of Vaylene's cohorts, but there was something highly unusual about her. They could be associated with Vaylene, which meant…

They could be associated with the Ylvan himself. However, as the Ylvan was captured and held in a camp in the other direction, it didn't seem as likely for them to be traveling this way.

As the pair stopped at the edge of the camp, Dran approached them, leaning on his staff. He studied them carefully before anyone spoke, but it was Venelwin who leapt up and approached them.

"Troubadour! I recall you from last night!" Venelwin turned to Dran and the others and continued. "This troubadour is among the best I've ever heard. He played for us as we ate, before Captain Flek sent me back here. I tell you, he is a musician of unequaled talent."

Dran flashed the pair a tight grin, Venelwin's testimony having done nothing to dissuade his suspicions. "Is that so? Would we have heard of you? Certainly a troubadour of such talent would have a reputation. We are not untraveled. May I inquire your name?"

There was the slightest hesitation before the troubadour responded. Most people wouldn't have even noticed, but Dran caught it. "Param," the troubadour replied, bowing without dismounting the horse. "They call me Param of the Northern Path."

"Ah." Dran eyed him closer. The man didn't look familiar. "Well, Param of the Northern Path, who is your lovely assistant? Does she sing? Does she play?"

"She, uh, she dances, actually."

Dran wasn't sure, but he thought this caught the troubadour something like a sharp nudge or a pinch from her judging by the brief but pained expression that crossed his features. Further, Dran thought the look she gave him might drive a steel spike through a man's skull. There was definitely *something* going on here. It could be as simple as a lover's quarrel, but that wasn't the impression he got. Dran wished he wasn't busy pursuing the Ylvan, because he had the most delightful feeling that this would be fun to investigate. In fact, he began the fun almost immediately.

"Well, as the two of you may or may not know, we are the *Maraggan*. A special force reporting directly to King Jerrick, sent only on the most important assignments. In fact," and here Dran lowered his voice and looked around conspiratorially, putting on an act, "we are in pursuit of two criminals right now. You wouldn't have encountered a young hunter and his companion from an obscure far northwestern village, would you?"

The young woman, who had yet to speak, shook her head. Param replied. "No, My Lord, not at all. We've been far to the east, in fact, and are only now traveling back west for the winter."

"I see." Dran paced closer to them. "May I ask you another question?"

The troubadour laughed nervously. "Why, as you are the King's own forces, it would seem you can ask us any question you wish."

Dran laughed loudly with exaggeration, and after a brief delay, the troubadour joined him. The young woman remained expressionless and silent.

Immediately from the laughter, Dran's face turned serious and grim. "My question should be easy to answer. How did you come to be in possession of one of our royal horses?"

The troubadour appeared shocked, and it was very good. Dran couldn't tell if it was sincere or not. "Why, this lovely horse? We just found him back up the trail a short distance. We were afoot—it hasn't been a profitable season, you see—and he appeared lame at first. Upon closer inspection, there was a sharp rock lodged in his rear hoof. We removed it and he was as good as new. Please consider him returned with our apologies." The troubadour bowed and handed the reins to Dran.

The troubadour spoke with such sincerity that it gave Dran pause, and he turned to Venelwin with a look of admonishment. If Venelwin had foolishly abandoned a horse without thoroughly examining it… but then again, he had been in a tavern before his return trip, so it was possible he had perhaps drunk too much. This was not an acceptable excuse by any means, but it could be a believable explanation. Venelwin cringed under Dran's withering gaze. "I checked, My Lord, but I found nothing." He appeared completely perplexed.

The troubadour took a long look at Venelwin. "Why, yes! I do believe I remember you and your friends. Good lads! Is this your horse?"

Now Dran was uncertain there was anything untoward about the pair, but he still wanted to know more. And he knew exactly how to find out.

"Well, thank you for returning our property," he addressed the troubadour, handing the reins to Venelwin to lead the horse away. "No doubt you would have brought it right to us had you realized it was royal property, am I right? Of course I am. But I have a proposition for you. We've been on the road for days. My men would benefit greatly from a performance this evening. Some songs, a little bit of dancing… You'll stay with us today, and we'll see that you're well fed. In payment for your performance this evening, we'll make a gift of this horse to you. It just so happens that we find ourselves momentarily in possession of a couple of extra. We can spare one for a performance by a troubadour of your reputation. What say you?"

"We'd be honored and delighted." It was the woman who spoke and accepted the invitation. The fact that she was the one to accept, and that she spoke at all, shocked Dran, and that was hard to do.

Reading the meanings of facial expressions was something he'd become good at over the years. It was abundantly clear that the young woman wanted nothing to do with them which, of course, only aroused his suspicions even further. Param, however, was much better at feigning enthusiasm. "That's what we do. Thank you for the generosity and the opportunity to improve our reputation."

Still perplexed about the pair, Dran kept up the act. "Wonderful! Please help yourselves to something to eat." He pointed them to the fire in the center of the camp. "And stay warm. I'm sure too much chill is bad for both a troubadour's voice and a dancer's limbs."

"You've been more than kind, My Lord." Param turned and strode toward the fire, the woman immediately behind him, both carrying full packs. But something else drew Dran's attention, strengthening his suspicions about the pair.

The woman had a fighting quarterstaff strapped onto her back. It was subtly carved with special markings that Dran could not read and wasn't sure if he'd ever even seen. They reminded him of something, but he couldn't be sure what. Magic symbols, perhaps? Not a prohibited weapon under the King's law, something about this woman's staff caused him concern. And the pair had traveled at night? Something was wrong here. Possibly very wrong. He would find out before he allowed this couple to depart their company. *If* he allowed this couple to depart their company.

Chapter Thirty-Three

They were devastated to learn the messenger had reached the encampment before they were able to catch up to him. Unfortunately, they had no idea whether the message he was delivering mentioned the capture of two men in Arskellion or not. Dran had asked about them, but it didn't preclude that he knew of their capture.

"We have to find out what news that messenger is delivering." Lynari stared at the camp from off the path, among the trees where they'd hidden for the moment. "I'm not sure what we can do to delay them or help Rhinan, no matter what his message is, so we may have to improvise."

"I'm 'the gambler' as you said, aren't I?" Param looked at her grimly. "I have a thought that just may work." He looked back at the horse. "We walk the horse we 'found' right into their camp, a simple troubadour and his assistant heading west for the winter. We return the horse when they recognize it, claim we removed a stone from its hoof, and see what we can learn about their plans."

Lynari considered this. Given that Param was, in fact, a troubadour, this didn't seem unbelievable. It was being in possession of the horse that concerned her. "Maybe we should just set the horse free?"

"I think returning their horse could endear us to them, perhaps get them to look more favorably upon us."

"I hope you're right. If Dran thinks we meant to keep that horse, he'll hang us."

* * * * *

After entering the camp and conversing with Dran, when they were sure they were out of earshot of Dran's men, Param said, "I wanted to cut his head off. It didn't show, did it? I gave it my best performance."

He was still wearing his fake smile too tight, Lynari thought. Dran was suspicious, she could tell. But Param had done a good job. "You couldn't have done any better," she reassured him. "Except the dancer part. Param, I'm no dancer."

"Well, you said we may have to improvise."

The men were all busy, so they had the fire to themselves to warm up.

"You can't improvise a skill like that, you idiot."

"You wanted me to make the plan. You agreed to it. Here we are, alive. I hardly think calling me an idiot is a proper show of gratitude."

Lynari glared at him a moment, then looked around to make sure there were still none of the elite soldiers nearby before answering. "The original plan was to prevent that *Maraggan* from reaching Dran and possibly telling him that Rhinan and Eodorr were in captivity. Not for me to become a dancer."

"Yet we didn't catch up to him before he got here,

remember? Your lame horse was slower to recover than you expected. That's the part where the plan had to change. A good plan has to be flexible, and it has to change as circumstances change. The circumstances changed, so the plan changed."

Lynari felt the sting of Param's words. She had to take some responsibility for this. Her spell to make the horse lame faded slower than she would have expected. The *Maraggan* had reached the encampment before they could catch him. He was impressive in his dedication and swiftness, that one. She'd have to acknowledge that. "Well, do you mind telling me the plan now? We need to find out what they know. We certainly can't hurry off to the mining camp now and find a way to free Rhinan and Eodorr."

Param reached out and pulled a strip of meat off a spit that dangled over the fire. Popping it into his mouth, he mumbled, "You said there would be too many soldiers guarding the mining camp for us to help Rhinan and Eodorr. Our next best way to help them is to delay Dran's arrival to take them. Is it not? And here we are, with Dran lame and us holding them up for the day so we can perform this evening. We've given Rhinan at least a day to work on his own escape plan and, if I know my friend, I can assure you he is doing just that."

Reaching for a strip of meat herself, Lynari had to acknowledge that Param was right. They could be creating a delay, or at the very least contributing to a delay, that would allow Rhinan more time. But then something occurred to her, and she punched Param in the arm as hard as she could get away with and not draw attention to them. This was relatively easy, as the men around camp all seemed very preoccupied with various tasks.

"What was *that* for?" Param looked wounded more than physically.

"Because somehow, between now and tonight, I'm going to have to learn to be an adequate dancer to whatever music you choose to play."

Param actually laughed out loud at this. "I am sorry. I have a plan for that as well. You see all these men practicing around the camp? Well, why wouldn't we do the same? We'll go off to the side, I'll play a little on my mandolute, and you can practice some moves very slowly until you have some adequate moves."

Lynari didn't feel good about this, but it was their best option. "I can move, Param. With grace and speed. You've seen that now. But it's all combat moves. Performance dancing? That's nothing I have any experience with."

Param leaned away from her and eyed her up and down. "Well, for one thing, these men have been on the road for a while if what Dran says is true. I don't mean any disrespect, but the quality of your dancing isn't going to be the first thing they notice. But—" he interjected before she punched him again, "you'd be surprised how similar combat moves and dancing really are. We'll practice, and I'll help. You'll be doing well enough to distract them by this evening."

Considering this, Lynari could see the logic in it. She was about to accept when Param opened his mouth further.

"It's just a shame we don't have a more revealing outfit for you to wear during the performance."

This time, the punch nearly left his arm too lame to perform later. It caught the attention of a couple of the men working nearby, who chuckled and returned to their duties.

Thinking for another moment before they set off to "practice," Lynari considered another problem. "So we entertain them this evening. What happens after that? It will look suspicious if we try to leave or sneak out at night, especially heading back east when we're supposedly heading west."

Param paused before answering. "We spend the night here." He gritted his teeth. "I suppose it's too much to hope we can take them all in their sleep the way we did in Arskellion?"

"I can enhance their drowsiness, but they'll likely have a watchman, and yes, there are too many for the two of us."

"Alright. So we spend the night. In the morning, they head east toward Arskellion or the mining camp to pick up Rhinan and Eodorr. They'll think we're simply heading to the west, but we slip off the path and among the trees and follow them, carefully. If they head into Arskellion, we head up to the mining camp and be prepared to help Rhinan when they inevitably get there. If they head straight for the mining camp, we follow and help Rhinan and Eodorr escape if they haven't already by then. It all depends on what the men in Arskellion learned. We'll still be quite outnumbered, but the chances improve."

Lynari shook her head. "You're not really much of a planner, are you?"

Param snorted. "I've gotten us this far, haven't I? And we're still alive, aren't we? Give me time."

Lynari looked around the camp at the able-bodied *Maraggan*. She saw Dran poke his head out of the small shelter he appeared to be resting in, taking a good look at the two of them.

"Time is a deceptive creature; it always appears larger than it really is. I'll grant that you are a skilled performer, Param, but Dran isn't believing it. Not even a little bit."

* * * * *

Param gently strummed his mandolute, instructing Lynari to step lightly here, sway gently there. She was surprised to find that she was more graceful than she would have expected. Param had been right—much of her combat training helped significantly with dancing. She still found herself stumbling at times, which infuriated her and she sent hard, sharp looks at Param when this happened, after which he would demand considerably simpler moves of her for the next few steps.

Fortunately, Dran's men were disciplined enough that they remained focused on their duties, and, therefore, did not observe the instruction from Param, nor notice exactly how inexperienced she was. And Dran himself had disappeared into the little shelter, seemingly recuperating from a leg injury Lynari credited to Vaylene's work. Param promised that if she could learn just a few specific moves, she would be able to swap them around and use them through the music he would play, and the men wouldn't notice when she performed. Not only that, as he kept reminding her, the men weren't much likely to care how varied her dancing was. But a certain amount of grace and flow would be expected, and she would have to achieve that in order to refrain from arousing suspicion that she was more than the dancing companion of a wandering troubadour.

When time for the midday meal came, Lynari and Param were able to beg their absence and enjoy it separately from the men so they could "prepare the evening's program." Granted this by Dran, they were able to speak privately while eating.

"Param…" Lynari hesitated, but Rhinan's friend needed to know something critical about their current predicament.

"I'm listening." Param turned toward her, ripping bread and handing her a chunk.

"I need you to understand something very, very important." Her voice became hushed, and she looked around to ensure they were, indeed, alone. "The existence of the *Hegana* must not be exposed to the King or any of his representatives. Not under *any* circumstance. Do you understand what I'm telling you?"

Param stared her in the eye for a moment, but she sensed he was far away. When he spoke, it was as if he had memorized something long ago and only now repeated it. "You must not be captured. You must not be questioned. There are more lives at stake and more consequences than any single mission would incur. As a friend or companion, even I must be willing to do what is necessary to prevent them from learning about the *Hegana.* I must be willing to take your life before they can gain any information from you. I must be willing to sacrifice my own life as you are willing to sacrifice your own. This is the pledge of being the trusted companion of a *Hegana.*" His focus then seemed to return to her. "Does that about cover it?"

Lynari stared at him, her jaw hung open. He was precisely correct, and had conveyed a perfect understanding of the importance of the situation with an oath sworn by those heartily trusted by a *Hegana.* Lynari would risk her life for whatever potential Rhinan's existence promised, but if it came to it, her life would be sacrificed on behalf of protecting the secret order of the *Hegana* before anything else. If for any reason she was unable to do this herself, Param would have to find a way, even if it meant sacrificing his own life. It was more than a huge responsibility, and it had to be clear to her that he was capable of taking the actions necessary should the situation come to that.

"That is what I meant, yes. How do you know all of this?"

"You recall when we met I recognized you as *Hegana*." There was sorrow in Param's eyes, his voice. "Do you think I would be alive if I knew of the order and there were any chance I would expose its existence? Do you think I would know what it means and what I have committed myself to by joining you, if I had not been… close… to a *Hegana* before?"

Lynari realized what he was saying. "You loved a *Hegana*. You were in this situation, and you lost. Dare I ask… was it by your hand?"

"No." Param's quick response was followed with a shake of his head. "No, and that is perhaps what tortures me. Had it been my hand, perhaps it would have been better than him having to do it himself. I tell myself I wasn't able, I had no choice, I was too far at the moment, but it brings me no comfort. Honnarvo deserved a better ending, but he was true to his vows, both to me and to the order." Param's eyes were wet when he finished speaking.

Lynari had heard of Honnarvo, and the legend of his self-sacrifice when captured near Masseltaine. It was truly rare, and few were those who had been forced into that choice. None had ever failed. In her mind, she questioned whether or not she could do it, feared dreadfully that she would fail. But here was Param, who wasn't sure if he could have done it, but regretted not being able to do it for someone he had been close to, had clearly loved very much. *Hegana* were not forbidden to have intimate relationships, yet she had never heard of Honnarvo's relationship with a troubadour. There was some surprise that Param had been romantically involved with a man, given his initial approach to her. She had to ask.

"Param, thank you for sharing that with me. I can't imagine being on the other side of this situation, only that it must feel like an impossible choice. But I can count on you?"

"Yes, *Hegana.* If there is the necessity, and any way, I will not fail you."

She believed him. With that out of the way, she pressed the issue about Honnarvo. "I have heard of Honnarvo. He is highly regarded. You were in a relationship?"

"For some time."

"I would have expected—"

Param cut her off. "You see me as I want the world to see me. As a woman-chasing troubadour. I love women. But I also love men, prefer them in many cases. I love beauty where I find it, inside or out. Please do not judge me as I have just pledged my life to you."

Lynari laughed, and Param appeared irritated. "This is funny how?"

"Because," Lynari managed to get out when she could catch her breath, "you and I are the same. I prefer the company of my own sex, but this does not mean I do not enjoy the opposite sex as well, for much the same reason you put so well: loving beauty where I find it."

Param looked at her for a moment. She assumed he thought she was jesting, but then he, too, began to laugh. To Lynari, the laughter felt good, and imagined it was good for him, too. They had met so recently, and it had been mostly ugliness since, so it was special to share this, to have this little piece of time to get to know one another, if only briefly.

The night would be upon them all too soon, and their

performance would have to be convincing. They still had to get in as much practice as possible, and so they continued their work. Lynari put every bit of physical exertion she could into focusing on Param's directions. If they could convince Dran and his men they were *both* performers (there was no question of Param—she already knew he was good), then there was a chance they could leave the *Maraggan's* presence. This would allow them to follow while making a plan to free Rhinan and Eodorr, or confirm that they had escaped on their own and try to find them.

In one of her stumbles, Lynari nearly fell at Param's feet. That's when she noticed it. The hilt of Rhinan's sword was exposed from Param's pack.

"Param."

He had paused in his playing when she stumbled, but he looked up at her when he heard the serious tone of her voice.

She cast a glance around the camp, and no one was watching. Disguising it as an arm movement, she pointed to the pack, hoping he would notice.

He looked down, and his eyes flew open wide.

Had anyone seen it? How long had it been exposed? And they *still* didn't know what the report out of Arskellion had been. Looking back up at her, eyes still wide, he said, "If any of them noticed, I'll think of something."

Lynari hoped so, because all that came to her mind now was the suicide oath of the *Hegana.*

* * * * *

Following their performance that evening, as the sun began to set among the trees, the lash of winter's icy whip drove the men closer to the fire and whatever fur-lined bedding they could wrap around themselves. Dran had threatened an early departure in the morning. Despite his profound limp, his determination was unrelenting.

Lynari felt the show had been a success. There had certainly been no complaints. The men enjoyed Param's playing and singing so much that, for a couple of songs that reminded them of home, they even sang along. She wasn't expected to dance for every song, which made it much easier. She found it far more pleasant than she expected. There was something powerful in this form of bewitching men, a talent which she had perhaps always possessed yet never fully realized or used.

As the men cleared up for the night, Dran himself limped over.

"Thank you for entertaining my men. It can't be easy, especially out here with the winter snowfalls driving down at us. You must both be chilled to the bone. Do you have enough furs and skins with you to keep you warm in the night?"

There was a hesitation before Param answered, and Lynari knew it was one more thing to raise Dran's suspicion. "As a matter of fact, we lost much of our supplies when we lost our horses. We do not."

"I see." Dran looked around the camp. "Well, I'm sure we can find extra for you. Gaimesh!" He called to one of his men, and the man approached. This man, of all of Dran's men, made Lynari most uncomfortable on many levels. His presence was like worms crawling under her skin. "It will be cold tonight. Will you round up some additional furs for our guests?"

"Yes, My Lord." And Gaimesh slipped away.

Dran limped over next to Param and sat on a boulder.

Daylight had not faded, but the shadows were long. Param was visibly uncomfortable. It weren't as if there were enough sorrowful things on the poor troubadour's mind.

When Dran spoke, his voice took on a conspiratorial tone. "I don't want to seem ungrateful, but one of my men noticed what he thought was the hilt of a sword protruding from your pack today. As the General of the King's elite force, I cannot be remiss in my duty. You'll understand that I must ask about it, given that blades are firmly outlawed unless you serve the King. Were you a soldier?"

It was a moment they had dreaded, hoping it would not have been noticed. Lynari cursed herself at their carelessness, feeling it was unfair of her to place much of the blame on Param. He was, after all, busy concocting much more of their current plan than she. Whether or not he was being very successful was another debate and remained to be seen. But not ensuring their packs were sealed tightly? While carrying a sword and not in the King's employ? It was a major gaffe for them. This was a prime law of the land, and here they were, two mysterious travelers flaunting this law. But in the end, it was Param who would have to cover it.

"Briefly, My Lord, and long ago," Param went into his most earnest voice.

"But you no longer serve the King?"

"No, My Lord," Param looked down at the ground. "I was not worthy."

"I see. And yet you carry a sword, restricted to those serving the King?"

"I admit that I do so intentionally, and I only ask that I be given the opportunity to explain myself, if I may."

"By all means, troubadour, proceed." Dran leaned back, with the appearance of preparing to be entertained.

"Providing I can have a look at it."

Lynari watched as, with all possible restraint, Param could find no way to refuse and inevitably removed the blade from the pack and handed it to Dran. "You see, My Lord, as a wandering troubadour, I must travel many places. As you know, there are rougher places than others. I avoid it, but I do draw near to the Unreigned Territory in my travels. I am a lone traveler, and this becomes a dangerous aspect of my profession."

"Lone traveler?" Dran asked, cocking an eyebrow and leaning his head to look toward Lynari. She couldn't help feeling that this was somehow getting worse. "I wouldn't consider myself alone with such a gifted partner."

Param did not even pause, though Lynari could tell he was improvising further on the spot to cover his misspoken words. "Well, My Lord, you see, protecting her is one of my reasons for the blade. I only hope you can see how one might feel compelled to do the same as I have in a similar circumstance."

"The funny thing, troubadour, is that I can." Dran eyed the scabbard up and down. "Yet it does not excuse breaking one of the King's most emphatic laws." He drew the blade forth from the scabbard, and Lynari inhaled sharply. The blade was of Ylvan make and, without a doubt, Dran would recognize it as such. It would make matters even worse.

In desperation, Lynari began to improvise more dance practice, though as such, she could only draw on her combat moves. Nevertheless, it drew Dran's attention, but not in the way she had hoped.

"You'll forgive me if I notice that it appears your dancer seems well able to defend herself, should the need arise." Dran watched her, but at least he took his eyes from the blade. "Those moves would serve her well against an assailant and, as I recollect, she carries a formidable quarterstaff. In fact, it is a lovely piece of carving, I noticed in my brief glimpse as you entered camp this morning. Perhaps you could show it to me now. I would very much like to examine the workmanship."

The General of the *Maraggan* was putting nothing over on Lynari. She had made this worse. She had thought it went unnoticed, but her quarterstaff had also caught his attention, and now he wanted to examine it. Rhinan's Ylvan blade still lay across Dran's lap, half drawn out of its scabbard.

Had there been more than two of them, Lynari would have seen this as the moment for action. If Param could surprise Dran, he could perhaps seize the blade back and use it on him before Dran even knew what was happening. She could pick up her quarterstaff, and the two of them would be armed and ready to fend off the remainder of the elite troop.

It was a lovely thought, yet there were over a dozen of them, and only she and Param to stand against them. The *Maraggan* were well-trained. This was not a situation where combat was the answer. And Param had appeared to use up his deceit unsuccessfully. Their options were reduced to running or surrender (which was not an option). Giving both herself and Param the opportunity to plan a running escape, Lynari bowed to Dran and simply said, "Of course, My Lord." She then turned and headed for her pack, stashed nearby beside a large rock. Her staff leaned against a tree next to the rock.

Gaimesh returned with an armload of furs. Her quarterstaff in hand, Lynari saw her moment. The creepy soldier stood over Dran with the armload of furs, so she sprang forward. With a swing of her quarterstaff, she struck a thundering blow against the back of Gaimesh's head, knocking him forward on top of Dran, half covering him in the furs. Param grabbed Rhinan's sword and the two made quickly for the horse they were being "given." They made it halfway to the animal before they were subdued by several of the men. Now Lynari feared the worst, and attempted to pull a dagger from one of the men, knowing that she must use it on herself. She hoped Param was taking the same action.

Her attempts, however, failed. She found her arms pinned and tied behind her with leather straps. When it was clear enough, she saw Param in the same condition, only he looked as if he'd taken a beating where she hadn't. Blood trailed down his face and his head hung. She wasn't sure if he was conscious.

Then her view of him was partially blocked by Dran, who limped between them and grabbed Param by his hair, pulling his head back. Param was conscious, but he also had a puffy eye. They hadn't treated him nearly as well as they'd treated her.

"Well, Param of the Northern Path, it would appear that you are something more than a simple troubadour. At first, I suspected that perhaps you and your partner," here he turned to glower at Lynari, "were bandits of the mischievous type. Possibly even using magic to lull your victims into a sleep or something, after which they would wake and find all of their goods had vanished with the entertainers. I have heard of, and in fact arrested and punished, those sorts of traveling bandits. But you two? There was something more going on."

The one called Gaimesh stepped up beside Dran at this point, rubbing the back of his head and aiming a murderous expression at Lynari. She could not face this man. If she could find a large enough rock that was sharp, she would throw herself over against it and smash her head if she could. She looked around, but could find nothing suitable within range. And Param? He was in no shape to resist anything. This was possibly the moment in all of history that *Hegana* had managed to avoid. Until now. And Lynari would be responsible for it. She had failed her order.

Gaimesh handed Lynari's quarterstaff to Dran, who already held Rhinan's blade in his other hand. "Now another thought occurred to me," Dran continued, holding both weapons. "We're pursuing two outlaws who have some level of magic skills. What if you are the exact two people we're pursuing, well-disguised by some powerful spell? And then you hand me a sword which is clearly of Ylvan make." Param's expression changed to one perhaps of surprise, and Dran reacted. "Ah, yes. I noticed immediately." Lynari had hoped her distraction would have prevented this, but even here she had failed.

Dran turned to her. "Your clumsy distraction was so obvious that I knew my suspicions weren't completely unfounded. But then," and he looked to Gaimesh, "you attacked one of my men. One of the King's *Maraggan*." Dran shook his head at her. "With this." He waved her quarterstaff at her. "I don't exactly know what this is, or where the two of you came up with an Ylvan blade, or if you've used magic on us, but we're going to find out. We leave in the morning to find out if the two outlaws we're searching for are, indeed, two men who were conscripted into the mining camp north of Arskellion. You'll be coming with us. I'd like to know what your connection to them is, but I have no doubt now there is a connection."

So that messenger *had* known about Rhinan and Eodorr's arrest and, of course, reported it to Dran who, no doubt, suspected it was Rhinan. The General of the *Maraggan* turned to the one called Gaimesh. "It's getting late, but I think there's still time to ask this troubadour a few questions. Or at the very least, let him know how we feel about being lied to and played for fools." This last line came out with a snarl that frightened Lynari in a way nothing else ever had. He looked directly at her. "Oh, don't worry, little dancer. We'll get to you later."

Dran limped back toward Param. "Gaimesh, I trust you have your tools with you?"

"Always, My Lord."

"Bring them." Gaimesh nodded and stepped away. The rest of the men were gathered around, awaiting orders. "We're going to keep these two bound tightly and under close watch all night. If anyone allows them to escape, that man *won't* be coming with us in the morning. Do I make myself clear?"

Every *Maraggan* to a man nodded and spoke an affirmation of, "Yes, My Lord."

Gaimesh returned with a large leather pouch. He stood next to Param. Lynari trembled for both Param and for the secret order of the *Hegana.*

"Now let's ask this troubadour where he came by an Ylvan blade. And perhaps if he's familiar with anyone by the name of Rhinan Ashuir. That's all I want to know tonight. We'll find out more tomorrow when we rejoin Flek and his squad and get to the mining camp."

Lynari felt sick. They had killed the squad Dran referred to. Would Gaimesh be able to discover this? At least Param wouldn't know Rhinan by his true name of Ashuir; thankfully, she hadn't told Param all of the details. He did not know Rhinan was Ylvan, either. He could answer in sincerity if asked about these things.

The panic rising within her was almost uncontrollable. She began to try practicing tactics *Hegana* were taught for such a situation. She had no magic that would help in this situation, but she reminded herself that she was chosen for a very important mission because she was a skilled *Hegana*. Her opportunity would come; she would have to maintain patience and, in so doing, recover the clarity of mind that threatened to flee from her like a rabbit in the woods.

Dran spoke to the big, creepy soldier again. "He's a troubadour. If we want answers, it's quite easy to target what he values."

Gaimesh nodded, a twisted, frightening grin on his face. He seemed to be concentrating in preparation for whatever he was about to do.

Dran began to limp away in the direction of his little shelter. "Oh, and Gaimesh?"

"Yes, My Lord?"

"Not the whole hand at once. He plays right-handed, so begin with the small finger of his right hand. It will cause the least disruption to his ability, leaving him hope as we press for answers. The slower you go, the more bargaining bits we have." Dran wiggled the fingers of his own right hand at Gaimesh for emphasis.

Gaimesh nodded. "Of course, My Lord. Wise approach." He opened the leather pouch, retrieving the sharp tools of his terrible craft. Most of the other men looked away as Gaimesh moved toward Param.

"And Gaimesh!" Dran turned back from a bit further away. "Stop with one hand for tonight. We need him able to travel in the morning. See to it that he's able to make the journey with us. Answers would be good, but if you can't get them, don't go any further. I know how dedicated you get when you work. Don't proceed beyond that point this evening. If you get those two answers I asked about earlier, then don't take anything extra. Like I said, remember to leave us more to bargain with later."

Gaimesh seemed to stop and think about this, appearing to Lynari as if he wasn't sure he understood, but then he shrugged and moved toward Param.

Still searching, there were no sharp rocks to be found, but Lynari found a good sized one behind her. Even with her hands bound, she managed to get her legs under her and throw herself backward onto it before any of the men could get to her. Her head hit the rock with a heavy impact, and she blacked out.

Chapter Thirty-Four

Another kick in the side from a soldier told Rhinan it was the second morning at the mining camp. He sat up, winced, and nearly went back down. His muscles ached excruciatingly from the previous day. He glowered at the soldier who grinned and turned away, sending a kick at Eodorr to wake him as well.

As the miners gathered around the morning porridge—some soupy/lumpy substance Rhinan couldn't define but also couldn't refuse—he became concerned. Eodorr was altogether too sullen. Not an overly cheery fellow on any regular basis, Rhinan's companion at least usually seemed to make the best of even the worst situations. This one had him down, and Rhinan was at a loss to provide any comfort.

While they ate hastily, urged on by the soldiers, Rhinan took a better look around the camp than he'd been able to before. At the back of the camp, upslope or northward, was a long log building which obviously served as the barracks for the soldiers. Next to it was another smaller log building that he'd seen soldiers go in and out of. Was it food storage? No, that was another log building on the downslope south side of the camp. Which was also where the food emerged from (and Rhinan thought "food" was perhaps optimistic for describing what they were being given to subsist on). He wondered what was inside that other structure. With his skills, he would find out under normal circumstances. That led him to another thought, but before he could finish it, the soldiers had them up and moving toward the mine.

As they entered the dark pit, a soldier spoke to Wogen and Brondur, who then led the way for everyone else. There were only a dozen miners, but twice as many soldiers. And, of course, the miners were unarmed, half-starved, and exhausted. Rhinan could see no effective form of resistance. As he dawdled, pondering possibilities, Eodorr was handed a pick and entered the mine. This left Rhinan and another man named Taploden (who appeared to have been portly at one time, now gone to sag), to begin the day hauling buckets of ore up and out of the mines and sorting it. This was discouraging news for Rhinan, as they had learned that Taploden was known among the miners as a whiner and a slacker. He had the further annoying habit of half humming/half singing to himself. None of them wished to be there, but Taploden would not do his bit to make it less hard on the rest of them. Now Rhinan was stuck with him on an ore-carrying shift. They were handed buckets and torches. Being sore already, it was bound to be a merciless day.

As it turned out, the soldiers had given Brondur and Wogen instructions to open another branch of mine tunnels near one of the sections the miners had closed off due to the Eyeless Ones. Learning of this, the miners were all on their guard, fearing the worst. Production would therefore be reduced from the day before, which made Rhinan's job easier, but the miners knew the soldiers would be unhappy with the day's results. Rhinan didn't know what that would mean, having only been there such a short time, but he presumed unhappy soldiers meant unhappy miners at the end of the day.

While waiting for the first bucketful, Rhinan approached Brondur. "Tell me more about these Eyeless Ones. If we encounter them, are there any tales of survivors? Has anyone made any observations that could be useful in defending against them?"

Brondur paused his picking for a moment and thought. "Well, they don't always kill the miners they catch. They've turned some loose, but none have been sure why they were lucky. Perhaps if you're very polite…" Brondur jested, winking in the torchlight just enough for Rhinan to see.

"But they don't usually release you once they capture you?"

Brondur shuddered. "They caught a soldier once who'd come down to inspect an area we wanted to shut away due to the Eyeless Ones. The next morning, we found the soldier outside, hung on a wooden stake, and he was… flattened. As if they'd stripped out his insides and left only the shell. I've never seen anything like it, and I sincerely hope never to again."

"But miners?" Rhinan persisted.

"If they take you, you are either released or you are not. But there has never been such a display with a miner that I've heard of. Just some are released and some are not."

"Do they perhaps react to the torches?" It occurred to Rhinan that if a people lived underground, perhaps fire would be a thing to set them off and enrage them. And if they did not like light, perhaps that's why the inspecting soldier was brought out at night and left as a show of warning. But only a soldier was left as a show of warning, so the Eyeless Ones most likely recognized the difference. And, possibly, saw the soldiers as the worse problem. Clearly, the Eyeless Ones were not mindless monsters. But if they could emerge from the mines at night, what prevented them from wiping out the camp altogether? Unless there were just too few of the Eyeless Ones, which he doubted, there was some other factor that drew them out of the mines, or there wouldn't be a camp left.

As suspected by the soldiers, the miners found a nice vein of silver where they'd been instructed to dig. This was, of course, no comfort to the miners who worried about the Eyeless Ones.

On their third or fourth trip up with their buckets, Rhinan and Taploden heard something move swiftly in the darkness beyond their torchlight. Each of the two men carried a bucket in one hand, and lit torch in the other. Straining to see, Rhinan thought it would be a good moment to step up the pace. Taploden, however, was not one to make haste.

Before they could resume, they were seized and dragged aside into an older, abandoned tunnel.

When it happened, Rhinan drew back instantly, not being held clutched in the grasp that had snared him. By the light of their torches, they were able to get a good look at the Eyeless Ones.

There were two of them. No taller than Rhinan, and certainly no more muscular, they were not terribly frightening until you studied their details.

Covered in a blue-gray skin, they were completely hairless. They also had leathery wings with points that reminded Rhinan of drawings he'd seen of those on dragons.

The hands at the end of each wing were sharply clawed, but it was their faces that inspired terror in Rhinan.

They weren't called Eyeless Ones for no reason. They had long jaws with sharp teeth—jagged, extended, pointed teeth that would easily rend flesh from the look of them. Above their mouths, where noses would be on a man, they had two lengthwise slits. Above that, the rest of their heads were normal sized but bald.

But eerily, there were no eyes on their faces whatsoever.

It was so unnatural that Rhinan, despite his experience with creatures in the woods, was unnerved. Especially when the two Eyeless Ones began to creep toward himself and Taploden.

Thinking quickly about his conversation with Brondur that morning, he dropped his torch and stomped it out. Taploden, on the other hand, waved his torch at the advancing Eyeless Ones as he backed away in terror.

"Drop your torch!" Rhinan hissed at him.

Too gripped by fear to understand, Taploden (having already dropped his bucket) continued to attempt to fight off the two Eyeless Ones. One of them backed him against the tunnel wall and grasped each of Taploden's arms with the clawed hands at the end of its wings. Taploden unintentionally dropped the torch then, where it lay on the ground, still lit. The Eyeless One then leaned his head forward, apparently sniffing Taploden's face. Then, in a sudden motion, the Eyeless One tipped its head just a bit, opened its jaws, and snapped forward. When it drew back, Rhinan could see that everything from Taploden's nose to his neck had been ripped away. The lifeless body slid down the tunnel wall to the ground.

Now the two Eyeless Ones turned toward Rhinan. In a

moment of desperation, he rushed forward and stomped out Taploden's torch as well, leaving them all in complete blackness. Rhinan hoped his hunch was right, and that perhaps keeping the light and fire away from the Eyeless Ones would make the difference between who they returned and who they did not. Then he was grabbed by the arms and slammed against the tunnel wall as Taploden had been, and knew that he'd made a grave error. Undoubtedly his last.

Then the most unexpected thing of all occurred.

"You… respect the Vimyr?" The raspy voice was high pitched, but it was clear to understand.

"I do not wish to harm… the Vimyr," Rhinan replied, using the term for the Eyeless Ones they obviously used to refer to themselves.

He could see nothing, but he became more terrified when he could feel the Vimyr's hot breath on his skin. Close enough to bite half his face off as it had Taploden. It was… sniffing… him.

"Very strange," it said at last.

Hoping that this meant he wasn't about to be bitten, Rhinan chanced to respond. "You can speak to us?"

And yet more surprises. Rhinan hadn't really expected more direct interaction, but the Vimyr replied. "We learn from you in our homes. Yes, we speak you."

In the absolute darkness, Rhinan could not guess what to expect next. He hoped he had a chance of being one of those released. Really it was his only hope. He offered one more attempt at communication. "We down here… we do not want to disturb the Vimyr's homes. We are… forced… to be in your homes." He hoped they understood these words. It could make a difference whether he lived or died. He considered rattling his shackled hands to illustrate his point, but feared they may take it as a sign of aggression and thought better of it.

"Some care. Some do not." The Vimyr sniffed him again. "You care. This is… permitted?" The Vimyr seemed unsure of the right word.

The other Vimyr then spoke. "Vimyr not want you here. Tell others."

Then there was a sharp, painful scratch of claws across his face which hit him so fast and so hard that he fell backward against the tunnel wall. He lost consciousness from the impact.

* * * * *

Eodorr sat beside him when he woke. His face burned, but Rhinan tried to sit up. "Don't do that," Eodorr said. "Just lie still."

Rhinan did as he was told, and Brondur walked over, leaning over him and taking a careful a look. A couple of soldiers followed.

"He is lucky," Brondur announced. "He has been returned, and this should leave no permanent damage." The big man poked a finger around Rhinan's face. Brondur straightened up. "Taploden, not so lucky. If they haven't returned him by now, it's less likely they will."

The two soldiers walked away to speak to the rest of their number.

Eodorr leaned forward. "The Eyeless Ones left you at the opening to the mine, just inside. It's like they wanted you to be found and helped."

"That's what they do with the lucky ones," Brondur added. "Leave them just inside the mine opening, injured enough to send a message. Did you learn why they let you go?"

Rhinan wiggled his mouth around, and his face hurt, but he found he could speak. "They can speak to us. They don't want us there. And, by the way, they are the Vimyr. Not 'the Eyeless Ones' as we called them before. They are the Vimyr. And…" Rhinan paused as Brondur's eyebrows raised and his own face felt another flush of anguish. "And, if you want to survive when you meet them, stomp out your torch. They take it as a sign you aren't there to harm them. It's considered respectful."

Brondur sat down beside Eodorr. "Well, well, well. Look who learned a lot today."

"I'm surprised you didn't know this before," Eodorr said. "It doesn't sound complicated."

"Look around here," Brondur growled. "How many of these men seem complicated to you? Your friend here has an eye for things. That helps. And who says we didn't know some of these things before anyway?"

"Oh?" Eodorr pressed the big man on the subject. "What exactly did you already know?"

Brondur hung his head. "Well, it's clear they don't want us in the mines. Fortunately for me, I've never been taken."

"Brilliant." Eodorr leaned back. "You were on the verge of saving your lives. If, you know, you had realized they're threatened by the torches."

"Well, we're not down there because we want to be," Brondur snapped. "And we can't see anything without the torches."

"They know this." Rhinan was exhausted of the conversation, but leaned up. "That's another thing. They *know* the soldiers are forcing us to go down there."

"Do they know *why* we're being forced?" Eodorr asked. "Do they care that we're stealing valuable minerals?"

"They didn't say." Rhinan lay back. "I don't think they care. It's like that's not the issue."

"Well," Brondur added, "You're off duty. You get a break until the soldiers feel you're well enough to send back down—which is probably one day. And, thanks to you, the rest of us get the rest of today off, too."

Rhinan realized it was late afternoon. He'd been out a while. He thought of poor Taploden. "I don't suppose you found Taploden?"

Brondur shook his head. "Never do. You either come back or you're just gone. That's how it works."

"It was terrible—" Rhinan began.

"Don't tell us," Brondur cut him off. "That's another one of the things we already know. No point in telling us about that. Poor useless windbag."

The other miners were given tasks within the camp, and Eodorr was pulled away to work. Brondur was left as the one person to care for Rhinan.

"They will talk to us if we put out the torches," Rhinan said.

"The Eyeless Ones?" Brondur looked at him as if he were half mad.

"The *Vimyr*," Rhinan corrected him. "If we can talk to them, there may be a way to reach them. Maybe even gain their help."

"They're cowards who kill us in the dark." Brondur was firm. "I wouldn't count on that."

Rhinan dropped his face into the palm of his hand. Then he took another look around the camp, once again noticing the odd structure beside the barracks. "Brondur, do you know what's in that?" He pointed to it.

Brondur looked over. "My axe, for one thing. Anything they take from us when they bring us in."

Rhinan made a mental note of this. "What about the ore for the King? We're pulling that out of the mines. Where are they keeping that?"

Brondur chuckled. "You get a lot of ideas, don't you? Same place. They keep a couple of chests in there. When they're full, they get transported out of here."

Rhinan sat up. "You mean there will be fewer soldiers here?"

"No, unfortunately. They run down to Arskellion for reinforcements before they send a team away with the chests."

Laying back down, Rhinan's mind kept rolling ideas around. There had to be a way out of this, but something was missing.

That something showed up right about dinner time. A man who obviously considered himself very important, accompanied by fifteen soldiers of the same type who attacked them at Brinaya's cabin, rode into the mining camp, dusty from a day's ride. They had two prisoners with them.

In Rhinan's mind, there was no doubt that, here at last, was Gethor Dran. One glance over to Eodorr, who nodded, confirmed it. It was all Rhinan could do not to fly directly at the pompous General and strangle him with his shackles. He fumed and he feared. This was now almost surely it for him, and despair took hold.

But only fifteen of the King's *Maraggan*? Where were the rest? Well, he knew where *some* were... back at Brinaya's cabin. Perhaps Vaylene had taken her toll.

Then he noticed something interesting. He got a better look at the two prisoners. One of them was Lynari. And the other, at long last, was Param Voss. If they could get out of this somehow, they now had a guide to continue eastward, and further from King Jerrick.

But Gethor Dran was here, and that was the biggest problem of all.

Chapter Thirty-Five

The mining camp was filled with Rhinan's ghosts, though of course only he could see them.

The soldiers were making a fuss over the *Maraggan*, guiding them up to the barracks, and making other arrangements for the evening. One of the *Maraggan* was dispatched southward, with orders to retrieve their number that he, Eodorr, and Lynari had seen down in Arskellion.

He was concerned about Dran finding him, but he still had the advantage, if only temporarily, that Dran had never seen him. Still, he could have been described to the General by someone, so he was careful to avoid Dran or any of his men. The miners were on their best behavior, but in all of this chaos, Rhinan had lost track of Eodorr.

What Rhinan did see was that Param was in poor condition. He'd been mistreated, that was obvious. There was dried blood on his face and his right hand was bandaged, which concerned Rhinan most of all. The bastards! If they'd done something to prevent his ability to strum his mandolute, Param's career as a troubadour was at an end.

Lynari, on the other hand, had been bound and gagged

tightly, but did not appear to be in such bad shape. There was a trickle of dried blood down the side of her face, but no other outward signs of injury.

The Ylvan ghosts (for Rhinan generally assumed they were now) murmured and faced the northern end of the camp where a couple of recognizable pouches were taken into the storage building and locked within. Rhinan's bow was also among the items, and Lynari's quarterstaff. Lynari and Param had somehow found each other, gotten Rhinan's possessions from the inn, and managed to get captured by Dran. There must have been a trap set or something that he and Eodorr had only eluded because of their poor luck with being conscripted by the local soldiers.

Shortly, as night drifted in, things began to settle into a less chaotic state. A light snow began to fall, and all of the fires in camp were lit. Rhinan's stomach rumbled, and he hoped that, before Dran realized he was here and executed him, he might at least get a good meal for once. It was possible they could put one together for the *Maraggan*, maybe even share it with the miners.

Even though they had never seen each other, it had been obvious to Rhinan right away which man was Gethor Dran. Rhinan glared at him when he could, allowing his darkest thoughts to formulate tortures for the despicable General. Dran was dark-haired and bearded, with a sour grimace for a permanent facial expression. His black and gold *Maraggan* uniform differentiated him from the few other men of the special force in that there was more gold and less black in the General's. He walked with a limp (Rhinan had never heard of that—perhaps another gift from Vaylene?), but he set everyone on edge. Despite his foreboding presence, Dran appeared jovial to the soldier hosts, leading Rhinan to the conclusion that he was in a good mood for someone like Dran. Rhinan supposed that having the two prisoners, Param and Lynari, had Dran feeling he was closing in on Rhinan. For all Rhinan knew, Dran was already aware that Rhinan was in this camp, but he hadn't spotted him yet. The only possible salvation for Rhinan was that, since Dran had never seen him, he might not recognize him. But he would use Param and Lynari to draw Rhinan out, if not some other method. Rhinan desperately wished for his bow and just one arrow. For Keirwyn. For Devram. For Brinaya. For countless others who'd suffered at the hands and efforts of this relentless, reprehensible excuse for a man. Rhinan would send an arrow through the man's throat from where he sat if he had his bow. He tried to hide his fury, appearing no unhappier with his predicament than any of the other miners. He was distracted from his rage when the rock gnome Wogen came and sat next to him.

"I can't tell you if the opportunity will come for you, lad, but I've been around a long time. A man like that? He gets what's coming to him, sooner or later. You only have to worry about how much damage he does before it catches up with him. And, of course, hope that you can stay out of his path."

Rhinan nodded. The Rock Walker made sense, but it didn't provide any comfort. Nothing would bring back all those who were gone. Before Rhinan could reply, they were hushed by a nearby soldier. It appeared Dran was about to address the camp.

Stepping forward from the west side of camp, Dran moved close to the larger, central fire. As the shadows of late afternoon fell, this illuminated him and created a dark, imposing image as he stepped up onto a table.

"Citizens of Lydania," Dran addressed the miners more than the soldiers, but he cast a good look around when he said it. Rhinan suspected it was to see if anyone showed any negative reaction to this label, under the circumstances. He kept his own head tilted downward, knowing that were his gaze to meet Dran's, all doubt as to his identity would be removed.

"We have come because we believe a man wanted by King Jerrick may be hiding himself among you. He may be travelling with a companion. They would have arrived within the last two days. If any man in this camp can point either of them out, he will be set free."

Before he could finish, several soldiers stepped forward. Of course they had seen Rhinan brought north from Arskellion with Eodorr—some of them had even been among the soldiers who brought them. A pair of the soldiers dragged Eodorr forward. Rhinan cursed quietly and turned to Wogen. The gnome could only shrug and shake his head.

There was some discussion between the soldiers, Dran, and Dran's men. The remaining miners began to raise their voices in anger. The soldiers had robbed them of an opportunity for freedom. There were still a couple of them who would gladly turn Rhinan in, and he could hardly blame them for a chance at freedom.

Dran spoke again, louder and harsh. "This is not the man we seek, but we believe this is his companion." Rhinan didn't know if Dran had seen Eodorr back in Cabelon, or if he knew who he was. But even if he'd never seen him, he could easily determine that this was the only other man brought in within the last two days, and it wasn't Rhinan. What would Dran do to Eodorr?

The soldiers began to walk among the miners, looking at

their faces. Rhinan still bore the scratches given him that day by the Vimyr. He hoped that would make him less recognizable. As one neared Rhinan and Wogen, the gnome, leaned forward onto his hands and knees. The soldier looked down at him as if to throw a kick, but was suddenly shoved from behind by Brondur.

The soldier fell right over Wogen, landing hard with a shout. A handful of soldiers rushed to the aid of their comrade, beating Brondur to the ground. Wogen escaped unpunished, but the ploy had worked—the soldiers passed on and Rhinan was overlooked. For the moment.

"We've also brought entertainment," Dran continued. "We believe this troubadour is an ally of the traitor we seek. For your enjoyment and as a reward for the hard work you provide your King, we're going to ask him to play for you tonight. Should the man we seek fail to step forward, it will be his last performance." A large *Maraggan* stepped behind Param, reaching around in front of him to hand him his mandolute.

Rhinan slid forward on the log on which he'd been sitting next to Wogen. They'd tied Eodorr up and sat him next to Lynari. Neither of them were in any position to help Param.

Then Rhinan realized that Param had spotted him. Param looked worried, but he shook his head at Rhinan, careful not to be noticed by anyone else. He then turned to Dran in a blatant act of defiance.

"I have played this camp at night before, My Lord," he spoke through gritted teeth. "You know I am Param of the Northern Path. Please believe that you do not want me to play here at night. None of us wants that."

"Captain Gaimesh," Dran turned to the large man

standing behind Param, "we're presuming a troubadour can still play missing the two fingers of one hand. Can he play missing *three* fingers?"

"Play, troubadour!" shouted a soldier.

Param met Rhinan's gaze again. He appeared to be more afraid of playing than he did of suffering the consequences of *not* playing. He'd played this camp before? But he didn't want to play now, regardless of Rhinan's predicament? For Rhinan, something he'd puzzled over earlier became clear. He nodded for Param to play.

It was clearly difficult and painful. Rhinan watched Param struggle to get started, but he began to play his mandolute. His strumming hand now lacked the last two fingers, and the bloody bandages indicated this was a very recent development. Nevertheless, Param's skills overcame, and he began a ballad.

"Louder!" shouted a soldier. This resulted in a nudge from the brute behind Param. Param swallowed, and sweat appeared on his brow, but he increased the volume of his performance.

Full night had fallen by this time. Rhinan would give Param a few moments to see if his suspicions were correct, then he would step forward in the dubious hope that his friends might be saved. As Param played louder, and nothing happened, Rhinan stood up.

"Ah, at last. Rhinan Ashuir, I presume?" Dran cocked his head to him.

And then, with a sign Rhinan had hoped to see, everything happened at once.

Something dropped from the sky, and ripped the large figure behind Param from the ground, carrying him away.

"Douse the fires!" he hissed to the other miners. "Hurry! And no torches!"

Beaten up as he was, Brondur dove at the large central fire, grabbing a bucket of drinking water as he did so. Following his lead, the other miners took the same action with the smaller fires.

After the big man—Captain Gaimesh, Dran had called him—was swept skyward, Dran leapt down from the table he'd been standing on and drew his sword. He looked skyward, and made a fatal slash at one of the winged creatures who were nearly invisible in the night. It fell at his feet, and he looked appalled. Rhinan recognized it was definitely Vimyr.

Rhinan began to suspect this when he thought of Param having played the campsite before, especially when he didn't appear to want to play. Perhaps, in the dark of night, it would be *music* that would draw the Vimyr out. They were timid, and they were *blind*, but when they could so clearly hear something as powerful as music, this may give them targets to come out and strike at.

Of course, this made Param a target as well. Fortunately, he'd stopped playing the moment Gaimesh was snatched, and the few Vimyr in the sky were now targeting soldiers with torches which they knew were the source of their troubles. For the moment, Param was safe. With the campfires going out, the only light was the faint glow of moonlight beyond snow-dropping clouds, which had the soldiers waving torches, giving the Vimyr the advantage for the moment. But the *Maraggan* and mine soldiers were clustering together to organize a defense.

Rhinan turned to Wogen. "If you want to be free this night, break into that storage shack and retrieve our packs and weapons. Do this before the Vimyr leave and we have a chance."

The gnome looked at Rhinan with a glimmer in his eye. "I don't know what you're up to, lad, but I like it." Then he yelled, "Brondur! Bring a couple of our strongest and follow me!" The gnome disappeared into the darkness.

Rhinan rushed to Param's side. They embraced warmly, two lifetime friends who had not seen one another in far too long to ignore the moment, even one this chaotic. Rhinan began to ask, "Are you—"

"Not as bad as I've let them think, but not at all happy."

Rhinan and Param turned and freed Eodorr and Lynari.

"Follow me!" Rhinan motioned them toward the north side of the campsite. "Quickly."

"You will stop where you stand in the name of the King!"

All four of them turned, and there stood Dran, a handful of *Maraggan* and some of the mine soldiers at his side. "Rhinan Ashuir, you and your accomplices are under arrest for treason to the crown."

From the side, out of the woods, came a vicious howl that sent a chill to the bones of all who heard it. The war cry of an angry beardog struck fear into the primal heart of most men, and no one present, other than Rhinan, was immune. When the huge beast leapt forward, both one of Dran's men and one of the mine soldiers went down beneath the charge, mangled beyond any hope of salvation.

Neither Dran nor any of the remaining men at his side had bows, and they all stepped back carefully, torches still lit.

Rhinan smiled. "Rip, follow?" He then turned to Dran with a harsh snarl. "You want me? Keep following. Either way, let the Lore Givers be my witnesses, one of us will hunt the other until one of us is dead. You evil bastard."

As if to emphasize the point, a Vimyr dropped from the

sky and swept away with another of the men standing with Dran.

With that sign, Rhinan turned away, leading Param, Eodorr, Lynari, and Rip rushing to the north end of the campsite.

Arriving at the storage shack, they found a grinning Brondur leaning on an axe that looked like it could fell a medium tree in one stroke. Wogen had a long pole with a hammer on the end of it. It didn't look like it would be of much use, but Rhinan saw that the gnome was happy. A few of the other miners stood by, picks and shovels in hand.

Brondur handed pouches to Rhinan. Lynari slipped past the men and retrieved her quarterstaff and Rhinan's bow and quiver of arrows. As she did this, Rhinan reached into the large pouch of his own. The sword and the *Pyvadis* were still there. He drew out the sword.

"Wogen, this is our best hope. I need you to hold out your hands."

The gnome eyed Rhinan suspiciously. "I'm not sure what you're thinking, lad, but I don't think I like it."

"Do it." Brondur scowled at the little Rock Walker. "You want those shackles off or not?"

Shrugging, Wogen held out his hands, the magical shackles stretched as far apart as he could get his hands.

Unsheathing the blade of Ylvan steel, Rhinan took careful aim at the center of the shackles. With one quick swing, he brought the sword down. It shattered the links in the center, and the shackles turned to dust. Wogen the Rock Walker was free.

The Vimyr had mostly vanished, leaving Dran and his men, plus the mine soldiers, to regroup and come at them. The soldiers had even grabbed bows to shoot at Rip.

"There!" Brondur shouted, pointing at a nearby boulder. The group hurried to it, and Wogen stood before it.

"Long has it been," said the gnome. He placed his hands on the boulder, and the foremost portion of the boulder began to shimmer into a gray, cloudy form, rather than solid rock. Heaving a sigh of relief, Wogen turned to them. "Follow me."

"Wait!" Rhinan called. "Brondur, can you help me steal one of those chests of ore?"

The big man grinned again. "How many would you like?" Within moments, the forester and three miners returned with two chests full of silver ore.

Rhinan grinned and nodded. That, too, would be some payback for the men and their families who'd been forced to work against their will as prisoners. However, before they could proceed, one of the miners was hit by an arrow meant for Rip. Dran and his group were creeping closer. Drawing his own bow, Rhinan turned and tried to find a clean shot of Dran. But the seasoned General was too wily to leave himself exposed. Rhinan fired an arrow, dropping the soldier directly in front of Dran.

"It's time," Wogen said. The Rock Walker stepped into the cloud, and through it, vanishing. Brondur followed immediately, alone dragging one of the chests.

"Go!" Rhinan urged Param, Eodorr, and Lynari. The trio stepped through. Another couple of miners, carrying the other chest, stepped through as well. This left only Rhinan and Rip.

"Rip, follow?" Rhinan stepped through the gray cloud, hoping the beardog would trust him as usual.

Once in the cloud, the air felt steamy and oppressive, as it did down in the mines. Worst of all, Rhinan could see nothing. He just stepped forward, one foot and then the next, a long, dark walk, until at long last he emerged from the cloud.

Rip emerged behind him, an arrow barely lodged in his haunch, but otherwise well. The beardog immediately tore the arrow out with his teeth and began to lick the wound.

Looking around, Rhinan was overwhelmed. They had stepped into a vast cavern, many horse lengths high and even longer from one end to another. It curved here and there, and even had several spots where platforms or outcroppings of rock were higher than the base at the center where they stood. Huge crystalline forms of various shapes and sizes jutted out around the cavern, creating illumination. Param held his bandaged hand, looking quite weak, but Eodorr, Lynari, Brondur, and Wogen all seemed to be fine. The other two miners, whose names Rhinan did not know, were also fine.

They had escaped Dran. Again.

But where were they?

"Wogen? Is that you?"

The voice echoed in the vast cavern. Rhinan realized they were surrounded by dozens of rock gnomes. One of them, a pretty gnome woman (A gnomette? Rhinan wasn't actually sure what the proper term was for a female gnome) stepped forward. She was looking at Wogen as if she were seeing a ghost (And Rhinan would know).

"Aye, Yeggam, it's me."

Yeggam rushed forward and embraced Wogen tightly. Wogen whispered sweetly to her, and Yeggam's eyes filled with tears. "We'd given up," she cried. "We thought we'd lost you."

Brondur had mentioned a wife and family to Rhinan, but

Wogen hadn't mentioned a wife, though Rhinan made that assumption about Yeggam. It could be his sister or mother, but the pair seemed to have more of an intimate nature. And it had clearly been a long period of time since they had seen one another.

Another rock gnome stepped forward. He wore a crown fashioned of some of the prettier crystals, polished and as multi-colored as a rainbow. This was obviously an authority figure among the throng of Rock Walkers in the cavern. "Eratho," Wogen addressed him and bowed.

"'Tis good to see you after such a long absence, Wogen." Eratho gave Wogen a firm handshake before he continued, "But you know the rules. You can't bring outsiders here. These others, we'll have to kill them now."

Wogen held up both hands. "Right. About that…"

Chapter Thirty-Six

At dawn, they found what was left of Gaimesh partially buried in snow among the trees nearby. Most of his face was gone. This was also true of several soldiers, as well as another one of Dran's men. Lastly, a beardog had shredded another soldier and one more of the *Maraggan.*

Dran had ridden into the mining camp with fifteen men, dispatched one to Arskellion to retrieve five more, and lost three in a battle with some horrendous beasts living in the mines and a beardog. His remaining team was now reduced from twenty to seventeen. Not even a score left from the original forty *Maraggan* he'd started out with to investigate what was supposed to be a routine pilfering accusation in an out-of-the-way town called Cabelon that they only pursued because of the victim's connections to Jerrick.

The only good news was that he'd sent for reinforcements from Masseltaine a few days ago, immediately following the battle with Vaylene. The reinforcements should catch up with them in Arskellion soon. And he still had Venelwin retrieving Captain Flek and four more of the *Maraggan* in Arskellion. Before long, he'd be at full strength or better, and then he'd set a trap for this Ylvan and his companions, of which now he counted approximately a half dozen plus, apparently, a "pet" beardog.

Chasing the Ylvan when he was using magic and had so many allies had been foolhardy. Of course, until last night's battle, Dran had had no idea there was a Rock Walker and a beardog among the Ylvan's allies. The former soldier who'd served the Constable in Cabelon, and the troubadour, those were less concerning. The mysterious woman was of greater concern to Dran, especially since he'd never had time to question her and now Gaimesh was gone. Gaimesh had been a most useful tool in many of Dran's criminal investigations. His loss would be impactful.

But Dran had to reassess his entire approach. There had to be a way to draw this Ylvan back to him. Or, for the flicker of a moment, he considered just letting the bandit continue his journey east. He'd likely be handled when he got to the Unreigned Territory anyway, and that was growing nearer. Perhaps Dran could turn his attentions to other matters. But that was not Dran's way. He wanted to be there when this case was resolved, especially after all the inconvenience it had created for him.

One of the "matters" was quick and easy to resolve: the soldier in charge of the mining camp. He'd been using a Rock Walker. Risky, but worse, he'd been using a magic implementation to restrain him. Magic use was forbidden. This applied to soldiers as well as commoners. And, due to his keeping a rock gnome among the miners, the entire Ylvan entourage had escaped capture last night. No, as a direct representative of the King, and enforcer of his edicts, it was Dran's job to punish this soldier. So they hanged him, protesting shamefully, from a snowy tree shortly after retrieving all of the dead. Dran made the ultimate example of the man.

Then Dran turned his attention to these Eyeless Ones. From what he could determine, they harassed the miners doing the King's work and were therefore a menace to Lydania. When he had time and a full staff, there would be a vigorous and efficient hunting party into this mine and these grotesque monsters would be eliminated. Completely. But that was for later.

For now, he prepared the *Maraggan* to ride down to Arskellion to prevent Venelwin and Flek and the others from wasting their time riding up to the mining camp. No sense in them coming there now. Also, by now, the reinforcements he expected from Masseltaine should have reached Arskellion as well.

While they finished up, he put his mind to determining where the Ylvan may have gone. Where would a Rock Walker take them? That was an open question. Who knew the ways of gnomes? For all Dran knew, the rock gnome had led them into some kind of deadly trap and his problem was already solved. There was little contact with them, so it was hard to determine what they might or might not do.

Then things got worse for Dran. Before they even left the mining camp, Venelwin came riding back hard.

He was alone.

He dismounted before Dran, looking pale. Wisps of his breath trailed away in the cold air. "Hard news, My Lord. Forgive me, but it must be conveyed to you."

Dran shook his head, limped forward, and growled. "Out with it."

Venelwin took a step back, but then stood up straight. He appeared sorrowful. "I'm afraid it's Captain Flek and the others. They were… Sir, they were slain mercilessly in their sleep. Two nights ago."

Dran cursed. Flek was among the most promising young *Maraggan*. "All of them? Slain how?"

Venelwin swallowed, then answered. "Throats cut. In their sleep. Well, mostly. It appeared one of them may have been awake. It did not seem he had been given an opportunity to defend himself."

"Assassins!" Dran took a moment to compose himself. His rage was such that he couldn't count on maintaining rational contemplation of all of the facts at hand. Gathering his thoughts, he considered that—from what he knew—the Ylvan was conscripted two nights ago. His thoughts went back to the mysterious woman. Was she a sort of witch? Another Vaylene? He would have to make it a priority of getting his hands on her if the opportunity presented itself again. This incident must have been performed by some of Ashuir's companions.

But were there more? How far did this extend? Were they already facing another Uprising? That thought caused even him to dread.

Dran regained his composure, forcing himself to become calm. So frightfully calm, in fact, that he knew it scared his men. Beyond his evident fury was a wrath so deep that it would drown his enemies. It didn't happen often, but he had now reached that point.

"Venelwin, I am promoting you to Captain to replace Flek. See to it that you do not disappoint me."

"Upon your orders, My Lord." Venelwin didn't seem too pleased, but he accepted the commission with grace. Dran didn't care, as long as he served competently.

"My first orders for you are to return to Arskellion with

haste. Take a couple of men with you and find out what you can about this business. Assassinations of our elite *Maraggan*? This is an act of open rebellion. It will be treated as such. I will bring the rest of the men right behind you after we pack up. If they are not there, I can no longer await reinforcements. I will meet with the Duke of Arskellia and commandeer a portion of his soldiers. This situation with the Ylvan is escalating, and we need to determine where he and his companions have gone. I am done with chasing him. We are going to get ahead of him. I just need the manpower—and horsepower—to find a point on his trek where he's certain to cross and we can be waiting when he gets there. Let him come to me. I now have the advantage of knowing who I'm looking for, unless there is more magic being employed than I suspect."

"At once, My Lord." Captain Venelwin turned to recruit two men and headed to Arskellion to investigate further. Venelwin hadn't been able to discover much upon learning of the murders, but Dran was sure there were more answers to be had.

Dran hoped he would be careful; he could ill afford to lose the men he already had, let alone more. After losing three men last night and now the five in Arskellion, the King's special force of forty soldiers, his *Maraggan*, was down to a simple dozen. From forty to twelve in a matter of days. Merely one Ylvan was wreaking havoc in Lydania.

* * * * *

Dusted heavily with falling snow, Dran rode into Arskellion in a foul mood with the remainder of his men. This was the King's *Maraggan*, the best of the best. Once again, it infuriated him that it had come to this. Dran was not one to tolerate such waste.

The ride down the mountain had been uncomfortable with the new snowfall and the bitter cold. Winter gripped the land, and Dran knew the season could work as much for him as against him. Just as the terrible rains had, back near Cabelon, it would slow his pursuit. But it would also slow his prey, and potentially make them easier to track. If, he reminded himself, tracking were still to be his tactic for capturing the Ylvan. It hadn't proven effective. Another plan was emerging in his mind.

But first, supplies and soldiers. As Dran and his men rode into Arskellion, capitol of the region of Arskellia, they were recognized by the lackadaisical city guard on watch. One approached Dran, inquiring how he could be of service. Dran ordered the man to prepare a set of rooms at the finest inn, and to get word to Duke Rendiff that General Gethor Dran would require an audience immediately.

The soldier turned to a comrade, who dashed off into the town. Dran did not know which task he'd been assigned, nor did he care. It just had better be accomplished with all due respect and speed. He himself was cold and hungry, and his temperament was at an all-time low.

Leaving another soldier in charge, the one who'd approached Dran requested they follow him. He led them through the streets of the town, covered in icy slush from the snow. Arskellion had a reputation of being a prosperous town, but also dangerous, and Dran preferred not to be in it if he could avoid it. It had grown in size since his last visit. Perhaps the prosperous element was outpacing the dangerous element. This, at least, would be some small measure of good news he could deliver to Jerrick when this mess with the Ylvan was finished.

The inn they were ushered into was lush and comfortable. The timber from the mountains to the north had been used for its construction, and evidence of lavishly made materials from other regions were evident in everything from drapes to cushions. A warm fire roared in the hearth, and tables of customers were served what smelled like divine food and drink. The soldier approached the man at the front desk, a well-dressed fellow who looked as if he himself were some sort of soldier. The deskman wasted no time in approaching Dran.

"We are honored by your presence, My Lord. We will prepare rooms for you immediately. What else can we provide you with? Perhaps a hot meal while the preparations are being handled?"

Dran looked at the haggard men behind him, and turned back to the host. "A meal would, indeed, be welcome, and quickly. And then our rooms as soon as we're finished."

First seating Dran and his men, the host bowed and whisked away, presumably to the kitchens. It was mere moments before steaming plates and bowls of hot food were brought out by servers and laid upon the tables for Dran and his men. Not one of them hesitated, and they ravaged the meal, half-starved.

Dran looked at his men as they ate. They'd been in their uniforms and armor for days. They'd cleaned up some while his leg was healing, but they hadn't been given the proper treatment they deserved as members of a king's elite force. Finished eating, Dran summoned the host and ordered him to provide his men with whatever they so desired. Baths, companionship, whiskey, wine, or ale. Nothing available was to be denied them.

The other soldier who'd been dispatched first when

Dran arrived, sort of a rat-faced man, entered the inn and timidly approached Dran.

"My Lord?"

"Duke Rendiff?" Dran was impatient.

"He is awaiting your visit. I can lead you to his manor at your convenience."

"Hmm." Dran grunted. He then followed the host upstairs, finding his own room suitable for royalty: a large, deep bed, lush rugs, thick velvet drapes, marble wash basin... Dran ordered the Duke's soldier to summon a hot bath from the host while he stripped off his armor and uniform. While bathing, Dran enjoyed a good portion of a bottle of fine wine. He sent the host to have his uniform repaired and cleaned.

When he emerged from the bath, Dran examined his leg wound. Without Gaimesh to treat it any further, it would have to finish healing on its own. Vaylene had cut him deeper than he'd realized. He was lucky; he'd seen similar injuries kill lesser men. As it was, he was beginning to wonder if he would ever walk without a limp. The thought stoked the fires of his raging fury.

His uniform was delivered, brushed and repaired as well as could be expected without being completely replaced. Dressed, Dran felt like a General again. Now he could face Duke Rendiff in the proper frame of mind.

A little too favored by the King, Duke Rendiff Arskell was someone with whom Dran would have to negotiate carefully. In charge of supplying the royal coffers with silver and ore, Rendiff had gained favor with Jerrick. Dran found the man an insufferable fop, but Jerrick enjoyed him. Dran outranked him (not due to his military status, but due to his lineage to the throne), but it wouldn't do to initiate any unnecessary animosity. So long as Rendiff knew his place. Dran had purposely kept him waiting long enough to make that abundantly clear.

The rat-faced soldier was waiting outside of Dran's quarters, and he snapped to attention when Dran emerged from his rooms. Cleaned up, Dran was even more imposing—which had been his plan for meeting with Rendiff all along. He cursed the pain in his leg and the new limp he could not hide

Led out into the snowy afternoon, Dran soon discovered that Rendiff's manor was only a few steps from the inn. While not palatial, it was a royal estate, currently covered in snow. Dran was ushered into a large foyer of carved wood and exotic drapes. The floor shimmered, paved with clay that included flecks of silver. *Someone has been skimming the mine's yields*, Dran thought.

Duke Rendiff appeared and greeted Dran. Approximately forty summers in age and slightly taller than average height, Rendiff kept himself in shape and well-trimmed. He spent too much time on grooming, in Dran's opinion, but he always looked fine. He wore a shimmering green robe and the best smile he could produce without actually meaning it. Behind him was a shorter man of elder years who doddered in his wake, appearing wholly uninterested in anything whatsoever as he gazed off in different directions and displayed no intention or motivation of movement.

"General Dran." Rendiff nodded in respect. "Welcome to Arskellion. It is an honor to receive a visit from the *Maraggan*." He then turned to the short, elder man and spoke. "Swebhode, refreshments please."

"At once, sir," the old man replied in a tired voice,

thoroughly disinterested. He shuffled off at an unhurried pace that nearly made Dran sigh out loud.

"Please, join me in the study," Rendiff continued. Dran followed the Duke into a vast room with a large, ornate table at the far end, a pair of cushioned sofas facing each other in the middle of the room, and a lovely carpet that appeared to be from farther south and east of Lydania, perhaps from the lands beyond. Or even Ylvan make, Dran thought, taking another look at the fine detail in the patterning. The back wall was an entire shelf of books, whereas the front wall was a series of narrow windows, fashioned in pretty shapes but designed to be defensible. Rendiff may be a pompous ass, but he was never a fool.

"Please be at ease," Rendiff said to Dran, indicating the sofas. "And tell me what brings you to Arskellia."

"Misfortune." Dran said it with feigned boredom, reaching over to a side table to pick up a small silver bookend that sat there.

Rendiff immediately dropped the pretense of pleasantries. "Of course, General. My condolences on the loss of your men. We have a skilled number of soldiers on patrol in this city and they are working even as we speak to find the murderers and bring them to justice."

"I appreciate the effort, and please don't halt it," Dran put the bookend down and leaned forward, "but I can assure you the assailants are long gone."

The confused look on Rendiff's face was more of his false presentation. Dran assessed that the confusion was real, but the expression of concern was disingenuous. Rendiff asked, "How can you be sure?"

"We're pursuing an Ylvan and users of magic." Dran watched Rendiff's reaction carefully, and it was obvious that he did not believe the thing possible.

"There are no more Ylvans since the Uprising. And magic users? I know they are out there, but they are not of any power or great numbers. Why, it would have to be a—"

"Rebellion." Again, Dran studied the Duke's reaction. It was one of abject horror. Exactly the reaction he was hoping to see.

"Do you mean another Uprising led by an Ylvan sorcerer?"

"I do not think it has reached that level," Dran replied. "But it could, if we do not put an immediate stop to it."

The Duke stood up, pacing. "What must we do?"

Dran sat back. "I require soldiers. Your very best. No less than you can possibly spare… all that you can spare." Dran paused to watch the Duke. Rendiff didn't like the sound of that, but he was frightened of another Uprising now. "We need a small army, Rendiff, and we need it at once. Only Arskellion can answer this call."

Rendiff looked out the front windows, staring at some distant and invisible location. "Yes," he said at last. "Of course, My Lord. I will prepare the men for your review as quickly as possible."

It was clear that the Duke was in no way pleased about the idea of losing a significant portion of his town's defense. But in the face of another Ylvan-led Uprising, prompted by a little of Dran's best manipulation, Rendiff's cooperation would be assured without a challenge or complaint. Which was exactly what Dran needed.

Swebhode entered the study, carrying a large silver tray of what appeared to be very fine dried meats, cheese, and fresh bread, with a pitcher filled with wine.

And Dran perhaps needed a bit more of that as well.

Chapter Thirty-Seven

"These humans," Wogen pleaded with Eratho, "every one of them, were helpful in freeing me from the bonds of the King of Lydania."

"Gnomes do not recognize the kingdoms of men." Eratho shook his head.

Wogen grew angry. "Nor do gnomes attempt to find and rescue lost members of their own kind, even after some months, apparently. But this does not change the fact that these subjects defied their own King to save me."

Eratho leaned back against a rock that was waist high for him. Rhinan figured it would be just above knee height for himself. He considered they may have to fight their way out of yet another predicament, but taking a good look around the cavern, he realized there were far too many of the Rock Walkers. All were well-armed with war hammers such as Wogen's, as well as short swords and other forms of weaponry. Not to mention their ability to drag you away through a rock and just leave you stuck there. Or, Rhinan shuddered, even leave you embedded *within* a rock. No, Rock Walkers were not to be tangled with if it could be avoided.

Then a thought occurred to him. He stepped forward and bowed to Eratho. "Your, uh, Highness…" He really had so little knowledge of the proper and respectful way to address Rock Walkers. "If I may speak?" Eratho looked up at him and nodded, and Rhinan continued. "When we left the mines where we and Wogen were imprisoned, we brought with us two chests filled with silver ore. Perhaps we can offer these to you in good faith with a promise never to speak of what we've seen here. Besides, we could never find our way back without the help of a Rock—" Again, knowledge of proper terms of address failed him, and he didn't wish to use a term which Eratho may find demeaning in some way. "Without the help of one of your people, we could never lead anyone here."

"What use have we for silver?" The Gnome King's tone was condescending. "We have not only an abundance of both silver and gold, but every glittering jewel that exists, in plenty, at our fingertips." He waved his arms around at all of the shimmering crystalline formations in the cavern. Rhinan could identify almost none of them, but it was clear they were valuable as more than a light source. It had been foolish of him to offer.

"The lad is right, though," Wogen continued. "They can do us no harm. In fact, they've shown us a kindness that proves such."

Eratho considered Wogen's words, rubbing his chin. His resemblance to Wogen was more than simply the features of gnomes… short and broad of stature, pointed ears, round noses. Like Wogen, Eratho was balding and his facial features shared similar sharp traits to Wogen's. "Wogen, you've been gone a long time. The Land Walkers in Lydania have become more troublesome for our people. We must not risk attracting their attention, and that means that the rule must stand. Despite their kindness to you—" and here he looked to all of the company standing beside Rhinan and behind Wogen, "—and no doubt helping themselves to your assistance in return, they must never leave this place. If we do not kill them, we must imprison them forever."

Rhinan was sure he could speak for Eodorr, Brondur, and the miners when he thought that they'd spent enough time underground as it was. Neither death nor imprisonment was an outcome he would face without a fight. He longed for his woods back around Cabelon, roaming free and hunting with Rip, even suffering his own madness of seeing the ghosts of what were most likely the dead Ylvan clans. He clenched his bow tightly, and reached for an arrow… an act that did not escape the notice of Wogen.

"Now, easy, lad," the Rock Walker said to him in hushed tones. "There is a bit of negotiation left. Let's not start something here we can avoid."

Wogen turned back to Eratho. "Brother, I may have been gone a long time, but how hard did you seek to find me? Hmm?"

Eratho held up his hands. "After a time, we assumed you had chosen self-exile. Your friendship with the Land Walkers," he looked up at Brondur, "led us to believe that you had abandoned your people. You never were of one mind with us."

"Liar!" It was Yeggam who stepped forward now. She screamed in Eratho's face. "You feared your own brother's claim to the rulership of our people, and you ignored my pleas for continued searches!"

Eratho turned as red with anger as Rhinan suspected rock gnomes could, even with their range of skin tones from stone gray to clay red. "Get back, woman! You forget your place!"

Wogen stepped forward with clear intent. "That is my wife you address, brother, and as such, do not forget she is royalty." Wogen's growl of this warning caused Eratho to flinch and step back. Wogen pressed forward. "Eratho, I did not return to challenge your rulership of our people. Have you so feared my presence that you allowed me to suffer these many months? All to retain your own power? If so, you have become as paranoid as the King of the Lydanian Land Walkers. As such, you are very clearly unfit to rule."

Wogen reached down for a fistful of dirt and flung it onto Eratho's chest in an almost comical gesture. "Eratho, King of the Rock Gnomes, I, Wogen, your brother and next in line for rulership, challenge your right to continue as King. I demand the Contest of Grembul. We will fight for the right to rule our people."

This had taken a serious turn Rhinan had not foreseen. He was stunned to learn that Wogen was a prince of the rock gnomes, but even more so that he would risk a fight with his own brother to save Rhinan and his friends. He did not know what the Contest of Grembul was, but Rhinan was concerned.

"Wogen, is there not some other way for us to resolve this?" Rhinan whispered.

"Rhinan, lad, you freed me. If I must put my life at risk to protect you now, honor demands that I must do so."

Rhinan sighed. Yet another good soul in harm's way because of him, the last of the Ylvan clans. Was there no end to this? Could he bargain his own life instead to let his friends leave?

Wogen was watching him and spoke. "If it weren't you,

it would have been something else eventually. Eratho has always been a bit… off. This is something I was running from anyway, but I should have taken care of long ago. This isn't because of you, Rhinan, but you've given me the courage I needed to finally take this action. Now I need you to lend me any more of that magic you may have for this fight." Wogen smiled and winked at him, then he turned away.

Looking to his other companions, none of them wore any expression of hope. Brondur appeared saddest of all, but the truth was, this Contest of Grembul, whatever it was, would likely determine the ultimate fate of each of them. Besides Brondur, only Eodorr and the two miners actually knew Wogen, and what a personal loss it would be if the outcome didn't go his way. The outcome being implied that the loser would die, whereas the winner would continue to rule, or assume rule, over the rock gnomes.

Yeggam looked saddest of all, having just been reunited with her husband only to perhaps lose him now. "This is how you welcome your own brother home," she sneered at Eratho. "May such brothers be rare among all peoples." She sat next to Brondur, and it was apparent they'd met before. The friendship of Brondur and Wogen obviously predated their imprisonment in the camp. It seemed odd to Rhinan, who would have expected that if a forester such as Brondur were to befriend a gnome, it would be a wood gnome before a rock gnome. Whereas rock gnomes ran from grayish to reddish in shade, wood gnomes (also called "Tree Walkers" for being able to use trees to travel in the way that rock gnomes used rocks) ran from light brown to greenish in hue. On rare occasions, Rhinan had seen them in the forests even as far away as Cabelon, but had never had any exchanges with any of them. Yet here was a forester, clearly a friend to a rock gnome. If nothing else, Lydania was a land of surprises.

Eratho appeared to be prepared for Wogen's challenge. He was slightly taller than Wogen, but not as burly. Wogen, however, had just returned from an extended conscription in a mining camp where he was worked hard and fed little. Holding a polearm similar to Wogen's long-handled, square-ended war hammer, Eratho stepped back into the center of the huge cavern.

There were rocks and crystals emerging from the top, sides and floors of the cavern. There were even tree trunks growing up from the base of the cavern, out through the top, undoubtedly appearing up on the surface as any other tree in the woods. All of these gave the two combatants plenty of cover and strategic concealment for their fight.

As Eratho stepped back, Wogen stretched his arms and swung his hammer about, loosening his joints. He smiled. It must have felt good to be back in his element, and have the freedom to once again do something he chose, even if it wasn't what he'd hoped to be doing. With a mighty swing, Wogen drove his hammer in an arc through one of the thick trunks of a tree that reached up to the top of the cavern. Rhinan's eyes widened, as this was no mere sapling. When Wogen's hammer swung through the trunk, it penetrated, removing a sizable chunk from the center of the trunk. There was a brief pause where the top of the trunk dropped down onto the bottom half of the trunk, appearing momentarily as if nothing had happened at all. Then, with the loud crack of large roots ripping out from above and a cacophony of earth and rock falling all around, the top of this tree fell into the cavern, pulling debris down from the cavern ceiling as it toppled. A group of gnomes on the far side where it fell scrambled nimbly to evade the massive chunk of tree. It was a feat far beyond what Rhinan would have given Wogen credit for having the ability to achieve, but he was apparently not the only one impressed by the opening display. Every eye in the cavern was widened by Wogen's demonstration of might, and even Eratho's expression betrayed a level of surprise and concern.

With a war cry, Eratho charged Wogen and swung his own hammer. Wogen deftly leapt above the swing. Eratho's hammer impacted with a large crystal, spraying fractured shards in several directions. Again, rock gnomes on the receiving end of the debris ducked for cover.

Wogen brought his hammer down with a blow that would have crushed his brother, but Eratho rolled out of the way. Wogen's blow struck the cavern floor, causing the entirety of the massive room to shudder from the impact. Rhinan could not believe the power these rock gnomes demonstrated. He wondered if the wood gnomes, the Tree Walkers, were as mighty. It was hard to believe what he was seeing.

Twisting quickly, Eratho managed to land a glancing blow on Wogen's hip. Though it had almost missed, it still sent Wogen spinning across the cavern floor where he broke off a few crystals in his path and landed against a larger boulder. If Rhinan calculated correctly, it was the boulder from which they'd emerged into the cavern.

Limping to his feet, Wogen leapt atop this boulder, awaiting Eratho, who charged at him again. With a mighty swing, Wogen brought down another blow that would have shaken the cavern, but didn't only because it met Eratho's own raised hammer, driving him backward in the process. There was a boom almost like thunder when the hammers clashed, and Rhinan and his companions winced.

Jumping down from the boulder, Wogen was still limping from the hip injury. Eratho rose from where he'd fallen at Wogen's last blow, and swung his hammer in a curved arc downward at Wogen. This would have crushed Wogen's right shoulder, clearly his lead shoulder, had it landed. As it descended, Wogen dropped to the ground and swiped out with his own hammer, sweeping Eratho's feet out from under him with what was clearly a painful strike, though it landed with little force. Nevertheless, the Rock Gnome King was lifted from his feet and dropped onto his backside.

Wogen quickly rose to his feet and charged his brother, almost certainly having the upper hand for a finishing blow. He stood above Eratho, hammer prepared to drop, and paused.

"Brother, I give you this one chance. Surrender your rule, and I will spare your life. Take it. I'm asking you in all earnest."

Eratho's response was anything but grateful. Though obviously in pain, he managed to shove his hammer into Wogen's gut, knocking him backward against the boulder on which he'd just been perched atop. Wogen hit the boulder with such force that it knocked his own hammer out of his hands, and the wind from his lungs. He slumped against the boulder, unarmed, sliding to a sitting position.

Eratho struggled to his feet and now stood over his brother, his own hammer raised. The rock gnomes began to grumble and cry "foul." From what Rhinan gathered, it was apparently considered against the rules, or at least poor form, to finish your opponent in the Contest of Grembul unless your enemy still held his weapon in his hands. Eratho shrugged off the complaints, and spoke to Wogen.

"You should have stayed away, brother. But you

returned to seek *my* throne?" Eratho's face was twisted into a furious expression. He brought his hammer down and, without his hammer in hand to defend or block, Wogen twisted in desperation to avoid the strike. His left leg was caught in the blow and crushed below the knee. The Rock Walker cried out in pain, drawing himself back against the boulder. Eratho seethed. "I will be perfectly satisfied to finish you a piece at a time."

The rock gnomes uttered protests, but no action was taken. From this, Rhinan presumed it wasn't against the rules, but just generally frowned upon. Himself, he considered it an act of cowardice. He could not contain himself, and shouted it out loud. "Coward!" There was nothing to lose here. If Wogen did not emerge victorious from this Contest, the fate of Rhinan and his friends was all but sealed at any rate.

His cry caught Eratho's attention, who chanced a quick glance at the Ylvan. He sneered, then turned back to aim at Wogen's other leg in a merciless show of torture.

In that fraction of time, Wogen reached behind him into the boulder. A small portion at the base of the boulder took on that gray, cloudy appearance as if a Rock Walk were about to take place. Rhinan's first thought was that Wogen was going to attempt to flee, but then he was surprised.

His arms raised with his hammer, Eratho prepared to crush Wogen's other leg, he was caught completely off guard when his unarmed opponent withdrew a short sword from the boulder and drove it upward into the heart of the Rock Gnome King. A stunned look came over Eratho's face as he dropped his hammer. He clutched at his own chest where gray rock gnome blood spilled forth in a heavy stream. He opened his mouth to speak, but no sound emerged as he tumbled forward onto Wogen. He died on his brother's crushed leg, his last act in life one of malicious cowardice.

Yeggam was upon Wogen before anyone else had fully realized what happened, and Brondur and Rhinan, Eodorr, and the miners were right behind her.

Wogen's eyes were filled with tears. "I didn't want to do it," he wept. "You heard me, no? I asked him to surrender his rule in peace."

"We heard, my dear," Yeggam sobbed. "Eratho left you no choice."

Brondur had bent down and heaved Eratho's body to the side, examining Wogen's crushed leg. "I'm so sorry, my friend. You'll be doing no Rock Walking, or any walking at all, for some time to come."

Wogen grumbled something unintelligible.

"Where did you pull that sword from?" Yeggam asked. "That was fortunate, to say the least."

Wogen chuckled, then winced, before he answered. "I slipped that into this boulder years ago. An old Rock Walker trick me pa taught me as a young one from some ancient tale he'd once heard. Find strategic rocks and imbed them with hidden weapons you may need some day. Well, I figured right here in this cavern would be as strategic as any, so that short sword has been there for many years. I'd hoped never to use it, but turned out me old pa was wiser than I ever gave him credit for."

Chapter Thirty-Eight

Fully geared up for a long winter's ride, General Gethor Dran, ten *Maraggan*, and a score of Duke Rendiff's best soldiers—hand-picked by Dran himself—made ready to ride east. Packs of food, weapons, furs, and other supplies were strapped firmly to the hardiest horses that could be rounded up in Arskellion. The town was prosperous, so soldiers, horses, and supplies were top notch. As far as an outer Lydanian city went, and despite his dislike for Rendiff, the force he'd assembled in Arskellion was as satisfying to Dran as it was going to get. Still, Dran was suspicious of Rendiff's prosperity, and planned to discuss it with Jerrick when he returned to Masseltaine... hopefully with an Ylvan from Clan Ashuir in chains or, more preferable to Dran, in pieces.

The morning sky was gray, tinged with vermillion, and Dran and his men were wrapped in heavy furs. Winter was upon them now, and though Dran would rather be sitting back in Masseltaine where it was somewhat warmer, lounging by a fire with a fine brew in hand while his men trained for the day, there was no chance he would return to Masseltaine now without the Ylvan, or absolute proof that the Ylvan was dead. In either condition, the Ylvan was now number one on Dran's life mission list. It was a short list—mostly because Dran tended to accomplish his missions with intimidating efficiency—and a list you would be unfortunate to find yourself on.

Dran decided to leave two of the *Maraggan* in Arskellion with Duke Rendiff: Captain Venelwin and young Thurrik. Venelwin, assisted by Thurrik, would be in charge of a contingent of Rendiff's soldiers who were still investigating the murders of Captain Flek and four other of the King's elite force. Dran suspected the murderer, or murderers, were companions of Rhinan Ashuir, but he wanted to make sure there were no Ylvan allies or sympathizers in the area. If there were, he wanted them found and eliminated. Duke Rendiff assured him that his own forces would continue to assist in any investigation and pursuit if necessary in order to meet that end.

As Dran and his force prepared to leave Arskellion, Captain Venelwin, Thurrik, Duke Rendiff, and his troop of soldiers who would be at Captain Venelwin's service stood at attention to see them off. Dran reminded Venelwin that he'd sent a man to Masseltaine for reinforcements, so their orders were to follow Dran and join his force when they reached Arskellion. He realized the weather would be slowing them down as well, but he felt confident that his message would urge haste on their part. It had occurred to him that the possibility existed the message may not have reached King Jerrick, but he preferred to remain optimistic.

Either way, with thirty good men, well rested and refreshed, he felt a new vigor for this mission. And he had a different plan as well. It had been a disaster of proportions he'd not experienced, which infuriated him to no end, but he felt that unfortunate part of the mission was going to be as left behind as better weather. Perhaps winter would be his ally.

As they rode out of Arskellion, Dran turned to Kilward, the only Captain in the *Maraggan* that was left with Dran. Relatively new to the King's elite force, Captain Kilward was a very capable commander, and Dran felt he might even be the sort to assume the position of general some day when Dran retired. Kilward, however, was impossible to read. It made him effective in most cases, but it also made him difficult to control. Therefore, despite his competencies, he'd never been a favorite of Dran's. Yet here he was, having survived when Siras, Gaimesh, and other qualified captains in the *Maraggan* had not.

"Captain Kilward, have you ever been as far as the Unreigned Territory?"

"No, My Lord. Begging your pardon and with all due respect, why would I go there? It's a horrible place, especially dangerous to royal representatives, and we don't patrol it."

Dran rolled his eyes. There were reasons he wasn't overly fond of Kilward, despite his competency. "Do you know *why* we don't patrol it? It *is* a part of Lydania."

Kilward hesitated before answering. "It has something to do with how things changed after the Ylvan Uprising. Eluciar, the lands where the Ylvan Clans dwelled, lie somewhere beyond the Unreigned Territory. It wasn't part of Eluciar, so it's never made sense to me that we don't patrol it."

"Ah hah." Dran eyed him. "You weren't too old when the Uprising occurred, but you may recall hearing of a region of Lydania we called Norham?"

"Norham, of course. The only Lydanian region to side with Eluciar and the Ylvan Clans in the Uprising. But it no longer exists. Wasn't it absorbed by another region?"

"No. Once the Ylvans were eliminated, King Jerrick sent a force—which I led—into Norham and we hung the Duke. We did not replace the Duke of Norham, because the Norham lands provided a good border between the destroyed Eluciar and some of Lydania. But mostly, it made a powerful example of what to expect when allying with the King's enemies. Without the rule of law, Norham fell upon itself and became a haven for all manner of ruffians, thugs, and villains. Left Unreigned, warlords rose to control what portions of the former Norham we hadn't plundered. Unable to formulate peace, which is what we anticipated, the Unreigned Territory became what it is today: a wide patch of land where scoundrels and warlords fight for control over scraps under the illusion that they are not part of Lydania. We foster this illusion. It keeps it from becoming a united region and providing any trouble to Lydania. And we can expect any serious enemy of the crown to flee toward it, making it easy to find them if we must."

"It sounds like a good place to avoid to me." Kilward snorted. "Let them devour themselves."

Dran grinned. "Well, you must have missed what I just said. If we're having a problem finding someone wanted by the King, we can expect them to show up in the Unreigned Territory. You haven't been in the *Maraggan* too long, so you've never been with us when we've had to go there. We're not welcomed, but we do remind them that they are under the rule of King Jerrick upon such occasions."

"That sounds… awkward." Kilward stiffened.

"It's not pleasant, but there could be warlords willing to work with us. If not, we will simply replace them. The land does still belong to Lydania."

"So you believe this thief we're chasing—the supposed Ylvan—is making for the Unreigned Territory?" Kilward expressed curiosity about Dran's plan. Dran considered this the sign of a sharp mind.

"Almost certainly."

"And I suppose that's our destination?"

"It is. And despite the miserable trek just to reach it, we're going to see if our Ylvan rebel is there, or has passed that way. Since the Rock Walker took him, it's the only place I have left to search above ground."

Kilward shook his head. "Well, I accepted the promotion to the *Maraggan* for adventure. We've certainly had our share, and it sounds like I can expect more."

Dran nodded and prodded his horse forward. "And the sooner the better."

* * * * *

Still in the foothills of the Percenes, Dran and his men rode eastward in worsening climatic conditions. It slowed their progress, wore down their horses and their morale, and made environmental resources such as hunted meat and firewood difficult to come by. Yet each day, Dran had them up early and riding, driving them like a man possessed. The worse it snowed, the harder he drove them. They came across the occasional village which, in service to the King, provided them with much of their winter stores, leaving the villages in precarious shape. The obsessed General could not afford to waste any more time.

They chanced upon a lone rock troll a couple of days out of Arskellion, the confused creature having wandered further down from the mountains than one would expect. The tall, rocky creature observed their passage, but made no attempt to attack. It was a bit hard to tell with a twelve-foot beast made primarily of stone-like flesh, but Dran thought it appeared to be starving: emaciated build, slow, weakened movements, and the like. Trolls weren't known for being particularly intelligent, but this one knew better than to attack a fully armed squad moving at a determined pace. Or, perhaps, it was just too weak to make the effort. Dran considered having a couple of the men circle back and finish the creature off, but considering the pathetic appearance of the monster, he felt the rock troll would almost certainly die on its own soon enough. If he were not busy with more important matters, he would be inclined to capture the troll and find out where it came from, hunt the rest of whatever small tribe it came from, and finish them all. But rock trolls were usually only a menace up in the mountains, and Dran wasn't heading that direction anyway. He did, however, take note of any soldiers who displayed fear or concern at the site of the troll. These men would be designated for lesser, more unpleasant tasks. He had no patience for cowardice.

Shortly after leaving Arskellion, the Percenes bent away to the north, and the eastward lands upon which they traveled leveled out in the region of Ramwick. The northern plains were still covered in snow, but at least the flat landscape helped speed up their progress. Dran was relieved, because they would soon reach the banks of the great River Arinell, upon which sat the city of Dunskern. That would be their last good stop for supplies and possibly even additional reinforcements. He would give the men a day or two in Dunskern. He wanted to wait and see if the reinforcements might catch up to them but, even though they'd been travelling at a swift pace, it seemed unlikely that at least a scout wouldn't have reached them by now. He'd suspected before, but now he was certain his message never reached the King. So any reinforcements to be had in Dunskern would be crucial.

Especially because Dran was aware of what waited on the other side of the River Arinell. The Blackmire Bogs, which could at least be easier to cross in the winter. Their worst hazard lay in those fens, but perhaps she would be in hibernation, and they could make their way across without disturbing her. Otherwise, she could prove to be their undoing. Part of this rapid ride had been in the hopes of reaching the Blackmire Bogs while snow yet remained, because it seemed less likely that she would make an appearance. But if she did, all the reinforcements he could get in Dunskern would be needed to survive and pass beyond the bogs.

And after the Blackmire Bogs… the Unreigned Territory. Even with a large force, the chances of an adversarial warlord, rather than one willing to work with him, was an equal possibility. If it came to that, he would need enough men not only to prevail in such an encounter, but still have enough reserves to present an imposing force to the next warlord. If they could not easily buy a warlord to work with them in seeking the Ylvan, they could be in for a rough time of it. He would need the best and the most men he could have on hand.

No, Dran reflected, aside from Dunskern, little waited for his men that they would enjoy for a long, long while. And he knew, though they did not, that some of them would not be returning. There was little chance of that much luck, and luck had not favored Dran of late.

Despite his best efforts, Rhinan Ashuir had eluded him

to an embarrassing degree. Dran was not incompetent, but the constant unexpected allies of his prey—everything from rebellious magic-using cults to Rock Walkers and even a beardog—had proven him unequal to a challenge that had always been so simple for him. For just a moment, Dran wondered if his age was now a factor. Perhaps he was not as effective as he had always been. But he reminded himself that, until this level of illegal magic use, his enforcement of royal policies had never been anything less than thorough. He believed in being prepared for all contingencies, but magic was a contingency for which one could never fully be prepared.

Reflecting on the group he'd known to aid the Ylvan, his mind went back to the mysterious woman with the quarterstaff. She was no troubadour's dancer, of that he was sure. What, then, was she? Was there a new threat in Lydania? When his suspicions were aroused, he was rarely wrong. He felt she was a key to something important. He regretted losing Gaimesh in the battle with those insufferable Eyeless Ones. They would be another battle for another time, but they would be dealt with. For once in his life, his "to do" list was growing, and he found it unnerving.

"Kilward?" Dran called his captain forward.

"Yes, My Lord?"

"I want to ask you something." Dran reminded him of the woman who'd accompanied the troubadour and of her staff and the carvings upon it. "Have you ever encountered or heard of such a thing?"

Kilward replied without hesitation. "Why, yes, My Lord, now that you mention it. In fact, another traveler accompanying a troubadour, some years ago. It was a man, and he was of a similar sort. It never occurred to me until now to connect the two. To be quite honest, I had forgotten the incident."

Dran's head snapped around to face Kilward. "Explain."

Kilward's eyes seemed to be searching within his own memory. "It was a routine patrol when I was a mere trainee. We were in the highlands, having heard reports of rock trolls harassing merchants along the northern path. We were in a village, and a young troubadour entertained us. He was accompanied by a companion—not a dancer—who shared many characteristics of the woman, including a similar quarterstaff."

"And what became of this man?"

Kilward faced Dran in alarm. "He was accused of something, theft I believe, and our captain went to question him. The man leapt with such grace and speed that he nearly escaped. Whatever he'd done, there was no serious accusation. He was not in any danger of harsher penalties than what he chose for himself. It was… disturbing."

"He chose a penalty for himself?"

"We had cornered him. Seeing his possibility of escape was no longer possible, the man withdrew a dagger and slit his own throat, dying on the spot. I've never seen the like of it…" As Kilward trailed off, lost in his memories, Dran had the feeling there was something he wasn't saying.

"What else, Kilward? What else about that man makes you connect him now to our prisoner? Speak, man!"

Kilward looked up at Dran, clearly puzzled. "I could be wrong, sir, but, now that you've recalled the incident to my memory, I could swear that this troubadour was familiar. Like I'd seen him before. Now I believe it was the *very same* troubadour accompanying that man years ago."

Dran cursed. "And you got no information from either

of them at the time?"

"The troubadour vanished at the time. There was no accusation against him, so we did not pursue. The man who stood accused was now dead. We had no answers, but the case was closed."

"Who was your captain at the time?" Dran demanded.

"It was Captain Siras, sir."

"Idiot!" Dran snapped, and Kilward leaned away from him. "Not you, Kilward. Siras. When a man takes his own life to prevent capture, he's hiding something. And something *big*. Remember how the woman slammed herself against a rock? Letting that woman escape was just as bad as letting the Ylvan escape. When we spring our trap, we must take her alive, and we must be prepared for her to take such an extreme action again. There is some level of fanaticism going on, and that is never good."

"May I ask what our trap will be, My Lord?"

Dran nodded. "I have no way of knowing where the Rock Walker took them. We have no direction of pursuit. But one thing I'm fairly certain of: Ashuir will wind up in the Unreigned Territory at some point, if only to pass through it. Eluciar lays beyond it, and—that being the ancestral home of the Ylvan clans—I would expect Ashuir to make for that cursed place."

"I can see your logic, My Lord. But won't he spot us in the Unreigned Territory? We'll stand out among the rabble."

"Well, if he hasn't already passed through, we'll settle in and wait. But we're going to have to blend in. We're going to have to live the lives of criminals for a while and keep a sharp watch and listen for anyone coming through that fits any descriptions of our Ylvan and his friends. They're certainly unique enough. If they all accompany him—and he'll need their help to make it there, believe me—we'll hear of their arrival and take them before they suspect we're even there. They won't be expecting the *Maraggan* to take up residence in the Unreigned Territory, I assure you. They'll think we've given up the chase."

Kilward nodded. "The only problem I can foresee is if he's gotten ahead of us and is already there or passed through."

"It's possible, but it's the only place I can be reasonably sure he'll show up. We have to look into it."

"Certainly, My Lord. The other problem is the warlords."

Dran chuckled. "Leave them to me."

Chapter Thirty-Nine

The River Arinell raged down from the northeastern end of the Percene Mountains, rending an exceedingly broad path southward for many, many leagues until it reached the lowlands and split three ways. The tributary of Lissida headed westward to Corm Lake at Masseltaine (named after Jerrick's father, the Lydan King who moved the palace there) and then onward to the Framman sea. The eastward tributary of Carrama stretched southeasterly from that point and formed the southern border of Eluciar. But Arinell herself continued straight southward, branching out in the lowlands, until she dove into the Ventrean Sea.

By far the widest river in Lydania, Arinell flowed peacefully enough past Dunskern at the northern leg of its journey. Having come down from the Percenes where they bent away north, the plains that the river crossed heading south calmed it considerably by this point, making it a useful outpost for the city of Dunskern. Her depth and width would have made her an ideal shipping route all the way to the Ventrean Sea if it weren't for the rough split in the lowlands. But she did serve her purposes. Among those were keeping the Blackmire Bogs on the far side as distant as possible.

As they rode into Dunskern, the gentle sloping terrain was spotted with rocky hills and scattered copses of trees. A fine layer of snow was draped across the landscape, and Dran found this promising. The city on the river's shore was fortified with great strength, as it had played a major role in Lydania's defense during the Ylvan Uprising. Crossing the River Arinell and taking Dunskern was difficult enough coming through or past the Blackmire Bogs, but the city itself was heavily walled and armed. Even riding down into the city, which ran much further lengthwise from north to south than it did westward from the river, Dran could make out the walls and docks on the water side of the city. Massive wooden structures faced the river at even spaces, capable of firing sharpened logs at an angle into boats with ill intent that attempted to cross the river toward the city. Dran had seen these logs ignited and fired from the devices, much like a giant crossbow. If a ship wasn't pierced by the force of impact, it was set ablaze by the tarry substance with which these sharpened logs were coated and lit prior to being fired. And the Percene Mountains provided an almost endless supply for these logs.

The city's lofty walls stretched around from the river side to the north and south, dwindling to an average height on the west side, the direction from which Dran and his men now approached. Even at the most average point, Dunskern was no city to be trifled with. It was not only Lydania's easternmost outpost since the Ylvan Uprising eliminated Eluciar and left Norham unreigned, but it was overseen by the Lord Mayor Ingon Summerhill. Few men held Dran's respect as Lord Mayor Summerhill. Dran had seen Summerhill lead a charge from the low ground, outnumbered and in a surrounded position, and emerge victorious. In his day, Summerhill was an animal in battle. They called him the "Dragon of Dunskern," a term Dran found ironic.

The city's gates swung open for Dran and his men as they approached. A small force of Dunskern's city guard rode out to meet them, led by Summerhill himself. It had been some time since Dran had seen his old war companion, and it disappointed him to see that Summerhill had let himself go. He was not in the fit shape Dran had kept himself in. It concerned Dran that perhaps the old dragon had grown soft, but those in his command appeared to be in firm control, so Dran cast aside his doubts and greeted the Lord Mayor with all due respect.

"Lord Mayor Summerhill, it has been far too long." Dran managed to sound magnanimous, despite his current surveillance of the man's condition. He was a firm believer in establishing his own position, even as a visitor. He represented the King's right hand, and no one in any seat of power should ever be allowed to overlook that fact. Even if he were himself limping on a painful wound that seemed to be worsening without the attentions of Gaimesh.

Summerhill rode toward him. He'd grown fat, and wore fine decorative garments of colorful silk with braided cording and bits of gems attached, and he wore jewelry—necklaces and rings. Even his men's horses were overdressed with décor. It was like the waste Dran had seen in Arskellion. "General Dran, you've hardly aged at all. How do you remain so youthful and vigorous, even after all these years?"

Dran grinned. "I seldom lose a battle, even with time itself."

This brought a chuckle from the Lord Mayor, and his jowls and belly shook as he laughed. "Welcome to Dunskern,

Gethor. Please bring your men in and allow us to provide them with the utmost hospitality."

The formalities out of the way, Dran waved his men forward.

"Andric," Summerhill addressed one of his guards, "see to it that General Dran's men are treated with the highest regard and provided with the best of everything Dunskern has to offer."

Andric bowed and indicated to Kilward, who stepped forward as Dran's leading captain, that the men should follow him. As they filed through the city walls, Summerhill turned to Dran. He had stopped smiling.

"It is an honor to receive you, of course, but it can't be any good news that brings you this far east heading a contingent yourself. I see fewer of the *Maraggan* accompanying you than I would expect. Word does not reach Dunskern as quickly as we'd like, but something is afoot. I hope you plan to brief me."

Sighing, Dran placed a hand on the old warrior's shoulder. "Ingon, I have much news to tell you. And great favors to ask. But let us rest, eat, and restore ourselves before I burden you with such things."

"Of course, my Lord. There is much pleasure to be enjoyed in our city, and you should avail yourself of it as immediately as one can. Other matters? They are but flies at a festival here in Dunskern."

Dran followed the Lord Mayor into the city, but as he looked up at the lackadaisical soldiers on the wall, and he considered Summerhill's attitude, he came to the sad conclusion that time had, indeed, been winning the battle against the old warrior. Summerhill was still quite capable, Dran was certain, but the man—a handful of summers older than Dran himself—had definitely grown soft.

* * * * *

Summerhill noticed Dran's limp, and Dran gave the Lord Mayor his version of Vaylene's ambush. Without hesitation, Summerhill sent another messenger dashing off for a healer to have a look at the wound. A short wait later, the messenger arrived with a confidant man of probably thirty summers. He'd studied healing at the Lore College in Masseltaine, and Dran wondered warily if he'd spent any time under Vaylene's tutelage. Nevertheless, after a thorough inspection, the healer recommended most firmly that Dran stay off the leg for a while if he wanted to save it. It had become infected. Dran had to employ his skills at maintaining his fury.

Given that Dran would be held up for a few weeks—but not the entire winter—Summerhill enthusiastically insisted upon holding a mid-winter feast in the Lord Mayor's estate that would also honor and celebrate the arrival of the King's *Maraggan.* Despite his desire to maintain as low a profile as possible, Dran could not talk him out of this.

Concerned that the Ylvan could be in the area, Dran ordered Kilward to have some of the *Maraggan* and a few of Rendiff's more competent men thoroughly combing the city at all times. Ashuir could have already passed through, he could show up at some point while Dran recovered, or he could be anywhere. It left Dran in poor spirits.

One thing Summerhill had not failed in as he had aged, and Dran had not recalled, was his penchant for finery. Dunskern's buildings were decorated and painted in exotic, shimmering hues from much further to the east and from the distant south. Diversity of people and architectural styles were everywhere. Many places in the city, street performers were distracting to the extent that Dran considered them to be underfoot. In some cases, men rode strange beasts other than horses—beasts such as the *Brascudos* with pairs of narrow horns like blades extending up each side of their snouts, with stocky builds—broader torsos than a horse but shorter legs. There were also rounded beasts, chest-high to a man, which were covered in their own rough shell—*Shell Mounts*—which featured a tail ending in a spiked club. Both quite useful as battle mounts, but rare—at least in Lydania. They came from distant lands, and Dunskern was clearly a draw to visitors from such places, though most of the travelers would probably have had to come up the River Arinell and through the Shilam Forest to reach this city. The lands across the river—the Unreigned Territory and the dead lands of Eluciar—presented problems of their own.

While Summerhill's private guard was exceptional, Dunskern's troops in general were not well trained. Given an opportunity to witness a demonstration of combat techniques, Dran was surprised to find that skills were lacking he would have expected Summerhill to demand of his soldiers. Especially given this was, as Summerhill liked to point out, the most important defensive city in the east of Lydania.

Besides his health delay, Dran's problem was two-fold. His first problem was that he needed more men. His chances of losing men in either the Blackmire Bogs (and he sincerely hoped not there) or in the Unreigned Territory were fairly high, and he would need to maintain an imposing force. The other problem that he now faced was getting Summerhill to give men up. The man was obsessed with keeping Dunskern defended (albeit lacking in quality), and Dran expected the Lord Mayor to be extremely reluctant to give Dran reinforcements. But watching Summerhill had given him an idea as the days passed and his leg healed.

The mid-winter feast was extravagant. Platters of meats with exotic seasonings, rare fruits, delicious breads, and vintage wines and ales were brought as if they were endless. Both men and women performers played, danced, and sang. Dran assigned Kilward to keep a sharp eye on every one of them. The entire grandiose display was held at the Lord Mayor's estate, a virtual palace with a dining hall, a ballroom, and lavish gardens. Had it not been winter, it would undoubtedly be breathtaking. The event was crowded with the upper crust of Dunskern's society. Dran was sick of the whole ostentatious ordeal early in the event, but he could not escape Summerhill.

"So, Gethor…" The Lord Mayor was well into his drink at this point. "Perhaps we should discuss what brings you all the way to Dunskern. You've never said. Was this just a convenient location to recuperate from your battle?"

Dran looked around quickly, taking note of anyone who could be listening. Not seeing anyone immediately paying attention, he grabbed Summerhill by the arm with intensity and leaned into his ear. "Do we have a private room where we can discuss this?"

Shocked, Summerhill stammered, "Why, yes, of course. This way." Dran (still limping, permanently, but in much better condition) followed the tottering Lord Mayor past the celebrating crowds of people and to a staircase leading upward. Soon he was locked in a spacious private sitting room with Summerhill.

After a quick search of the room and a look outside to make sure no one was at the door, Dran was certain they were alone. "We have a security problem in Lydania, and I need your assistance."

"*Me*?" Summerhill's eyes widened as he pursed his lips, leaning back in surprise. "I live to serve. What do you require? And may I ask why?"

With a heavy sigh, Dran grabbed the bridge of his nose with his thumb and forefinger. "I tell you this, Ingon, in the strictest confidence. Only King Jerrick and I know this, but I am trusting you with this information because you were the greatest warrior in the King's army in the Ylvan Uprising, and you were my inspiration." Dran was laying it on thick, but he could tell that Summerhill was suitably impressed by the flattery.

"It is within my vows to serve the King to protect and keep confidences."

"Ingon, there is a living Ylvan. I am either on his trail, or I am setting a trap for him. I am not sure which. I don't know his whereabouts, but I do know he will come this way to reach the Unreigned Territory... and possibly even Eluciar."

Summerhill was stunned almost to sobriety. "There are no Ylvans in Lydania." Dran watched as it dawned on Summerhill that he was being told the truth. Then Summerhill smiled and rubbed his hands together. "An Ylvan, you say? Wen's tongue! Why you could knock me over with a feather." Dran almost laughed, feeling certain that this might be true after smelling the drink on Summerhill's breath. "So how do we set up a trap here?"

"Oh, no." Dran was quick to rule that out. "Far too dangerous, and we know that a Rock Walker is among his allies. He can pass Dunskern and reach the Unreigned Territory and leave us sitting here like fools."

Summerhill looked confused. "Then how can I be of service?"

"Ingon, I need men. And plenty of them." For fodder, Dran withheld. Again, there was no doubt he would lose some of these men, but it would be vital to maintain an imposing force at any cost. Summerhill's men were less well trained than Rendiff's, which meant he now had expendable resources.

Summerhill drew back. "Why, Gethor, you know the King relies on Dunskern to protect the northeastern edge of Lydania. We've established this fortress town on the River Arinell to prevent anyone…" and here he gave a Dran a knowing look, "or any*thing*, from menacing the kingdom. The only thing I cannot spare is men."

Dran was afraid of this. "You see I only have a small number of the King's *Maraggan* with me, don't you? Ingon, I swear to you that I have sent to have reinforcements prepared." Dran knew they would have arrived long ago if they were actually coming. No doubt his scout never got through to Jerrick. But Ingon didn't need to know this. "They can be here in days. I can leave *Maraggan* in your command." It was a baiting ploy, but Dran knew Summerhill would see it as a gesture to his prestige.

This seemed to start Summerhill thinking. "But you intend to cross the Blackmire, *and* you intend to enter the Unreigned Territory?"

"Think of it, Ingon. The King will be forever in your debt, and our mission will succeed because you sent men to help prevent another Ylvan Uprising—"

"But there *are* no Ylvans!"

"There is one. And we'd like to insure that he will be the last. Look, Ingon, I can order you to turn troops over to me. You know this. Ordinarily, I would. But in this case, I feel you'll do the right thing without having to resort to any unpleasantries."

Chagrined, Summerhill stared up at Dran. "Well, of course, I'll do the right thing. You'll be sure to return them safely, won't you? I know the dangers over there, Gethor."

"I'll take care of them," Dran assured him.

"And the King will know I helped with this?"

"I will tell him myself."

"Very well. How many men will you require? And how soon do you plan to leave?"

Dran had him. It had gone as he had hoped, and he'd succeeded in acquiring what he needed again. "I will require at least twenty good men. The best. And—now that I'm up and about—we should leave as soon as possible, while the Blackmire is still under snow. Perhaps a day from now."

Summerhill rubbed his chins. "So be it. In the morning, choose your men during their training exercises. I will ensure they all show up for your inspection."

Dran smiled at the old warrior. He felt almost sorry for the old fool. He'd once been such a capable soldier. "That will be perfect—"

There was a loud banging on the door. "It's Andric, My Lord!" called a voice from the other side.

Dran turned and opened the door. Andric was taken aback and seemed unsure if he should speak or run.

"What is it?" Dran snapped.

"It's the western wall, My Lord." Andric addressed Dran rather than Summerhill. He clearly knew the chain of command. "We are under some sort of attack."

"Attack?" Summerhill stepped forward. "On the west wall?"

"Two men, felled by arrows." Andric cringed. "Perhaps more. We are still investigating."

Dran turned to Summerhill. "I'll handle this. Why don't you stay here where it's safe?"

"Oh… well, if you think it best." Summerhill looked as confused and frightened as someone who'd never even seen battle.

Furious at this news, Dran stormed past Andric to find Kilward and rally the troops he had with him. Whoever was attacking from the west, it was probably related to Ashuir. This could be an opportunity. Or even more disaster.

Chapter Forty

The rock gnomes did not wait for Wogen's leg to heal before he was bestowed the title of Grembul, the King of the Rock Walkers. Many of the rock gnome officials fussed over ceremonial preparations, but only at the risk of Yeggam's wrath, who saw to her husband's recovery with militant vigilance.

As he healed, Wogen not only offered, but requested, that Rhinan and his friends remain in the caverns with the rock gnomes for the time being. The new Rock Walker Grembul pointed out that it was winter above, and they were safe here among friends. He wanted to be the one to rock walk them to their next location, and even join them on their journey further east. He had sworn to aid Rhinan in his quest, and Rhinan considered this not only an honor now that he knew Wogen's status, but certainly beneficial having witnessed the gnome's capabilities. It was hard for Rhinan to refuse the injured sovereign, and so it came to be that they waited out the winter months underground. At any rate, it was far more pleasant than the mines. It was actually quite fascinating, Rhinan found, as he explored. The large, precious gemstones that grew like wildflowers in the connected system of caverns provided both luminescence and beauty—not at all dark and gloomy as he would have expected (and if he happened to find a few smaller-than-fist-sized gems lying around loose on occasion, his travel pack swelled a bit). The vast systems of tree roots were not only fun to guess at the type of tree, but to climb and swing from in the larger caverns. There was no meat, but the rock gnomes served hearty dishes of vegetables, fruits, and nuts they gathered from who-knew-where.

Among the Rock Walkers, Rhinan and his friends were celebrities as friends of the Grembul—and curiosities as well, as most of the rock gnomes avoided any interaction with Land Walkers anyway. Most of them were surprised to learn that Land Walkers didn't make a habit of stewing rock gnomes or, worse, drying them out, painting them in bright colors, and decorating their homes with them. Rhinan and his friends found these tales humorous, which in turn delighted the Rock Walkers and clearly provided them with some level of relief. Rock Walkers averaged about the height of Rhinan's midsection, but the Rock Walker children were much tinier. They, of course, took especially to Param; he kept them entertained with tales of the Lore Givers and all sorts of other adventures.

Param was a constant concern for Rhinan. He'd meant to be the one to break the news about Brinaya to her son, but it hadn't turned out that way. Lynari explained how it came about, and Rhinan understood, but he could see that the shock would take some time to heal.

And healing, for Param, involved far more. A troubadour by trade, losing the lower half of his right hand could have ended his career. The Rock Walker children were the best help for Param in dealing with this adjustment.

Param still played his mandolute for them with skill. By the luck of the Lore Givers, no further damage had been done to him.

As for fighting, due to King Jerrick's laws, Param never carried a sword. He was adept, but his lengthy dagger was important as a wandering showman to protect one's earnings from the opportunistic bandits that preyed on such individuals. Param often travelled in caravans of merchants and other entertainers, even earning some gold pieces while he moved between villages and towns and cities. But defense was necessary. He was also an archer of some skill, having had plenty of training from Rhinan, and it turned out his hand injury did little to reduce that skill. They were able to shoot at targets of cloth woven by the rock gnomes and hung in out-of-the-way caverns, which helped Rhinan keep his own skills sharp as the winter passed.

As far as sword and dagger play, Lynari and Eodorr helped Param immensely. The time underground was put to good use. Param made progress, and it became apparent his sword skills would be almost as good as they'd ever been should he need them. It would, of course, depend on the sword, but they were able to find ones that gave the troubadour plenty of opportunity to practice. As a town guardsman, Eodorr had trained beside soldiers in the Lydanian army before his assignment at home in Cabelon as an official, so his skills were considerable. Lynari, as it turned out, was adept at many weapons from her quarterstaff, to daggers, to small, bladed fist straps she carried.

There was an interesting personal dynamic among the three. Eodorr's enchantment with Lynari clearly continued, but Lynari and Param had spent some time together and it seemed to be of concern to Eodorr. Rhinan knew that

Eodorr had never considered himself very exciting, so he tried to compete with Param. This made their workouts a bit, Rhinan would say, bumpy. Trying to train and heal Param, Eodorr still wanted to prove he was an impressive warrior himself. Sometimes this fit into the training, and other times it annoyed Lynari, who would then spend time meditating. Param, on the other hand, seemed to enjoy the discomfort he sensed in Eodorr, so he played up his flirtations with Lynari when the opportunity arose. It would obviously irritate Eodorr, and Lynari would admonish Param.

Lynari, on the other hand, was impossible for Rhinan to read. The trio was entertaining, and Lynari never let it develop into anything concerning, so Rhinan felt it best left alone. He offered to speak to Eodorr if he ever wanted to or felt the need, in a general sense, and was given a polite response of gratitude, but no such conversations took place.

An unexpected conversation of another sort, however, did. Eodorr was glum quite often, and it turned out that it didn't have as much to do with the bond between Lynari and Param. He admitted to Rhinan that he was struggling with what he'd discovered about Lydania on their journey. He felt responsible as an official (even though it was minor, informal, and in a small village). Rhinan would find him brooding about it. Eodorr swore often to continue to aid Rhinan on behalf of Keirwyn, and to see justice done for Keirwyn, Devram, and Brinaya (causes Rhinan himself was firmly behind), but it went deeper. In his deepest sorrow, Eodorr even went so far as to ask Rhinan if Keirwyn himself might have known how the King was ruling Lydania. Was he now in doubt of Keirwyn's integrity?

Rhinan assured him that, though Cabelon was small, Keirwyn had his hands far too full to be concerned with much of Lydania beyond it. In fact, Rhinan told him, he didn't recall having seen Keirwyn venture far from Cabelon either, and it was unlikely their mentor had realized how bad things had become, aside from the ban on weapons and magic. Rhinan himself had taken little interest in the affairs of Lydania, finding it hard to relate to people anyway. And few travelers passed through Cabelon, so there wouldn't have been much news of events further out in Lydania. In any event, it would be unfair to blame the old Constable for anything the King did. There would have been little Keirwyn could do, and he did his best to preserve the safety of those in his charge in Cabelon. *Even if,* Rhinan speculated, *that protection may have meant keeping a lot of information to himself.* Not entirely certain that Eodorr was convinced, it broke Rhinan's heart to think of his friend perceiving Keirwyn—a father figure to both of them in many ways—in any diminished sense.

Eodorr spent time either sulking, or trying to persuade Rhinan that something must be done for Lydania. A former bastion of regulations, Eodorr surprised him perhaps most of all. In fact, Eodorr's usually responsible nature had been an influence on Rhinan, and he felt changed because of it. But Rhinan couldn't disagree about saving Lydania, though he pointed out that he was on the run as an outlaw and, as such, was in no position to save others until he'd first saved himself. But having spent so much of his own life apart from others, and now spending so much time in the company of others? Even though he still feared for their safety, he found them far more accepting of his own madness than he would have expected.

In fact, he began to suspect his madness may be leaving him. His ghosts had not made one appearance in the rock gnomes' caverns. Always having feared that others in his life were in danger as long as the ghosts haunted him, he began to hope—for the first time in his life—that perhaps it was safe. Despite the loss to those he'd cared about on the journey here, and the dangers that lie ahead, he was coming around to the idea that perhaps the ghosts themselves had never been the actual danger.

One day, as Wogen lie alone, Rhinan visited the rock gnome Grembul. He took the chance he'd rarely taken, but not only had he come to trust the rock gnome, he suspected that it was possible a rock gnome, if anyone, would know about the gem he still carried about his neck. First explaining how he'd come by it, he withdrew the *Pyvadis* and showed it to Wogen, careful not to let him come into physical contact with it.

The Rock Walker was thoroughly perplexed by the thing. "No, lad, I can't say I've ever seen the like of it in all my travels. It's as if it came from far away, beyond any place I've ever been. And it's been tampered with—you see the interior that looks like a tiny sea, don't you? That's got to be magic." It was the same conclusion everyone else who'd seen it had come to. Sorry he couldn't be of any further use, Wogen recommended Rhinan keep the thing close, and keep it secret (unlike the other gems piling up in Rhinan's travel pack. "Yes," Wogen told him, "of course I know, and of course it's fine. Just don't weigh yourself down—you may need to make a nimble escape again, and I wouldn't want you burdened."). But if the *Pyvadis* was important enough for his parents to save for him, it was important enough to keep protected. And it would be seen by anyone as valuable, without a doubt. Rhinan didn't bother to tell him that the gem had a way of protecting itself from the wrong hands, though he wondered if this would apply to Wogen. It certainly hadn't applied to Lynari.

Brondur, large as he was, spent a lot of time trying to keep out of the way. The rock gnomes were extremely patient, but it was clear the big man was an obstacle at times. He mostly wanted to help Yeggam heal his friend Wogen. And the other two miners they'd rescued, Tarmil and Mocelag, did everything they could to be useful to the Rock Walkers. Though good-hearted men who'd suffered the conscription and the mines, neither were very bright, but they did get simple tasks that kept them busy.

Finally there was Rip. At first, Rhinan was concerned that the beardog would rage if kept underground. Initially healing from a light arrow wound, the big furry beast wandered into an unused cavern and curled up in a ball and went to sleep. And slept. And slept. Rhinan couldn't recall seeing Rip in the winter time, so he assumed this was what the beardog did: hibernate. One day, Brondur attempted to approach the sleeping beast, gently, apparently about to reach out and gently brush it with his hand. Rhinan caught him just in time.

"You don't want to do that, Brondur."

The big man turned to Rhinan, confused. "I've never seen one in the wilds. They say they're almost all gone now. I just want to know… how it feels."

"I suspect he won't much mind that when he's awake. But even I don't disturb him in his usual sleep. And for him to sleep this long? I think it's important, a hibernation. And we all like having our arms, don't we?"

The two men chuckled lightly and left the room. Rip would stay there, undisturbed, until he woke up. It seemed even the Rock Walkers knew better than to risk disturbing a sleeping beardog.

Most interesting of all was the friendship Rhinan struck up with a particular young Rock Walker named Dalgin. The slender rock gnome had a mischievous smile and an abundance of curiosity. While helping Rhinan cut beautiful arrow tips from some of the more suitable gems in the caverns (Rhinan was creating a large supply of some of the most valuable arrows ever made), Dalgin would question Rhinan repeatedly about the western regions of Lydania.

Though Rhinan would tell him only what he could (they had made a point of not telling the rock gnomes he was believed to be the last remaining Ylvan), there was no satisfying Dalgin. Bored with the underground, Rhinan was delighted when Dalgin offered to take him on brief rock walks to places nearby and show him around. It would get Rhinan out, and give them more time to talk. Both considered it a win.

But, by decree of Wogen, none of the rock gnomes with the ability to rock walk (as it turned out, rock walking was a special skill that not all rock gnomes have, and it must be practiced and perfected in the way a baby learns to walk) were to take any of his friends out of the caverns. Therefore, once Rhinan and Dalgin came to the decision to slip out for a quick walk, they had to find out-of-the-way places of the caverns to depart from and return to. They found a spot not far from the sleeping Rip, and it became their meeting place for excursions out of the caverns.

Wrapped in warming furs, they would rock walk to nearby areas of interest, Dalgin pointing out things such as frozen waterfalls and snowy hills and fields. They would travel further and further on these walks as they felt safer in getting away and returning, their absences unnoticed.

On a day nearing mid-winter, Dalgin did get Rhinan to

admit which direction they would head once Wogen was well. Once he realized it was east, it became much easier for him to narrow down their most immediate likely destination.

"Dunskern? It's a big city!" Dalgin seemed excited. "You'll find visitors there from many lands near and far. Exotic merchants..."

"What makes you so sure we want to go to Dunskern just because we want to head eastward?" Rhinan asked the eager rock gnome.

"If you go east and south, you come to the Shilam Forest, where the wood gnomes live. We don't go there, ever. It's a peace treaty. You'd have to travel much further south to avoid that. There's very little due straight east, and north of Dunskern, there are only plains that lead up to the base of the eastern curve of the Percene Mountains. Rock Troll territory. You don't want to go there, do you? Please tell me you don't."

"No," Rhinan admitted. "You're correct. Our path lies to Dunskern." He didn't offer that it would continue *past* Dunskern, but Dalgin was excited enough about the city not to ask.

"It's wonderful! Would you like to see it?"

"Well…" Rhinan hesitated. If Dran had reached Dunskern, he could be waiting there for them. It was an incredibly risky idea to visit the city. He had an idea, though, that it might be a good idea to get a look at the lay of the land in case Dran *was* there. A little scouting mission. "Tell me, Dalgin. Is there a spot outside of Dunskern we could rock walk to? I don't want to enter the city without the others. That would spoil it, wouldn't it? But I would like to see it from the outside."

Satisfied with that explanation, Dalgin let Rhinan know

that there was a boulder not far from the west end of the city walls that the Rock Walkers used frequently. It was close enough to get a look at Dunskern, but far enough to keep out of sight of the city if that's what Rhinan wished. Dalgin was youthful, but he was clever enough to infer from his conversations with Rhinan that perhaps the companions would prefer to keep a lower profile.

This sounded suitable to Rhinan. The winter snows had not melted, so they again bundled up in light-colored furs, hoping to blend in with the frosty landscape, and took a walk. By now, the walks themselves were not as disconcerting as the first one had been. They reached the other end fairly quickly, leaving Rhinan with the sense that perhaps the rock gnome caverns weren't terribly far from Dunskern. A rock walk could swiftly cover a lot of territory, but Rhinan had come to understand that the time involved in reaching the destination was indicative of the physical distance.

Arriving at the end of the rock walk, Rhinan and Dalgin emerged from a boulder on the western side of a small, grassy rise. Over the rise, Rhinan caught his first glimpse of Dunskern.

The city stretched wide from north to south, well-walled with very light gray stone. Aside from Omriel, this was the biggest city he'd ever seen. It was larger, in fact, and he wondered how it compared to Masseltaine. He stared in awe, finding it difficult to imagine so many people in one place. On the far, eastern edge of the city, running from the north to the south, was the mighty River Arinell, legendary for its width and depth.

The city gate was a giant double door of thickest wood, reinforced with iron. It swung open outward, left open as merchants moved into and out of the city for the day. Rhinan assumed these gates would close at night, which would be quite soon. Looking more carefully, Rhinan noticed there appeared to be a type of portcullis built into the thickness of the castle wall behind the gates that would perhaps slide across to reinforce them, most likely inserting into the castle wall on the other side. There was a guardhouse on the ramparts of the battlements, one on either side of the massive gate. The walls were taller than the gates, with the battlements rising above the gates. It was clear that the ramparts stretched across this section, and almost certainly about the entire wall around the whole city. Every few feet, the battlements themselves arched downward so that either soldiers or archers within could both fight through the lower portions and find protection behind the higher should the city come under attack.

As Rhinan studied the city, an alarming sight caught his eye. One of the black-and-gold clad *Maraggan* stood upon the ramparts above the gate, one of the soldiers from Arskellion at his side, and two soldiers he assumed were Dunskern men. He was overtaken by all of his grief and anger, a new rage building within him. One of his fears confirmed, Dran was ahead of them now, probably blocking their path across the Arinell. He cursed.

Realizing these men on the ramparts were too far away for most archers, it was not beyond his skill or range. Few were the men who could make such a shot. If he took the shot, he didn't want to miss. But taking down one more of Dran's men and then simply disappearing? It was well worth the risk. Every time one of Dran's men was removed, their chances of proceeding increased, and now their way forward was blocked.

Rhinan strung his bow. He turned to Dalgin.

"Dalgin, get that rock walk open for us."

Without waiting for an answer from the young rock gnome, Rhinan drew and fired one arrow through the battlements, catching the *Maraggan* in the side of the throat. Before his other three companions could recover from their confusion and duck for the cover provided so well by the battlements, Rhinan had lodged a second arrow in the Arskellion soldier's face.

Turning to flee into the boulder for a rock walk, Rhinan caught Dalgin staring at Rhinan's handiwork with awe. "That was amazing!" Dalgin exclaimed.

"Be amazed later!" Rhinan shouted. "Get us out of here!"

There was a sound of arrows, and one pierced Rhinan's heavily furred cloak, but did him no harm, lodging between his chest and arm. He turned to Dalgin, and the rock gnome had fallen with an arrow in his midsection.

Turning toward Dunskern, Rhinan noticed belatedly that there were archers stationed in the two guardhouses on the rampart above either side of the gate. He returned fire at them without really aiming, not hitting anything but the guardhouses, forcing them to be more cautious in taking shots.

He swiftly scooped up Dalgin and ducked for cover behind the boulder. With night falling any minute, Rhinan knew he could easily disappear into the tree line just south of them before pursuit could be sent out to capture them. But with those archers, he would never make it that far carrying Dalgin.

The rock gnome was conscious, but severely injured, and Rhinan wasn't sure he could rock walk in that condition. "Can you rock walk?" Rhinan whispered in desperation.

"Unless you can use your ability, we'll be caught out in the freezing night or captured by soldiers at some point."

"Let me try," Dalgin said weakly.

"What happens if you fail?" Rhinan asked. He had no way of knowing which direction to travel back to the caverns. Under normal circumstances, he could use his wildland skills to simply hide and preserve them, but these were no normal circumstances. They were stuck. Rhinan cursed himself for his impulsive actions. "Do we wind up part of a rock?"

Dalgin laughed, choking up blood. "It's possible, but unlikely. I'll find us a closer cavern that I can reach. It just has to be some place I've been before. We can't rock walk to an unknown location."

Their fate almost certainly sealed if they remained here, Rhinan had no choice but to take the chance Dalgin offered. He held the Rock Walker close enough to reach the boulder, and Dalgin opened the cloudy portal. By the difficulty he was having breathing, Rhinan could tell that Dalgin's condition was worsening. With a leap of faith, Rhinan stepped into the opening, carrying the rock gnome, uncertain if they would survive this rock walk.

Chapter Forty-One

Two bloody corpses lay at Dran's feet. An arrow pierced the neck of one (which Dran recognized as a member of his last ten *Maraggan*—one of the men Kilward had assigned to search and keep watch for signs of the Ylvan) and another lodged in the head of the other. Yet again, another of the King's elite forces had been lost. The other was a soldier of Duke Rendiff's relatively qualified troops.

With night descending, and hidden archers beyond the walls, Dran knew it would be foolish to pursue the attackers. And there was nothing at the moment he could do about it. He was most displeased.

"Kilward!" he bellowed. "Keep our men off the walls. You personally handle this. Stay here in Dunskern when we leave tomorrow to cross the river."

Kilward stepped forward. "Yes, sir. I will require some of… Lord Mayor Summerhill's men." Dran heard the disdain in Kilward's voice. "Searching the area will be dangerous without adequate troops. And we still want to keep the city watched for the Ylvan and his companions."

"Of course," Dran's voice sounded tired even to himself.

"I'll leave orders with Ingon to cooperate with you fully and provide any assistance you need. I'm leaving you in charge on behalf of King Jerrick… his royal majesty. Ingon won't like it, but I want someone in charge that I can trust. I don't feel Ingon is the warrior he used to be. Frankly, I find he's grown too accustomed to comforts, too fond of exotic objects, and far too sloppy as a military commander. I say these things to you in the strictest confidence, though I am certain you've noticed them for yourself." Kilward appeared satisfied, if not pleased.

Now down to himself and eight of the *Maraggan*, Dran would have to choose Summerhill's men carefully in the morning. He could not afford to cross the river with a weak host. There were too many risks and he would either be pursuing Ashuir again, or laying a trap and waiting for him. Either way, in the Unreigned Territory, a virulent show of force would be necessary.

Andric was at hand, despite Summerhill's absence. Dran stared him down and gave him a list of orders. "Andric, dispatch the following to Lord Mayor Summerhill: Cease any festival celebrations still in progress at once. Dunskern is officially under the King's command effective immediately. Captain Kilward will be in charge of all city decisions until further notice. Unnecessary nighttime guard personnel are to retire for the evening. Every soldier, including Summerhill's private guard, will report to the training stadium at sunrise in the morning. *All* of the men should be prepared for a lengthy road trip so that we may leave as early as possible, as we don't know who will be chosen. Penalties will be issued to those who are tardy." He emphasized this last sentence, leaning toward Andric. "Is that clear?"

"Yes, My Lord." Andric stepped back, hesitating a

moment. "Will that be all?"

"It will."

As Andric headed off to carry the orders to Summerhill, Dran was relieved he wouldn't have to face Ingon himself. The old fellow had gone to porridge, but Dran recalled the warrior of old. It prodded him to ensure that he never let himself fall to that condition.

Kilward still stood dutifully at his side. "See that these two men receive proper last rites. I suppose Duke Rendiff's man should be returned to Arskellion, but we can't send anyone now. When the time comes, we'll send a courier to Rendiff with a full report of his soldiers."

"I will see to it."

"I'm turning in for the evening, Kilward. As of now, I leave Dunskern in your command."

"By your orders, sir."

It was highly unusual for Dran to leave any of his Captains in charge of a city, especially while he still remained within it himself. But Dran was tired, and his leg hurt. He just wanted to rest. Tomorrow would be a long day.

* * * * *

Dran feared the men would sense his apprehension as they crossed the Blackmore Bogs. Winter still strong, they found the swamp covered in a layer of snowy ice, not to mention a dense fog, when they crossed the Arinell on several large barges packed with over fifty men and horses. Part of Dran's fear was that it wouldn't be enough, but he also feared what lay in the bog. Mostly flat, the landscape was scattered with the shadows of bent and warped trees visible through the fog, and Dran became jumpy when he thought he saw one move—even if it was just due to the breeze off the river.

Little created such wariness in Dran, but this was not a place to linger. Kilward had run every soldier and guardsman through a quick demonstration of skills at the break of dawn, and Dran had chosen from Summerhill's men those that appeared the most enduring, nimble, and strong. This had included a few private guardsmen. Summerhill was insulted to have his city raided for men, but this was part of his oath to the King. Without any further word to the Lord Mayor, Dran loaded his own handful of elite forces, Rendiff's men, and the additional men from Dunskern onto barges. Dran looked back at the city as they left it behind, impressed once more with the eastern walls. Despite his personal deterioration, Summerhill had suitably maintained the eastern side of the city, and Dran was glad it was not something he would have to assault.

The Arinell's cold water moved slowly in the winter, which made the crossing less challenging and they made exceptionally good time. Nevertheless, it was so wide at this point of the river that it was similar to crossing a lake, and it took almost a full day to cross. There would still be daylight once they reached the other side, however—a fact that gave Dran immense relief.

Spread across a wide stretch of the bog, the men were careful not to step on any soft spots in the frozen surface of the swamp. Dran's worst fear wasn't losing a man into the muck that lay beneath the frozen surface, but disturbing that which he knew lurked below. He warned the men to reach the far end of the swamps as quickly as they could, disturbing as little as possible and using all caution.

The company was almost all on solid land on the far side of the bog when one of the Dunskern recruits began to curse.

His horse hit a thin spot in the ice and broke through. The horse began to scream as the rider struggled to bring it under control. The more the horse struggled, the further they both sank into the muck.

Dran hollered to the few remaining men out on the swamp. "Get off that ice if you want to live!" Taken seriously, he was obeyed and all of the remaining riders reached the far side. Another of the new Dunskern recruits turned to Dran. "Shouldn't we help him, sir?" The man started back to help the struggling soldier.

"Halt. It's already too late."

Before the words were out of Dran's mouth, the horse vanished beneath the icy muck, and the man screamed in agony. In less than a second, the man, too, disappeared beneath the muck swiftly as if something yanked him under. Dran cringed and looked away.

Dran saw his men staring in horror and confusion. Nevertheless, there was no doubt in his mind that most of the Dunskern men had heard the bog legends. Dran turned his horse eastward, and called out, "Ride! Now!" Getting them away from the scene was the best thing he could do. He wore an expression of anger and snapped at anyone who hesitated. It would get them moving and take their minds from any inclination to go back out on the bog to investigate. The damned fools had no real idea what a favor Dran was doing by rushing them onward, leaving the bog behind.

* * * * *

The first village they arrived at in the Unreigned Territory was obviously poor. The streets were unpaved, covered in muddy slush from the snows and the occasional passage of men, horses and wagons. The buildings were in poor condition, some with holes in walls or rooftops open to the elements. Dran was surprised the inhabitants hadn't frozen to death. A good portion of this decay could be repaired, money required or not, if only they had the support of the King. These people had no morale, possibly no will to live, excepting possibly the warlords who roamed the territory. But this was what happened when you rebelled against your King… if you were lucky. If not, you disappeared, like all of the Ylvan Clans. Well, almost all of the Ylvan Clans.

A hunched woman bundled in patchy furs hurried past Dran's host of horsemen, glancing furtively back over her shoulder at the number of soldiers. She looked terrified. Perhaps, Dran thought, she had chosen to be on the other side during the Ylvan Uprising, as opposed to being merely caught in this land by misfortune. It was long ago, but this was no young woman.

"You there!" Dran called out to her. She stopped, staring forward, then turned to face Dran, gazing up at him on his horse.

"Is Lydania come to reclaim this land?" she asked. Her eyes darted around the village, as if she were afraid to be seen speaking to these men.

"This land belongs to Lydania," Dran corrected her. "We just don't patrol it."

"That's our curse." The woman looked down, fidgeting with her furs.

"It is." Dran recalled Norham, once a thriving land. Allied with Eluciar and the Ylvan Clans, Norham was left to rot after the Uprising. On rare occasions, he'd been out to patrol this area, but only to ensure it wasn't thriving again.

Clearly that hadn't changed. "This village… it is called Wulmond, is it not?"

The old woman shrugged. "Depends on who you ask."

Dran felt his patience wane. "I'm asking you."

"I have always known it as Wulmond, yes."

Dran sighed. "My men require shelter for the night. Are there inns here, or must we seek a larger town?"

The woman stepped backward. "I'm sorry, sir. I can't answer that for you." And so saying, she turned and scurried away as quickly as she could, which wasn't very quick.

Dran considered this. He didn't recall Wulmond being very large. Probably the old woman was mad, and a larger town would provide more options for shelter. Dran intended to quarter the men at homes and businesses, and he didn't care for the look of those in Wulmond. It was too late to move on, and a meal was needed, so they dismounted and prepared hot food from their supplies, camping for the night right in the street. Occasionally, a villager would pass, but they appeared more eager to avoid Dran and the soldiers than anything else. Of course Dran was still wearing the uniform of the King's *Maraggan*, and they were a sizeable force, so people probably assumed that King Jerrick was coming to resume patrol of the land. Which, from what Dran could see, would be a favor to the wretched denizens.

In the morning, the men mounted and continued their eastward trek. Beyond the village, the land was jagged and rocky, with short, spiky trees and small shrubs. The terrain changed with altitude. The snows seemed less heavy. Ahead of them, the route they followed curved upward again, and what lay beyond the rise could not be seen.

Dran called a halt. He selected and ordered a pair of small contingents to scout ahead and others to hunt for game, which he expected was scarce.

As the men prepared to leave for this duty, a group of four strangers on horseback came over the ridge ahead. They rode straight toward Dran and the soldiers. Dran decided to wait on them and see if they had any useful information. As he waited for their approach, Dran sent his designated scouts north and south to see if any other local riders were in the area.

The four locals were rough, unclean, and questionable. Dran had to remind himself that this was not patrolled land, and therefore lawlessness abounded. Of course, four men against fifty would be foolhardy, so he didn't expect any trouble. Having these men ride up to such a large force so boldly wouldn't be very surprising if they appeared to be honest men, but nothing about these men struck Dran as honorable. They were bearing weapons at their sides—swords—which made them outlaws.

The man in the lead of the four pulled back a fur-lined hood. "You wear Lydanian uniforms. Has the King decided to reclaim this land?"

Again, Dran was irritated at the insinuation that the region was not part of Lydania, and he did not care for the man's brash attitude. "This is Lydanian territory," Dran stated sternly. "We seldom patrol it, but the laws of Lydania still apply. Your swords are prohibited. I'm Gethor Dran, the General of the King's *Maraggan*. Surrender your weapons, and then I will require some answers."

The man laughed. "You think men who carry weapons won't use them, is that it? You leave this land to feed upon itself, wandering in every so many years and expect us to bow to your King? This is not part of Lydania anymore. This land has no king."

With the speed of a much younger man, Dran drew his sword, spurred his horse forward, and impaled the man directly through the chest. As the man fell from his horse, the other three men backed their horses up.

"I am *sick* of having my authority challenged by worthless scum!" Dran screamed, spittle flying from his mouth. He knew his eyes were wide and he must appear to be a madman, but he didn't care. He would wipe out every armed man in the Unreigned Territory if it came to that. Looking the other way for these rapscallions to fight amongst themselves was one thing, but he would not tolerate any disrespect toward representatives of the King. He'd had quite enough of that.

"We're under attack!"

The yell had come from one of the scouts he'd sent northward, riding as fast as he could back to Dran's group. He only made it halfway before he was shot in the back by an arrow.

At virtually the same moment, the scout from the south came riding back screaming unintelligibly. He didn't make it, either. Another arrow dropped him from his horse as well.

Whirling with his sword still drawn, Dran cut open two of the three remaining men before him, toppling them to the ground. The last man of the four strangers who'd ridden out turned his horse and galloped back toward the ridge.

That's when Dran saw the trap. On the ridge were a number of mounted men. Upon seeing their scout riding back toward them, they spurred their horses forward and rode straight at Dran and his men.

Taking in the situation quickly, Dran realized there were also riders coming at his group from both the north and south. The landscape in both directions dipped enough for a few men on horseback to have been concealed. There weren't many coming from the sides, but they were firing arrows. Some of Dran's men fell.

"Circle!" Dran called, and his troops formed a complete circle on their horsebacks, drawing bows of their own. "Fire!" Dran called, and arrows launched in all three directions. Many of the marauders fell.

Dran was caught out in the open, almost surrounded, but he could also see that he had the numbers on his side. These were desperate men. More arrows slammed into his circle of men, but they had put up shields and leapt from their horses, using the animals for cover. A few horses went down, but not more than a man or two. "Fire!" Dran shouted, and another volley of arrows launched, wiping out several more of the oncoming marauders.

The bold marauders slammed into Dran's forces, their momentum and fury forcing his troops back. The Dunskern troops weren't well trained. The marauders had spears, which allowed them to penetrate into Dran's forces and take more than they should have.

Still on his own horse, Dran caught sight of the man giving orders to these marauders. He was a big man and clearly in charge. Dran called two of his last eight *Maraggan* to his sides and they rode for the big man.

Glancing back, Dran saw the other marauders were doing better than they should have been. His own troops were failing him. There were plenty of men left, but they would have to fight harder. He then saw the remainder of his *Maraggan*, a mere six men, rally the troops and begin to push back the marauders. It looked like the marauders would be defeated, so he felt he could concentrate on their leader.

As he neared the marauder leader, an arrow took one of

the two *Maraggan* riding with him. One of his *Maraggan* back with the main group took out the responsible archer with a shot of his own, just before a marauder took him with a spear. His shot, however, allowed Dran and the other *Maraggan* still with him to reach the marauder leader. Outnumbered two to one, his forces failing in their bid to sweep Dran's force by surprise, the marauder leader surrendered.

"What's your name?" Dran demanded.

"They call me The Boulder," the man replied.

"I see." Dran pointed his sword at The Boulder. "I order you to dismount. Now."

Calmly, as if he did not fear for his life, The Boulder did as he was ordered.

"Call your men off," Dran snarled, "if any of them wish to live."

The Boulder let out a strange holler, and the fighting ceased. Dran took another glance behind him, and did not like what he saw. He'd lost more men than he expected.

Turning his horse to face back to his troops, with the other *Maraggan* who was with him, they flanked The Boulder. "Start walking," Dran ordered.

The Boulder walked to the cluster where Dran's remaining troops and the last few marauders stood. Unwitting men would walk calmly into their own worse fates. The marauders, of which there were now about a dozen, and Dran's men, of which there were about thirty—almost half of those he'd began with—listened as Dran spoke.

"You know this man as The Boulder?" Dran shouted, eyeing each of the marauders. His fury was at full strength, which he knew was a terrible sight to behold.

After a moment's hesitation, the marauders silently nodded.

"He is your… warlord?"

Again, the marauders nodded.

Sitting on his horse behind The Boulder, Dran swung his sword in a swift arc. With one stroke, the Boulder's head tipped sideways, falling to the ground as his body crumpled.

"Not anymore." Dran looked to each of the marauders. He waited for a reaction, but all he could sense was their fear. He nodded to his *Maraggan* partner to pick up The Boulder's head. Doing as he was told, the soldier handed the head to Dran. "The Boulder's head will decorate my lodgings." He held it up for a moment, then dropped it into the bag strapped to his horse, which also still contained the head of Vaylene. Now he would carry two heads.

As he looked around, he noticed the last of his own elite forces, who'd led the answering charge, lay dead. Besides himself, there was the *Maraggan* who rode beside him. Of the forty *Maraggan* he had when this whole calamity began, there were now exactly two of them left. And he was one of them. He howled in fury. The remaining troops had no idea how to react, shifting uncomfortably and casting nervous glances elsewhere.

"As for the rest of you… I was going to spare those of you who survived, if you agreed to join my force." Dran looked to his own men. "But no. Kill them all."

The remaining marauders had no time to defend themselves. Most of the remaining soldiers were Duke Rendiff's, and they were efficient. The last of The Boulder's marauder troop died attempting to flee.

Dran addressed the remainder of his own men. "I am the new warlord here. I am Dran the Slayer. And this is now *our* territory. We're going to find the Ylvan or wait for him here."

His troops looked frightened. He felt that was suitable.

That worked for Dran just fine. Let that word spread around. It would keep the other warlords away. He would have to move fast if the Ylvan were here. But Dran had decided that here is where it would end.

Chapter Forty-Two

"What are you going to do with your beardog?" Wogen asked Rhinan. "We'll never get through the city without them spotting you with that big, ferocious beast."

"He's not *my* beardog," Rhinan reiterated. It felt like he always had to tell people this. "Rip goes where he chooses."

The pair, joined by Param and Eodorr, stood at the spot beside the boulder overlooking the western gate of Dunskern, right where the rock gnome Dalgin had been shot by an arrow that winter. They were surveying the town, and looking for signs of Dran's men. They'd been watching since the cool, crisp spring morning, but there had been no signs on the walls of anyone but the usual Dunskern soldiers.

"Rip usually won't go into a town or city," Eodorr noted. "When we go in, he may wander back west into the Percene foothills."

Rhinan bit his lip. The beardog had been his hunting companion for years. On this journey alone, the huge animal had saved his life on more than one occasion. Rip may not be his beardog, but he was his… friend. Abandoning him for the rest of the journey felt wrong. But he also knew his companions were right. The Unreigned Territory was sparsely forested, and there wouldn't be enough hunting for the beardog. The best thing for Rip at this point in the journey was to convince him to turn back. It would likely only endanger the beardog—and all of them—to have him along.

"I'll see if I can urge him to leave us." Rhinan gave a heavy sigh. "All I can do is try."

"Look there!" Param hissed. The troubadour's sharp eyes had spotted a man on the wall above the open gates who didn't appear to be one of the regular soldiers, nor was he one of the King's elite force.

"That's a member of the Lord Mayor's private guard," Wogen explained. "His name is Andric. He is neither a fan of the Lord Mayor or the King of Lydania. He knows we're coming through tonight, and he's going to see to it that we have provisions and passage across the River Arinell."

"So what you're saying," Param grinned, "is that we shouldn't shoot him?"

Rhinan shot a dark look at Param. Param continued more seriously. "Well, I suppose we shouldn't shoot anyone off the walls from here, hmm?"

"We should get back," Wogen said. "We have the rest of the day to make final preparations, and they close those gates at dark. We'll need to have all made our way into the city before then, or we'll be left behind."

Wogen faced the boulder and opened the cloudy passage. He had claimed his leg was fully healed, and with the weather turning for the better, he had urged Rhinan to continue his journey now that he could join him. Having now surveyed Dunskern enough for their plan to proceed, Wogen stepped into the boulder and Rhinan, Param and Eodorr followed.

None of the rock gnomes had been to any location across the Arinell, so it was therefore necessary to find normal passage. As Dalgin had told Rhinan, they couldn't simply rock walk to a spot on the other side without a rock gnome having knowledge of destination he'd previously been. Fortunately, Wogen had some underground connections in Dunskern and they ran pretty high in official status. Andric was literally the second in command, and Wogen told Rhinan that he had always been able to rely on him.

When the four re-emerged in the rock gnome cavern, they were greeted by Lynari, Brondur, and Wogen's wife Yeggam. Rip sat behind Brondur, who'd struck up a friendship with the beardog since Rip awakened from his hibernation a few days earlier. Fascinated by the creature, Brondur was one of the few people, like Lynari, that Rip took a mutual liking to right away. Finally, Dalgin stepped forward from behind the large man and large beast, also fully recovered from the serious wound he'd received scouting Dunskern alone with Rhinan that winter.

Seeing them all there gladdened Rhinan's heart, though he'd grown tired of waiting in the caverns for Wogen to heal. But it was spring now, and hopefully a better time to move on. The hope that Rhinan clung to strongest was that Dran would have given up on him by now and gone off to some other pursuit.

He considered Silarrah. There was no way of knowing if Silarrah had been forced to play a part in the search for Rhinan, but if she had... Rhinan did not like to think of it. He would tell himself that she was safe and warm back home, doing what normal daily tasks she did, and perhaps missing him. Hopefully she was not too hurt that he had not yet been able to return. It had been months since he left in early autumn, and now it was early spring. If Silarrah thought of him at all at this point, she probably expected the worst. He would rather be back at home with her, but the mystery of his parents and his heritage still needed to be solved. And then there was Dran and King Jerrick, and Rhinan would never be safe in Lydania with either of those men in power. He fumed about that, but he felt powerless to change it.

With help from the Rock Walkers, Rhinan and his companions had made forays out for supplies they would need on their journey. Much of it was food that could be dried or prepared so that it would not spoil, as hunting in the Unreigned Territory was rumored to be scarce. They also gathered disguises that would make them harder to spot if Dran's men were watching. They spent the afternoon making preparations to leave, and then gathered in the great central cavern of the rock gnomes' system of tunnels.

Rhinan made sure he had his bow, as well as the Ylvan sword his parents had left him, hidden away in a long, thick coat of dark fur. Tucked within his tunic remained the *Pyvadis* that seemed to react to weather, or unwanted touch. Clearly an object of magic. Rhinan hoped to understand it someday.

Also wrapped in furs were Lynari and Param, the three of them hauling a cart of more furs. They would appear to be merchants from the western woodlands. Lynari's quarterstaff was tucked beneath the furs in the cart, safely hidden but reachable should the need arise. Param's mandolute went into the pile, as he refused to part with it, along with a sword he'd been given by the rock gnomes.

Brondur had put work into felling trees, stripping the logs, and piling them onto a second cart. Eodorr would pose as his brother, and they planned to pose as merchants hoping to trade wood to artisans. The disguise meant Brondur could openly carry his massive axe, but Eodorr's sword was also hidden beneath the merchandise.

Wogen would carry a sack of gems into town for sale, rock gnomes not an unusual sight in Dunskern. Surprisingly, his hammer was not considered a weapon of war, but more a mining tool, so it would not be confiscated. Rhinan recalled how Wogen could use it and knew that was an oversight on the King's part.

With each of them disguised as a merchant of some sort, they would enter separately and hope to arouse no suspicions whatsoever. The guards at the gate weren't overly observant at any rate, and Wogen assured them this was a safe plan. Their goal was to reach the waterfront at sunset. There would be bargemen who traveled up and down the river willing to ferry them across the Arinell at night, provided the river wasn't too high or too rough. This was Wogen's chief concern, as it was early spring and the melting snow runoff to the north could create risky conditions for the crossing.

There was no backup plan. If they could not convince one of the bargemen to get them across this night, they would have to return to the rock gnome tunnels until the river calmed down. It was a mighty river and unpredictable in the best of times. But it had been a mild winter, and Wogen's sources felt optimistic.

Once they were across the river, of course, they were all in new territory. Their only plan was to hire a guide to lead them to Eluciar. Finding a guide they could trust in the Unreigned Territory could prove challenging. None of them knew what to expect, other than various rumors they'd each heard. It was something they'd deal with when they got to that point.

The time had come at last to set out. All gathered in the

main cavern, where the small carts of furs and logs were waiting. Wogen was still off somewhere filling a sack of gems, so the rest of the companions waited.

"You don't have to come," Rhinan said, looking at all of them. "You're safe here, and the Rock Walkers can likely get you to places closer to your homes. I am the Ylvan. It is me they're after. The rest of you, they will most likely forget."

Lynari spoke first. "Dran will not forget me. If he caught you today, I would be next on his list. He seemed far too curious about me for me to do anything but my sworn duty, which is to stay by your side. Even if Dran wasn't so interested in me, my assignment as a *Hegana* is to observe you. I will not do otherwise."

Param spoke next. "I would have been with you from the start, my old friend. Even though I can't be of the use you'd hoped for once we cross the river. And what do I have to go home to now?"

Eodorr agreed with Param. "Our home is not what it was when we left. Besides, I made a promise to Keirwyn, and I intend to keep it."

Brondur even chimed in. "You helped us escape the mines. We'd still be toiling away if not for you, and I'm sure I speak for Wogen, as well. He didn't hold us here while his leg healed just to pass the winter. He's sworn, as am I, to repay a debt that means seeing you safely wherever you may wind up."

Tarmil and Mocelag, the last two miners rescued by Rhinan and Wogen, had stayed the winter to aid the companions' preparations while keeping a low profile as wanted fugitives. They also offered to continue on, but Rhinan had sternly turned them down. Like Brondur, they had families, and the Rock Walkers were going to get them home. Neither of them had the bond with Wogen that Brondur did, nor with Rhinan, so he was able to persuade them. Besides, he told them, too many "merchants" arriving too closely together could arouse suspicion, and it may be best not to have them among the companions. They would undoubtedly have proven useful in the Unreigned Territory, but Rhinan could not justify it. Mocelag was from a distant land as it was, and his journey home would be far. Tarmil, however, did make him one offer: he was from the west, and if the Rock Walkers could get him there, he would find Silarrah in Omriel and let her know how Rhinan fared. As he had told them all many parts of his story, they had been especially moved by the depth of his feelings for Silarrah left unexpressed. Tarmil's offer brought tears to Rhinan's eyes, and he gratefully accepted the offer if Tarmil promised to be extremely careful not to endanger himself or Silarrah. The miner was confident that he could accomplish this.

Wogen and Yeggam entered the chamber. The crown sat upon Yeggam's head, for she would rule as queen in Wogen's absence. This was unprecedented among rock gnomes, but Yeggam was popular, and all knew her to be of sharp mind and firm hand. Wogen had slung a sack over his left shoulder, still favoring his "healed" right leg just a bit. (Yeggam had wanted Wogen to wait a bit longer, but there was no more keeping him down.) Seeing the companions all gathered and prepared to set out, the rock gnome couple turned to one another, clenched in a hug, their foreheads touching, speaking in low tones that Rhinan could not hear. This might be the last time any of them were seen alive, and Rhinan could not escape the feeling of responsibility. He'd spent his entire life alone, away from others, fearing that his ghosts meant danger to those around him. And now, here he was, accompanied against his will by people willing to put their lives in jeopardy for him. He did not know how he came to deserve such devotion, especially when others had already lost their lives on his behalf.

At last, Wogen and Yeggam split apart, and Wogen approached Rhinan. He jerked his head toward Rip. "It's time, lad." He sat down the sack he was toting.

Rhinan felt a lump in his throat. His eyes were wet. "It is," he agreed. Changing the mood, he cast a glance at Wogen's sack. "Are you sure you have enough?" he jested.

"Are you?" Wogen winked at him, reminding Rhinan of their earlier discussion of the abundance of gems in the caverns and Rhinan's occasional tendency to help himself to things that he considered less necessary to others.

Without a word, Rhinan merely grinned in response.

Wogen stepped to the central boulder in the cavern. Facing it, he opened the pathway.

Rhinan stepped forward and turned back to where Rip sat, larger than the rest of the companions and yet—in Rhinan's eyes—a helpless animal in many ways. Rip was licking a paw. Rhinan waved to the beardog, and Rip stood up and approached him.

Wogen stepped through the cloudy portal. Taking a deep breath, Rhinan followed, knowing that Rip would follow as well.

The walk was a bit longer than some, but when they emerged, they were among trees. Rhinan could see the foothills of the Percenes to the north.

"How far west are we?" he asked Wogen.

"Should be just far enough to avoid any patrols out of Dunskern. And, if he heads up into the hills, plenty of hunting and shelter."

Rip stood waiting to continue. Rhinan faced him, staring into the big, broad, furry face. The beardog could shred him with one swipe of a paw, or rip him in half with a snap of the powerful jaws with huge, sharp teeth. Despite their massive size, the creature could move so swiftly you would not outrun it if it were hunting you. A beardog was an animal to be wary of.

Rip leaned forward with his nose and nuzzled Rhinan under the chin. He was ready to hunt.

His eyes so wet that he could not see clearly, Rhinan reached up and rubbed the beardog beneath his ears. Rip made a guttural sound that might have frightened most others, but Rhinan knew it was a friendly response. In a rare display with the beardog, Rhinan reached out and hugged the big creature, then stepped back.

"Rip, hunt!" He faced up into the trees, and drew his bow from his back as if to string it.

With a couple of grunts, Rip began to lumber up the hill into the tree line.

Wogen turned back to the boulder from which they had emerged, opening the walkway again.

Up the hill, Rip turned, either because he sensed the portal or to see if Rhinan was with him, he could not be sure. The beardog made a sound that Rhinan recognized as his curiosity groan, emitted when he was confused.

Wogen stepped into the portal and, taking one last look back at Rip, Rhinan called to him. "Hunt! Careful!"

As he stepped into the walkway behind Wogen, Rhinan could hear the beardog howl. It was his sorrow howl, but there was nothing Rhinan could do for him.

Then the portal closed as they continued the dark rock walk back to the cavern.

Chapter Forty-Three

By the time they reached the cavern, Rhinan was weeping. Yeggam immediately took him to her side, much shorter though she was, and offered him the comfort of a mother with a son who'd lost a pet.

"You don't understand…" Rhinan said to all of them of his emotional display. "I've never had much in the way of family. Rip has been with me for years."

"Excuse me," Param said, stepping forward and placing a hand on Rhinan's shoulder. "How many times did you spend with my mother and me, hmm?"

"I know." Rhinan placed his hand on Param's. In truth, the words meant to comfort only hurt worse at the thought of Brinaya and all the kindnesses she'd shown him in his life. In fact, if there were ever anyone besides Silarrah he felt inclined to speak to about his madness—seeing ghosts—he felt it would have been Brinaya. Not even Param. But all he could reply was, "It will always be appreciated more than you know, Param. More than I can repay."

"It's not to be repaid," Param said. "It's what family does."

"And you have family in all of us now, lad," Wogen said. "Though I'll apologize in advance for that."

Yeggam shot her husband a menacing look, but the rest of the companions laughed.

"We need to leave now," the Rock Walker King said as he lifted his sack. "We've got to get into the city and make our rendezvous." Giving Yeggam one more hug, he opened the rock walk portal. "This many of us with the carts will require a bit of endurance, so I've asked Dalgin here to help us on the walk. He'll return here once we're all at the other end. *Won't you, Dalgin?*" Wogen stressed the question.

"Yes, your majesty." Dalgin hung his head, and Rhinan knew he would not go against an order from Wogen. But he also knew Dalgin would rather join them if he could. Wogen had forbidden any others from the journey, feeling it would draw too much attention. And, to ensure Dalgin's compliance, he'd charged the young rock gnome with transporting Tarmil west once the others had been gone long enough to be clear of Dunskern.

It was a short rock walk to the boulder near Dunskern. Dalgin bid them good luck, shook Rhinan's hand, and rock walked back to the cavern.

The companions waited in hiding and watched from a distance as each group took their turn slipping into the city. Being the least suspicious, they sent Brondur and Eodorr in first, watching them enter the gates and be questioned by the guards. Brondur said something that made the guards laugh. The big man clapped a friendly hand on one of the guard's shoulders, and the guard's legs nearly buckled. Still laughing, the guards waved them on into the city.

"All right," Wogen said to Rhinan, Param, and Lynari. "I'll go in next, and they'll still be fixated on me when you come along, so be right behind me." So saying, the Grembul of the Rock Walkers strode up to the road, and whistled as he approached the guards. They appeared more interested in his sack than they were in him, when it came down to it. He opened it for them and, even from a distance, Rhinan could see the wonder on their faces as they shook their heads. But they waved Wogen in.

They'd gotten up to the road with their cartload of furs, all three of them still bundled in furs themselves. Their cover story was that they came from the south, so even the early spring was cold for them, especially here along the wide River Arinell.

The guards halted them, and they were, as Wogen had predicted, still paying more attention to him than they were to the group of southern fur traders. The two young men gave Rhinan, Param, and Lynari odd looks, but waved them on without a question, seeing their cart full of furs.

As they passed, one of the young guards called to them. "Hold!"

Both Rhinan and Lynari stepped closer to the cart, prepared to reach in and withdraw weapons if it came to it. But it was Param's professional charm that came into play. "What can we do for you gentlemen?" The troubadour gave his most gleaming smile.

"You're from the south, aren't you?" asked the guard.

"Yes. Much warmer than here."

"I don't suppose you have any *jarlet* pelts in there? My girl would love a *jarlet* mantle for next winter. She whined for one all this winter."

Param didn't answer immediately. Rhinan wasn't even sure. He knew *jarlets* were knee-high creatures of the south with soft, warm fur, and that you didn't see many of them this far north. But they'd scoured various areas in gathering the pelts in this cart, and he couldn't recall. Possibly neither could Param, and the last thing they needed were the guards trying to sort through to find one. Not only were the weapons piled beneath the furs, but also Param's mandolute—and they all knew Dran was looking for a troubadour. If the guards should uncover any of their items, it would be trouble.

"You know," Param said thoughtfully, "the *jarlets* were scarce this winter. We haven't brought in a *jarlet* pelt since last winter, but I can keep my eyes out for one. I'll be sure to come this way again, and I'll remember you. Perhaps your girl will have her mantle by next winter after all. And it'll be *you* she keeps warm, hmm?" Param gave him a wink. The guard smiled, and that was enough. They were waved through into the city.

Param slipped Rhinan a quick look of relief.

"To the waterfront," Lynari said. "We've got to meet the others, and it's nearly sundown."

Indeed, the *Hegana* was correct. The sky was fading from copper to bronze with the setting sun. The city was full of buildings and people and no time for Rhinan to explore or, if the opportunity arose, possibly even pick up an extra necessity or two for the journey. Coming down into the city, the river was visible at the far end, but the other side of the River Arinell, at least at this point, was too far to see.

They made their way to the waterfront, arriving as the sun was fading and torches were being lit along the docks. There were several river boats and barges along the docks, across from which were numerous taverns and pubs. Toward the northern end of the docks they found Wogen, Eodorr, and Brondur awaiting their arrival. Beside them stood a man of about Brondur's height, only much thinner, wearing a long frock which Rhinan had seen many bargemen along the docks wearing. Apparently it was common river wear. The man looked weathered but by no means weak.

"This is Kam Fain, our captain this evening." Wogen introduced him, but made no attempt to introduce Rhinan or his companions. Obviously, that was part of the deal with Fain.

Behind them was a large river barge. It was low to the water, long, and shaped somewhat like a stretched oval. It had rusty bolts, and it smelled horribly of fish and mold and who-knew-what. There were two other men on the barge, the crew of Fain's. Already on board were more than a half dozen horses. Eodorr would be pleased, and it would be helpful in speeding their journey along. Obviously, some of these were pack horses, not for riding. Two of the horses were already laden with sacks. Rhinan could only guess the sacks were filled with food that Wogen had arranged, as he had undoubtedly arranged the horses and the transport using gems in the sack he'd been carrying. Now it was reduced to a large pouch on his belt. One thing Rhinan knew: he would forever be indebted to the rock gnome Grembul.

The risk to his companions still gnawed at Rhinan. He approached Fain. "You've been to the other side of this river before?"

"Sure have," Fain assured him.

"In this barge?"

"It's the only one I got."

Rhinan looked at the water. As Wogen had hoped, it was running relatively smooth. They would begin at the north end of the city, so Rhinan assumed it meant that, by the time they crossed the southward-running water, they would come out across from the southern end of the city.

"How is the other side?" Rhinan asked.

"It's a bog." Despite his warning, Fain didn't seem too concerned about whether they made it beyond the Blackmire Bog or not. "Don't think you'll care much for it. My suggestion would be to get across the bog as quick as you can and keep moving. Don't mess around there."

Wogen jumped in. "Why don't you load those furs on the barge now, hmm? They may be of some use to us on the other side."

Param and Rhinan pushed their cart across a narrow ramp onto the barge. Lynari followed. The barge wobbled gently on the water under their feet, but it still didn't feel as if the waters were rough.

At that moment, a man came down a flight of stairs from a city street higher up than the docks. Rhinan recognized him as the man they'd seen on the wall. Andric, Wogen had called him. He seemed in a hurry and made directly for Wogen.

"You should launch now," Andric said to Wogen, looking back and forth between the rock gnome and Fain. "Captain Kilward is on his way down for his evening inspection of the docks. You haven't much time."

"Captain Kilward?" Rhinan asked.

Wogen waved him back onto the barge. "Time to go. Fain, are we prepared to launch now?"

Fain scratched his head and looked down at the rock gnome and back at the barge. "Soon as we're aboard."

Andric nodded, looked straight at Rhinan, and said, "May the Lore Givers guide your path." And with that, he turned and hurried away.

Wogen and Fain aboard, Fain's crew untied the barge and began to push away from the dock. Fain included, they each carried extremely long, thick barge poles which broadened and flattened on the ends. They began to employ these with great effort to get the barge moving across the water.

As they floated out into the Arinell, a man descended the stairs that Andric had just come down, and it chilled Rhinan to see him. The man wore the black-and-gold uniform of the *Maraggan.* It was one of Dran's men, accompanied by two private guardsmen of Dunskern's Lord Mayor. Rhinan recognized their uniforms from when he and Dalgin had surveyed the city that winter.

There was no particular hurry to Captain Kilward, as if he was not concerned a bit with anything going on at the docks.

But a very strange thing happened that threw everything into turmoil at just that inopportune moment.

A large creature in the water swam up to their barge. The animal was sizeable enough to jolt the barge when it impacted. Fain and his men ran for a small shelter cabin in the center of the barge. Rhinan saw barbed spears leaning against the cabin. Fain and his crew were prepared to fight the beast off. As they dashed for the spears, the creature tried to climb aboard the barge. Even in the darkness, Rhinan couldn't mistake the animal's identity. Rip had reached the river and swum out to catch up to him, now trying to gain footing and climb aboard the barge.

"Hold!" Rhinan yelled, running to the beardog's side. Brondur, Param, Lynari, and Eodorr were all at his side immediately, assisting the effort to bring Rip up onto the barge.

Fain looked to Wogen, holding out his arm to stop his crewmen from killing the thing invading his barge. Rhinan was relieved, but Fain seemed perturbed. "What is this?"

Wogen sighed. "It's a beardog the like of which I would never have imagined existed." The rock gnome Grembul shook his head. "He's with us. He'll be no trouble."

Fain didn't seem convinced about that. Wogen reached into the pouch at his waist, pulled out a fist-sized gem of red, and handed it to Fain. "Will that cover it?"

Staring at the gem in his hand, Fain shrugged. "I suppose it will."

That resolved, Rhinan looked back to the docks. Captain Kilward and his men had watched the entire event, taking no action. Lining the docks and mounted to them were plenty of large ship-sinking crossbows aimed out over the river. All Kilward would have to do was give the order, and one of those would fire at the barge, and the entire company would be in the water. Instead, the Captain laughed, turned away, and headed off to a tavern behind him on the wharf. Rhinan didn't understand it, but he was grateful to be overlooked. However, Dran was still out there. Did this man not realize who Rhinan and his companions were? Even with a beardog on board? It was the only logical explanation he could come up with, but it still didn't quite add up.

Rip sat on the deck, shivering with wet fur. Rhinan grabbed furs from the cart they'd brought, laying them on the beardog to help dry him.

"Why couldn't you have stayed behind, you foolish creature?" Rhinan couldn't help being glad to see the beardog. After all, he may be worried about all of his companions, but what was one more?

Chapter Forty-Four

Crossing the River Arinell on the barge from Dunskern took the entire night. Fortunately, the river remained relatively calm and there were no incidents. Rhinan managed to curl up against Rip in some of the furs and get some uneasy sleep, but what little sleep he had delivered only the blackest of dreams. He found upon waking that Lynari was curled up on the other side of Rip in the same way, still sleeping.

The pre-dawn morning was cold and hazy. The darkness itself seemed to coalesce and thicken over the oozing swamp, blurring the rising sun to dullest luminescence. The fog was so thick he wondered if Fain would be able to see the shore before they struck it. After all they'd been through, dumping their supplies and horses, not to mention themselves, into the river was unthinkable. Anticipating that the barge captain had plenty of experience with this, Rhinan was able to put his mind at ease.

Rising and walking to the front of the barge, Rhinan found Wogen, Eodorr, Brondur and Fain and his crew staring ahead into the fog. In the murky water, there was a layer of floating moss and spiky plants and odd shrubs. Something was wrong, but he wasn't awake enough to determine what it was.

"You hear that?" came a voice from behind him. It was Param.

Rhinan listened. Then he quickly realized what Param was implying. "It's too quiet," Rhinan mused. "The sun is rising and there should be some wildlife… birds, at least… making sounds."

They all watched as the barge moved in through the foliage, the water still too deep for the horses to disembark and be ridden. The crew tested the depths every so often.

Lynari joined them. "I could use some of that bog moss," she whispered to Rhinan as she studied the muck. "You know… for certain spells."

"We can scrape some up once we get ashore," he assured her, scowling at the thought of touching it.

Lynari watched his reaction with clear disappointment, but before he could say more, a thought crossed her features that seemed to excite her. She dashed off to grab the crewmen. Rhinan couldn't hear everything she told them, but he thought he heard the word "recipe." The crewmen, with shrugs of confusion, simply complied and used the paddle end of their long rods to pull out a handful for her. She was delighted.

As the sun rose higher, the fog cleared a bit. Short, bent trees draped with moss were scattered in the surrounding bog, and there was even more of the odd shrubbery. The water grew murkier, which delighted Fain. "We're closing in on land," the captain informed them.

At last, one of the crew men pulled his pole from the muck and turned to Fain, shaking his head.

"That's as far into the bog as we can go," Fain told Wogen. "I'm sorry. It will be drudgery, and slow going, and cold and wet, but you'll have to ride from here."

Wogen turned to the rest of them. "Everyone choose a horse. We're on hoof from here."

Rhinan was concerned about Wogen riding a horse, given his smaller stature, but there was a shorter horse among the stock—not by much, but enough for Wogen to ride. The rock gnome saw Rhinan watching him and commented. "What, you think gnomes don't ride?"

Not knowing what to say, Rhinan turned and found a horse to his liking. "That's a good one," Eodorr said. "He's balanced, you see? And good, strong legs." Eodorr reached down and touched the horse's legs. "And he doesn't spook easy."

Rhinan felt better. If anyone knew horses, it was Eodorr. "Thank you, Eodorr. I'm sorry we spent so many years at odds. You're a good friend to have."

Eodorr grinned and stepped to the next horse, leading it to Lynari. She'd already had her eye on it as it turned out. Rhinan grinned. She hadn't needed any help from Eodorr when it came to horses.

Param mounted a sturdy stud, followed by Eodorr on a mare. Brondur had chosen the largest of the horses on board, but he didn't mount. He waited and helped the crewmen extend a ramp into the swamp. It hit the muck and sunk in a few inches. None of them liked the look of it, but they would have to make the best of it.

The two extra horses had been laden with food and furs. Wogen lined them up on long leads of rope behind him with Eodorr following. Rhinan rode behind Eodorr, followed by Rip, Param, Lynari, and Brondur bringing up the rear. Rip looked hesitant to abandon the barge for the bog, but Rhinan was sure he would follow when the time came.

Wogen directed his steed down the ramp, slowly testing the depth of solid land. His horse sunk into the muck almost to its knees. This would create a terribly slow passage out of the Blackmire Bog, and Rhinan could see by his frown that Wogen didn't like it.

They all disembarked, no one perhaps less happy with the muck than Rip. He shook a massive paw to remove the mud that clung to it, mostly clearing it, only to find that his other paw was covered in the same muck. He groaned, but he stalked forward on all fours with the group.

Wogen turned and waved to Fain, and they watched the barge back out of the swamp.

Once it disappeared into the fog, Rhinan realized they were all completely lost. They would have to make their way eastward beyond the bog and then find a guide to Eluciar. And in Eluciar, there was no guarantee they'd be safe. Most legends described Eluciar as a once-beautiful land left barren after the Ylvan Uprising. If it was that bad, Rhinan had no idea where to go after that. Besides, seeing one of Dran's men back in Dunskern? He couldn't be sure what to expect. Was Dran still following him? Had Dran given up, returned to Masseltaine? He was not sure he would ever feel safe as long as Dran was out there somewhere, hunting him.

"Let's get out of this bog as soon as we can," Wogen told them. "I don't think any of you are any happier in a swamp than I am, and I'm a lot closer to it." It would have lightened their mood, but no one seemed affected by Wogen's attempt at humor.

Lynari rode up next to Rhinan. "I don't like this place," she said stiffly. "I can't say if it's magic, but it's not natural."

Listening again, Rhinan responded. "It shouldn't be this quiet."

And then, suddenly for Rhinan, it wasn't. His ghosts chose that moment to appear en masse, murmuring and holding out their hands. He cringed a bit in reaction and Lynari noticed. He realized she'd seen this before, and it was becoming something he might not be able to hide from the *Hegana.*

"Rhinan, what is it?" she demanded. "It's never good when I see you like this."

Attempting to ignore the ghosts, Rhinan said, "Let's just get beyond this bog before nightfall. None of us wants to camp in this mud, do we?"

The ghosts persisted as they rode through the mossy mud, grass, shrubs, and scattered bent trees draped with moss.

The sun never completely broke through the fog. By midday, it was a miserable ride with poor visibility, cold, damp air, and the horrible smell of death. Rhinan couldn't get his horde of ghosts to leave him be.

And then the horses spooked.

To their left, northward, the swamp water was deeper. When Rhinan saw something move past them in that water, all he could determine was that it was large. *Very* large.

"Ride fast!" came a shout from Wogen. "Ride hard!"

As one, the companions drove their horses as quickly as they could, despite the muck slowing them down.

"Lynari, is there anything you can do here?" Rhinan hoped some of the *Hegana's* simple spells could help them. He glanced at her and saw she was staring at the swamp water to their left, an expression of horror on her face. It terrified him to see her terrified. Lynari was not one to fear easily.

All she could do to answer him was shake her head. "No. This requires powerful, violent magic, lore I have not learned and is rarely if ever taught."

Rhinan drew his bow and nocked and arrow. Param did likewise. Eodorr had his sword drawn, as did Wogen, and Brondur held his big axe upon his shoulder.

It didn't take long to realize that Wogen was looking for a large rock somewhere in the swamp. He clearly felt he would have to take them back across the river to escape whatever he deemed this danger to be.

Going back was as likely deadly for Rhinan as staying here, but it did give him an idea.

His ghosts, however, screamed like banshees and circled him as if they could do him any good.

Rip roared.

And then it emerged.

With an enormous splash of muck and water, and a deafening, gurgling roar, a serpentine creature of pale mottled brown and green in color wriggled up from the swamp, rising above the companions. It was flattish in form, with wide, jagged spikes down each side of its body between front and rear legs that ended in webbed feet and sharp claws. Covered in slime-coated scales, it even had a flattish tail it twitched about as it reared up. Its head was as wide as two men end-to-end, and the length of the entire creature was easily that of six or eight men. The incomprehensible stench of the monster was so overpowering that it induced a nauseating weakness in Rhinan. It opened its wide slit of a mouth, bits of rotting vegetation and other things he preferred not to consider both spraying out in pieces and hanging from jagged teeth that lined its expansive maw. He noticed that the teeth were angled backward in the mouth, making for what would be a terrible rending if the giant thing got those teeth into you. But it could almost certainly swallow you whole.

"*Swamp dragon*!" Wogen hollered.

Many things happened at once in the face of this giant monster—a *dragon*! Rhinan could hardly take it all in.

The swamp dragon snapped forward, almost slithering gracefully on top of the swamp muck, sinking those hideous teeth into one of the pack horses. Then it withdrew, screaming horse in mouth, beneath the swamp water. Bloody bubbles rose, creating the only sound in the stunned silence of the group's momentary pause.

"Ride!" Wogen yelled again. "Keep riding!"

In that instant, the swamp dragon rose up again, towering above Wogen, chunks of horse flesh visible in its angled teeth. It drew back on its hind legs and opened its mouth.

"Dive!" Wogen screamed. He leapt from his horse and landed in the muck, and all followed suit in the same instant.

Laying in the muck, Rhinan witnessed a stream of what appeared to be steaming, lumpy bog mud spray forth from the swamp dragon's mouth. Whatever it was, it was hot enough to incinerate Wogen's horse instantly. Wogen had rolled safely away, being small enough to do so, but the other pack horse was also caught in the stream. A layer of the steaming hot, tarry expulsion clung to the front end of the horse, and the horse writhed in agony, unable to breathe through the coating as it burned to death.

The rest of the horses scattered, fleeing the swamp dragon.

Rhinan fired an arrow, but it glanced off the swamp dragon's slimy scales. Param tried the same. Lynari clenched her quarterstaff, but had no effective means of attack. Rhinan hadn't seen her use any offensive magic, so he didn't expect her to be able to help fight a dragon in any safe combat style.

Sword in hand, Eodorr ran straight at the swamp dragon, Brondur behind him, axe prepared for a mighty blow. They caught the dragon's attention just as something hit the dragon and knocked it sideways.

Rip snarled his most ferocious growl, his claws actually digging into dragon scales.

Screaming with a gurgling cry, the swamp dragon twitched and hurled Rip several feet into the air and away out of sight.

The beardog's attack, however, gave Eodorr and Brondur the opening they needed. They hit the swamp dragon simultaneously, Eodorr's sword scraping scales and Brondur's axe chipping others. Rhinan could see that—as with all dragons—getting through the hide would be a battle of endurance. And they didn't have enough arms here to battle a dragon.

Turning its attention to the two men, the swamp dragon reared back and opened its mouth for another expulsion. No way would the two men survive that breath attack at that close range.

But then the swamp dragon jerked again, another gurgling, rumbling scream. Wogen had brought down his hammer on the swamp dragon's tale, and it shook the dragon enough to back up. It swept its tail, however, and Wogen flew away to the side somewhere, disappearing as had Rip.

Rhinan considered his father's sword. It might well be useful, but it was in a pack on the horses. Could he even find it in time? The horses had been killed or run off.

"The eyes!" Param yelled. He fired another arrow, and it struck the swamp dragon just behind its left eye. Bow still in hand, Rhinan fired for the right eye, and lodged an arrow in the membrane surrounding it. The swamp dragon screamed again.

Brondur and Eodorr struck again. Brondur's axe chipped a scale completely off this time, and Eodorr, taking advantage of the weak spot, plunged his sword into the opening.

This clearly hurt the swamp dragon. It swiped with a clawed hand, raking Brondur across the chest, heaving him backward into the swamp.

Rearing back one more time, the dragon snapped his head forward with great speed. Its jaws opened, snatching Eodorr from the ground. It shook him back and forth.

Rhinan and Param fired arrows again, striking the left eye. Both arrows struck their mark, right in the center of the eye. The swamp dragon threw Eodorr off into the bog, screamed loud enough to create waves on the mucky surface and wriggled back into the waters.

Rhinan and Param stood with arrows drawn, watching the waters of the swamp for any signs of the monstrous swamp dragon. Lynari held her quarterstaff, ready to smash at anything that rose to attack them.

Within a moment, it was clear to Rhinan that the swamp dragon wasn't returning, as his ghosts had disappeared again. The companions had failed to kill the swamp dragon, but it was an astounding feat to have driven it away by taking out an eye. Had Rhinan and Param not been as good with a bow as they were, there would be no survivors. Rhinan had always taken his bow training very seriously. Perhaps it had all been for this day.

A groan caught their attention, and the trio turned to search for their friends in the bog. They found Brondur first. His chest was deeply wounded, but his armored vest had prevented a fatal wound. He was able to sit up, but in no condition to help them look for other survivors.

Wogen called to them from the fog, "Did you kill it?" he asked, hope in his voice.

"Drove it away for now," Param answered.

As Wogen emerged, Rhinan saw that part of his face and his left arm were badly injured. Rhinan wondered if that had been from the tail whip. Wogen looked up him, saw him staring at the wounds.

"The swamp dragon breathes a molten muck," explained the rock gnome. "I was splattered when it hit the horses. Lucky for me, I'm a rock gnome. We're fairly resistant. Had this been any of you, you'd be swamp dragon food by now. But I'll be fine."

Relieved, Rhinan turned to look for Rip and Eodorr, the only two of their number unaccounted for besides the horses, which had fled earlier. He panicked. "Eodorr! Rip!"

Further off, there was a groan that was clearly the beardog. Rhinan ran toward the sound, Param, Lynari, and Wogen on his heels.

The beardog was sitting up. He'd been thrown, but he wasn't injured. He moaned and looked down into the mucky swamp grass.

Eodorr lay at his feet.

Rhinan rushed to his side, the others right beside him.

It was hard to look at Eodorr. The swamp dragon's teeth had torn a deep gash from one shoulder down to the abdomen, and his sword arm was just… gone. It was like half of Eodorr was missing from the waist to the neck.

"Lynari!" Rhinan's panicked voice rang out in his own ears. "What can you do?"

The *Hegana* was already pulling herbs from her pouch

and uttering an incantation. She moved forward, but it was clear from the panicked expression on her face that she wasn't even sure where to begin.

Eodorr was conscious. He tried to speak. Rhinan leaned down. "I wasn't good enough. Keirwyn..."

"You stop that!" Rhinan snapped. "You've saved me several times over. I could never have gotten anywhere without you. That's what Keirwyn wanted. You've done him proud. Now stay with me. We're going to get you out of here."

He turned to the others. "By Wen's tongue, will someone find a rock in this cursed bog?" He looked at Wogen, who turned away, hanging his head. "There has to be a rock here!"

Lynari's tears told him what he did not want to know. Param reached forward to hold Rhinan. Rhinan screamed. He was inconsolable. It was like that day they had all been children playing in the forest. The ghosts had appeared when his parents were slain. He relived that moment of shock and pain.

He collapsed sobbing into Param's arms, their childhood friend lying at their feet, passed from the world, off to join the Lore Givers where he would learn all things for eternity.

* * * * *

They'd rounded up three of the horses, and in the process, come close to the end of the bog. Before moving on, Rhinan managed to find and retrieve the Ylvan sword from the pack on the half-charred horse. Lynari attended Brondur, his injuries bad, but not unhealable.

They finally found a large rock rising from the muck near

the edge of the bog. Wogen assured Rhinan he could use it to take them back across the river to the caverns, or any spot he'd been to before. This was agreeable to Rhinan, but Rhinan made Wogen promise him a favor.

They put Brondur on one of the horses, but used the other to carry what they'd salvaged of their packs. Wogen asked Lynari, "Can you keep Brondur well for the walk back?"

"I believe I can."

Wogen faced the rock, and opened a gray, cloudy portal. He looked at Lynari, and said, "Go, Quickly."

Lynari, leading the horse bearing Brondur, stepped into the mist. Eodorr's body was strapped over another horse, and they sent that through next. Wogen turned to Rhinan, and Rhinan nodded. Wogen, shaking his head, stepped into the cloudy portal.

Param turned away from the rock, staring at Rhinan and Rip.

"Hurry," Rhinan said. "I don't know how long Wogen can keep that open once he's stepped through. I have to coax Rip to follow me."

Param stepped to the side. "I'll follow you."

"Don't be ridiculous, Param. Get going."

"You can fool them, Rhinan. They don't know you very well. Trust me when I tell you that Lynari would never leave your side if you hadn't tricked her. But I'm a professional fool," here Param grinned, "and I know you better than they do. Did you really think you could fool me? We've been friends since childhood. You *can't* fool me, and if Silarrah were here, you couldn't fool her, either."

"There's no time for this, Param," Rhinan pleaded. "I'm going where I may not be able to come back. There's no reason for any of the rest of you to continue. I've lost enough people who care about me. Including Eodorr."

"Oh, and I've lost a couple of fingers," Param waved his hand at Rhinan. "But I can still be pretty handy in a fight. No jest intended. And besides, what have I got to go back to, hmm? During the winter, I sit beside the fire in my mother's cabin, eating her cooking and composing new ballads for the next season. None of that is left to me now. Sending me home would be a cruelty. I should be with my best friend."

His tone had grown quiet as he explained this, and Rhinan felt ashamed. Param, too, had suffered so much for being Rhinan's best friend. And now his thoughts turned again to Silarrah. He still had no idea if she were safe or not.

At that moment, the dark twinkling in the boulder vanished, leaving a normal boulder again.

"Well, I suppose it's settled anyway, now. I made Wogen promise not to wait for me." Rhinan made sure he caught Param's eye. "But I hope you don't regret this."

"We've got one horse to carry our packs," Param said. "We're walking out of a bog on foot, and it's getting dark. I *already* regret this."

Chapter Forty-Five

Param seemed unusually quiet, and Rhinan assumed it was out of respect for his grief. They had both lost a friend, but Rhinan and Eodorr had traveled so far together, grown much closer. Param had not shared that experience, was not particularly close to Eodorr, but he knew that Rhinan was suffering from the loss.

The pack horse strode between them, and Rip lumbered behind, occasionally wandering off to hunt. The land beyond the swamp went from dried grasses to shrub brush and dust. Short, spiky trees were sprinkled across the landscape. To either side, jagged, rocky hills stretched away in all directions, waves of rock rising higher and breaking lower. Rip would disappear behind a rise and reappear on the next one as he wandered further away. Large, filthy birds neither man recognized passed overhead in flocks. Rhinan and Param brought them down with arrows, providing pretty much all the meat they had. There were still some dried meats and vegetation in the packs on the horse, but it was very little. The horse wasn't doing too well, either.

"We should have passed a village by now," Param finally said. "There are villages in the Unreigned Territory. Some trading. I may not have been here, but I've heard that much."

Rhinan considered this. "Would Eluciar be further north or south? Perhaps we shouldn't be traveling directly east."

"Unfortunately, I would have only been able to get you to Dunskern. I've never crossed into the Unreigned Territory in my travels, and I don't know exactly which way Eluciar lies. I believe it is further south and east from the Unreigned Territory, but I can't be sure. The best help I can give you is finding a guide for us when we have any people to choose from."

It had been only a couple of days, but it felt longer. Water would become an issue soon.

They caught a lucky break when they came across a nomadic camp of travelers in tents with a wagon. Lying on a ridge, watching from afar, they didn't see anything that made them think the nomads were bandits. There weren't many of them, and they had women and children with them, but they were also armed. In the end, they had to risk approaching them. They needed direction, or they risked wandering this forsaken land until they died there.

They decided that Rhinan would keep Rip out of sight behind a ridge, allowing Param to approach and appear less threatening. Before he set out, the troubadour reached into one of the packs and pulled out his mandolute, still in one piece.

Rhinan shot him a curious glance, and Param replied with a shrug, "You never know."

"Just remember there's a troubadour missing two fingers being sought by the King's elite force," Rhinan warned him.

"If Dran's out here after all this time, I think we'd have known by now. I'll ask them if there are any Lydanian patrols."

In truth, the Unreigned Territory was about what Rhinan had imagined: Barren. Empty. Left ungoverned by its King, it had become a tragic and desolate region. Rhinan feared even worse for Eluciar.

He watched as Param waved to the camp, approaching in the least threatening possible manner—making plenty of noise in his approach and no attempt to charge. Of course, the nomads did not know Param had backup. Rhinan sat with an arrow nocked in his bow, and he had fastened the Ylvan sword to his side the minute they left the swamps behind. Laws were not enforced here, so what difference did wearing an outlawed weapon make?

A man from the nomad camp wandered out to meet Param, and they spoke for a few moments. Param then turned toward Rhinan, waving him to come along. Hesitating, Rhinan wasn't sure what to do with the pack horse and Rip, knowing that neither would stay put if he went down there. Rip acted like he didn't trust Rhinan not to "forget" him somewhere (Rhinan assumed that was how the beardog viewed the incident on the other side of the river), so he stuck pretty close, even when he wandered to hunt.

Putting the arrow back in his quiver, Rhinan led the pack horse toward Param and the nomad. Rip followed, and it was the nomad's body language that betrayed his feelings about the beardog. He stepped back and sort of half-crouched. Param waved at him, indicating there was nothing to fear. It looked to Rhinan like this only worked part way, but the nomad stood back up.

"Our friend here," Param said to Rhinan as he approached, "thinks we'll be robbed by warlords. Merchants out of other parts of Lydania aren't favored here."

Rhinan studied the nomad. He wore shabby clothes and

appeared hungry—thin and malnourished. Beyond him, the little encampment wasn't more than a dozen nomads, and about four of them were children. The rest were also in tattered clothing and looked just as weak and in need of food. They'd probably eat Rip if they had the strength to bring him down, but it was clear they didn't.

This was the price of crossing King Jerrick. This was Jerrick's idea of justice. Starving children. Rhinan realized it was a result of his own peoples' rebellion, but if this was Jerrick's manner of ruling, Rhinan understood the Ylvan Uprising. He seethed with rage. Turning to the pack horse, he pulled out several of the furs and pushed them into the man's arms. "Will you accept these as payment for pointing us to a nearby town? We need a guide to get us through the Unreigned Territory as quickly and safely as possible, and we're hoping to find a guide heading further." He didn't want to specify Eluciar as their destination. No point having more information about them out there than was necessary. He doubted Dran was in the area, but it was not a chance he would take.

With widened eyes, the man enthusiastically accepted. He pointed them a bit more north than east for the nearest town where they could probably find a guide willing to lead them wherever they needed to go. Especially for some of the furs they had to offer. As they wandered away in the direction indicated, they could hear the excited chattering of the nomads at their good fortune. Rhinan hoped they would survive, not simply fall prey to bandits or warlords. He wished he could do more.

By the following afternoon, they found the town. It was nothing like they were used to seeing in Lydania. Most of the buildings were in some state of disrepair, the citizens looked as poor and hungry as the nomads they'd met, and fewer people were on the streets than a town that size would normally contain. Nevertheless, it was a town, and it had the amenities that Rhinan and Param desperately needed. Rip wandered away, but the two men led the pony into the town, drawing all manner of looks from the citizens. "This doesn't feel safe," Param whispered.

Rhinan had far less experience with towns than Param, but he was willing to take his friend's word for it. Nothing seemed right about it, and he just wanted to get out of sight as quickly as possible. "They'll have an inn, won't they?"

"One would hope." Param peeked along the side streets as they strolled down the main street, acting as if they'd been here before and it was nothing new. "Ah!" Param exclaimed at last, pointing to a tavern. "We can find out in there… and have ourselves a drink, perhaps."

Rhinan was so thirsty he could barely speak. A drink of any sort sounded like salvation at this point. Neither he nor Param knew Brewing Lore, not to mention they had no ingredients, so they were parched.

At the tavern, they looked at one another, then at the pack horse, then back at one another. "You go," Rhinan said. "You've got the golden tongue. Remember we can pay, but we want to remain as unnoticed as possible."

Agreeing, Param pointed at Rhinan in affirmation, winking to indicate he had the situation well under control. He grabbed his mandolute out of the packs again and went into the tavern.

Standing with the pack horse, Rhinan kept an eye on the few townspeople who happened to pass. Most of them noticed him but looked away quickly. It seemed they didn't want anyone to know they'd noticed him. A man on horseback passed at one point, dressed in dark clothing, and stared hard at Rhinan as he passed. The man wore a sword at his side. Rhinan assumed this was one of the local warlord's men. Being noticed by them was likely trouble. He wished Param would hurry.

With a sudden burst of noise and debris as the door shattered, the troubadour ran out of the tavern. "Run!" he yelled.

Rhinan had his bow out, an arrow nocked and aimed at the tavern by the time he realized Param had stopped running. A hand had grabbed the back of Param's tunic. Enough of the man was exposed that he and Rhinan could see one another. The man looked as nondescript as anyone else in the town, but his expression was angry.

"You might want to unhand my friend, sir." Rhinan wiggled the bow, the arrow pointed at the man's face.

"You might want to lower the bow," came a voice from Rhinan's left hand side. Another nondescript man held a bow, an arrow pointed at Rhinan.

"I'd listen to *my* friend," came a new voice, this one on Rhinan's right hand side. There stood yet another man, sword drawn, casually examining its blade. "Now what's this all about, Beelor?"

Rhinan lowered his bow, but kept the arrow nocked. Beelor had released Param, but now he shoved the troubadour forward. "It was my *wife*."

Param smiled and shrugged. "How was I to know?"

The man with the sword stepped forward and used it to slice through the strap of the pack on the pack horse, dropping their packs to the ground. "Think what's in those packs will make up for it, Beelor?"

Beelor eyed the packs, then glared at Param. "Doesn't

matter now. If you say we take 'em, we take 'em."

There was a loud thumping sound, and the man with the bow on Rhinan's left side landed on the ground, unconscious.

Behind his limp form stood an older man, sword in one hand and dagger in the other. He was rugged looking, a deep scar from the side of his left eye down into his left cheek, mostly gray, shaggy hair, and not as emaciated as most of the locals seemed to be. He wore good leather and stood firm. "You think Slayer Dran's troop won't want whatever's in those packs, Feldas? Or did you forget who the warlord is around here?"

Rhinan's blood ran cold. Dran. Somewhere here in the Unreigned Territory. He would have bet against it, but his gambling luck was always a bit of come-and-go. This was the worst news, however. Dran was still pursuing him, or he wouldn't be here.

Feldas stepped back. "No, we don't want any trouble with those scrappers. You gonna squeal to 'im, Bruccan? Didn't think you were in with any warlords."

Param turned and yanked Beelor out of the tavern doorway, shoving him at Feldas.

"I don't have to squeal. They'd likely hear about it anyway." Bruccan stepped forward, prying the bow from the figure he'd knocked unconscious. "You might want to take this one with you."

Beelor and Feldas stepped forward and lifted the unconscious man, moving on past the tavern and down the street.

"They're small time," the old man called Bruccan told Rhinan and Param. "But if you want to keep those packs, I'd suggest you pick them up and follow me."

"And who are you?" Rhinan asked.

"Just call me Bruccan. And you're welcome, by the way. But let's hurry it up, hmm? I don't need encounters with any warlords, especially Slayer Dran. He's risen up over the winter, and he's supposedly vicious."

Rhinan and Param each grabbed a pack. "Did you ask about a guide, at least?" Rhinan asked.

"Didn't get the chance," Param responded. "I was trying to talk my way out of something that happened a long time ago."

"You've sure got a past," Rhinan quipped.

"Where do you need a guide to?" Bruccan interrupted them.

They both paused, but Rhinan decided this man had helped them. Perhaps he'd be able to help them find someone to lead the way to Eluciar. "We'd like to see the old Ylvan lands of Eluciar."

"That's been a wasteland since the Uprising. Why would anyone—" Bruccan stared at him for a moment, frozen. He looked Rhinan up and down. He stopped when he saw the pommel of the blade at Rhinan's side. He finally spoke again. "That an Ylvan blade?"

Rhinan glanced down at it. He decided it better not to know, so he lied. "Might be. I can't be sure."

Bruccan sighed. "I've been there. Eluciar. I can guide you myself."

This was a stroke of luck, and Rhinan had just been considering his gambling ups and downs. Yet here was a man who'd not only saved them, but who could guide them to Eluciar? "How much?"

"Well," Bruccan looked him over again. "Maybe we can get out of here and discuss that later."

"You're. NOT. Going. Anywhere."

The rough voice came from a figure on a horseback, as several more rode up and surrounded them. In fact, Rhinan saw the man that had ridden by earlier among them. They were rough looking men, many of them pointing arrows at Rhinan, Param, and Bruccan.

Turning to see who was addressing him, Rhinan assumed this was a warlord of the Unreigned Territory. The man wore a black hood that kept his face shadowed, but he had long, dark, wild hair, streaked with gray, visible as it crept out of the hood. Also visible was a long, dark beard streaked with gray. Clad entirely in black cloth and leather, the man threw back the black hood.

He looked weathered and rough, as so many of the people they'd seen since crossing the river, some sort of madman who would kill Rhinan if he could. He was almost unrecognizable, but it was definitely Gethor Dran.

And he and his men had them surrounded. There was no escape this time.

Chapter Forty-Six

"Search them," Dran commanded. "Leave nothing on them that isn't clothing."

Rhinan counted about a dozen men. None of them looked like the type you wanted to tangle with. He set down his bow, wondering if this was how it all ended. Several men approached to remove their weapons.

He had only seen Dran the one time, but this was not the same man he'd seen briefly at the mining camp. That man was a crisp general, disciplined to the tightest degree and filled with solid, clear thinking. This man had a pair of weathered, severed heads, one hanging on either side of his horse's rigging. This man clearly no longer cared for regulations, but seemed to have one singular purpose. And Rhinan suspected *he* was that purpose.

Wild Dran looked over Rhinan, Param, and Bruccan. "So this is what's left? I suspected the swamp would be a hardship." The general gave them a cruel grin. One more reason to hate Dran, and Rhinan was keeping a list.

The men took the bows and arrows carried by Rhinan and Param, as well as their swords. The men also cleaned Bruccan out of weapons which included a sword, two or three daggers (including the one for throwing they found in his boot), a small stone axe which was sharp on one side and rounded on the other, and the weapon he had been leaning upon—half staff, half blade. The men also took the pouches from the pack horse. The soldiers looked inside and let out crows of delight seeing the pelts and gems within.

Lastly, they were roughly searched. The man patting down Rhinan discovered the lump under his shirt. The man looked Rhinan in the eye with a sneering grin, and reached down the front of his tunic.

As Rhinan expected, his ghosts appeared and the sky darkened. While only he saw his ghosts, the darkening of the sky was apparent to all. Dran looked up and called out to the man to halt.

"Remove the item," Dran addressed Rhinan. "Or I'll pick it up after I cut off your head. I don't have to bring you back alive. Frankly, I would love an excuse."

Taking Dran at his word, Rhinan reached into his tunic and withdrew the *Pyvadis*. His ghosts murmured loudly, and he did his best to ignore them.

When the gem was withdrawn, Dran's eyes widened and his jaw dropped. "No!" he hissed. "How is it possible?"

Dran knew about the Pyvadis? The man who was chasing him all this time should have been the man *he* was chasing. What if Dran had the answers *he* needed? Handing a pouch to one of the men, Dran looked Rhinan in the eye. "Drop it into that pouch. Carefully." To the men behind him, he ordered, "If he makes any sudden moves, fill him full of arrows."

Cautiously, the man approached and held out the pouch. Rhinan met his eyes, and he could tell the man knew that he would take a portion of any arrows fired if Rhinan failed to follow the orders. For a moment, Rhinan considered it might be worth it. But not without having some answers from Dran. He did exactly as he was ordered, and dropped the *Pyvadis* into the pouch. It never touched anyone but Rhinan, and the inside of the pouch. The man handed the pouch to Dran, who tied it to his belt. The skies cleared, but the ghosts lingered a while before wandering off to wherever they went when they weren't haunting Rhinan.

Param's mandolute was tossed into their pile of confiscated items on the ground. Seeing it, Dran took a closer look at Param. Then he smashed the mandolute on the ground before speaking. "Troubadour, we meet again. Don't worry. I've got questions for you, too." Dran smiled at Param, and it chilled Rhinan. Nothing good was going to come of this.

Finally, Dran looked at Bruccan. He squinted for a moment, then his eyes widened again. "By the Black Halls of Norrik! If this isn't the most interesting day I've had in months. *You*? Here? How long? Never mind. It all makes sense now. King Jerrick will be most interested to speak with you."

Rhinan was thoroughly confused. Dran knew Bruccan? What would the King want with him? He didn't suppose it mattered. Even if he managed to get out of this somehow, he'd likely just lost his guide. But he wouldn't leave this man to Dran, even knowing nothing of the man. If he couldn't get Param and Bruccan out, he'd stay with them all the way to Masseltaine, if that's what it took, to bring this to a conclusion. He'd had enough of Dran.

"Bind them, and bring them back to camp," Dran said. "I want two men watching each of them, and carefully. If they escape, whoever's on watch dies first." They were tied well, thrown over horses, and ridden out of the town.

As evening approached, they entered Dran's camp. It must have begun as a village at one point. There were some wooden structures and large tents of thickly woven cloth. A fire burned in a pit at the center, but there was no one to be seen. These few men with Dran… this was all that he had left of the *Maraggan*? Or were they even his original men? Had Dran become a warlord in the Unreigned Territory? To Rhinan's eye, this is how it appeared.

"Lock them in the livestock shed," Dran ordered. "Leave them bound, and secure the shed beyond hope of opening. I want half of you watching it the first half of the night, and the other half to watch it the other half of the night. Bear in mind these men have habitually escaped, so expect anything."

Rhinan was hauled down from the horse, and heaved into the wooden structure. The floor was covered in filthy straw, and there was nothing else in the building. He was joined by Param and Bruccan. As he listened, the doors were spiked shut from the outside. The voices of several men could be heard nearby, settling in for the evening.

Rhinan sat up, and he and the other two men inspected the interior of the shed carefully. It was ragged, but with guards outside, even if they forced their way out, they wouldn't get very far, even though it only took the three men moments to unbind one another. At last, they sat down on the straw and looked at themselves.

Rhinan's ghosts appeared to him. A number of them faded into the shed and back out. They murmured as usual, but while they were sometimes more distracting, this was one of the times they were less of a distraction. Rhinan was grateful for this much, but could not figure why they were there.

Looking for a distraction of his own, Rhinan allowed his

curiosity to get the better of him and decided to question the old guide. "So Bruccan. You know Dran. And the King as well, I take it? As long as we're imprisoned, what're you out here in the Unreigned Territory for? Why do they want you? If it's none of my business, it won't hurt my feelings for you to say so. Just making conversation."

The old man leaned back and smiled. "None of your business? No. But let's play a game. I'll ask you a question, then I'll answer one. Or we can start there, see where it leads us. You see, in order to answer your questions, I may need some answers of my own first."

Rhinan glanced at Param, who shrugged.

"Fair enough," Rhinan agreed.

The old man sat forward and looked Rhinan over, the same way he had back in front of the old tavern. "All I ask is that you be truthful. You have no reason to lie to me, I can assure you. Remember, I'm in the same pot of stew as you. But if you want answers, as I said, it's likely I'll need a few myself first." The old man's scarred face was hard to read, but it appeared he meant what he said. "You asked me two questions, so I'll begin with two. But they're basic."

The sun was sinking outside, and the shed was growing dark. Soon, they would be in pitch blackness. It would be harder to gauge a man's expressions in the dark, so Rhinan grew impatient for answers. The distraction would be helpful with the ghosts.

"Tell me two things," the old man began. "Where do you come from, and how old are you?"

These were much easier questions than Rhinan had asked, and the simplicity surprised him. Even Dran knew these answers, so there was no risk in being straightforward with Bruccan about it. "I come from a small village far away in the north of the Domin Mountains, a place called Cabelon. I am almost twenty-eight summers."

Bruccan stood, pondering Rhinan's simple answers. He began to pace, and he seemed troubled. "Cabelon."

"You know it?" Rhinan asked. "Not many do."

"A bit. I was there once. A naïve young soldier in service to the King, I visited that town. About twenty summers ago."

Rhinan stood up. A tumultuous thought gripped his mind. It was so unthinkable it paralyzed him. He was very still when he asked the next question, remembering the day twenty summers ago that changed his life forever, led to the madness which brought him ghosts or the visions thereof, and forced him to avoid normal companionship to keep others safe. "You're sure it was twenty summers ago?"

Param stood as well. He got between Rhinan and Bruccan. "Let's hear him out," the troubadour said. "I'm very curious about that visit and what we may learn from it." The same thought had occurred to Rhinan, despite his rising tendency to act on impulse. "It's your turn to ask a question," Param reminded him.

"Your service to the King," Rhinan began. "Did that involve your visit to Cabelon?"

"I was a young soldier back then," the old man explained. "All of my service was to the King."

Rhinan fumed. "That is not the answer I am looking for, and I think you know it."

Bruccan sat down again, began playing with the straw. "Always choose your questions as carefully as you choose your answers."

He was about to rephrase his question, but Param stepped in yet again. "I believe the next question is Bruccan's." Rhinan had rarely heard the tone of voice that

Param used, but he imagined it was one the troubadour practiced. It confused the listener, at once putting him at ease and also putting him on guard. It was clear that Bruccan did not miss this inflection, either, as he scooted away from Param.

"This is not *your* game of questions, troubadour." The old man stared far away, delaying his next question. After a period of contemplation, he asked, "Do you have reason to believe yourself an Ylvan?"

Rhinan lunged at the old man, but he stopped himself. "You bloody well know I do, don't you?"

"I suppose it's more a confirmation than a question." The old man sighed heavily. "We both know there's only one way I could possibly suspect that, don't we?"

Filled with rage, years of pain and anger bursting from within him, his ghosts murmuring at full scale, Rhinan leapt upon the guide.

"It was you, you worthless cur! You insufferable assassin!" Rhinan shouted, and pummeled the scarred man with his fists. "That's how you know Dran!" After taking several blows that left his face bleeding, actually as strong as he looked, Bruccan fought Rhinan off.

Param made no move to interfere until the two stood again, face to face. "Rhinan, I can relate to how you feel. But if it were me, I would want to ask this man one more question, and it's your turn."

"*Why?!?*" Rhinan screamed into Bruccan's face. It was all he had, all he could think of that Param must be referring to. "Why did the King send you to assassinate my parents?"

Bruccan stepped back. "You already know this answer, don't you? Because they were Ylvan. Though I can provide many details you likely do not have." The old man paused, and Rhinan waited impatiently. Bruccan's shoulders drooped and he hung his head. "I am a dead man, whether I die at the King's hands or at yours. This day was inevitable. I only prolonged it a while by hiding most of my life here in the Unreigned Territory.

"Rhinan, I have no right to ask you, of all people, for a favor. But I ask this favor not for myself, but for you. Will you allow me to tell you what I know? I'm not asking for my own peace of mind or your forgiveness. I am well beyond both. You deserve to know what I can tell you of the circumstances that led to… led you here."

He hadn't thought of it a moment ago in his rage, but Rhinan knew that he did, in fact, want to know anything he could about what happened. And why. He could beat Bruccan to death, maybe, but the guide was strong and capable of defending himself. And what Bruccan said was true for Rhinan as well: he would either die here in this shack, or at the hands of the King. He may as well hear out the man who'd assassinated his parents.

"Tell me," Rhinan said. "Tell me everything."

As Bruccan was about to answer, there was a terrible scream outside. One of the guards, then another. A third guard hollered, and then one of them came through the wall head first, shattering wood pieces everywhere. He landed at their feet, dead.

It was followed by a familiar howl of fury. Rip.

"I believe that's our cue," Param said, reaching down for the dead man's sword, stepping over his body and out of the shed. Rhinan nodded to Bruccan, indicating he should follow.

Outside the shed, the camp was chaos. It was dark, and the beardog was wreaking havoc. The few remaining soldiers, as well as Dran himself, were caught in a battle soon joined by Param and Bruccan, who'd picked up a blade for himself.

Rhinan, silently, snuck around the shed in the darkness. Unseen, he found the only solid structure besides the animal shed… most likely this would be Dran's quarters. Opening the door, he slipped inside. He heard shouts, and knew neither Param nor Rip would slip away. He just hoped the darkness would protect them and that Param would keep Bruccan close. Whether Rhinan chose to kill him later or not, they still needed his help to reach Eluciar.

In the dark cottage, Rhinan's eyes adjusted to the light of a single candle left burning. There was little of interest in the cottage but a comfortable bed and some weaponry. On a table were the two dilapidated heads that had been strapped to Dran's horse, and with deep sadness he was able to recognize that one was Vaylene. He could not identify the other, but it was a man's head. He couldn't imagine Dran living like this. It must have been a desperate winter. The general of the King's *Maraggan* had perhaps gone a bit mad himself.

Spotting what he came for, Rhinan grabbed their packs and weapons. He chanced a quick look inside the packs, and saw the *Pyvadis* glowing within one. Present, too, was his Ylvan sword. He took the packs and began to leave, then stopped. He turned to the candle, tipped it over, and made sure the wooden table caught fire. He hoped the entire structure would burn.

Outside, he saw Rip using his sizeable teeth to rend a man to death. Param and Bruccan both fought viciously against Dran's soldiers.

Spotting horses, Rhinan untied the leads on three. He called to Param, who dragged Bruccan away from the melee. They leapt onto the horses and, with Rip loping along at their side, fled into the darkness.

Chapter Forty-Seven

This was the second time he'd had the Ylvan in hand, after nearly laying hands on him countless times. And yet, again, his men had proven themselves incompetent and unequal to the task of capturing or holding the man. Fuming with nearly blind rage, Dran was completely out of ideas, but he was certain of one thing: that Ylvan wasn't going to get too far too fast in this territory.

Then he noticed the smoke rising from his quarters, the flames licking the darkness. The Ylvan.

He turned to the men he had left guarding the shack. Two yet lived, though they were injured. They couldn't take down a simple beardog by the firelight? In uncontrollable fury, he turned on them and drove his blade into their hearts.

He couldn't believe the beardog hadn't gotten himself killed by the swamp dragon, but that was no excuse for the men being caught off guard. It had been a rough winter, waiting in the Unreigned Territory and scrounging as necessary to survive. They'd fought other warlords and defeated them. Of all the warlord bands in the area, Slayer Dran was now known as the one you didn't want to cross paths with.

The rest of his men—only a handful now—stood staring at him with jaws hung open. They drew back as he glared at them. He didn't even know anymore which of these men had come into the Unreigned Territory with him, official soldiers, and which had joined his troop from other defeated warlords over the winter. The fools all feared him. Well, they should. He would kill them all if it was worth his time. But he had an Ylvan to catch, and he'd come to know this region—even in the dark of night. He'd follow immediately.

"Go home!" he shouted at them. "You are hereby relieved of your duties. Never let me see any of you again!"

The few remaining men turned quickly, mounted horses, and rode off as swiftly as they could. Without hesitation, they'd abandoned him to a man. Not surprised, it was a relief to Dran at this point. He wouldn't have to look after anyone but himself now.

Alone at last, Dran thought now he might have a chance to actually catch Ashuir and not have it fouled up by any sniveling excuses for soldiers. He tried to enter his burning shack, but it was engulfed to the point that anything left inside would be ruined. And he doubted anything he *really* wanted was left inside anyway. The Ylvan was a thief, after all. That's what had started this whole mess. Or was it that the thief was an Ylvan? He laughed at his own jest.

He picked around the camp for quick supplies: food, a bow and a quiver of arrows, little more. He would travel light. His sword was strapped across his back now—a warlord style he'd picked up as they waited these few months.

Slinging a pack on one of the remaining horses, he set out south-eastward, sure he knew what direction the prisoners would be heading. Bruccan would be leading them.

Bruccan. It was no real surprise to find his old Captain here. Bruccan had served directly under Dran many years ago, and the thought that Bruccan might be living in the Unreigned Territory had occurred to Dran. But he'd never considered it might be worth pursuing him. Not until this Ylvan came to light. Now it all made sense. Bruccan had to have known of Rhinan's existence. His absence all these years proved that he had chosen to keep it a secret. But why? Had he been in league with that Constable? Bruccan had "deserted," but that hadn't been a chief concern of Dran's after the rest of that affair. But this? It was treason. And now he was *guiding* the Ylvan? Bruccan would be punished worse than the Ylvan himself. The Ylvan was an unwitting traitor, but Bruccan? Bruccan had chosen to defy his King. And Dran could not have that. He would dismember Bruccan, and slowly.

Infuriated at the scent of embers from his quarters still burning in the night, he spurred his horse forward at top speed. There were only three of them. And a beardog. He would have to handle the beardog first. He checked the bow, made sure it was strung. The mistake his men had made had been to let that creature get too close to begin with. It was a mistake *he* would not make.

* * * * *

As they rode swiftly in the dark of the night, Rhinan was sure Dran and his men would pursue them. Until Dran was dead, this would never end. And until Jerrick was dead, it would probably continue even then. As an Ylvan, he would be a fugitive forever, perhaps never see Silarrah again. The only way to handle this was to face Dran, and he knew there was only one way he could best Dran… with an arrow. And then, to truly end it, Jerrick's rule must end. This was a decision he'd already come to after everything he'd seen since leaving Cabelon.

In their silence, Rhinan recalled the "game" he and Bruccan had begun in the shed. "You asked me a favor," Rhinan reminded him. "I grant it on the condition that you owe me some explanations."

Bruccan gazed over at him. "I can only explain what I know, which is clearly much more than you do. But yes, let me tell you what I know as it relates to you."

Rhinan turned to Param. "Param, can you drop back and keep a close watch, or at least listen for Dran's men? I have no doubt they'll be in pursuit, and we'll need all the warning we can get." Rhinan's only plan was to hope that Param would hear Dran riding up, and then they could hide and Rhinan would take Dran off his horse with a single shot in the dark. After that, it all depended on how many men were with the General and how close they got.

Nodding, Param dropped back and looked over his shoulder. Rhinan felt secure in Param's ability to alert them as soon as it would be possible. And Rip was close by as well.

"Did you get the *Pyvadis*?" Bruccan asked.

Shocked that he knew of it, Rhinan decided there was no sense in denying it. "Yes."

"Good. Don't ever let that get back to the King, or he'll destroy it."

"Let's start with that gem," Rhinan asked. "What is it? Why is it so important?"

"Can't start a story in the middle," Bruccan answered.

"Fair enough." Rhinan watched the older man carefully. He was tough, capable, and had considerable knowledge of the land they were in. If he wanted to make an escape, Rhinan's only way of stopping him would be with an arrow, which might end the possibility of getting the answers Bruccan claimed to have.

"I was a young captain in the Lydanian army," Bruccan began. "Eventually, I proved my worth and was transferred to the *Maraggan*, the King's most prestigious force. Gethor Dran was a close confidant and friend to the King. So as one of his captains, I was privy to certain information. The elite force was assigned missions of a more… personal… nature to the King. Secret, if you will.

"In those days, believe it or not, magic was legal and Jerrick had an entire council of wizards. This council was also secret, known to but a very few, including the *Maraggan*. Your father, Markin Ashuir, was on that council. As the Lore Master of the school of magic at the Lore College, he was, in fact, the *head* of the council."

Vaylene the Healer had already told Rhinan that Markin worked with the King, though it was not public knowledge. But this was a new dimension, and Rhinan did not care for the implications.

Bruccan continued. "All of the Magic Lore in Lydania at the time was of an elemental nature, and Ylvans were particularly adept. Rhinan, have you ever asked yourself why the Ylvans rose against King Jerrick?"

Thinking for a moment, Rhinan knew what everyone knew. He repeated the story to Bruccan. "The Ylvan sorcerer Narkan Tanglas craved power, ensorcelled the Ylvan clans in Eluciar, and attempted to overthrow the King of Lydania because he was seeking the lost lore of Lydania—magic never meant to be used by anyone but the Lore Givers themselves. He attacked because he falsely believed the King to be in possession of this knowledge, though he had no reason to think so." Even as Rhinan said it, he knew that Bruccan was getting at something else… the truth was far less simple, and Rhinan was beginning to feel he wouldn't like it.

The old guide chuckled. "Well, that is *mostly* true."

Growing impatient, Rhinan snapped at Bruccan. "I don't understand. Which part is supposed to be false?"

Param spoke up. "Hurry. We are being followed. Far back, but whoever it is, they are moving fast."

"It's true that Narkan Tanglas sought knowledge of the lost lore he believed Jerrick to have in his possession. But *why* would he think that?" Bruccan asked.

Rhinan had no answer for this. Did Tanglas know of the King's council of wizards? That could be it.

"I see you are beginning to understand." Bruccan gave him a half smile. With his scar, it was almost fearsome to behold. "Tanglas attacked because he thought Jerrick had knowledge he didn't have. The falsehood is that Tanglas had no solid reason to suspect the knowledge may be in Jerrick's possession. You see, unlike the Jerrick you know today, *the King was obsessed with magic in those days.* Why do you think he had an entire secret council devoted to it?"

Jerrick? Who had banned all magic? Obsessed with it? It was too much to believe.

"As it happened, King Jerrick had indeed given his council of wizards a task, and the *Maraggan* were sent to help them. We were to find the lost lore of Lydania—ancient magic that was powerful, violent, ungentle and, well, unnatural. But this lost lore… it was more powerful than the magic of the day, and Jerrick craved that power. As head of this secret council of wizards, and a curious man for lore, your father was part of this search. So the false part is that

Tanglas had no reason to believe Jerrick might have this knowledge or some way to gain it. He had a *very good* reason, and *that* is why he attacked.

"But do you know how he found out? You're not going to like this, Rhinan, but your father and Tanglas were friends. Your father told Tanglas about the secret council of wizards. He meant well. His plan was to bring Tanglas onto the council to add another Ylvan."

Rhinan felt his rage growing as the man who'd killed his father rode next to him, accusing his father of inadvertently setting off the Ylvan Uprising. The thought of killing Bruccan, once his tale was finished, formed in Rhinan's mind. Why not? It would be justice for his parents' murders.

"So the war began. And it was bloody. I fought in it; I'll never forget it." The old man grew distant as he paused, reflecting on a time long ago.

"Then something happened that changed everything," Bruccan hung his head. "But it did lead to the end of the Uprising. You see, an unknown assassin slipped into Jerrick's palace and murdered his wife, the queen, and his son, the prince. The grief drove Jerrick mad."

"You?" Rhinan asked, his temper smoldering.

"No. I was never an assassin. I was a soldier. And I served the King in those days. I would not have murdered his family. They were dear. Though no one knew who, it was certainly an act of Tanglas. But in answer to losing his family in this way, Jerrick turned to your father for help in his grief and rage, for he knew of your father's friendship—now *former* friendship—with Tanglas. He asked Markin to use what he knew of the lost lore—for there was *some* knowledge of the lost lore among the wizards—to find a way to destroy Tanglas. Markin agreed. Tanglas had gone too far, and the

Uprising had to end.

"There was an ancient spell of the lost lore—developed with help from the rock gnomes, I believe—but it was terrible. It created a prison for the soul of the victim—within a gem—for eternity. The victim could not live, nor could the victim die and join the Lore Givers." Bruccan paused and looked to Rhinan. "Yes, that is the gemstone that hangs around your neck."

Rhinan was horrified. The prospect of an eternity trapped between life and death… But also the very notion that Tanglas was trapped in this gem he'd been carrying. Even more puzzling: What about the rest of the Ylvan Clans? What happened to them? Rhinan assumed that they were his ghosts, but how?

Rhinan was sure Bruccan had no idea of the ghosts, but he had more to say about the *Pyvadis*. "Markin fashioned the *Pyvadis*. All he needed to do was activate the spell in the gem, and it would capture the life essence of Tanglas. Jerrick asked Markin for the gem, to hold himself for a while, considering whether or not to use it. Markin agreed… it was a terrible fate, and one that should only be used should the war efforts appear to be failing—which, at that time, they were not. Dutiful, Markin gave the *Pyvadis* to the King.

"Now remember that Jerrick had an entire council of wizards at his disposal. Combined, most of them were not as powerful as any one Ylvan wizard. But Jerrick turned to some of the more faithful of them, and asked them about Markin's spell. As Dran's captain, I overheard something even I could not believe of Jerrick. He asked them for a horrifying alteration. The King wanted the *Pyvadis* expanded to hold *the entirety of the Ylvan Clans*, regardless of distance and irreversibly, once the spell was activated. Without your father's knowledge, some of the wizards on the council changed the spell. It became a prison to an entire race of people."

Bruccan paused to let this sink in, leaving Rhinan speechless. The unspeakable act was beyond his comprehension. His parents were assassinated when he was a child—by the man he decided more and more he would kill when he finished speaking, the man having been a part of all of this—but he could not fathom the idea of committing such an atrocity. Was it to be believed? Could this *Pyvadis* hold the entire Ylvan Clans? And if so…

"Jerrick ordered the wizards to use the altered spell. He didn't even consider your father and mother, living in Masseltaine at the Lore College. He sacrificed every member of the Ylvan Clans. Within moments, every Ylvan in every part of Lydania, including those in Eluciar, disappeared. Those who saw them claimed they cried out in utter anguish as they faded from vision. And as a further punishment, he had his wizards send an eternal, crippling drought upon the land of Eluciar itself.

"And then our King Jerrick, finished with magic forever, turned on his own council and had us murder the wizards. Every one of them we could find. We killed them all. And the School of Magic at the Lore College was closed and outlawed, as was any practice of magic. Furthermore, being that weaponsmiths in Lydania had armed the Ylvans, the King outlawed the forging of weapons unless they were hired by the King and working for the Lydanian army. And that was the end of the Ylvan Uprising."

Rhinan was sickened and confused. He couldn't believe the King, even in such mourning, could condone such an unspeakable act. But there had to be more to the story. He, himself, was Ylvan. If the *Pyvadis* trapped all of the Ylvans, how was *he* here?

"They're gaining on us," Param whispered loudly. "At least one of them. How much further to Eluciar?"

"Oh, we're approaching the land." Bruccan turned to Param, looked past him. Rhinan, still not trusting the old guide, wondered if he were expecting any help of his own. For all Rhinan knew, there was another band of warlords out there that Bruccan was a part of or that he even led himself. They'd ridden most of the night, and sun would be rising soon. Should they expect attacks other than Dran? "We'll be there by dawn." Rhinan wasn't sure if this was confirmation of his mistrust, or simple coincidence.

"Now let me tell you what you must be wondering." Bruccan turned back to Rhinan. "I heard this all from Dran, and it's all I know. We learned of it a few years after the end of the Uprising, but it's the information I was given to act upon."

With a grimace, Rhinan indicated that Bruccan should continue his tale.

"As it turned out, not all of the wizards who worked on the spell agreed with the King's plan. One of the more powerful wizards, Odryn Dayas, had reached Markin with the terrifying news. Markin was able to fashion a spell to protect himself and his pregnant wife before the *Pyvadis* was activated. Odryn had a brother in the Lydanian army who was being assigned the position as Constable of a distant outpost in the far northwest. Quiet place. Cabelon."

"Keirwyn!" Rhinan let the Constable's name out in pain.

"Was that his name?" Bruccan asked. "I never knew. But Odryn convinced his brother to steal this prison gem of the Ylvan Clans. At the same time, he convinced the Ashuirs to relocate to Cabelon where they would never be discovered. No one in Cabelon had ever even heard of Markin Ashuir. Except, of course, Keirwyn, but Odryn trusted his brother to look after the Ashuirs. A wizard himself, Odryn then disappeared, hearing that the rest of the King's council was being hunted and killed.

"Jerrick naturally assumed that Markin and his wife, Herilyn, were vanquished with the activation of the *Pyvadis.* It was years later, on a routine patrol, that one of Dran's other captains—a man named Siras—discovered the Ashuirs were alive and living in Cabelon. He reported this to Dran who, in turn, reported it to the King. We had just fought the Ylvan Uprising a few years before that time. Many people had been convinced that the Ylvans were evil and dangerous. I sincerely apologize, Rhinan, but I was afraid to hear that Ylvans yet survived. I fought in that war, and it was terrible. When Dran assigned me to ensure the pair were finished, I accepted the assignment. It would truly be the end of the Ylvans."

Gritting his teeth, Rhinan placed his hand on the Ylvan sword at his side. He knew the motion would not escape Bruccan, but he was more than ready to kill the assassin. Yet he would hear him out first.

"When I arrived in Cabelon, I slipped into the home occupied by the Ashuirs. I killed them as quickly and painlessly as I could. I had been told to find and retrieve a gem—the *Pyvadis*—but it wasn't in their home. Someone else had to be in possession of it, hiding it. But in searching for it, I realized the Ashuirs had a child. My assignment was to kill a wizard and his wife; it never had anything to do with killing children. I wouldn't do it, so I could not return to the King for fear of exposing the child's existence.

"I made sure that word got to the King that the Ashuirs were dead, but that no gem was present. He must have believed it or confirmed it in some way, because I was never hunted down. I fled to the region that had been Norham, but by then was being called the Unreigned Territory. Jerrick allowed it to be raided by plunderers, bandits, and pirates as penance for siding with Eluciar in the Uprising. There was no law, and it was a place I could hide the secret that an Ylvan yet remained in Lydania.

"That is everything I know about you. And here you are, about to be the last Ylvan to set foot in Eluciar."

As Bruccan finished his tale, the sun was rising. It was hazy in this land, the light dim and murky. Rhinan's mind was swirling with the hidden truths and secrets about the King, his parents, Lydania, the Ylvans, and this gem… He wanted to kill Bruccan for killing his parents, but now he also knew that he owed Bruccan his life. In fact, Bruccan had sacrificed much of his own life to protect Rhinan's very existence. It was a conundrum Rhinan knew he would struggle with for the rest of his life.

"For what it's worth, I think your father would be proud of you for making it here."

At the mention of his father, Rhinan whirled on Bruccan, his hand on the sword, still tangled about what to do with the old man. "Do not speak of my father, Bruccan. Not in any way, not ever."

The old assassin looked chagrined, but pointed ahead. A jagged, rocky ridge rose ahead of them. They could not see beyond it. "Just over that ridge is Eluciar. In case you decide it's time to kill me now, you've arrived at your destination."

Bruccan sounded resigned, and Rhinan wasn't sure he could do it. He cocked his head. "I've never thanked you, you know. Not for helping me get here. For sparing my life when I was a child. You knew I was there, but you told no one, and you chose not to kill me."

"As I've said, I was no child killer. I was sent to end a threat to the kingdom, and at the time, I believed it to be true. But I couldn't murder an innocent child. If not for Jerrick's obsession, you'd still be running around in Cabelon."

His mind whirling with all these answers he'd been seeking, Rhinan was conflicted about what to do next. He was still unsure if he would kill the old man. "You may be right. I would still have no idea who murdered my parents or why. I wouldn't even know I was an Ylvan. I can't say if that is a blessing or a curse. But you spared and saved my life, Bruccan, so I will consider the account settled for killing my father. But you killed my mother, too, you damned wretch. And for that, you still owe me."

Unwittingly, Rhinan had drawn his father's Ylvan blade from its sheath. He examined the workmanship of the weapon. Not once since Eodorr had brought it to him had he taken another moment to admire the craft and the workmanship that went into the blade. He thought of the long-abandoned smith shop back in Cabelon. This craft was another thing the King had taken from the people of Lydania.

"You're scarin' me, boy." Bruccan drew his horse nearer to him. "You look like an angry mountain troll. But I understand."

"Rhinan!" Param exclaimed.

Rhinan and Bruccan both turned. An arrow flew from behind Param, landing with a thud in Bruccan's chest.

"Ride!" Param yelled.

Even injured as he was, Bruccan was able to get his horse moving and keep up with Rhinan and Param as they rode to the ridge and over it, finally crossing into the land of Eluciar.

Rhinan hadn't expected much, but he wasn't prepared for what lay before him.

Chapter Forty-Eight

The territory of Lydania known as Eluciar was legendary. Rhinan had heard his whole life how glorious it had been. Bright, living green lands with fresh waters and abundant wildlife. Cozy villages, creative people with special gifts for art and magic, and a peaceful disposition. The outermost, and furthest region from the capitol within the Lydanian kingdom, and a majority would say the most beautiful.

But then came Narkan Tanglas. A power-craving sorcerer who used what bits of the lost lore of Lydania—forbidden magics supposedly long-since forgotten—to gradually seize power and, ultimately, to persuade or enchant the Ylvan Clans to follow him. Convince them that King Jerrick of Lydania was a tyrant whose sole intention was oppression. The result was the Ylvan Uprising, but they weren't strong enough. Not fully capable of enchanting every member of the Ylvan Clans to his cause, the sorcerer fixed it by having the King's family murdered and bringing about the oppression he had warned them about. The King's response was swift and harsh, but even harsher than anyone expected. The Ylvan Clans were erased from Lydania, some magic spell created—initially by his own father—under the King's orders. What followed was the actual oppression Tanglas had mostly imagined. And the utter destruction of the beautiful land of Eluciar.

Forgotten since the Ylvan Uprising, virtually uninhabitable, it was a difficult journey to reach the province. Even Rhinan's tracking skills would have failed him here. And with no resources in the land, it was pointless. For Rhinan, it was his last bastion of hope for safety from King Jerrick who had learned, as had Rhinan himself, that he was the last living member of the Ylvan Clans, the lost natives of this land.

Coming over the rise, Rhinan gazed down into a valley of pure desolation stretching some distance away. Blackened, barren land covered with rough shards of dull stone and scattered, twisted thickets of short, scorched, gnarled trees. There was no life in this place. No chance for survival. In order to escape King Jerrick, he would have to flee Lydania completely. And from here? Crossing Eluciar was not likely to be a journey one would survive.

At the thought of survival, he snapped out of his feelings of remorse and self-pity. Next to him, Bruccan had slid from his horse to the ground, an arrow protruding from his chest. Rhinan dismounted and squatted next to him, expecting that Dran and his men were not far behind. Param was already at his side. Rip was somewhere, but Rhinan did not see him.

Wracked with guilt at the idea he considered killing the old man himself, and yet somehow feeling that here at last was retribution for a lifetime of madness and sorrow, Rhinan knelt above Bruccan when the former soldier-turned-assassin-turned-guide fell from his horse, the arrow clearly a deadly shot. The man who killed his parents, and yet by ironic logic was responsible somehow for Rhinan's being alive, lay dying in his arms.

The scar-faced Bruccan looked up at him, his eyes apologetic and pained. His expression turned to one of peace. He met his fate without another word as if he welcomed it.

But it was Param that caught his attention. "Rhinan?"

Looking up, Rhinan could see his ghosts like never before. They were usually muddled and murmuring, but now they seemed more defined, more solid.

And there were so many of them. They stretched away down the valley.

What amazed Rhinan was that *Param was looking at the ghosts.*

No one but Rhinan had ever seen his ghosts. Ever. Yet here was Param, looking around wide-eyed and clearly terrified at the sight of the ghosts.

"What in the Black Halls of Norrik is going on?"

"You… you can *see* them?" Rhinan had spent his whole life hiding the secret of their existence, and yet now, here in Eluciar, Param was reacting to their presence.

Param nodded, unable to tear his eyes away from the multitudes of ghosts that stretched out across the barren land. "This is where your people come from, Rhinan. Is this normal? Do you know?"

He wasn't sure yet if he should jump for glee. All these years, they'd been more than a figment of Rhinan's imagination, and this was validation he'd never expected to receive that he wasn't simply out of his mind from the death of his parents.

Overwhelmed and overcome with the emotion of a lifetime of being victimized by a simple misunderstanding of his own childhood's lost innocence, tears welled up in

Rhinan's eyes and he began to weep. His parents' murders had been avenged, probably at the hands of his worst enemy, the man who had ordered their deaths, and the same man who had been pursuing him with the intent to kill him. Gethor Dran.

Rhinan realized that there was a glow coming from within his tunic. The *Pyvadis.* This inexplicable thing was glowing here, now in Eluciar, as the ghosts became visible to his friend. He withdrew the gem from his tunic, his own tears falling upon it.

The blue, watery area in the center of the gem was churning as it never had before. It was like a mini storm inside the gem, which seemed to be crumbling.

The skies above them burst with thunder, and lightning streaked across the sky. An intense rain began to fall, soaking Rhinan in a land long fully parched. Fascinated, Rhinan could not take his eyes away from the melting gem. Param was still fixated on the ghosts.

It was Rip that growled a severe warning from behind him.

Still kneeling, Rhinan looked up to see Dran a few lengths away, aiming an arrow directly at him. The rain made Dran's long black and gray hair and beard look even wilder. He was alone, unaccompanied now by any soldiers or bandits or companions. Param had lowered his bow in his wonderment at the ghosts, and could not have gotten a shot into Dran before Dran finished Rhinan. The King's General had caught up to him in his Clan's homeland, and Rhinan just didn't care anymore. Still weeping, he let the stone fall to the ground, raising his arms in surrender.

As the *Pyvadis* hit the ground of Eluciar, wet with Rhinan's tears and the downpour that had appeared so suddenly in a land long dry without it, a miraculous and inexplicable event occurred.

Rhinan no longer looked at Dran, and neither did Param. In fact, even Dran was no longer looking at him. They were watching the land itself.

First around the gem, then spreading out around Rhinan, Bruccan's body, Param, Rip, and swiftly reaching Dran, lush, green grasses sprang from the earth. This spread away from them, unfurling across the valley, covering the blackened land, restoring it to resplendent life. The twisted thickets of short, scorched trees unwound and rose to full heights, their branches shooting outward and bursting with full leaves and blossoms. And it was happening so swiftly it was impossible not to watch.

Eluciar was coming back to life. Without knowing, Rhinan could feel that this was one last magic with which his father had imbued the *Pyvadis* upon having it returned to him by Keirwyn after its terrible use by the King. The gem held the power to resurrect Eluciar.

All three men watched, transfixed, as the valley before them transformed from death to life. Rhinan saw that Param was as shocked as he was. Even Dran, who had seemed impervious to anything, stood with his jaw hung open, the bow he'd aimed at Rhinan now dropped to his side.

As the land sprang back to life, the *Pyvadis* itself transfigured into a glowing mist that flowed toward Rhinan. As the glow reached him, he could feel it become a part of him, like warmth. Only there was something deeper, something he could not understand. Something changing him.

And now the ghosts rushed to Rhinan. They swarmed him. Rhinan's tears turned to those of joy, feeling that if the land was being restored from lifelessness after all these years, then surely the Ylvans were about to be returned as well. His people would return; he would not be alone in the world in the way he had always known he was, though he had never known why until Bruccan's tale. He would no longer be the last of the lost Ylvan Clans.

It occurred to him that Dran would be ripped to shreds by these Ylvans, as they returned from the border of death and sought vengeance on one of those responsible for their tortuous imprisonment. He wondered for a moment if his parents would be there, but then he remembered that they were not caught in the gem's imprisonment spell, and he doubted he would see them. There was a twang of pain, expecting the Ylvans to return, but his parents were truly passed into the land of the Lore Givers and would not be among them.

As the ghosts drifted past him, they acknowledged him with what appeared to be gratitude. They smiled, they nodded. The ghosts for once had clear faces and their murmuring was gleeful, not dreadful. He prepared himself to meet the Ylvan Clans.

But the ghosts passed Rhinan, and then wandered off into the beauty of Eluciar, disappearing. As they faded for what he somehow knew inside was the last time, his expectations were dashed. They were not returning to life. Heartbroken, it dawned on him that, of course, these had never been ghosts at all. They were the Ylvan Clans, but according to what Bruccan had learned, they were imprisoned in an irreversible magic spell that held them between life and death, an even worse and horrible fate. And returning the *Pyvadis* to Eluciar… this somehow released the spell to move forward, but not to restore their lives. It had set them free to pass into the afterlife, to peacefully join the Lore Givers in eternal learning of all things. Had his father known this? If so, why had his father not brought the *Pyvadis* here years ago? There was something he did not know, that perhaps even Bruccan with all of his knowledge of the events that led to this gem's creation did not know.

Sorrow gripping him even further, Rhinan watched his ghosts… the Ylvan Clans… fade away forever, released at last. Weeping with a loneliness he could never eliminate, filled with an emptiness from which he would never recover, he realized with deep grief that he was, after all, the last of the Ylvan Clans.

Chapter Forty-Nine

Magic. Ylvan magic at its strongest. This storm reminded Dran of the one back near Cabelon, and he was certain Rhinan Ashuir was responsible then and responsible now.

Only this time, there was no escape for the Ylvan. After Dran shot Bruccan, they'd crossed into what used to be Eluciar, fully preoccupied. This allowed Dran to dismount and creep forward between the jagged rocks. He snuck up on them and, as they were distracted by the storm, he walked almost right up on them. There were only two of them and the beardog behind them. He drew an arrow and aimed straight at the Ylvan. Dead or alive, it no longer mattered. He would return to Masseltaine with heads on his saddle if that's what it took. But none of them could move toward him without him piercing the Ylvan with an arrow.

The Ylvan held the glowing gem in his hand, but he dropped it and raised his hands in a show of surrender. Without any more fools around to foul this up, Dran was elated that his long mission would finally be at an end.

He had been so focused on the Ylvan that he hadn't looked outward over the dead valley. Hordes and hordes of ghosts drifted about. The *Pyvadis* had let them loose! He knew at once that this was disastrous. It was more Ylvan magic, but it did not comfort Dran. He could fight anything he could stick with an arrow or stab with a blade, but ghosts were not in his area of expertise.

Worse, the land around the gem, and then around the men and even around his own feet, was suddenly thriving in a return from the dead. Life flowed outward across the valley, swiftly and powerfully. He had never seen magic on this scale, and it even drew his attention from the Ylvan.

One of the ghosts parted from the others. Unlike the other ghosts, who were beings of light primarily transparent to the landscape, this ghost was a dark shadow, and it emanated an oppressive power Dran could somehow detect in what was left of his feelings. It dove straight at *him*, rather than the Ylvan who seemed to draw the benevolent attention of all the other ghosts.

As the ghost approached, its features became clear. Standing transfixed, Dran had no idea how to fight this ghost. Not this time. Not like before. You needed magic for this, but the magic had been banished and he had no King's wizards to help him.

It was Narkan Tanglas, the Ylvan sorcerer who'd started the Uprising. The very soul that *Pyvadis* had originally been created to contain. The *Pyvadis* that someone had hidden for years, leading to this moment of tragedy and ruin. The ghost spoke to Dran in a hiss that mysteriously came from an unknown place further away than the ghost. But it was loud enough for Dran to hear.

"I see you remember me."

"We disposed of you," Dran retorted in anger. "Why do you not rid us of your existence? Your time is done. Be gone with you."

Tanglas' laughter was an unnerving sound, even to Dran. "I've been released." Tanglas leered at Dran, mocking, and shrugged.

Drawing his sword, Dran plunged it into the ghost in a desperate attempt, yet it was to no avail. With no means to fight this enemy, Dran was overcome with an emotion that took him a moment to identify: Fear.

"That steel cannot harm me, Gethor Dran."

"So you remember me as well?" Dran asked. He wasn't sure how much he'd crossed paths with Tanglas directly, but it struck him as odd that the Ylvan sorcerer that led an Uprising so many years before would remember him specifically. The fear in him grew. There was something personal to this.

"Let me show you," hissed the ghost of Narkan Tanglas.

The world in front of Dran disappeared completely. Tanglas' ghost, Eluciar, the Ylvan and his companions… it all went away. It was replaced by what felt like a memory, but more overpowering. Yet it was no memory Dran had any recollection of ever experiencing.

Young King Jerrick was assigning duties to Dran and the other officers present. Dran was his right-hand man and most reliable officer, of course, as well as his friend. The Uprising had been faltering, but the King's army had still not found a way to crush it completely.

Dran knew all of this to be true, but he could not place his own mind in the memory.

Assignments doled out, Dran bid the King a good night. He was the last to leave the council chamber where all the King's planning was done.

He did not know why, but Dran found in this nonexistent memory that he took a corridor in the palace that did not lead to his own chambers. He recognized the way, but as everything else in this "memory," it was something he hadn't actually been a part of.

He came to the door he was looking for. There were two guards outside of it.

"My Lord, Dran," one of the men said to him in official greeting.

Without response, Dran drew his blade and, with a swift and powerful stroke, the guard was decapitated. Before the other guard could act, Dran had impaled him, leaving him without a voice as he slumped against the wall and drooped to the floor, dead.

Dran recoiled from this vision. This was not his memory. This vision belonged to someone else. This had not happened at the hands of Dran.

Dran entered the chamber, the queen was putting the prince to bed. She turned toward Dran.

"Gethor?" she looked concerned. "Is everything alright? You look troubled." Her gaze drifted to the bloody blade in his hand and she drew back. "What has happened? Is Jerrick—?"

With another powerful stroke, Dran removed another head. Only this time, it was the queen's. Rushing forward, he impaled the prince where he lay in the bed.

The shock of all of this brought Dran to his knees. This was not him! But this was exactly how the King's family was murdered, how they found them. The ghost of Tanglas was sharing the murderer's memories with Dran. The murderer had never been caught, and it was always assumed it was Tanglas, entering the palace with some form of magic. Dark Lore, perhaps the creation of a Face-Thief. Why would Tanglas share his memory of the events with Dran from Dran's own viewpoint? Was this a confession, at last proving the sorcerer must have been the guilty party as they had always expected? Only the murderer could recall these visions with such accuracy.

But the "memory" vision did not end yet. Still seeing from the killer's eyes, he stood up and noticed his reflection in a mirror. Splashed with blood, the reflection was clearly Gethor Dran himself, at the age he was when the King's family was murdered.

"No!" Dran screamed, swinging his blade uselessly through Tanglas' ghost. "It wasn't me! It was *you*!"

Dran was back in Eluciar, ghosts fading away in a land recovering its life and beauty. On his knees, Dran was weeping. He'd been a friend to Jerrick, and his wife and son… Their murders had been terrible. Had Tanglas used Dran for this? It absolutely could not be. It was a magic trick. Tanglas was trying to trick Dran into feeling responsible for the murders.

"Do you not wonder how I was so easily able to assume control of you?" Tanglas inquired. "For it was you I used."

Still in denial, unable to accept any truth in this vision, Dran came up with a simple answer nevertheless. "Magic. Magic, of course. Magic is destructive. Magic must be eradicated at all costs."

"No." Tanglas' ghost shook his head. "You misunderstand magic and its uses. But there is a level of the Lore of Magic that is lost in Lydania. Jerrick was seeking it, and I was as well. Some of it is not lost, and there were bits of it I could use. One such lost Lore of Magic allowed me to assume control of your body all those years ago."

Utterly helpless, Dran could only try to think of ways to destroy the ghost. Seeing Rhinan a bit further away, still overwhelmed by the fading ghosts himself, Dran realized that the Ylvan he'd been pursuing for so long and trying to kill was actually his only hope of eliminating *this* ghost. The man he'd sworn to capture or kill, and possibly even magic itself, was the key to defeating Tanglas here.

The ghost of Tanglas spoke again, swirling around Dran, whispering in his ear now. Dran could not wave him away. "You were an easy target for me to control for one reason, and one reason only. And I want you to know this before I take what I need from you. I was able to take control of you because of your Ylvan heritage."

Dran stood in shock. "I am not Ylvan. How big a fool do you think I am? Look around you. If I were Ylvan, I would be one of them. There is no Ylvan in my blood!" But something bothered Dran about the accusation of his heritage.

"You may thank *me* that you have not spent years trapped between life and death." The ghost was angry, sneering at Dran. "I happened to be in your body when the spell was cast that drew all of the Ylvans out of the world. By some magical fluke, it ripped me from your body and left your worthless mind in that shell. It only took *one* Ylvan from a body. I saved you from a terrible fate."

"No!" Dran screamed again. "No, no, no! Lies and magic and deception!" He attempted to back away from the ghost, but he had no way to hold the ghost back from pursuing him.

Tanglas laughed again, his laughter penetrating Dran's bones like icy wind. "I would tell you to ask your grandparents, but they are long gone. But feel it. It is in you."

Completely broken, Dran collapsed to the ground. It was true, and he could not deny that he felt it. There was a faint trace of Ylvan blood in him. The Clans he'd spent so much of his life trying to wipe out, and he was partly one of them.

Then he remembered something the ghost had said. "You need something from me. *What do you plan to take from me?*" He saw Rhinan and the troubadour and the beardog, and there were still some ghosts. He attempted to cry out to them. His last effort was to call for help from his enemies, but he found that he could not. He could not move at all.

"Isn't it all very simple, Dran? I am a ghost without a body, so I will assume permanent control of yours. So thank you for being here, because that other one over there?" Tanglas' ghost gestured toward Rhinan. "He is too powerful for me. I could not hold him, or defeat him, as I never could have his father. But you… you shun magic. You're easy, Gethor Dran. You're *weak*."

Already immobilized, Dran instantly felt a pressure in his mind, like a squeezing, as if a horse were stepping on his brain. His life essence was being crushed out of existence. No power to fight this kind of attack, he tried to scream from the pain, but could not make a sound.

He could feel Tanglas inside his thoughts, violating his consciousness, his own external awareness of the world struggling, but failing and fading. A paralyzed form, he was a dead body to his own mind. And then his internal awareness of all things—his memories, his knowledge, his skills… everything… he felt it ripped from this dead body within his mind and into the existence of Tanglas. Blackness took over his consciousness, leaving no will to struggle, only an urge to survive. Then the last of any kind of awareness or knowledge—who he was, where he was, or what he was—was stripped away until there was nothing left but a powerless desire to continue to exist. But even that dwindled, painfully, as his consciousness was crushed and absorbed.

There was nothing left of Gethor Dran in this body, or anywhere else. He simply ceased to exist.

Chapter Fifty

Almost dutifully, every Ylvan ghost passing into the realm of the Lore Givers drifted past Rhinan. There were so many of them. All of these people—*his* people—wiped out at the whim of a grieving king.

Recalling how he first saw them, it reminded him of his home in Cabelon. He had his own griefs… his parents… and how he missed Silarrah and the scent of her hair on the wind and the way she looked at him. Param playing his mandolute and singing. He missed hunting in the forest with Rip. He even missed the way Keirwyn would admonish him. He regretted the time he had not spent with Eodorr for so many years, and he regretted not visiting Brinaya more often. Most of this was lost to him now. For all he knew, it was possible that it was *all* lost to him now. Except that Param and Rip were here, at least for the moment.

But he had spent his entire life in fear of these ghosts, and they were simply his people, trying to reach him. He'd been watched over in some way. He took what comfort he could from that as they began to wane in number. Before long, this beautiful land of Eluciar would be empty, though it would be alive again. Others would find it. It would be a populated land again, just not by Ylvans.

As the land was restored to life, one of the first acts would be to bury the dead body of Bruccan. The land did not care, but Rhinan found that he did.

His anger rose. Jerrick. All of this because of a paranoid regent. And Dran.

As the heavy rains continued, he turned to the General. Despite the downpour and the winds and hazy fog, he could see Dran lying in the grass a few feet away. He'd forgotten the *Maraggan* in the swarm of departing ghosts, each saluting Rhinan in their way as they were freed from their prison between the living world and the afterworld.

But Dran was down. Rhinan looked at Param who was still watching the ghosts. Rip sat licking his paws, oblivious, unconcerned for the moment. Had someone else gotten to Dran at last?

Then he saw Dran rise to his feet. He appeared to examine himself for injury, and then looked up at Rhinan. Swiftly drawing an arrow, Rhinan was prepared to put the General down for good. Then Dran did something Rhinan would never have expected: he held up his hands in surrender, empty of weapons.

Dran stepped slowly toward Rhinan, moving differently than he normally did, and Rip growled his most dangerous warning. Param swiftly turned, nocking an arrow of his own and aiming at Dran. Rhinan kept his arrow pointed at Dran's throat. With his skills, Rhinan could put an arrow through one of Dran's eyes at this distance without even trying, perhaps even with his own eyes closed.

Dran stopped moving, close enough to be heard only by Rhinan over the din of the storm. "Dran will now stop pursuing you, Rhinan. And I do not intend to kill you. Dran acted on the King's orders, so much of the anger you have is misplaced. This land," here Dran waved his arms out across the lush Eluciar, "remains a part of Lydania as long as Jerrick rules. I would leave you to it, but the King never will. You will have no peace here or any place you go, but it will no longer be because of Dran."

Confused by Dran's speech, Rhinan could not figure out why Dran referred to himself as if he were someone else. Rip seemed on the verge of pouncing, and Rhinan wasn't sure he could call off the beardog if he did. Or even if he should call him off. He kept his bow aimed at the King's number one man. "What of all the vicious things you've done, Dran? You don't get to walk away from that."

Dran smiled, and it made Rhinan's flesh crawl. But he responded, "Oh, Dran has paid for those actions. Let me assure you. Dran is gone."

It took a moment for Rhinan's mind to work it out. He looked around for remaining ghosts, but they were all gone. And then with horrifying realization, he recalled that one of the ghosts in that *Pyvadis* had been Narkan Tanglas: the very sorcerer who'd begun the Ylvan Uprising. And one who knew of the darker, lost lores of Lydania, of which included the act of being a Face Thief, or a body occupant. *And Rhinan had just freed him with the rest of the Ylvans.* Only, unlike departing with the rest of the Ylvans, Tanglas had clearly chosen to take up residence in Dran's body.

This man was no longer Gethor Dran. Rhinan shuddered in horror at even his worst enemy meeting such an appalling fate. And if not for Rhinan, there wouldn't be a powerful Ylvan sorcerer on the loose in Lydania again. He no longer wondered why his father never returned to Eluciar with the *Pyvadis*. It must have been a terrible burden on his father knowing that he must keep the entire Ylvan Clans prisoner in order to prevent the foolish act Rhinan had unwittingly committed.

As all of this tortured Rhinan's mind, he froze for just a moment.

The man who was now Narkan Tanglas turned and walked away into the mist of the storm.

Tears and rain clouding Rhinan's eyes, he let loose an arrow. But Tanglas had vanished, almost as if he were one of the ghosts.

Param and Rip joined him. "We can catch him," Param said. "If we hurry."

Rhinan shook his head. He explained to Param that the Ylvan sorcerer, Narkan Tanglas, had taken Dran's body, and Dran was gone. Dead, for all intents and purposes.

"Are we going after him?" Rhinan could tell that Param was genuinely concerned. "You've set him free. You may be the only one who can stop him now. According to Bruccan, it took your father to do it before, to end the Ylvan Uprising."

Again, Rhinan shook his head.

"I understand." Param relented. "You've revived Eluciar… ancestral homeland of your people. You've freed the ghosts lost between life and death, giving them the peace they deserved. You might be safe here for the rest of your life. Why not take what happiness you can from that, stay here, stay safe? Rhinan, you're the Duke of Eluciar now." Param grinned at him in jest. "Maybe even the King, if Eluciar is no longer a Lydanian region. But you'd need an army to hold it…"

The rain had stopped, but a strong wind swept across the grassy plain as silence fell between them. Rip wandered a bit further away now, exploring.

From the moment Keirwyn had sent him running, Rhinan had only wanted answers. Why would King Jerrick be so interested in him specifically? He had those answers now. Brinaya had exposed the truth of his heritage as an Ylvan. Lynari had told him of his potential relationship to magic, Vaylene had revealed that his father Markin had been the Lore Master of the Discipline of Magic at the Lore College, even working with the King. The same King who later outlawed magic and hunted and slaughtered those who used it. But there had been so many gaps that didn't make sense until the very man who killed his parents, Bruccan, filled them in. The deeper truth about why there had even been an Ylvan Uprising. The secrets of the King's clandestine council of wizards, of which Rhinan's father had been one, and their search for a darker, older and more powerful lost Lore of Magic, in competition with Narkan Tanglas. How a mysterious gem had come to eradicate the Ylvan Clans, and yet Rhinan had been hidden and protected by a few, including the mercy of his parents' assassin. And how that had put the gem into his own hands, so that he had ultimately survived the King's extreme wariness of Ylvans to carry it to Eluciar. The *Pyvadis* that had imprisoned the Ylvan Clans, his clans, was gone, and with it went the ghosts that had haunted him his entire life.

He had also gained answers to questions he hadn't even thought to ask. His own madness—his "imaginary" ghosts that no one else ever saw—hadn't been hallucinations. And his life of solitude hadn't protected anyone. And most of all, hiding in the forest when a ruthless king oppressed an entire land after wiping out the Ylvan Clans of Lydania? Well, that hadn't done anything to improve the situation, even feeding the hungry by hunting for those in his little village and helping Silarrah with the orphans when he could. He'd been a good man, if unreliable, but he'd failed Lydania, even if not the Ylvan Clans. He'd especially endangered Lydania now, he felt with a pang of guilt, responsible for the release of Tanglas.

Rhinan had come to hope that reaching Eluciar would help him find the answers to all of his questions, but now new questions plagued him. The gem mysteriously released the Ylvan Clans, and the gem mysteriously brought the land back to life. But none of this would have been part of his father's spell, for—if Bruccan were correct—his father's spell would only have imprisoned Tanglas. He assumed his father, once back in possession of the *Pyvadis*, had added the restoration of Eluciar to the gem's abilities, but he didn't *know*. And the gem itself had left him feeling… *different*.

If the King had meant to be rid of the Ylvan Clans, it had been a terrible act of cruelty to trap them rather than simply finish them. When altering Markin's spell, had this secret council of wizards done more or less than the King had commanded? Why would the *Pyvadis* only free them to move on to the afterworld? Why not restore them to the lives they were robbed of? Had there been a mistake by the council of wizards, or had there been sympathy for the Ylvans, perhaps an unwillingness by any of the wizards to prevent them from a peaceful death or to be the one to actually destroy them? Perhaps this had been one of the King's deepest fears, for it released Tanglas. Rhinan wondered if Tanglas was off to seek his own vengeance against Jerrick. He also wondered how many of these wizards there were, if any of them survived, and if so, where they might be found.

If Rhinan wanted answers, he knew where to start. It all

came back to King Jerrick. It was the King who had set these events in motion. He had sent Dran after Rhinan, resulting in the deaths of so many that Rhinan held dear. Before all of this, Rhinan had thought himself content with his solitary life. That was no longer satisfactory. He had been wrong. He was lonely, and he wanted to belong to someone. For a moment, he'd dared to hope that he had some chance of restoring Ylvans to the world. That hadn't come to pass. He was still alone, but unlike in his past, now it was an aching emptiness. King Jerrick's madness, his obsession, had taken so much from Rhinan. His parents. Keirwyn. Brinaya. Eodorr. And other friends. And he still did not know if Silarrah had suffered in any way… if she, too, had been taken from him. He recalled his promise to return to her if he could. It seemed so long ago. But now? He wasn't even the same man who had made that promise anymore.

He began to entertain a thought that had come to him earlier. King Jerrick had taken almost everything from him. Yes, he wanted answers he felt he could get from the King, but he also wanted more. He wanted to take everything from Jerrick in the way that Jerrick had taken so much from him. Whatever the cost, he would see a king pay for what his oppression had done, not just to Rhinan, but to all of Lydania. All of his anger, all of his pain, now raged within him, a volcano of vengeance. He would find a way. The King had hunted him; now he would hunt the King. And one thing Rhinan knew about himself was that he was an *excellent* hunter.

Param spoke again. "But you still aren't safe here, are you? That King will never let you rest. And now you're not even the last Ylvan, are you? And the only other Ylvan? He's the very reason *why* the King will never let you rest, and my guess is that Ylvan is not likely to let you rest for long, either."

His friend was right. Even if he hadn't decided to hunt the King, Rhinan would never know peace unless he did. And once he'd dealt with the King, gotten the answers from him that he needed, then Rhinan could decide what, if anything, to do about the Ylvan sorcerer Tanglas. It would undoubtedly require extensive knowledge of the Lore of Magic, knowledge which Rhinan did not have and did not want.

But the *Pyvadis* had done something to him as well; he could feel it. There was an inexplicable… vibrancy… within him.

He needed Lynari.

Rhinan gazed out at the lush green landscape of fields and trees and life. This had been a dead land when he found it. "No, Param. It's the most beautiful thing I've ever seen, but I would not be happy here. I think I've learned that there is no happiness without justice. These Ylvan Clans… my people… they deserve justice."

The King would be his first priority. The King and his corruption.

"Whatever you choose to do now, Rhinan, this is your time to be amazing." Param clapped him on the shoulder. "Few are such times in one's life."

Rhinan looked down. Besides his bow and arrows, his father's Ylvan sword was all he had left. "What was that you said earlier about an army?" he asked Param. He would need many more swords to face the King. This would present a problem, the smithing of weapons by anyone but the King's forces being strictly forbidden. He would have to find a way to solve that complication.

But for the moment…

He saw Rip wandering nearby. The beardog would not let him out of his sight. And there might be game in this land now, too, right?

"Rip!" Rhinan yelled, stringing an arrow. "Hunt!"

To Be Continued in

The Lost Weaponsmiths of Lydania

Additional Information about "Rip"

The creature Rip is based on a factual animal that existed from the Aquitanian Epoch until the early Pleistocene era in our world. It is known as an Amphicyon or, more commonly, a bear-dog. According to Wikipedia, the Amphicyon was similar to both bears and dogs. The largest species looked more like a bear than a dog. I have, of course, taken liberties with the likelihood of its nature. There is a lot of information online about the bear-dog, and there are a lot of cool, extinct creatures from our world that make great fantasy cryptids… get Googling! (*Artist for this image unknown*)

As for his name, it's a tribute to my favorite episode of my favorite old television show, *The Twilight Zone*. Written by Earl Hamner, Jr., "The Hunt" features a very rural old man and his dog, Rip, who go raccoon hunting in the middle of the night. Rip features prominently in the episode which is not only touching, but has one of the best all-time story twists, in my opinion.

Note From the Author

Thank you for reading *The Lost Clans of Lydania,* first book in *The Lore of Lydania* trilogy. The second book in the trilogy—*The Lost Weaponsmiths of Lydania*—will be released in 2018!

Book release info and other notes and updates can be found by signing up for my mailing list (I won't spam you, and I don't pass your info along to anyone else) at **http://eepurl.com/bOJ-PL**

And you can find me at:

Facebook: **https://www.facebook.com/AlinSilverwood.Author/**

Tumblr: **https://alinsilverwood.tumblr.com/**

About the Author

Alin Silverwood formerly worked for Marvel Comics (as Gary Barnum or G. Alan Barnum) editing titles such as *The Incredible Hulk, Ghost Rider,* and *G.I. Joe*, as well as writing comic stories. He has also worked for Paramount Pictures and currently writes and edits for Mattel/Hot Wheels. He also released *Tangled Worlds*, a collection of short stories reminiscent of *The Twilight Zone.* He enjoys making people uncomfortable, ghosts and haunted places, fantasy and cryptids, superheroes, and—especially—Steampunk. He is a resident of Portland, Oregon, and this is his first novel.

Also by Alin Silverwood

The Lore of Lydania

The Lost Clans of Lydania
The Lost Weaponsmiths of Lydania (Coming in 2018)

Short Story Collections

Tangled Worlds

Made in the USA
San Bernardino, CA
11 December 2017